## ACKNOWLEDGEMENTS

Many relatives and friends have helped with the research for this book and I would like to thank them all. I am particularly indebted to my mother, Mrs Blanche Sharp, and to Mr and Mrs Ernest Sharp of Montacute, Somerset, who told me many of the old legends.

My grateful thanks to Mr David Parchment, Mrs Stella Wilson, Mr and Mrs Gordon Board, and Mrs Jill Colledge, for their patience and kindness in answering my many questions; also to Mr David Bromwich, Librarian of the Somerset Local History Library, for his invaluable assistance.

I am deeply indebted to my newly-discovered American cousins for their enthusiastic assistance, and the wonderful material which they have provided. My special thanks to Donald and Patricia Salter, and Mrs Esther Salter Watson, all of Wisconsin, U.S.A.

I would like to acknowledge the generous Bursary given to me by East Midlands' Arts which has greatly facilitated the writing of this book.

# PART ONE

They came down into Yeovil by way of Babylon Hill, anxious to be across the boundary, clear of the county of Dorset, and safely into Somerset before nightfall. Dorset was intolerant of travellers. Only last year a gypsy had been murdered on his way from the Packe Monday Fair in Sherborne.

They began the descent into the town, their wheels braked safely against the strong pull of the incline. The restraining dragshoes clattered against the flints and stones of the uneven surface, but the experienced mares were not easily panicked. The men walked beside the horses; the women trudged behind in the rear of the waggons. The children were growing weary, and they dawdled in the hedgerows. Dogs and goats were tethered, and they ran beneath and behind every flat-cart and caravan.

As the long bright straggle of waggons and coloured horses coasted down into Yeovil, the old cry flew up at their approach. 'Gypsies! The gypos are comin'. Lock your doors. Hide your children!'

Meridiana Loveridge walked behind the last waggon. She halted on the summit of Babylon Hill and looked down into Yeovil. The steep banks of Windham and the blue rise of Nine Springs held the town in a hollow palm. Somerset, a

11

green place; good cropping for the horses, fat hens and rabbits, sweet apples. She knew all its secret treasures. The dingles where the wild iris grew; the banks of wild orchid; the combes in the Blackdown Hills where the nightingale sang in the darkness.

Fever Hospital Lane was their regular camping site in Yeovil. A safe place to pitch, since the people of the town, fearing contamination, rarely strayed out into that direction. The waggons and carts wound down into the valley, and drew onto a dry, grassy clearing. The old hospital loomed dark through the elm trees; evening had come down swiftly, but within minutes there were several fires crackling, and the smell of frying bacon in the lane. Ten families were travelling together, and more were expected to join them along the way. This night-stop in Yeovil was to be their last pitch before over-summering in Buckland St Mary.

The winter had seen a thinning-out of their numbers. The damp and fogs of the previous November had carried off an uncle and a grandfather. The bitter frost and snows of January and February saw the premature births of three still-born babies. In March, two chavvies had died, suddenly drowned in their own blood. The gorgio doctor told the mothers that their children must have been consumptive for a long time.

They had burned the grandfather's and uncle's waggons, destroyed the clothes, and the bender tent in which the chavvies died. They had buried their dead in Dorsetshire churchyards and turned their faces, stoically, towards April. It had been a season of grief and mourning.

The overnight pitch was a brief one. They rose early. Fires were re-lit from the still-warm embers of the previous night. The women brewed gallons of strong sweet tea, and fried the last of the bread in the fat that remained from the supper-bacon. They would not eat again until late in the evening.

12

The men attended to the horses and livestock, and then faced-to around the fire while they ate and made plans. They were anxious to move on while the fine weather lasted. There were steep hills to be climbed in the Blackdowns, and profitable hawking to be done by the women in villages along the road.

All was made fast before moving. The thin old plates and cups were packed carefully away; the sooty kettles and pans were placed inside the pan-box underneath the waggon. Bender tents were dismantled and loaded onto flat-carts. The steps that led up to the waggons were unfastened and suspended from hooks beneath the food cupboard. Horses were fetched, put between the shafts, and harnessed. The fires were doused, and a patteran of twigs and grasses was left for the instruction and guidance of any Rom who might follow on behind them.

The Loveridge waggon was a fine bow-top, with the frame built of ash wood and the bow made of stretched green canvas. The door and frame were decorated with painted scrolls of red and yellow, and the carved heads of dogs and horses. It had been purchased from the proceeds of horse-dealing and many hours of fiddle-playing by Jesse and his sons, in taverns and at village weddings.

Preparations for this journey westwards had been under way for many days. Jesse Loveridge had repainted his waggon, and his sons had greased the axles and had the horses specially shod. Meri and her mother had washed and boiled the family's linen, and hung it to dry and bleach in the April sunshine.

This journey to the Blackdowns was not only for the summer work of haytime and harvest, there was always a great coming-together of travellers in the spring of the year. Councils were held, and any bad conduct was looked into.

13

Marriages were arranged; and Meridiana Loveridge had been footloose for too long.

She was her family's jewel. Among the assets of the Loveridge tribe she ranked above the horses and the donkeys. In a family of tall women she was already, at the age of seventeen, taller than her mother. Meridiana was straight-backed, dark as any Eygptian. With a compelling gaze, and a head swathed in thick black braids, she drew every male eye in the western counties.

The morning road was sweet with promise. Meri wore her best Scotch plaid and starched white pinna'; red, blue and yellow ribbons were plaited in her hair and flying loose about her head and shoulders. She walked alone behind her father's waggon. She believed in signs and portents, in the power of the mind to transmit a desire and seed it in the mind of another. For Meri to want was to have. The distance between all and nothing had never existed for her. In Montacute there lived a gorgio who was the beauty of all the western counties, and she would have him.

They had not yet spoken together. She had called at his mother's door at fortuitous times, when he was returning from the quarry, or at work in his strip of garden. In one stolen corner, away from the precious cabbages and potatoes, he cosseted a single rose bush. Last June she had seen him rewarded with blooms of scented damask.

They came into Montacute in mid-morning. The houses lay golden and silent in the sunshine; the smell of wall-flowers was thick on the air. A few ducks swam about on a pond; a boy with a stick stood sentry on them while the gypsy waggons passed by. The men of the village were at work in field and quarry; the women and children, heads bent to the glove-making, were prisoners within their houses.

14

Meri knocked at the door of Number One, Wash Lane. She smiled and cajoled, although she did not need to. This woman was afraid of gypsies. The sale here was easy and without satisfaction. Meri lingered on the doorstep, she rubbed one bare foot across the other, and shifted the basket to her other arm. Mrs Carew looked apprehensive but determined.

'I shudden hang about yer, if I was you,' she told Meri, 'our Luke's gone away to work. He idden livin' yer no more.'

The road up to Buckland St Mary was long and steep, and without joy. Together with her cousins and mother, she hawked posies of wild flowers and clothes-pegs in Ilminster and Chard. It hardly mattered now if housewives bought from her or refused. The thought of Luke Carew twisted and bored into her mind until her head ached.

Eliza Greypaull watched the gypsies' ascent of Buckland Hill, always a dangerous business with the sweating horses pulling on the heavy waggons. She saw how two families worked together; how the horse of one was taken from its harness, and placed in traces in front of another. When the top of the hill was reached, both horses were walked back down to fetch up the second waggon. She had heard the gypsy-men call this practice 'doubling-up'.

Meri Loveridge was considerate of the family horses. Eliza saw her walking behind her father's bow-top carrying a chunk of wood mounted on a stick. At intervals during the long ascent she blocked the wheels for several minutes, allowing the horses to rest.

The bright April day had closed down in drizzle, and Eliza's petticoats and dress were soaked through and clinging around her ankles. The lane into Dommett Wood was green and dim, narrowed in its beginnings by hedges of

15

untrimmed blackthorn which grew inwards and shut out the daylight. Further in, the pathway widened into a clearing; a secretive shuttered place edged with holly and beech trees, and still slippery with the leaves of previous autumns.

The waggons swayed and creaked into the lane. It was a forbidden thoroughfare for gorgios; Buckland people rarely walked there. Stories were told of evil things seen and heard in the clearing. The farmer whose land nudged up to the lane had hung a high gate in between the blackthorns to prevent his cattle straying. Over the years, the gate had also, by association, acquired its own superstitious legend. No one ever leaned or swung upon it.

The lane drew Eliza. She moved as close to her father's gate as she could, without actually touching it. She lifted the fleecy shawl from her shoulders and covered her head. As she began to move away towards home, she could see Meri Loveridge running fast through the trees towards her.

They met as if it were only yesterday that they had last spoken together. They stood one on either side of the blackthorns and whispered urgently across the thicket.

'You'm not wedded then?'

Eliza covered one freckled hand defensively with the other. 'Next month. On the first day of May. To my cousin Philip.'

Meri frowned. 'May weddin's is unlucky. I could make 'ee a charm against marriage troubles, we could chop for that shawl you'm wearin'.'

'All right then. But don't wear it round the village, will 'ee, Meri? My mother's bound to recognise it.'

'You'm still feared o' your mother?'

'Aren't you?'

'I's seventeen. I do's what I wants to.'

Eliza knew that Meri told lies, that she was without shame, a brand to be plucked from the burning. The

16

Reverend Soames had said so. She was also, by Eliza's standards, deprived, in spite of her sloe-eyed beauty. The farmer's daughter lifted the shawl from her head and handed it across the hedge. 'I got some boots as well, Meri, if you wants them.'

'Your boots 'ud never fit my feet, Liza, an' anyway, I wudden never wear 'em.'

Eliza knew that she was not beautiful, and no one had ever told her that she was pretty. She was like a quick bright bird, neat boned and small, with tiny tenacious hands that would never relinquish their grasp, once engaged.

She needed her tenacity. Red hair, so they said, was unlucky. It showed a jealous and deceitful nature. So Eliza must be especially careful to appear magnanimous, and always be seen to tell the truth. Her complexion was the fine paper-white that would freckle at the first touch of sun, and her eyes were a rare and opaque shade of green. In a village that believed in pixies and fairies, and the power of ill-wishing, a young man would need a powerful incentive to court and wed Eliza Greypaull.

Her brothers were decently black-haired; they were short stocky men with furrowed faces and powerful shoulders, who moved about the land with purpose. They were men of limited vocabulary; their speech was short but pointed. The one word used between them more than any other was 'family'. That Eliza would marry her cousin Philip was a natural assumption; after all, romantic love was a privilege enjoyed only by the labouring classes, or the lords and ladies in their castles.

Her wedding gown would be stitched by her cousin Walter of Fowles Mill Cottage, who was also a Greypaull and the village tailor. Eliza had never worn silk; bolts of various colours had been brought up from Taunton by Tom

Every, the village carrier. On this Sunday morning her brothers gathered round the parlour table to view their glory.

Francis favoured the blue. James preferred lilac. Robert and William, who spoke as one, decided on a striped pink-and-white. But Eliza reached out a committed hand to touch the gold, and Walter, who had come over to pin and measure, lifted the bolt and draped a length of the silk around her shoulders. Was it her colour? She looked at herself in the parlour mirror and the slow pink of pleasure rose in her face. Oh yes! The delicate silk, the exact shade of wheat straw, helped to quiet the angry tint of her hair and lighten the pallor of her skin. It added dignity and stature to her tiny person. Her dowry, already sewn into an embroidered bag made of purple velvet, would be carried to church by Eliza's father. It amounted to two hundred and fifty new gold sovereigns.

The Greypaulls observed the Lord's Day. No cooking was allowed on the Sabbath. Pies and puddings had been baked and boiled on Saturday evening; meats had been ready-roasted. Cows had still to be milked, and stock fed and watered, but on Sunday mornings the four labourers and two house-servants employed by Eliza's father were obliged to attend on God in company with their master and his family. The Reverend Soames demanded a full muster, and where Greypaulls were concerned he always got it.

After a high-tea of lardy cake and cold roast mutton, the family gathered uncomfortably around the piano. Eliza, who at the age of five had learned the first principles of music from Mrs Angelina Soames, strummed 'Home Sweet Home' and 'Drink to me Only'. Her cousin Philip stood close beside her and turned the pages of her music.

Philip sang in a high pure tenor that soared above the

18

accompanying growls of his tone-deaf cousins. If she loved anything about him it was this voice. His parents had promised a rosewood piano as part of their wedding-gift. The instrument had already been selected at Mann's Music Emporium in Taunton.

Philip had nothing to say to Eliza, save a word or two about the promised piano. It was only when he sang that her cousin came alive. She supposed that she had no mystery for him either. He already knew the dramas of her twenty-four years; that she had almost died of the croup when she was seven; that she defied her mother by consorting with the gypsy they called Meri; that no man, save Philip, had ever offered for her.

If Philip's courtship of her was less than lukewarm, she was not surprised. Eliza did not expect romance, and she did not get it. Philip was not at all what his father had expected of a first-born. There was his colouring which was flaxen, and his build which was tall and insubstantial. The Grey-paulls, save for Eliza who was a woman and hardly counted, were all uniformly dark and compact. Daniel Greypaull had once, in a fit of temper, suggested that Philip his son might even be a changeling.

Philip was good-natured and accommodating; he needed the little lift of warmth that came his way whenever he had pleased somebody. He bent with the breeze; to his mother, Rachel, he was still her golden child. His features had never toughened into manhood. He still had a dimple in his chin into which she could place her little finger, and, no matter how short she clipped them, the yellow curls still corkscrewed around his ears and cascaded across his fore-head. At the age of twenty-eight it was high time he was married.

Philip truly did not want to marry Eliza. He had said so, but not to his father. Courage only extended as far as his mother.

'I don't find her pleasing.'

Rachel had banged the flat-iron down onto the trivet; she had folded a pillowcase with nervous fingers and grabbed up a shirt from the washing basket. 'Liza's what you need. There's no nonsense 'bout our Liza.' She shook the old tin water-sprinkler and peppered the shirt with a violent shower. His mother's words had ridden on a smile, as they always did for Philip, but he sensed that in this, his first spoken rebellion, she would not be his ally. The flat-iron had hissed across the linen, raising steam. For the first time he had noticed the chapped and roughened skin of her hands. Farm women needed to be hardy. They bore their children too swiftly, and often died early from exhaustion. Eliza had the frame and brittle bones of a sparrow. She was angled where a woman should be rounded. He could not see how he would ever bring himself to touch her.

His father had named him for his great-uncle, a ploy which had been intended to bring land and money with it. Stories of this bachelor uncle had coloured the long winter evenings of Philip's childhood. It had been recorded in the *Taunton Courier* of 1828 that, in his seventy-ninth year, great-uncle Philip had lain all night on the grave of a ravished and murdered child, convinced that by so doing he would see her killer in a vision. The newspaper had described the old man as 'a poet and a soothsayer'.

If the murderer had obliged his great-uncle it had not been recorded, but to the young Philip Greypaull it had seemed like a brave and splendid gesture. Sometimes, even now, on his way into church, he would stand by the little girl's grave and imagine the soothsayer uncle lying prostrate all night on the mound of earth underneath the yew tree.

Fir-capped ridges and deeply wooded combes encouraged magic, and many people considered this whole county of

Somerset to be bewitched. The Blackdown Hills had a special reputation. Even in this Year of Our Lord, 1857, with Queen Victoria and her Consort so prosaically on the Throne of England, the people of Buckland St Mary were still faithful to their old pagan habits. Every cottage and farm had its legend of a haunting. Intermarriage between close family members was approved and frequent; incest was suspected in some cases, but never proven; madness was rife in the district.

The sanity of Philip and Eliza's family was, of course, unquestioned. The village carpenter, the tailor, and many yeoman farmers, bore the name of Greypaull; but to truly understand the Greypaull men you would need to count the hours and the years of their lives lived apart on scattered hill farms. You would need to reckon with an isolation so severe that it could fold the edge of an exploring mind back upon itself, so that the boy grew into a shy, introverted man who was only at ease among his own kin.

You would need to handle the parchment of Greypaull family Wills to appreciate, in among the legal language, the true depth of mischief that was caused by inheritance. The power that was wielded by legator over legatee.

Sometimes, ill-luck would come down quite unfairly on a woman, on a parcel of land, on a family.

Mischief had first been let loose on the Greypaulls by their great-uncle Philip. His Will had extended to six large pages of closely scripted parchment. The hand of the poet was clearly to be seen in the wording, but the mind of a man concerned only with power had dictated the content.

The Land Enclosure Act of 1827 had ensured that this Philip Greypaull, yeoman and octagenarian, was safely the richest and most influential man in the parish. Four farms and several enclosures of fields were in his gift to distribute, and great-uncle had his favourites.

It had been whispered that Eliza's father had toadied, had

21

made himself indispensable to an old man who had long ago used up his three score years and ten. Whatever the reason, John, favourite nephew, had inherited all the farms and most of the money, while Philip's father, Daniel, had received a single insulting bequest of nineteen pounds and nineteen shillings.

It was the farm known as Larksleve that was most at issue. As Daniel had said, he could have forgiven his brother John almost anything save possession of this prime sixty acres. Daniel had been born at Larksleve. He had believed that his grandchildren, at least, might grow up and grow rich there. But he also knew his own brother; what John had, John held on to.

Twenty-five years of bitterness lay between them and, since they were respected farmers and Churchwardens, and Daniel was Overseer of the Poor, and John the Parish Clerk, such enmity had hardly been seemly. Sermons, preached from the pulpit on a Sunday morning, had been aimed quite openly at John and Daniel. The Reverend Soames had spoken to them singly and finally together. This last homily had resulted in a family council at which there had been a deal of plain speaking.

'Right then, bor!' John had said, 'I got the land, I got the money – I also got a daughter who be so ill-favoured no farmer's son'll offer for her. Not even wi' a dowry of sovereigns. 'Tidden no fault o' my maid, but that red hair an' they freckles – well, you know what folk do say about 'em. They do reckon that unlucky.' He grinned at Daniel. 'Now you, bor – you whelped a pup what's stayed a puppy. You shudden never have called 'un Philip, didden do 'ee no good, did it? Twenty-eight years old, an' he's not so much use round the shippon as is my liddle maiden.'

Daniel protested, but John halted him. 'I've seen him, bor! Measured him alongside my own boys, measured 'un beside his brother Samuel. I've yeard stories about 'un. They say he do like the Taunton women, that he goes card-playing in the Turk's Head tavern.'

Daniel growled and muttered, but John overrode him. ''Tis like this, bor! You got a son as needs his arse kickin'. I got a maid as nobody'll wed. Our Liza's a tidy worker, her'll handle Master Philip. What say us puts 'em together, brother? I'll sign Larksleve over to thy son Philip, an' chuck in a dowry to soften his marriage-bed. How'll that suit 'ee?'

Daniel Greypaull had not hesitated. He spat in his palm, stuck out his right hand and the bargain was struck.

The farm called Larksleve lay above the village. It had taken the local thatcher and a firm of builders from Taunton to make the house weatherproof again, and fit for a bride to come back to. It was a pretty house. The outer walls had been newly whitewashed and the doors and window-shutters painted a soft shade of blue. The roof gleamed yellow with the newness of last season's reed. There was, as yet, no cultivated garden.

These desirable acres had first come into family possession in the year 1761, when a certain William Greypaull, ffarmer, had purchased them from Stephen, Earl of Ilchester, for the sum of sixty pounds. There was a document, still held by a firm of solicitors in Chard, which bore the signature of the Earl and the great seal of the Bishops of Bath and Wells.

The Greypaulls chose to believe that this first William of Larksleve was the ancestor common to them all, except perhaps to Eliza, whose flaming hair and strange green eyes had always been accounted to the lusting of some ancient Danish invader.

'A praper liddle Dane,' the midwife had cried, at first sight of Eliza's curly head. The hair was seen as a curse. It was kept clipped short and covered by a frilled white cap. It was just possible, said her mother, that control of its length and concealment might weaken the potential for evil of the colour.

Pinned down between her mother and her aunt Rachel, Eliza was taken to Larksleve to discuss the colour of curtains, a carpet for the parlour, and the need for a good strong kitchen table and adequate ingle-settles.

There were features of the house that charmed her. It was smaller and cosier than Castle Farm. The hallway was broad and flagged, with a spiral staircase of scuffed black oak leading up in to four small bedrooms. The inglenook spread along one whole wall of the Larksleve kitchen; it recalled the hearth at Castle Farm, when she was a child, with a joint sizzling on the roasting-jack, and the bellows casting shadows in the firelight. From every Larksleve window she saw only a pattern of small green fields marked out by hedges and surrounded by many trees. Home would no longer be visible to her after marriage; except for her cousin Philip, Eliza would be quite alone here.

In company with his father and uncle, Philip also walked his inheritance. They talked about crops and stock, and the state of the sheds, while he, insignificant and superfluous, was eclipsed by them. Occasionally he nodded and pulled at his lower lip as if his opinion had been sought. In an upper meadow Daniel Greypaull halted and clapped his eldest son on the shoulder. Spite towards his brother John peeped between his eyelids and was swiftly hidden. For the first time in his life Philip heard a congratulatory word from his father.

'Won't be long now, eh bor? Won't be long now till this boy o' mine makes us all very happy.'

Philip's father had excused him from the early milking so that he might go into town to be measured for his wedding

24

suit, and this time Rachel had her way. If her son was to be married then he should be suitably dressed for the occasion, and not by the village tailor, but by a fashionable gentle-men's outfitter in High Street, Taunton.

Ten miles of winding road brought him down to Taunton. It was not often that he was permitted such free-dom; a visit to the town had usually to be made in Daniel Greypaull's shadow. The tailor laid swatches of various coloured weaves before him, but Philip had received his orders. 'Dove-grey,' his mother had insisted, 'with a lavender ruffled shirt and gloves to match.' She had once seen a photogravure of the Royal Family in which Prince Albert, beloved Consort, was wearing exactly such an outfit.

'It had better last him a lifetime, then,' Daniel had grumbled. He himself intended to be buried in the navy-blue serge of his own wedding suit.

Eliza's wedding gown was almost finished. The neckline was high and ruffled, the bodice narrow and close-fitting. The skirt was full and ended in a short but elegant train. A veil of gold lace had been sent up from Taunton, and Candace, her cousin Walter's young wife, had sewn slippers of matching gold silk to fit Eliza's tiny feet. Her brothers were fearful for her, but only Francis dared to say so. He also approached trouble by the safest route, through his mother.

'He's no good for Liza.' The words held a depth of meaning understood by both, but not dwelt upon by either. Elizabeth patted flour onto bread dough and looked embar-rassed.

'He bain't no farmer, Mother. You knows that, well as I do. He do go runnin' round all the inns of Taunton. He do play cards an' wager, so I've yeard. He do go with loose women.'

Elizabeth pinched and slapped the dough, her hands were frenzied but her voice was cold.

'Us don't know that, Francis. 'Tis all hearsay. Liza'll tame 'un.' Her tone softened into pleading. 'Us'll help 'un – eh Fran? Me and Liza got to set that house to rights out on Larksleve, an' there's ploughing to be done still in top fields.'

'And what about Philip, Mother? What'll he be doing? Sleeping-off his cider back o' Dommett Wood?'

Daffodils swayed wild and yellow in the fields; the sides of the combes rose sharply, hinting at disaster and confirming the hardness of underlying rock which had lain concealed for a thousand years.

In Dommett Wood eighteen waggons were drawn into a circle. Overnight, two waggons were parked across the lane to prevent the horses straying. The gypsies did not trust John Greypaull's gate which could easily be opened by mischievous children.

The women rose first, stretching and yawning and rubbing the sleep from their eyes. Rain had given way to a brilliant morning. Meri gathered willow and thin green ash-sticks for a quick fire; she took the water-jack across to the stream and filled it. The big iron kettle was suspended from the chittie above the flames, and the tea was brewed strong and dark, with plenty of sugar. Meri's mother fried bread and strips of thick fat bacon. They never ate at mid-day.

The men were always served first. Already they would have checked upon and tended to the horses. They ate swiftly, with their fingers, from thin old plates made of fine bone-china. The journey from Dorset had almost emptied the cratch. Today, the women must beg or barter for bread. They seldom took trouble to bake their own.

Meri had abandoned her plaid and ribbons for a sober dress and clean white pinna'; a single rope of amber was her only decoration. She arranged her bits of lace and clothes-pegs with professional care; a well set-out hawking basket might tempt Buckland housewives. She and her cousin Lavinia always worked together.

On their way through the wood, they found Philip Grey-paull, yeoman's son, lying underneath a blackthorn; his fine bay mare cropped quietly at the end of the lane. Meri prodded at Philip with a sharp big toe, and the two girls giggled together.

'Oh-ho my fine rai – well aren't you a tasty picture? Down-along to Taunton yesterday, was you, Philip Greypaull? Your Pa'll have a fit when he sees the state o' you.' Meri had seen this rai several times around the fair-grounds and in the streets of Ilminster and Taunton. His bobbing curls and curving mouth were not to her taste. She thought about Luke Carew who, according to his mother, had left Montacute and was therefore lost to her for the present.

Eliza, on Meri's instructions, had stitched the love-charm inside her old blue garter. It looked like a bit of rabbit bone, all splintered and jagged. It chaffed her leg as she walked, but Meri insisted that pain was essential if the magic was to work.

Eliza had tried many spells to discover her true love. Last Midsummer's Eve she had sat before her bedroom mirror, in the glow of two new wax candles, and eaten a rosy apple, very slowly. According to Meri, her true love's face should have bloomed in the mirror beside her own, but Eliza had munched her way through four red apples and nothing had happened.

Meri had recommended applications of fresh mare's milk

as a sure cure for freckles, and, at great personal risk, had approached a newly foaled mare on Eliza's behalf. But the few drops of liquid that eventually lay in the bucket had not been enough to fade freckles so dense as Eliza's.

Meri wove spells inside Eliza's head. She had seen all the fearful and romantic places that Eliza knew about only from hearsay. The Loveridges were well travelled in the western counties; they must cover all of forty miles in any good year. Meri talked of the man she called Luke Carew as if they were already promised.

'But,' Meri said simply, 'I's willing to take Luke - an' as for Pa - if us runs away for a night then there's nothin' he can do to change it.'

Eliza took time to think this over. She said at last, 'That don't sound quite right to me, Meri. That Luke - shudden he be the one to do the choosing?'

Meri's chin wagged with scorn, 'They'm dragging that Philip to your marriage-bed wi' his neck tied up in a halter, bain't they?'

Luke Carew of Montacute, unaware that he was the chosen of Meridiana Loveridge, considered his responsibilities. At the age of nineteen, he was the eldest of nine children and the main support of his widowed mother. His father, an ostler who had been trampled and killed by a bolting drayhorse, had lain buried for the past twelve months in the Montacute churchyard.

Luke's mother worked at home, at the glove-making, as did his five sisters. Even Mary-Ann, who was six, and Louisa, who was only four years old, could earn sixpence each in a week if they were industrious for twelve hours in every day. His brother George was a carpenter's apprentice. Nathaniel and Edmund, aged five and three, were still underfoot and incapable of earning.

At the age of twelve Luke had been apprenticed to the craft of mason. His father had paid over his 'footing' – a nominal shilling. Luke was proud to be one of the Company of Masons. He found their disciplines self-fulfilling. Fines were imposed for any bad conduct which might reflect on the dignity of their craft. No shirt which had not been clean-on on the previous Sunday could be worn by a man in the quarries on a Monday morning. A skilled mason could earn thirteen shillings in a good week.

Luke had lately become a time-served man; his final shilling had been paid and a traditional spree with cider kept up with his workmates. But not to excess, the masons were no longer members of Court Guilds, but some customs still survived. Any carelessness or incompetence in his work would be promptly fined. But if Luke should fall ill for any considerable time weekly collections would be taken up to assist him and his family.

Luke had watched the master-masons. He envied their skill with chisel and mallet. He himself was ambitious. His craft had set him higher than his father the ostler, above the village wood-cutter or the agricultural labourer.

When his name was put forward to work on the rebuilding of a church in the village of Buckland St Mary it was the proudest hour of his nineteen years.

Life sat easily on Luke. He was taller and broader than the other young men in his village. It was hinted by his neighbours that his thick black curls and swarthy skin were an inheritance from gypsies, but his mother denied this. Luke spoke when he had something worth the telling; the village girls teased him and called him slow. They resented his devotion to his mother, his silences, and his impregnable beauty.

A sight of the gypsy they called Meri had occasionally

flitted in between Luke's eyelids; he had noticed, with distaste, that she was bold and forward. She dressed in outlandish colours. The Scotch plaid and flying ribbons and the sinister amber necklets had no charm for Luke, who could approve only the modest dress and bearing of women like his mother.

The lanes between Montacute and Buckland St Mary were busy with carts and horses laden down with Ham Stone. The contract between church and quarry was a valuable one. The word in Montacute was that the Reverend Soames was a wealthy man who hoped by the building of a brand-new church to tame his pagan congregation.

Luke had been lodged in the house of the carpenter, William Greypaull. To begin with, the 'foreign' masons had been treated with suspicion, but, as work on the church had progressed, relations between Montacute men and villagers had gradually grown warmer. Luke's arrival in Buckland St Mary had coincided with the completion of the new chancel and transept. His height and strength, he was told, would be needed in the dismantling and rebuilding of the new bell tower.

It was while he was perched several feet above the village, removing old stone from the crumbling tower, that Luke had first seen the smoke of gypsy fires in Dommett Wood. The gaudy plaid and coloured ribbons he had recognised at once as belonging to the tall one they called Meri.

Meri rose early; at dawn she was at her most receptive. She moved through the fields like a shadow, slipping between humped oxen who were still frozen in the shapes of sleep. She believed that lines of force existed between lovers and her feet, of their own volition, took her downhill towards the church. She stood in a gap in the wall, half-way in between the new church and the old one, and there he was, standing up before the altar.

'Young man,' she whispered sharply, 'come you here, I wants you!'

For Luke the presence of a gypsy in church was sacrilegious, but he had no words of his own that would fit the situation. He resorted to the Biblical thunder he had learned in the Sunday School of Montacute's Baptist chapel. 'No further,' he roared, 'thou art an abomination in the eyes of the Lord.'

'I wudden come in there if you was to pay me,' she said slyly, 'even though Parson do say I ought to.'

'Do 'ee?' Luke was stranded between what was fitting and the possible saving of a soul. She studied him from beneath her eyelids.

'Parson do come out to see we when us comes up to Buckland. He do give our rawnies a shillin' if they lets him pour water on their chavvies' heads.'

Luke was overwhelmed. Without thinking about it, he had assumed that his God would only have truck with respectable people. There were, of course, the missionaries who went out to darkest Africa to convert the blacks. His uncle Simeon, an ordained minister of the Baptist faith, was such a one. But, dark as they were, he could not quite bring himself to categorise the Loveridges as heathen natives needing to be saved.

'Have you been saved?' he asked Meri.

'Not as how I know to.' She tossed her head in a way that alarmed him. 'Me an' Pa don't want your Parson's shillin'. Churches is only for bad people.'

'That's a lie! Church is for everybody.'

She wagged her chin in delight, and pointed her finger at him. 'Then why do 'ee shout at I, an' say "no further"?'

Luke's broad face reddened.

'That's flummoxed 'ee proper, my young rai,' Meri's

31

bare toes spun around in the dust in a wild tarantella that set her full skirts flying. He could see her smooth brown legs right up to the knees. He averted his eyes and began to walk away, but she thrust the upper half of her body through the gap in the wall.

'That suit 'ee better then?' She giggled. 'Good part of me is in church – wicked half is left outside!'

His consternation was unbounded. Gypsy-girls were not known for the modesty of their speech, but what was acceptable talk among men in field or in tavern should never be indulged in by a woman; and so close to the holy altar.

'Heathen!' he shouted. 'Lewd and sinful woman!' The Baptist minister in the Montacute chapel would have been proud of Luke Carew in that moment.

The mocking grin slipped down from her features leaving wonder behind it.

'You'm frighted o' I, Luke Carew,' she whispered, 'you'm frighted, bain't you?'

Leaving home and travelling up to Buckland to live and work among strangers was stretching Luke's comprehension of the world. Until now, his span had needed only to encompass Number One, Wash Lane, the Ham Hill quarry, and the Montacute Baptist chapel.

The first contact with a gypsy had confounded his mind; they were not, he learned, the outright heathens he had always assumed them to be. 'Parson . . . do pour water on our chavvies' heads,' Meri had told him. Himself a committed Baptist, Luke thought he should feel only approval of this practice, but found that he could not; he struggled with his un-Christian doubts. As far as Luke could judge, Holy Baptism had made no visible difference to their behaviour. The gypsies still lied and stole. They frightened timid women, like his mother, into buying goods which they neither needed nor could afford. They told fortunes for money, which, in Luke's brand of judgement, was the greatest sin of all.

A surge of the same crusading zeal that had driven Simeon, his uncle, to board ship and set out for the dark continent now washed over Luke. Perhaps he had been 'sent' among these people, and not only to help with the rebuilding of their church. Luke picked up his chisel and his mallet and turned his face towards the sun. One way or another, he was about to undertake the Lord's work.

There was the dove-grey suit to be collected, and the ruffled lavender shirt with gloves to match, and this time his father had insisted that Samuel should go with him. Samuel, who was three years younger than Philip and beloved of his father, would ride down into Taunton only on a market-day, or when he had an aching tooth that needed pulling.

Dark haired and conscientious, a true Greypaull, Samuel was the consolation of his father. He suited Daniel as closely as a good glove fits the palm. It was Sam who worked tirelessly in field and shed, who talked knowledgeably about stock and prices. Second sons had their natural order of importance, and Samuel knew his place. He accepted that his brother Philip should be the first to marry. The love he felt for his elder brother was the same rough affection he could feel for the sacrificial lambs in the collecting-pens in Taunton market. There was a tender patch deep in Samuel's chest whenever his mind strayed across to his cousin Eliza.

Philip, who was always the last one to leave his bed, hardly spoke on the outward journey. They stabled their horses in a gloomy silence. But the final fitting of his wedding-suit wrought a miracle in Philip. Stripped of his breeches and broadcloth jacket, and clothed in the dove-grey

33

outfit, he strutted transformed before the tailor's mirror. Samuel felt embarrassed for him.

Out on the street, Samuel's unease increased. Passing strangers winked and nodded at his brother, half of Taunton seemed to know him. But when Philip halted in the Turk's Head doorway, Samuel stood fast.

'Come on, Sam. They won't rob you.'

'I got no money.'

'But I have.' Philip patted his breeches pocket and Samuel heard the chink of gold on gold.

'I reckon Mother gives you her egg-money!'

'I don' ask her for it.'

'No? I've watched 'ee hangin' round the kitchen, lookin' peevish. You knows her can't abide that.'

Philip flicked a bit of straw from his brother's coat collar. 'Women,' he said, 'you'll have to learn how to handle 'em, Sammy. They'll do anythin' you want if you goes right about it.' He drooped an eyelid, grabbed at Samuel's elbow, and pushed him through the Turk's Head doorway.

It was a tiny bar-room, warm and smoky, with brown chenille curtains that shut out the daylight and a layer of fresh sawdust on the floor. Lightly-clad girls lounged across the bar, their legs straddled carelessly in attitudes of invitation. In the light of the single lamp they looked dangerous to Samuel.

'C'mon,' he muttered, 'we mun bide yer. They's wicked women.'

Since their arrival in Taunton, Philip had lost some of his country burr. In a knowing voice Samuel hardly recognised, he said, 'More sad than wicked I'd say, Sammy.' He gazed into Samuel's burning face. 'For God's sake, man, stop acting like Parson.' He thrust the box that held his wedding-suit across the table. 'Here – hold onto this. I'll fetch you something to heat your blood up.'

Samuel crouched in his corner. He cradled his whisky

glass in his palm; he could not drink, he dared not. One of them would have to stay sober enough to carry home the parcels and lead the horses. Philip was drinking faster now. A high flush rose in his face and his blue eyes glittered.

'Cider for all,' he shouted. 'Come and love me, girls. I'm getting myself a farm and a wife next week.'

Farmers who had finished their business in the market spent ten or fifteen minutes in the bar-room, drank up their porter or cider, and called for their horses and waggons to be brought to the inn door. From his corner seat beside the window, Samuel could see the long line of traffic stretched out across the Tone Bridge; he could hear the squealing of pigs in netted farm-carts, and the voices of drovers away in North Street as they manoeuvred their flocks of sheep and cattle out onto the Staplegrove Road. Responsible men did not linger long in Taunton, they were anxious to reach their farms and villages before nightfall. Philip had left the bar in the company of a tall girl whose style of dress and coquettish behaviour had alarmed and disgusted Samuel. Time passed, and Philip did not return. Samuel approached the barman.

'Where's my brother?'

'Who'll that be, then?'

'Philip Greypaull. He went out o' that door wi' a girl in a pink frock.'

The barman grinned. 'He won't be back for some time, then. Best sit you down by the fire, an' have another drink. Unless you fancies a girl for yourself. Not many left by now, though. The best of 'em 'ull have been picked-over.'

Samuel sat down. He waited for half an hour, never shifting his gaze from the door through which Philip had vanished. Once again, he approached the bar.

'Cud 'ee go an' fetch 'un for me? 'Tis gettin' dark, an' us got a tidy ride back up to Buckland.'

The barman polished a glass, breathed on it heavily, and rubbed again. He shook his head. 'More'n my life's worth,' he said, 'to go up they stairs when the girls is working. You shud o' got yourself fixed up. I warned 'ee 'twould be a long wait, now didden I?'

'But us got to be back home pretty soon. There's the evenin' milking – an' his weddin' suit, an' all they other parcels to be carried.'

'Weddin'-suit? Him? Who's the poor maid, then, what's takin' on the likes o' Philip?'

'Thass none o' your business, just tell me how long he usually bides yer.'

'All night, as a rule. 'Tis a Friday, see. On a Friday night us has our "Free an' Easy" in the supper room upstairs. Your brother won't never miss that. He's a part of the entertainment.'

When Philip at last returned to the bar, Samuel stood up and gathered the parcels together.

'Better call for our horses,' he muttered, 'Father'll kill us for bein' this late.'

He kept his gaze upon the table-top and would not look at Philip.

Philip said, 'You didden sit here all afternoon did you?'

'Yes.'

'But why? There was plenty for you to choose from. You got to start sometime, boy, an' it might as well be here an' now.'

'No!'

'Why not? Not scared of 'em are you? There's just time afore us goes up to supper. There's Beulah? Now her's a bit older than the others. Jus' what you needs, first time.'

'I want to go home. Father'll be waitin'.'

'Damn Father! If you goes, Sam, then you goes alone. Loosen up, boy.' Philip shook his head. 'All right. Us'll go up for supper, an' then straight home. That's a promise.'

Their knees were cramped beneath the mahogany top of a wrought-iron table; plates heaped with faggots and peas had been set before them, and tankards full of cider. The entertainment took place on a small raised stage at one end of the room. The audience, which was exclusively male, howled the comic singer from the room. They applauded the fire-eater, and the sword-swallower, cheered the three-piece band, and stamped their feet in an ecstasy of pleasure when the chairman announced that the final act would be Miss Mary Wallace and her identical twin sister, those two indistinguishable 'Living Statues'.

The Living Statues were draped, Grecian fashion, in strips of flesh-coloured silk so narrow that they hardly counted. Philip stood up and banged on the table with his empty tankard. 'Look at them,' he shouted to Samuel, 'now you can see exactly what you bin missin'.' The final entertainment was to be provided by the patrons. When the chairman called for a volunteer, Philip Greypaull was first to leap onto the stage. He sang a song called 'I'm a Young Man from the Country – But You Don't Get Over Me', and followed it with 'Martha the Milkman's Daughter' and 'Sister Mary walks like This'. He brought the house down. A stage-coach driver leaned across from an adjoining table, 'He'm too good for an amatchoor,' he shouted, 'make his fortune, he would, up in London.' Philip came back to the table. He sat down amid a chorus of stamping and cheering. 'What did you think then?' he said to Samuel.

'Father wudden like it, neither would Eliza.'

'I bain't askin' Father, nor Eliza. I be askin' you, Sam.'

Samuel said, 'Why don' you sing proper songs – you got a good voice.'

'Do 'ee reckon I'd do well in London?'

'How shud I know? All I knows about is sheep an' cattle.'

'I bin asked, Sam. By an important man what was in yer

last week. He wants me to go with him. He got a big place up in London – a music-hall, he called it.'

'Thass foolish talk, Philip. 'Tis all arranged for you to wed wi' Liza. You can't go back on it now. You got your suit made, an' folks have sent wedding-presents – '

'Why can't I go back on it? They had no right to fix me up wi' cousin Liza.'

''Cause if you was to fail in London, our Father would never take you back. He don't believe in the fatted calf for the prodigal son.'

'I don't want marriage, Sam.'

'What do you want, then?'

Philip waved a hand at the dingy walls, at the atmosphere thick with smoke, and the noisy cheerful drinkers. 'I want life, Sam. Life – short and sweet and merry.'

'An' what about Eliza?'

'You can have Eliza – if you wants her.'

Samuel thought about Eliza, about the fiery curls that escaped the confinement of her frilled cap, about her green eyes, and the triangle of her small face. He thought about the cleanness of her, the way she smelled of lavender and milk, and new hay. He allowed his mind to go further, he wondered how it would be to place his hands upon her shoulders and feel the fine bones move underneath his fingers. He imagined them running together in the fields by moonlight, and felt the heat of shame rise in his face as if she were already his brother's wife, and he, in thought, had already broken the tenth commandment.

'Us had better be gettin' back home,' he said. 'Father'll be out of his mind by this time.'

'You can tell 'un the horses went lame,' said Philip, 'he'll believe it if you say so.'

Without a manor house or an aristocratic family in the

parish, the local farmers and craftsmen had done their best to take care of a scattered community; what they had lacked was the guidance of an educated hand. Until the arrival in 1832 of the Reverend John Edwin Soames and his wife, Angelina, the village of Buckland St Mary had been without benefit of resident clergy for more than fifty years. It had been a very wild place. Murders and outrages upon children had been committed; superstition and witchcraft had run loose, like lightning in the hills. The parish had needed strong clergy, and this was precisely what they had obtained.

This J.E. Soames was a man of some distinction. Educated at Winchester and Cambridge, his beautiful copperplate handwriting had now dominated Parish Registers for the past twenty-five years. It was rumoured that he was a spartan; that he ate no luncheon and broke ice on his bathtub in the winter. But the parish of Buckland was said to be so dear to him that he refused all offers of an easier living. When the fabric of the medieval church became unsafe, it was J.E. Soames who put up the money for rebuilding.

Timber to be used in the new church had been purchased long ago, in the winter of 1845; all local oak, grown and felled within the parish. William Greypaull, carpenter of Buckland, had taken the newly cut rafters and beams and set them to soak in ponds beside the School House, in order that they might be thoroughly seasoned when the time came.

The time, it was considered, had finally come eight years later. Rebuilding had now become necessary, urgent even. On April 30th 1853 a notice had appeared in the window of the Lamb and Flag.

We, the undersigned, Churchwardens, convene a Meeting of Ratepayers to be held at the Lamb and Flag Public House, to take into consideration the important subject of taking down and rebuilding the Church.

Signed: John Pyle. John Greypaull.

Once the decision had been taken, no time was wasted. The first stone had been laid on July 26th 1853 and the old church was carefully dismantled, section by section. In this year of Our Lord, 1857, it had been possible for the congregation to move into the new chancel and transept, while the rest of the fabric had still to be completed.

The Reverend Soames was unwilling to marry cousins. He pointed out from the pulpit on a Sunday morning the disastrous consequences of too much intermarrying. John and Daniel agreed with their rector, but, they declared, there was no taint of madness in their blood.

The Reverend's decision was made more difficult by the fact that Daniel was an Overseer of the Poor, and John was Parish Clerk and both were Churchwardens, and it was J.E. Soames himself who had recently reconciled the two brothers.

The first banns for Philip and Eliza, bachelor and spinster of this parish, were called on the first Sunday in April. It was fortunate, perhaps, that great-uncle Philip, poet, soothsayer and notorious eccentric, had died in 1831, just one year before the advent of the present rector.

Philip was proof that her parents knew best; he was her inevitable future - as they had pointed out when the subject of marriage to him had first come up - no one else had offered for her.

Just lately, Eliza had felt the weightiness of Castle Farm. The safety of grain in her father's barn, the stock in his sheds. All those rows of preserves in her mother's pantry, the jams and jellies; the linen and blankets stacked in cupboards and chests. All that providence and good husbandry; not an acorn, not an apple, not a daughter wasted. Hard times had made her parents careful, they still talked about the 'hungry forties' when prices were low and many crops failed.

All the days and months at Castle Farm were labelled according to their yield, their estimated harvest. Every season had its haul, its bounty. Every golden hour was crammed into bottles, preserved in salt or sugar, or strung up to dry on pungent lines in the kitchen. Vegetables and fruits were selected for their life-span; 'quick' ones were eaten, but 'keepers' were valued and saved against the winter. In springtime the best of the blossom was torn from the hedgerows and made into wine for Christmas. Eliza's mother was always at least two seasons ahead; nothing escaped her zeal. Every scrap was utilised, every gap breached. She was not likely to weep at her daughter's wedding. Eliza would be seen as a crop, gathered later than expected, but at least gathered. She would hardly be missed in kitchen or dairy. Her mother would still have Hannah Cooper and Loveday Venn, who were paid servants and stronger in wind and limb than Eliza.

Eliza had spied upon the summer encampment in Dommett Wood. She had seen how cuffs and kisses were doled out among gypsy chavvies in equal proportion. She would never have suspected that she was unloved if she had not witnessed the love of the Rom for their children. Parental devotion, thought Eliza, had little to do with silk gowns and lavish dowries.

From the safety of her father's field she had often spoken with Meri Loveridge, but always across hedges and in moments sneaked from allotted tasks. Meridiana was skilled in crafty persuasion; she could talk the cloak from Eliza's shoulders, the shawl from her head. But in certain ways she was quite without guile. There was usually time for a word or two beside the blackthorns when Eliza drove the cows from the Home meadow after evening milking.

41

'It didden work, Meri. 'Tiv only raised a blister on my leg.'

'Thass good! I told 'ee it 'ud have to be painful, and anyhow – I never promised nothin' certain.'

'I know you didden – but still!'

'What happened, Liza?'

'He stood beside the piano. Turned over the music, like always.'

'Never put a hand on your shoulder? Nuthin'?'

'No.'

'Me and Lavinia see'd 'un t'other morning. Laid out drunk as Christmas he was, in the ditch. He'm not much cop, Liza. What you want him for?'

''Tis my Pa an' his Pa – '

'Oh ah! Like that is it? I's done my own choosin'. I got him all spied out an' tied down.'

''Tis all right for you. You're pretty.'

'Well, they freckles is fading since the mare's milk! Anyhow – you'm offered along wi' a farm an' a dowry. Tell I again, Liza. Tell I all about it.'

Eliza repeated her tale of a golden gown, silk slippers, and a purple velvet bag crammed with sovereigns. It was the only truth she had.

The charm-filled garter being old and blue was accepted by her mother as a necessary item of bridal attire. The golden dress was tweaked into place, the slippers eased onto her feet, her white cheeks pinched to bring up some colour. The veil was pinned in heavy gathers to conceal her hair. She was not allowed to go near a mirror.

The farmhouse had been scrubbed and burnished, even the sheds had been whitewashed; who knew where the visiting farmers and their wives might poke their noses? The wedding gifts were set out, row on row around the parlour.

Carriages and horses were restive at the front door. Alone with her eldest brother, Eliza whispered, 'Will it be all right, Fran?'

'Course it will. Why shudden it be?'

'Don't know. I just got this feelin' – '

'What feelin'?'

'He don't want me, do 'ee? He's taking me to please his father and get back Larksleve.'

''Tidden too late to say no to 'un, Liza.'

She looked down at the silk and lace, at the hand-stitched slippers. 'I should a' knowed it when I ate the apple, an' I never saw his face in the mirror.'

Surreptitiously she felt for the ridge of the magic garter. 'I can't jilt 'un now, Francis. What 'ud people say? Just look at all they wedding presents!'

It had been agreed that Joseph Hayes, the sexton, should be paid an extra pound for keeping the church and the burial ground in good order throughout the period of the rebuilding. The gaps in roof and walls where the old church abutted on the new were sheeted with waterproofed canvas. The two halves of the building stood companionably together, and Joseph was earning his twenty shillings. The red carpet that led up to the altar had been thoroughly brushed, no Ham stone dust gritted beneath the feet. Everything shone. The new chancel walls were unusual, being carved in diaper upon Bath stone. The handsome screens between chancel and transept were of Ham Hill stone with marble columns and white lias capitals. The new choir seats were made of solid oak and beautifully carved by William Greypaull.

Today the church was filled with the farmers of Buckland St Mary and their sons; their wives and daughters preened beside them in new bonnets and dresses. But no one looked finer than Eliza. Clothed in gold and stepping high, she did not allow the reds and blues of the new stained windows to overwhelm her. Neither was she dimmed by the banks of flowers, the arrangement of which had kept her female cousins busy since early morning.

Eliza's face, beneath the soft mesh of the veil, had a wistfulness that might have touched John Greypaull's heart if he had troubled to look down at her. Her quick glance sideways skimmed beyond the bridegroom, she was aware of a dove-grey shoulder, a lavender ruffle, a yellow curl. The face she sought for reassurance was that of Samuel, who was standing-up for his elder brother, Sam grinned and she, gold veil and faint awe notwithstanding, grinned back at him. The responses were rushed through in an embarrassed whisper, the wedding band was pushed across her knuckle, and the veil thrown back. The dove-grey shoulder dipped towards her, and Eliza was kissed briefly, on the cheek, by her cousin Philip. But the drama they had all come to see, the real business of the day, was to do with the dowry. Every head was craned, every eye was upon John Greypaull as he parted with the purple velvet bag that contained a token amount of his conscience-money.

Her father's barn had been emptied and swept clean for dancing. An old man who played the fiddle had been brought out from Combe St Nicholas to provide the music. The wedding dress was shrouded in a clean white-bedsheet and laid carefully away between mothballs.

Stripped of her finery, Eliza was left alone to contemplate the accomplished fact of Philip. He had begun his celebration without her, he was already three parts drunk. She moved alone among the guests and said 'thank you' nicely for their presents and good wishes. Purposefully unsentimental, she had tripped through the daylight hours in golden slippers. But now, in a plain blue dress, her red hair uncovered, Eliza's defences were breached. Philip had

44

reached that stage of inebriation in which his voice was at its finest, but only Samuel knew this.

A singing man must suspend his intake of liquor, if only for the space of his song. To save Eliza's shame, Sam begged a verse or two.

'My love is like a red, red rose,' sang Philip, 'that's newly sprung in June. My love is like the melody that's sweetly played in tune.'

The Buckland farmers halted their drinking; the wives their chatter. The young people gathered round him to listen; Philip held them in his hand. The reverent, up-turned faces inspired him. When the song was ended, they stamped their feet and shouted for more. Philip felt warm and unusually important; his glass was refilled a dozen times.

The song had been a new one to Eliza. It was not among their Sunday evening repertoire; and she wondered where he could have learned it.

He was carried out sack-like across his brother's shoulder and dumped beside her in the carriage. Samuel took the reins and they drove slowly up to Larksleve in a mortified silence. Philip was carried dead-drunk across the threshold of his life. Eliza followed, like an afterthought.

They laid him upon the canopied bed, on the fine white sheets and tapestry bedspread that had been a part of his parents' gift. The dove-grey suit was rank with vomit, the lavender ruffles were torn, the yellow curls dark upon his sweating forehead.

They sponged and cleaned him like dutiful parents who were obliged to tend an unpleasant child. Samuel, tongue-tied and angry, went away, and Eliza climbed into the window embrasure and sat, chin on knees, until sunrise. From this bedroom window she could see the sheds that had

45

lately been repaired and the sloping fields which her four brothers had ploughed and seeded.

Spring wheat was through, threading the drills with lines of level green. The path before them had been made straight and paved with sovereigns, and Philip Greypaull slept, like a child, an arm curled around the pillow, the other out-thrown in unconscious appeal towards Eliza.

They had not even danced together, so quickly drunk was he. She twisted the ring around her finger and felt old; older than her own mother, who had danced and laughed the whole evening. She wondered how it was to know yourself to be pretty; to be so powerful in that knowledge that you dared to put your hand upon a certain man and claim him. She remembered Meri, her handsome face taut beneath the black line of brows, her terrifying simplicity.

She had seen Loveday Venn pulled away from the dancing by Jed Hayes, the cowman, seen the girl leave the safety of the lighted barn for the risky darkness, her smiles edged out with fear of what Jed might do - or not do. A longing tore through Eliza to run and run through the silent meadows, to dance, abandoned, underneath the moon. To lay a confident hand upon a man, to feel his arms around her, to be young and reckless, not knowing quite what that dangerous man had in mind.

Luke Carew walked in Dommett Wood on a Sunday evening. The house of the carpenter was noisy with relatives after evening service. The visiting Greypaulls talked of nothing but money and land enclosures, and where a penny of profit was likely to be gained.

The conversation in the Lamb and Flag was equally distasteful to him. Buckland men dwelt on pixies and hauntings. It was frequently remarked in Luke's hearing that his taking down of the medieval bell tower was a sacrilegious business, likely to bring ill luck on the visiting masons. According to the landlord of the inn, the demolition of a church attracted evil spirits, sometimes old stones were carried away mysteriously overnight. It had happened once before when a new church was being built at Broadway. A man needed all his courage, said the landlord, to walk through the churchyard, or in Dommett Wood, after dark.

Luke probed towards his own unease. He missed the plainness of the Montacute chapel, the fiery preaching of its pastor. The chatter of his little sisters. He was not exactly unhappy. The carpenter's wife made a tasty dinner, and his spare shirt was always washed and ironed for a Sunday morning. His workmates were Montacute men, known to him from childhood, and he was practising his mason's skill.

It was this place, this village which disturbed him. Perched on the bell tower, his facility for observation had been unique; there was more here than a hint of Sodom and Gomorrah. He had been the unwilling witness to many strange practices and small crimes that were thought to be known only to their perpetrators. His pastor had preached the contagion of madness and the dangers of defilement. Luke carried his Bible whenever he could; the feel of its grainy leather, the weightiness of it, brought the sanity back to his queasy mind.

Magic and sorcery lurked in many places, and when Meridiana Loveridge stepped out suddenly from behind the blackthorn thicket, he could feel the short hairs rise up on the nape of his neck.

He tried not to look at gypsy girls, but the uniqueness of Meri had him baffled.

Luke clutched the Bible close to his chest and tried to step past her; but she moved with him. They performed a shaky gavotte on the narrow path until Meri giggled.

'Bide still, you ninny! I won't eat thee.'

Her voice had lost its usual gruffness, the order sounded almost seductive. The Bible was suddenly clammy against his chest. She prodded at it with a stabbing finger.

'What you got there?'

'My Bible.'

'Like Parson Soames do talk about, in church?'

'I be chapel. Mos' Montacute fellers be chapel.'

'Whass diff'rence?'

'Chapel idden so – well, 'tidden so – fancy!'

'I likes fancy.'

'So I notice.'

'Whass wrong, then, wi' fancy?'

He tried not to look at her slender ankles, at the dark sheen of her arms, bare up to her elbows. 'Fancy be sinful,' he told her. ''Tis the Devil's trap.'

The sloe-eyes widened. 'Young man – you do sound jus' like Parson.' Her tone was respectful, but her lips were curving. 'Read somethin' for I, then! Tell about the Devil.'

'Whyfor you want to hear about the Devil? Be better if I tell 'ee about God.'

She swayed towards him, whined a little. 'Old Beng do torment we travellers somethin' wicked. He'm always hanging round, waitin' for to catch us.' She dropped, cross-legged, to the path; he hunkered and leaned his back against a beech tree. He allowed the Bible to fall open where it would. It made little difference. Luke could read only the small words.

His memory, however, was faultless. Once heard, he could recite any Bible passage. His assumed skill impressed Meri.

'I s'pose 'ee can write words as well?'

He turned to the fly-leaf of the Bible and showed it to her. 'See that – that says, Luke Carew, Number One, Wash

48

Lane, Montacute, Somerset.'

'I knows,' she said softly, 'I knows where you live. I bin there.' She touched the amber about her neck. 'Whyn't you come to our tents, Luke Carew? You'm good as Parson wi' that Bible. Better, I shudden wonder.' She paused, and when she spoke again, her voice had an undertow that pulled him. 'We'm wicked, all of us, save the chavvies. We do thieve taters out the farmers' fields, an' tell lies. We do go dukerin in the pubs, and chop for love-tokens. You cud tell us about your Devil, cudden you?'

The time was to come when Luke would say, with truth, 'Lord, the woman tempted me.' But that time was not yet. Sitting underneath the beech tree, in Dommett Wood, he could feel the dry tinder of his soul catch fire from the gypsy's spark.

When Meridiana Loveridge took his hand, and led him towards the tents of her people, Luke went with her, even as Abraham followed Sara.

To come upon them, unawares, was to be an experience that would stay with him for ever. That first sight of the fire, the blue flames leaping, the smoke wreathing upwards into the beechwood, the glow cast on lifted heads and arrogant features, stirred some old memory in him that was not his own. A dog growled, somewhere in the darkness, and was promptly silenced.

Her introduction of him was abrupt. 'This yer's Luke Carew. He'm a Preacher. He do tell about Beng.' Meri spoke to her people with the drawling vowel sounds and the soft slurr of the West Country. They answered her in a language that Luke had sometimes heard spoken, in times of stress, by his own father. The swift exchange secured him a seat at the fire and a cup of dark tea, sweet with honey. Meri sat herself down, just a breath behind him. She dug him sharply in the ribs and ordered, 'Tell 'em 'bout the Devil, then! They'm all ready an' listenin'.'

He was hesitant to begin with. He clutched the Bible in one hand and the thin old teacup in the other. A part of his mind was still wrestling the point of misrepresentation, but she had, in fact, introduced him as a preacher and not as a parson. His duty now was to fulfil her prophecy of him.

Luke had practised his delivery of the Word in derelict sheds and in open fields. Knowing that he was not likely to be overheard, he had preached, head thrown back, throat roaring, to the Ham Hill rabbits, to a field of barley. He had dreamed of a pulpit, a chapel, a rapt congregation. These dark faces, angled and sharpened by the firelight, were neither antagonistic nor receptive to him.

'The Devil,' he began, 'lies in wait for our souls. He be all around us. He do come as a ravening beast, devouring us lambs. He do watch his chance, an' then he do pounce on we. He be all the more dangerous 'cause us never can see 'un.'

'I did, sir. I see'd 'un.'

The interruption came from a little hunched man, whose face bore a puckered scar that ran from chin to eyebrow. Luke shook his head, confused. The rhetoric of the Montacute pastor was never broken into. 'You did? You see'd the Devil?'

'Aye, sir. I see'd Beng as clear as I sees thee now.'

A murmur ran around the fireside. The bland faces became closed and graven. An old grandmother said in a shaken voice, 'Us didden never ought to talk 'bout Beng. That'll only bring 'un runnin'.'

Luke jumped up. He loomed above them, magnificent in the firelight. 'Thass where you be wrong,' he thundered, 'thass where you be all mistook. Us got to fight the Evil

50

One, look 'un straight in the eye, an' say "Satan, get thee behind me".'

'But what if 'un pokes at we from behind? Parson do tell that Beng got a liddle iron prodder, wi' a point on, that he do go roun' pokin' at folks wi' it. What if Beng do lame our horses, eh? What if he do give our chavvies the falling sickness?'

They nodded their agreement and the scarred man continued, 'I see'd 'un. I see'd Beng. He'm a gurt black hound. He got a blue light burning round him. He runned atwixt my ponies an' they all went lame nex' day.'

This evidence, first-hand and unarguable, carried weight among the assembly. They fell to discussing it among themselves.

Luke sat down again. He turned back to Meri. 'They idden listenin' to I no more,' he complained, 'looks like I better be goin'.'

She placed her hands on his shoulders and prevented him from rising. 'You got to tell 'em about your Devil. Gorgio Devils is diff'rent. Thass what you come up yer for, idden it?' She was right of course. His uncle Simeon, in Africa among the heathen blacks, would never have given up at the first setback.

Luke raised his voice and waved his arms about. 'My Devil is bigger'n yourn,' he shouted, 'my Devil is a gurt green dragon, wi' smoke an' fire coming out his nostrils.' He paused and then continued in a whisper. 'If you was to see my Devil, you wudden never live long enough to tell about it.'

He was never to be sure quite how it happened, but he knew that he had them. They turned awed faces towards him, they hung on his outstretched fingers; they believed.

He was walked to the edge of Dommett Wood. They left him with protestations of undying friendship. He was commanded to return among them, without delay. It was only Meridiana Loveridge who stood apart and silent. Concealed in the blackthorns' shadow, she touched the amber necklace, and smiled.

Six weeks in Dommett Wood had seen a recovery among the gypsies. The only effective law in Buckland St Mary was that of the Reverend Soames, and he was well disposed towards them. With the knowledge that they were not likely to be harried or moved on came a relaxation of mind and body. They took time to stretch and yawn, to sit idly on upturned buckets and face the sunshine. Their chavvies no longer woke and coughed in the tents at night; their little chapped legs had healed over.

The spring had been cool and wet; the hay crop would be heavy. Farmers would need extra hands and the Rom men were anxious for the work. Secure in the knowledge that they would not be requested to pack up and move out in haste, the rawnies unwrapped their valuable possessions: the heirlooms that had come down through several generations, the bits of eggshell china, the silver buckles, the faded Spanish shawl, the origin of which had become uncertain, so old was it.

Luke returned to their atchin-tan every evening. They were impressed by his height and strength and a certain steadfastness in him.

They were not, as he had always believed, a dirty people. Neither were they altogether vagabond or feckless. But they were untidy. Luke, accustomed to treating the mallets and chisels of his trade with care, was upset at the sight of axes and knives tossed aside and left to rust among long grass. The detritus of human habitation, bowls and buckets, bits of rag and paper, lay before the entrance to each tent and vardo. His instinct was always to tidy away, to set in order.

They had shown no curiosity about him. It was known

that he worked in the building of the new church, and that he lodged with William Greypaull, the carpenter. The Rom were a proud people, any extension of their hospitality was bound to be significant, and privacy was almost certain to result in interrogation. On the night that Jesse Loveridge invited Luke to enter his vardo, the gypsy had a look of portent about him. Luke climbed the short ladder that led up to the waggon and his shoulders caught in the half-door.

'They grows 'em big where you come from, brother!'

' 'Tis the quarry, the work. I bin usin' sledgehammer, see, since I were twelve-year-old. That do make for big muscle.'

'You got fam'ly?' It was the first direct question he had been offered, Luke accepted the seriousness of it.

'I got a mother, five sisters an' three brothers.'

'Father?'

'Dead this last year. Trampled by a dray-horse.'

'He worked wi' horses?'

'Ostler.'

Jesse Loveridge nodded. Luke could feel a tightening in his stomach muscles. They were coming to the nub of the matter.

'You bin comin' amongst we for many evenin's, brother. Us have watched 'ee. Careful. As you knows, I got a daughter what is my heart's joy. I don't give her up too easy, but us reckons time is come. My Meridiana is much taken with 'ee, brother. In the normal way o' things her would fetch a tidy bride-price.'

Luke flushed. 'I got no money. I sends my wages home to mother. There's eight to feed, an' no father – '

Jesse lifted his right hand. 'Very proper too. You'm a good man, Luke Carew, never mind about thik old Bible.' He leaned over and looked into Luke's anxious face. 'Young man – us is ready an' willin' to take 'ee as son-in-law. Us

53

reckons as you'm more gypsy than the ribs o' God!'

It was a terrifying statement, and Luke was not able to confirm or deny it. There had been talk among Montacute people that the first Carews to appear in the village had wandered in, with no more than a few pots and pans and a tent, seeking shelter from a wicked winter. But Luke's mother, that Particular Baptist, had always denied this. He said, 'Well, if 'twer true, then 'twas my father, but, like I said, he bin dead this past year.'

Jesse Loveridge spoke softly. 'Cut a gypsy in ten pieces, brother, but don' ever think he'm killed. All you got for your trouble is ten more gypsies.' Jesse stood up. 'You can bide yer, in the waggon, while us has our Council. My Meri can come an' keep 'ee company.'

Meri's mother was house-proud. Every surface gleamed, colours dazed his senses. A fringed silk shawl thrown across a settle; a blue velvet cushion; black polished stove; brass railings; old cups and plates in rich plum shades, with gold rims and handles; a striped woven rug on the floor in shades of green and yellow.

Not an inch was wasted. The stretched canvas of the bow-top was lined with a patterned material, underneath it, every gap and corner was fitted out cunningly with beds and cupboards. Shelves, guarded by rails to prevent their contents falling, held old brass lamps and tasselled pictures. The single bow-window was curtained with lace, which was looped and tied back with bits of pink ribbon.

The only embellishments Luke had ever known had been in the lush interiors of wealthy churches. The two rooms of Number One, Wash Lane must house a family of ten. He had lived all his life among the gloving; the stench of newly cured leather always in his nostrils, an earthen floor beneath his feet, and windows shut fast against fresh air.

54

Even in the carpenter's house, the stonemason had been confined to the kitchen. He ate below salt, and slept on a pallet of straw in a cupboard-bed close to the fireplace. The Greypaull's parlour was reserved for the reception of the Reverend Soames and his wife and sisters, and the hymn-singing around the piano on a Sunday evening.

The distribution of living space among the Rom became clear to him. Meri and her parents slept within the waggon. Her many brothers slept outside, in the tents. In this way morality was satisfied, and Meridiana Loveridge was watched over.

'You likes fancy a bit better now?'

She slipped silently into the vardo, pulling his gaze back towards the sunlight. He had not heard the slap of her bare feet on the ladder. Grandmother Loveridge had come to chaperone them; she sat sideways across the doorway, and puffed gently at her little clay pipe.

Luke had never encountered Meri within walls. His only experience of beauty had been the damask rose bush. Proximity intensified the lure of her brilliant dress, of skirts that showed her ankles, of the puffed sleeves of her blouse that revealed her elbows.

Several of the young rais were hammering a length of wood deep into the ground.

'What's that for, Meri?'

'Thass a peeled stick. Thass for a Council. Our men do sit roun' the stick an' talk. We cudden hold Council before. We bin waitin' on the Woods fam'ly comin' in from Wales. They'm here now.'

'What do 'ee talk about in this Council?'

'Weddin's mos'ly. Like how much a rai'll give as a bride-price. Like what is gonna marry what – stuff like that.'

He could see the Rom men hunkering down around the

55

peeled stick. The deliberate unconcern in her voice confirmed his unease.

'Whose weddin'?'

'Thine an' mine, Luke.'

'I never said I'd wed thee!'

'You mun got to.'

'Why for?'

'I told Pa you whistled for I – middle o' the night. That you laid wi' I in the far woods. That you kep' I away from the tan till mornin'.'

'But I didden, Meri!'

She glanced towards her stone-deaf grandmother. 'I knows that, you gurt ninny. I crep' out when Ma an' Pa was sleepin'. 'Twas easy – they sleep like old dogs. I bidded away all night. I come back while they was eatin' brekfus'. I was all draggled an' drippin' wet. So you got to wed I!'

'I'll tell un' the truth.'

'Pa won't lissen. He do want I settled – 'tis safer. They Woods boys is little an' skinny. The biggest one don't reach up to my shoulder. Granny hev said as that 'ud be a mismatch.' Her gruff voice softened. 'You'm a beautiful man, Luke. I never see'd a man so tall an' powerful. I wants 'ee – I wants 'ee so strong I can't sleep no more for thinkin' on it.'

'You shudden talk o' such things. 'Tidden decent – no 'tidden! Anyhow – man got to do the askin' – not maiden.'

'Well, ask I then, Luke Carew. Ask I to wed thee.'

He rested his head in his hands. 'What'll I do? I bain't yet twenty. I idden ready to marry. What my Ma'll say when she finds out, I don't know.'

She had waylaid him on woodland paths, peeped at him from beneath the bell tower, lured him towards the tents of her people. Now, they had him pinned down in the vardo. Grandmother sat across the only exit, and Luke's courage was withered by the circle of gyspy-men, who were still seated around the peeled stick.

There was also the temptress. When she touched his fingers he felt it right down to the soles of his feet. There was danger in this abandonment of feeling. The lowering of thresholds might allow unholy desires to seize him. Already, there was a whiff of burning brimstone in the air. When she lifted his hand to touch the amber necklace fire and ice pierced his body.

The amber was body-warm. It lived its own life, independent of her. It was the exact shade of wild cat's eyes, a rare green-yellow. 'I wants 'ee,' she had said, 'I wants 'ee so strong I can't sleep no more for thinkin' on it.'

The Council was over. The men rose and looked towards the vardo. Grandmother shuffled back towards her own waggon and Jesse Loveridge beckoned Luke Carew towards him.

There was a good deal of smiling and clapping of hands upon shoulders. It would seem that Luke had got himself a bargain. The bride-price, whispered Meri's father, had presented no problem, something honourable could be arranged between them. A certain amount of muttering and many black looks were observed among the Woods family, who declared their intention of pulling-out of the tan first thing in the morning. It was said that a mint-new waggon, built by a wheelwright in Bridgwater, was at that very moment awaiting collection by the Loveridges. It was to be Jesse's wedding-gift to his only daughter.

Luke had heard that they leapt over bonfires and jumped across broomsticks. His marriage to Meridiana was to be no more than a solemn breaking of bread between them and the eating of it. The drinking that followed was the true celebration. Luke and his bride had no vardo to which they might retire when the party was over.

Laughing immoderately, and reeling from the unaccustomed beer, he was schooled by his new brothers-in-law in the necessary skills of building his own bender. A pile of hazel-wands had already been cut from the wood and laid ready. Eight parallel holes had been made in the earth, four on either side. A wand was pushed into the ground and bent over to locate its corresponding hole. When the arcs were completed, a blanket and then a waterproofed canvas were thrown across and securely pegged down to make a simple dwelling. A depth of clean straw was spread within, and Luke Carew's marriage-bed was ready.

Between bud-burst and blossom-drop she had enslaved him. She had lied to ensure that he would be obliged to wed her. At sight of the little bender standing underneath the moon that same old memory stirred in him that was not his own.

Luke had always been secretive, both from necessity and by nature. If you were born into a two-roomed cottage, and you were the oldest of nine children, then a certain hiving-off, a detachment, was demanded if the spirit was to reach towards the sunlight. He told no one of his liaison with Meridiana Loveridge. He saw no need to do so.

It was a simple matter for him to return each evening to the carpenter's house as soon as his day's work was finished. Luke washed himself at the pump, ate his bread and cheese supper, and then retired to his pallet of straw in William Greypaull's kitchen.

The carpenter and his family went early to their beds. When the house settled down, and the village street was deserted, Luke returned to the tents in Dommett Wood. No questions were ever asked by his workmates. Luke had always been the first among the masons to pick up his mallet and chisel in the early morning.

The Greypaulls had looked leniently on the bridegroom's over-indulgence. 'If a young man can't get drunk at his own weddin',' said Elizabeth, 'then I should like to know when can he?' Since every other adult guest, save herself and Samuel, had been in a condition similar to that of Philip, Eliza's mother had found no argument among them.

Samuel, alone, was unforgiving. That old tenderness he had felt for his brother, a willingness to excuse him his little failings, had now been replaced by a festering anger. Marriage had not yet made a man of Philip; nor a woman of Eliza. It was Samuel, bringing back a straying cow to Larksleve in the early morning, who became aware that the new Mrs Philip Greypaull was spending her nights on the horse-hair sofa in the parlour.

Eliza, pitched uncomfortably between tears and terror, needed a friend; and there was only Meri. She walked down to the lane that led to Dommett Wood, and called out to a chavvie, 'Tell your Meri to come up to Larksleve. Say Eliza wants her. Say to hurry.'

Meridiana came triumphant up to Larksleve, plaid dress, white pinna', ribbons flying. She hovered at Eliza's kitchen door, hefted the hawking basket lightly and rubbed one bare foot nervously across the other.

'I didden know if I shud – '

'Come on in. He idden yer. He's down to Taunton. To market.'

'You didden ought to let 'un.'

'I can't stop 'un.'

Meri rested her basket on the kitchen table. She eyed the shotgun rack ominously above the chimney-breast and looked uneasily towards the door.

' 'Tis all right, I tell 'ee Meri. He don't never come back till late evening. Anyway – I be mistress now. This is my

59

house.' Eliza squared her narrow shoulders and looked brave.

Meri said, 'The chavvie said to hurry. Wass up then, Liza? You'm lookin' sickly.'

Tears welled in Eliza's eyes, they dripped from her chin and gathered in the thin hollows of her neck. Meri, who had never shed a tear in her seventeen years, was nonplussed. She edged away towards the open door, and this time she looked embarrassed.

'Don' take on then, Liza. You'm a wife now, wedded and bedded.'

'But I idden. I be wedded but not bedded.'

'That bain't natural.'

'He got drunk, see, on his weddin'-night. Sam an' me had to put 'un to bed. After that, well – I didden know what to do – I sleeps every night on the sofa, an' he sleeps in the bedroom.'

Meri looked thoughtful. 'You can't play they sort o' tricks in a bender.'

Eliza twisted her hands together. 'I didden ought to be tellin' you; you being a single maid an' all.'

'But I idden no more, Liza! I be wedded – an' bedded proper.'

'You got married?'

'Aye. I catched 'un easy. He come like a lamb in the end. He'm the beauty of all the West. He'm like blackthorn flowers shakin' brave against the wind. I never see'd a man like him, not even up along to Bristol.'

'Not the mason?'

'The very one.'

'But – he bain't gypsy. He come from Montacute. He lodges wi' my uncle William. I thought you said your Pa 'ud never let you marry out of – '

'Don' you ever say that, Liza Greypaull. He'm Rom, you hear me! He'm more gypsy than the ribs o' God. My Pa said so.'

'How do you know?'

'Us goes to Montacute. They always got a bit o' money put by, they women what do the glovin'. I do's a bit of dukerin in the King's Arms Tavern. I once yeard 'em talkin' about Luke Carew. They reckoned his father were a gypsy. 'Tis a gypsy name – Carew. My Granny said so!'

Eliza lowered her eyelids. Her sandy lashes brushed freckles. 'You'm bedded then, Meri? Proper?'

'Aye.'

'An' he come like a lamb?'

'He did-so!'

'I dunno what I can do.'

'Do 'ee like 'un? I mean – have 'ee ever kissed 'un?'

'No. Well – my Ma and Pa was always about, an' anyway he never tried to. I don' even like 'un all that much. He's – well he's like a liddle baby. Sometimes, when I know he's asleep, I goes up an' looks at 'un, sleepin'. 'Tis like lookin' at a puppy. You can't blame pups for what they do. They don't know any better.'

'What about that bone I give thee?'

'That only made a sore place on my leg.'

Meri tapped her heavy necklace. 'I didden reely ought to – Liza. But he'm a hard nut, an' us got to crack 'un.' She slipped the circle of green-gold amber across her braids and placed it around Eliza's neck.

'Only one night, mind. You got to give it back in the mornin'.'

'What'll this do?'

'That'll bring 'un runnin', all smiles an' kisses. But you got to believe on it, Liza, or 'twon't work.' Meri looked troubled. 'If my amber beads don't get Philip Greypaull movin' – then nothin' else will.'

To be his own man was a new sensation. Philip leaned back

61

on the bolstering knowledge of the fourteen milch-cows in his meadows, of the eight Spotted Wessex pigs in his sty, of the four dozen assorted hens and their strutting cockerel in his farmyard. Locked safely away up on Larksleve, and holding a quantity of wealth, was the purple velvet draw-string bag. It no longer held quite as many sovereigns, but then a yeoman farmer could hardly go into market without having the chink of gold about his person.

He rode into Taunton by way of Bishop's Hull. The town had never looked so fine to Philip. He turned into North Street and crossed the bridge that spanned the Tone. The river ran sweet and sparkling in the sunshine. The clock on St James's Church struck ten. He had one whole glorious day before him. The streets were loud with the voices of animated people, the rumble of farmcarts, and the ringing hooves of high-stepping carriage horses. His mare took him into St James's Street, towards the Turk's Head stables. Philip's blood stirred at sight of the familiar turbanned head on the inn-sign. Horse and master were equally at home here.

A visit to the cattle market would be obligatory. His father and uncle would expect an encounter and a brief reckoning-up of Philip's recent progress. He calculated rapidly on sweating fingers: hay nearly ready for the scythe; cows milking down well; hens laying; sow about to farrow; the shelves of the cheese-house filling up nicely.

What he was not prepared for was the man-to-man ribaldry of his uncle and father. Servants of the church not-withstanding, they nudged and winked at him like any lewd tavern keeper.

' 'Tidden they cheeses us be worried about,' grinned John Greypaull, ' 'tis thee bor, what do faze we! Our Liza do look fair wore out. Us hev calculated on gettin' our first grandchild roun' about Easter. Like I jus' said to Dan'l – thy son Philip mus' be more of a man than us gives 'un credit.'

Philip liked his women to be soft and rounded. Eliza would never please him. His tastes had been formed long ago in the brothels of Taunton. To give his father the slip on a market or fair-day had never been easy, but Philip had loved to gamble, to cheat a little, to have secrets.

But he also craved the warmth that would edge his way when he had pleased somebody. Just lately, he had missed his mother, his brother, Samuel, and his little sister, Madelina. Philip needed kisses, warm arms about his neck, Sam's grin for reassurance. On Larksleve there was only Eliza, who, like the oxen, was content to labour through the hot white hours of summer without complaint. He was afraid to gauge the quality of her, and shamed by her patient acceptance of his indifference, at the same time annoyed by it.

He knew that she crept to his side in the early morning; he had waited, feigning sleep, for the time when she would creep in beside him. The expectations of others had always driven Philip to seek bolt-holes. He suspected that he was incapable of bearing this bitter marriage yoke which his father had hung upon him. Sometimes he had even considered Lyme Bay and the promise of the tall-masted ships which lay at anchor. Sea-fog would penetrate many miles in land, and he had known evenings, high on Buckland Hill, when the salt mist had swirled into his mind and promised him freedom. But then he had heard the mariners' tales, told by old men in the Turk's Head bar, and thought better of it.

Eliza had milked fourteen cows singlehanded. There had been a certain satisfaction in the necessity for so doing. Satan would surely find mischief if her hands were idle. She took her milking stool and pails into the Home meadow; she leaned her head against each beast's soft flank and crooned the only bars of Philip's new song that she could remember.

'My love is like a red, red rose,' sang Eliza, 'that's newly sprung in June.' The melody at least made the milk run faster into the bucket.

She set cream to rise in pans, scoured the dairy, fed the hens and pigs. She mended the fire, and set the pie to warm against her husband's homecoming. She could never be certain whether he would be drunk or sober.

His step was firm across the cobbles; he stabled his horse without her assistance. She smiled nervously across the white tablecloth, fumbled the silver onto the kitchen table.

'You be early, Philip.'

'Nothin' much doin' down to Taunton. I run into father an' uncle John. I ordered a new hay-waggon. Us'll need that soon – they be cuttin' already, further downhill.'

Eliza, bathed and weary, slumped half-asleep across the table. Dressed in a plain cotton wrapper, her hair uncovered, she already had a look of his work-trammelled mother about her, and yet, in the triangle of her face, he could see the innocence of his little sister, Madelina.

He touched her shoulder and Eliza moved beneath his hand. She turned round to face him and the movement brushed his hand up against her neck.

'What's all this then? Fancy beads?'

'I don' often wear 'em.'

He ran the amber through his fingers; surprised at its warmth, he lifted and pressed the heavy necklace on the cool skin of his face. The action pulled Eliza inevitably towards him. She reached up tentative fingers, traced his jawline, touched his eyelids. He looked into her strange green eyes and, for the first time, he saw her clearly, the tenderness in

64

her, the promise of refuge. If he could only bring himself to please her, to give a little, she might allow him the warmth and cosseting that was essential to his nature.

'Come, Liza,' he whispered, 'you do look fair wore-out. Let we go to our bed then.'

Jesse Loveridge's acquisition of his own living waggon had been achieved by means of some skilful trading with a Midland gypsy met at a horse fair, one who had admired and desired Jesse's string of coloured Exmoor ponies. But the waggon he was to give to his only daughter on her marriage would be brand new. It had long since been commissioned from a local wheelwright and was almost paid for. Each time they had passed through Bridgwater town, Jesse had called at the wheelwright's yard to inspect the progress of his gift. A sum of five sovereigns, demanded by the craftsman, had to be paid over at intervals to cover each stage of the work. On his last visit, the wheels had been completed and work on the interior fitting of beds and cupboards was about to be embarked on. The final payment had now to be made and the waggon collected.

Jesse, and his eldest son, Ephraim, made ready for the twenty mile journey down to Bridgwater. Extra hands would be needed on the return trip, and Jesse insisted that Meri and Luke should go with them. They were to travel on Saturday, pitch overnight in Bridgwater, and return late on Sunday evening. Such a plan would involve Luke in lying; explanations of his absence from work would be called for on the next Monday morning. But he knew that such twitterings of his conscience would mean nothing to the Loveridges. He did not even take the trouble to voice them.

The trip was made with the flat-cart and their two strongest horses. Travelling light, loading only the necessary two benders, Jesse and Ephraim's fiddles, the kettle, the frying-pan, and four cups, they arrived in the town in late evening. The wheelwright allowed them to pitch in a corner of his yard. Water was readily available, and the grais were tethered in an adjoining meadow. Bread and tea, and a hunk of fat bacon, had been purchased along the road. A fire of aromatic wood-shavings quickly boiled the kettle and saw their supper frying. 'A kushti-tan,' grinned Jesse, and his children agreed. It was only Luke Carew, footsore and conscience-ridden, who sat morose and silent at the fireside. He had that day discovered that gypsies ride only on level ground, or when the slope is gentle. Many steep hills lay between the Blackdowns and Bridgwater, and Luke, whose great strength was mainly in his arms and shoulders, had found the long up-and-downhill marches in the summer heat more exhausting than the work of a mason. He could not match the easy barefoot stride of the Rom. His heavy work boots were a burning torture; the muscles of calf and thigh screamed out for rest. The brisk pace, he thought, might have been set up deliberately to test him; he would rather be drawn and quartered than complain.

Once the benders had been erected and the supper eaten, Jesse and Ephraim took up their fiddles and made for the inn. At their departure Luke tried to ease the boots from his feet. The sight of the blisters and the bleeding rawness, called a swift rebuke from Meri.

'Whyn't you tell?' she scolded him. 'Whyn't you say somethin'?' When she ordered him to 'Bide yer!' he almost grinned. He thought it quite likely that he would never move again. She was back within the hour, her arms full of strange smelling leaves which she applied, binding the greenstuff to his swollen feet with strips of white cotton torn from her petticoat hems. ' 'Tis they old boots what do make the trouble for 'ee, Luke.'

'I bain't no gypsy,' he muttered. 'I never walked before from sun-up till sun-down. I do wear boots ever since I bin a mason. I cudden go barefoot no more, if I was to try to.' He hung his head. 'An' I might as well tell 'ee what else I got in mind. I don' reckon we be married. Not proper. Not by parson. That do keep I awake nights, Meri.'

'We be so married, Luke Carew! Married more proper than your parson cud do it. We broke the bread an' ate it,' she hesitated, 'an' if you so minds, after seven summers, then you'm free to leave the tan. I won't keep thee.'

' 'Tidden no good like that! I got to see a parson. I can't never go home to my Ma no more if I bain't married proper.'

'You cudden go home no more, anyway,' she whispered.

'But I got to go one day, when the bell tower's built.'

She looked at him across the fire, traced with her mind's finger the dark planes of his face, touched the black curls that hung thick on his forehead. His great head was bowed in confusion; his hands, palms upwards, signalled his defeat.

She said softly, 'I see'd a parson up-along, on town Green. He'm travellin' in a dinky liddle waggon, wi' writin' writ on it. He'm telling about God an' such. He'm sellin' they Bibles.'

Luke tried to stand up; he clutched at her arm and staggered. 'Show I, Meri. Show I where's the parson!'

It was as she had said; the evangelist had pulled his caravan on to the town Green. It was indeed a dinky little waggon. Painted bright blue, with a spindle-railed preacher's pulpit built onto the back end, and the framework lettered all over with texts, it had the drawing power of a travelling circus.

Luke read the painted words. He moved slowly between the uplifted people and sounded out the individual letters. He rolled them experimentally upon his tongue, before declaiming them to Meri. 'The Lord is my Shepherd.' 'The Evil shall Perish.' 'Come all ye Sinners and Be Saved.'

The last exhortation was all that it would take to convince him. While Bibles were changing hands for pennies, Luke approached the itinerant holy man, hauling Meri with him.

'Us wants to be wed, right away. This minute!'

'You's'll have to buy a Bible.'

'Two! Us'll have one for each.'

They were decently married, across the Book and with a prayer, at sun-down on the Green of Bridgwater town. Luke unhooked a hoop of the gold from Meri's ear and slid it across her finger. He was too elated to notice that this Primitive Wesleyan Methodist, lay-preacher and Bible salesman, was not thoroughly conversant with the marriage service. By morning both his feet and conscience were less troubled. The Lord had sent deliverance to Bridgwater in a little blue waggon. The greenstuff applied by Meri had wrought another miracle in his feet. He could even put his boots on.

They all faced-to around the morning fire. Jesse had paid over the final ten sovereigns to the wheelwright, and then bargained for the return of two gold pieces.

'One for y'r honour's good luck – an' one for the drom.'

The new waggon stood brave and tall in the sunshine. Built entirely of wood, it was larger than Jesse's own canvas-topped vardo. It had been painted dark green, and fitted throughout with beds and cupboards. It had a small black stove, two windows, and a half-door. As yet, there was nothing fancy about it, nothing that a Particular Baptist could reasonably object to.

Philip was in no hurry to remove his jacket and roll his sleeves up. It had always been others who had set the times for ploughing and sowing; Daniel and Samuel who had sniffed the wind, felt the threat of rain in sinew and pulse, and decided when the first swathes of hay and corn should fall.

Left alone, Eliza knew that Philip would vacillate, find a dozen excuses for not beginning; escape down to Taunton. Lately, she had felt a pride rise in her, a wish to see her shelves lined with cheeses, her foldyards filled with livestock, her cart-houses, barns and stables crammed with waggons, grain, and horses. She knew that in her parents' eyes she and Philip were no more than stewards of this land, custodians of this house and its outbuildings. Accounts would still have to be rendered at the year's end.

Philip was susceptible to persuasion. Gentle cosseting on her part might coerce him into rising early, remaining reasonably sober, sharpening hay-knife and scythe, and making a start. The hay was their first and most vital crop of the season; and now there was a drying wind, clear skies, and that extra dimension in the air that informed Eliza that the time was just right for their haysel.

'Perhaps us had better begin, eh Philip? Fine days mayn't last much longer.'

'I was waitin' on Father being finished. He might spare me our Sam for a couple o' days.'

'I don't think us can wait for your Samuel.'

'All spare hands be already hired-out, Eliza.'

'There's still Jasper Loveridge to be had.'

'That gypo'! I'd as lief cut the hay by meself - by moonlight, as let any o' they thievin' liars on Larksleve.'

'There's bin many a time when my father's brought his hay in by moonlight. Us can't really wait,' she said gently, 'any longer.'

The unexpected sight of Philip Greypaull scything hay single-handed in Cherry Furlong so delighted his father that help was immediately offered. Samuel, and a younger

69

brother, Ben, were despatched with speed from Warren's
Farm. Not to be outdone by his brother, John Greypaull
sent Loveday Venn, from his own dairy, to help Eliza. At
the end of three weeks, there were respectable hayricks in
the Larksleve stackyard and several more cheeses maturing
on Eliza's shelves.

The Larksleve fields had been worked and seeded in spring
by Eliza's brothers. Wheat had been drilled in February,
oats and barley in April. The root crops of mangold and
turnip had been sown in May. Now, between haysel and
harvest, it was up to Eliza and Philip to weed and pick
stones from between the crops. There was also the seven-day
burden of milking and cheese-making, the weight of which
fell exclusively on Eliza and Loveday.

Pressure was already upon Eliza to emulate her mother, to
guard against waste, both of time and substance. So much
had been given by both sets of parents. She and Philip had
been allowed this good start, this legendary beginning.

Dairy utensils had been donated by her mother. The
churns and milk-pails (each cow had its own) the beautiful
dishes for cream, the marble slabs, the hair sieves and
skimmers, the moulds and the butter-patters had all come
from Castle Farm.

From Philip's mother had come the salting-trough, the
scales and cheese-press, and the calico window-blinds that
were hung, wet-through, at the dairy windows when the
summer heat was at its fiercest.

The house was also full of heirlooms. Daniel and Rachel
had bought the piano, and sent over a scrubbed-top table,
Welsh dresser, oak ingle-settles and carver chairs from their
own kitchen. They had also furnished the bedroom. The
parlour-gift of her parents was a source of comfort and pride
to Eliza. The window blinds, so her mother had instructed,

were to remain permanently lowered in this room to guard against fading. Through the perpetual gloom, Eliza found consolation in the flowered carpet, the blue horsehair sofa, the cabinets filled with wedding-present china, the what-not and its aspidistra.

It was only when Philip was to be seen in his fields, and Loveday absent from the farm on some errand, that Meri would venture to cross the Larksleve threshold.

'How be, then, Liza. You'm thinner than ever.'

''Tis a hard time, Meri. Us can't keep upsides wi' groundsel an' chickweed. Us fetched a gang of children up from the village to do some weedin', but they seven-year-olds take some watchin'. More trouble than they be worth, so Philip do say.'

'How be the Master?' Meri giggled. 'Do 'un still have need of my amber?'

Eliza blushed. 'Reckon as how us'll manage wi'out that now. How's Luke then?'

Meri looked thoughtful. 'Now thass a question I amn't sure of. He'm pulled all ways. His Ma don't know yet as we be married, an' they Montacute fellers hev found out, an' they'm joshin' Luke somethin' awful. My Pa says Luke shud leave that old church, but 'un won't lissen. Got to keep on sendin' his money home every Friday, Luke says.'

Eliza skimmed cream with a steady hand. ''Tidden all roses, is it, Meri?' She held out a hand for the milk-can, which the gypsy just happened to have brought with her. She watched the stream of blue liquid splash into the can.

'Sometimes,' she said, 'I feel a bit like the whey: all my goodness skimmed off.' She snapped shut the lid of the milk-can and handed it to Meri.

71

'Do 'ee ever feel frightened, Meri? Do 'ee ever dream about being up behind a bolting horse, an' the traces broke in your hands, an' the road in front running steep downhill, all the way?'

Meri's eyes were sharp with old wisdom. 'You'm frighted o' your Ma and Pa. Thass your trouble. They give you all this, an' now you got to keep it nice an' tidy. You always got to be milkin' they cows, an' makin' cheeses. 'Tidden never worth it, Liza!' Her eyes grew dreamy. 'You an't never packed up, an' harnessed the grai; you an't never seen the drom stretchin' out in front like a shiny ribbon. Ah Liza! That do lift the heart in a body. To hear the big trees talkin', an' the fieldfares call in the hedges. To wonder what you'll see aroun' the next bend in the lane.'

Eliza began to scour milk-pails; she swished the mare's-tail brush around with an angry motion. ' 'Tis next year what is worritin' me. He bain't no farmer, Meri. Everybody knows it. 'Tis shamin' for all the family. He's all right for the time being, 'cause 'tis all new to 'un. Him never havin' had his own place, an' still havin' the dowry money. But what'll I do when 'un won't get out of bed? When 'un goes off boozing again down to Taunton.'

Meri considered. 'You cud kill 'un, I s'pose. Or chop up his harness. You cud burn the house down. That 'ud show 'un!'

She followed Eliza into the kitchen. 'You gorgio women be too soft wi' your men. You wants to take the kettle-iron to 'un. Break his fancy nose. Pull out they liddle yellow curls by their roots. An' lock up that dowry-money, Liza! They Taunton pub-girls won't never want Master Greypaull, if 'un got no gold in his breeches.'

'What'll you do wi' Luke Carew if 'un don't come up to scratch?'

Meri nodded. 'He'm already half-Rom by blood. Us'll root out that gorgio rubbish what is in his head, all that

72

Bible readin'. Luke won't be chipping away at they old stones for much longer. Pa an' me 'ull train 'un to break ponies, an' make clothes-pegs.'

Luke had all of the chapel-goer's superior fervour. Harnessed from childhood to the driving zeal of the Particular Baptists, he had assumed the instant capitulation of Meri's people to his style of religion. But he was meeting with a resistance which was hard to define. They were polite. They listened to him, like children who were absorbed in a story, but he was beginning to suspect that they were incapable of making the vital transition from Biblical theory into daily practice.

Each chavvie, he discovered, had been baptised many times, in separate parishes, by a clergy whose willingness to pay for the privilege had been taken advantage of, without discrimination. It was all the same to the Rom if the baptismal shilling should come from High Church of England, Primitive Methodist, Particular Baptist or Congregationalist. Luke had tried to point out the fallacy of multiple baptism.

'Once be enough,' he said firmly.

'But that don't hurt 'em none,' he was told, 'that way they is double took care of, an' Parson's missus do bring cakes an' bits o' clothes.'

'Then why is it 'ee don't get married in church?'

'Some does, brother. But us reckons that is only for "show". 'Tis what us do promise each to each what matters.'

There were other areas in which they would confound him. The women, so immodest in their speech, were careful of their deportment within the tan. He saw how they always passed behind a seated man, how a woman would never let her hair down to comb it when men were present, how the mothers chided their growing daughters to sit 'legs together'.

The unstable temperament of these people was no real revelation to him. His own father had been such a one, high-tuned as a fiddle-string, swift to anger, a man who would lie more readily than he would tell the truth. But a loving father to his children, for whom he had always reserved a special tenderness.

It was the facility of the Rom to cheat, beg and steal that troubled Luke most. Even their lurchers were trained to retrieve and, in some cases, to go out and catch game. But whenever he mentioned the law he was told, 'But they is man-made rules, brother. Us does no harm. A man buys a field, brother. Oh yes! But that don't give him right to the rabbits what burrow under the grass, or the birds what fly above it.'

'You sometimes steal turnips and potatoes from the farmers' fields.'

'They is the fruits of the earth, brother, and what proper father can see his chavvies' hunger?'

Luke's secret had finally been leaked to the Montacute masons through gossip in the Lamb and Flag inn. The masons were not altogether surprised. They knew him for a kind and quiet giant, preoccupied with religion, and careful to avoid entanglements with women. That he should have gone to the gypsy tents with conversion in mind and then fallen victim to the enticing Meri was at first a fine source of amusement to them. Until they remembered Charity Carew.

'Wudden like to be standin' in your boots, boy, when your Ma gets to hear about all this!'

Luke's mother arrived in Buckland St Mary on the following Monday. She came riding in on the cart with the first load of Ham stone. Thin and angry, her greying hair scraped into a knot on her neck, she confronted him behind the almost demolished bell tower.

'Tell I 'tidden true!'

' 'Tis true, Ma.'

'I jus' cudden believe it. I had to come yer and hear it from your own lips. They be saying you took-up wi' they dirty hedge-crawlers. That you be married to one o' they.'

Luke tapped the mallet on his outstretched palm. 'I wed wi' the tall one, her they calls Meri.'

'I knows which one 'tis, Luke Carew. 'Tis thik proud one, wi' the plaid skirts an' the ribbons. Her what do tell fortunes in the pubs for money. Her what was always bangin' on my door lookin' for 'ee.'

'Her don't tell fortunes no more, Mother. I be teachin' her the Bible.'

'That won't make no diff'rence.' Charity rubbed tears away, angry at her own weakness. 'They bain't like Christian folk. They be feckless. They gives no thought for the morrow.' She looked down at the stones which littered the hallowed ground.

'I had trouble wi' your father. Jye could never bide quiet along to home. Always restless, especially when 'twas holiday and fair-days.'

'Tell I the truth, Mother. Were Father gypsy?'

Charity Carew, unwilling to commit herself to the lie direct, looked uneasy. 'I cudden say for sure. Well, 'twas all a long time ago, an' folk do talk some nonsense. Jye was twenty-year-old when us wed. He were ostler to the Isaacs family in Yeovil. There was talk that his folk had been travellers – but that don't mean nothin' to you an' me, Luke. 'Tis on'y you I be concerned with. To think you should have gone to live wi' one o' they hedge-crawlers, they diddecoi heathens!'

' 'Tidden like that. Us lives decent, in a brand-new waggon. Her father had it made special down to Bridgwater. They is good people. They got some funny ways – well, that's on'y natural. I tells 'em Bible stories, Mother, an' they do listen.'

'You be a mason; your shillin' was paid when you were twelve-year-old. You be a craftsman what has fell in wi' thievin' horse-dealers.'

Luke pointed to his chisels and mallets. 'I be still a mason, Mother. Nothin' ever goin' to change that. But I loves her, an' nothin' ever goin' to change that either.'

The Ham stone had been unloaded and stacked in a corner of the churchyard. The Montacute carter was about to begin the journey home. Tears ran down deeply grooved channels in Charity's face.

'I bin so proud o' thee, Luke. You always bin such a good son to your mother. You bin as steady as they old church stones.'

'Nothin's changed, Mother. I be comin' home jus' so soon as the bell tower's finished.'

As the cart rumbled out of the churchyard, Charity called back across her shoulder. 'Thy rose, Luke – thy damask rose is full o' flower.'

Luke's commitment to the masons, his faithful departure for work every morning, continued to point out the essential difference between himself and Meri's people. On Sundays he delivered the Word to attentive chavvies and their mothers. The need for constant application to the Bible had improved his reading skill. He had heard himself lately described among the Rom by the flattering name of Lavengro. His commitment to Meri was total and full of sweetness. Whenever doubts skimmed across his view of heaven, he told himself, ' 'Twere meant, her an' me, meant

76

that us two should come together.' Confirmation of this belief was given to him by other people.

There was a Sunday evening when strange waggons pulled into the lane. Three families, on their way from a Dorset wedding, had decided to pitch overnight in Dommett Wood.

'Thass my aunt an' uncle,' whispered Meri, 'thass James an' Drusilla Boswell, an' their children. He'm the King o' the Gypsies. He'm my mother's brother. Am't he a fine sight?'

The waggons were manoeuvred into position; the grais were unharnessed and left to graze in the lane. The benders were assembled and fresh straw laid within them. The kettle was set to boil for tea, and the visitors gathered around the fire to eat and drink, and smoke their little clay pipes. They brought messages and news from distant places.

From the shadows Luke watched James Boswell and his wife Drusilla. They were a stylish couple, middle-aged, full-fleshed and handsome. The man wore a suit of dark green cloth. The jacket was cut with a yoke and back belt; it had five double-stitched patch pockets with button-down flaps. There would be, Luke suspected, other pockets sewn into the lining, poacher's pockets. The trousers were cut high and drop fronted, there were seven rows of stitching around the flap, and five rows of stitching on the turn-ups. The trousers were cut especially close to the knee, for riding horseback. James Boswell wore a scarlet and yellow striped diklo knotted at his throat and a tall hat of soft black felt. As Meri had said, he was a fine sight. She tugged at Luke's arm: 'Look there – the buttons on his jacket is silver half-crowns – and they on his sleeves is shillin's.'

Drusilla Boswell wore black satin, an elaborate, full-skirted dress with a pleated and embroidered apron. The silk shawl around her shoulders was fastened with a golden crown brooch, and half-sovereign earrings dangled from her ears. Her necklaces were of coral and amber.

Luke was pulled forward and introduced as Meri's new husband. James Boswell stood up and shook him by the hand, and discovered that Luke was the taller, by two inches. 'A handsome couple,' said the King of the Gypsies, ''tis easy to see that you two was made for each other.'

Although he lived with the Rom, Luke was not yet one of them. He still thought of the new green vardo as belonging exclusively to Meri. He had expressed surprise at the wealth exhibited by the Boswells.

'Good times, an' lean times,' she told him. 'Sometimes, in bad seasons, they's as pushed as everybody else.'

The rules of life lived within the tan seemed to him to be chancy, if not downright irresponsible.

'You got no reg'lar wages, Meri.'

'The men do make stuff for we to sell, an' us to knock on house-doors.'

'But there's times when you don't sell nothin'.'

'The men do sell ponies, an' make chops.'

'I've seen what happens, Meri. They goes straight to the pub wi' the profits.'

She shook her head. 'Well, thass where you'm wrong, then. Our women be bankers.' She lifted up her pleated silk apron and showed him the canvas bag slung around her waist. 'Thass where us'll have to keep our money when us got a chavvie. 'Tis a wife's job to keep the gold safe underneath her pinna'. There'll be no more money goin' to your mother. That'll have to stop, Luke.'

He found her an awkward question. 'What about the fortune-tellin'?'

She held out her fingers and studied them; her face had a rare look of fear about it. 'Sometimes – they do ask we to look in their hands. 'Tis mos'ly silly maidens what do want a husband. But I don' never tell nothin' bad. No, I never does! When I sees the dark side I never speaks it.'

'What dark side?'

'Wi' some folks I gets a sight o' comin' sorrows. 'Tis like a shadow sittin' on their shoulders.'

'Thass wicked, Meri, so 'tis! Only the Lord God can know the trouble what is comin'.'

'I knows it too.'

'Then do 'ee tell I,' he mocked her, 'then do 'ee tell I what is comin'.'

She touched the rough skin of his palm. 'Thy rough gurt paw can't show much. 'Tiv all bin rubbed off wi' they old stones. Anyhow – I can't never tell for fam'ly.'

'Why not?'

' 'Tis time we skinned our supper-rabbit. All this talkin' makes I hungry.'

To begin with, he had asked her where the food had come from. Now he knew better. He had become like them in as much as he accepted what was put on his plate, or in his hand, as being the gift of God. Their bread had usually been begged in exchange for a prediction of some sort. The buttermilk would have come from the dairy on Larksleve, from the poor red-headed scrap whom Meri called Eliza. The rabbit had been laid proudly at their feet by Jesse Loveridge's lurcher.

Meri's fingers dealt with the rabbit. She cut off its head, skinned and gutted it, wiped it clean, and then skewered it to roast beside the embers. 'A good-fleshed chuchi,' she observed, 'now do you go, Luke, an' cut I a bit o' green cosht.'

He went to the hedge and cut out a length of green wood. He watched as she placed it into the very heart of the

79

fire. A savoury blue smoke began to rise from the sappy stick. It curled upwards and into the flesh of the roasting rabbit. Meri nodded her satisfaction.

His efforts about the tan had not always been so successful. Once, she had sent him to gather wood and he had returned, his arms full of dry branches. As he had bent to mend the fire, she had thrown herself upon him screaming, 'Thass elder! O dordi, dordi! Us dassen't burn elder, 'twill bring Beng down on us.'

'But, 'tis on'y wood,' he had argued, 'you said to fetch wood, so I fetched it.'

'Holly,' she had said slowly, 'or ash.' She had counted up the safe trees on her fingers. 'Beechwood or apple. They'm the good trees. Green ash or withy sticks is good to start fires. Oak an' pine'll keep a slow fire burning.' She had taught him to read smoke. 'When it goes straight up, thass for fine weather. When it goes so far up, an' spreads out – thass for cold weather comin'. When the smoke creeps about in the grass on its belly – thass for rain.'

Sometimes, he would try to imagine her living within walls and under thatch, and could not. He did not need to have his palm read. He could smell the trouble coming.

Domestic harmony, said Eliza's mother, depended on female submission, and what use was rebellion against a husband when the laws of the land, made and applied by men, were conveniently slanted to settle matters in their favour. To be seen and not heard was a requirement which did not always end with childhood. But there were ways, hinted Elizabeth, in which a clever woman could manage her husband. Since God did not repeat himself, and every man was unique, Eliza had better take a long and critical look at Philip Greypaull.

The use of Eliza's dowry was encouraging a jauntiness in

Philip. He sat straighter in the saddle, congratulated himself on a successful haysel. He would never, he assured her, be buried in his wedding suit. He began to wear it on fine Fridays when he rode down to Taunton market.

Daily tasks kept Eliza's world steady on its axis. There was more Greypaull in her than her family had suspected. Her pleasure was in the happy slap inside the churn of butter that had 'come' without too much effort. Satisfaction was to pour this morning's milk into last night's yield, add the rennet, and stir until curd floated in whey.

Cheese-making was a matter of instinct, of taste, feel and smell. Her mother had the knack, and so did Eliza; she cut curd, drained whey, dipped her elbow into steaming water to test for the scald. Then she chopped the curd again and ground it; she set the muslin-shrouded squares beneath the press, and sighed her satisfaction. The shelves were filling up. Her last task of every day was to visit her ripening cheeses and turn them. They were, from start to finish, her own hands' labour.

In August the harvest gangs were recruited within the parish. Groups of twenty and upwards, men, women and children, moved from farm to farm hiring out their labour. On Castle Farm the Lord of the Reapers would be Hannah Cooper's father. He was John Greypaull's senior farmhand, respected for his firmness, his ability to set the positions of reapers in the field and to control their output. In return for his strictness in keeping to the midday rest hour, and his consideration in seeing to it that food and drink were available to all, he was well liked by his fellows, and paid an extra pound by John Greypaull.

The gypsies stood out among the reapers as brightly as poppies between the ripened grain. The knotting of a scarlet diklo at the throat, the flash of a crimson silk pinna', a certain flamboyance in their style was all it would take to inflame Philip's temper.

'I won't have your father's harvest gang on Larksleve!'

'Us got small choice,' she said gently, 'they comes every year, and anyway, 'tis good of father to help we.'

She studied him across the supper table and her heart contracted at his drooping mouth, his petulant expression. The next stage, unless she could distract him, would be a childish outburst of rage, followed by a bout of hard drinking.

Eliza rose at four every morning. She lit the fire, set water to boil, and summoned the cows into the Home meadow. Then she returned to the side of the canopied bed, gift of his parents, and attempted to wake him. She milked the herd, fed pigs and calves, and called Philip once again.

She confided to Meri, 'I all but spoons the breakfast down him, an' sits him on his horse. He be always half-dead in the mornings. He do go up in field still asleep.' She paused and stretched out her hand. 'Do 'ee take a quick look to next year, Meri. Tell I what is wrote there.'

' 'Tis good, Liza. Truly. 'Twill be a girl-baby, strong an' healthy. A dinky liddle maiden. Truly!'

The corn, sown in February by Eliza's brothers, was about to yield Philip a heavy return. The harvest gang moved from Castle Farm and across to Larksleve. They came while the mist was still white in the combe, whistling and singing, young men and their families, nursing mothers with babies, tiny children just able to stagger among the pointy stubble, old men and women, all anxious for a chance to earn the extra few shillings that would buy clothes and boots for the coming winter.

The reapers were at their stations, sickles sharpened. Led by the Harvest Lord, who set the pace, they swung out into the standing corn like swimmers in a golden ocean. The women and children followed in their wake, tying-up and stooking. No matter how many times she saw it, the sight of a grain-harvest just beginning never failed to move Eliza.

At noon they broke for an hour to 'keep field in the heat'. The whistling and singing of the morning hours was hushed by tiredness. Firkins of cider were drunk, bread, cheese and oatcakes eaten. Many reapers crept off to the shade of trees and hedges to snatch half an hour of sleep.

The weather was with them; every day hot and sunny. It was not until they reached the final field that clouds, coming in from the sea to the south, warned the Lord of the Reapers to set up a faster pace. Eliza, bringing cider and food to the harvesters on the new hay-waggon, saw old Betsy Cooper clutch her head, scream once, and fall down across the stook she was tying.

A death in the harvest field was inconvenient, not to say unlucky. John Greypaull pulled at his lower lip and scowled. 'Best put thy old mother in the lea of the hedge,' he told the Harvest Lord. 'Cover her over wi' some sackin'. Us can't bide to bother wi' her now. There's rain comin', an' us got to get this corn in.'

The Harvest Home for both farms was to be kept up by Eliza's parents. She and Philip were not even consulted. 'No sense in you two goin' to all that bother,' said Elizabeth, 'one feasting'll serve for all.'

Once again, the great barn was swept clean for dancing. Trestle tables were erected and spread with white cloths. There was roast beef, salt pork, plum puddings, new bread and yellow butter, whole cheeses. All the evidence of their masters' devotion to husbandry and hard labour was set out before the workers. John Greypaull was toasted in cider and beer, and cheered to the rafters.

Eliza danced once, with Samuel, and recalled how, on her wedding night, she had wondered how it would be to lay claim to a man, to run with him through the meadows underneath the moon.

Philip, who had not been asked to sing, saw his father-in-law take all the credit for the Larksleve harvest; and Betsy Cooper, who had died in the field, lay forgotten in a shed behind the churchyard awaiting a pauper's burial.

The first letter ever to arrive at Larksleve came from a cousin, Rhoda Salter. The envelope was long and bright blue in colour; it bore an American postmark, and Eliza held it, unopened, for several minutes, savouring its strangeness. Receipt of the letter addressed in Rhoda's own handwriting was confirmation, at least, of her arrival in New York. The events, Eliza now recollected, which had led up to the taking of this journey were sad, and yet sweetly romantic.

Rhoda was the daughter of Eliza's uncle, the carpenter, William Greypaull. In the year of 1853, Rhoda's elder sister, Sussanah, had married a butcher named George Salter and emigrated with him to New York. Sussanah bore George two children, the first of which lived only one year. Homesickness, grief at the loss of her baby, and the difficult birth of a second son, all combined to undermine Sussanah's health. She had died in New York, in the summer of 1856.

Sussanah had been a good wife, and in their three years of marriage George had loved her dearly. Now he found himself alone, struggling to establish his butcher's business in a foreign land, and left to raise an eight-month-old baby. He gave deep and serious thought to the problem. The Greypaulls were a respected family; Sussanah had been thrifty, obedient and loving. She had also had a younger sister. George wrote a letter to William Greypaull in which he proposed marriage to the carpenter's younger daughter,

84

Rhoda. The wedding, he suggested, should take place in Charlotte, New York.

Eliza opened the envelope, and withdrew two large and densely written pages.

Charlotte, New York.

Dear cousin Eliza,

At last I find time to pick up my pen and write you a letter from Charlotte, New York. I took ship for America on February 13th and I will say nothing of that crossing but that I was Ill Throughout. Mr Salter was there to meet me at the Quayside, and we were married one week later. Mr Salter is a kind and considerate Husband, him being already Broke-In to the married state in the three years he was wed to my sister. It did grieve me, Eliza, to come into what had been Sussanah's house, altho' Mr Salter had been thoughtful and put away her clothes and likeness. I feel that my poor sister's grieving Spirit do still dwell among us, and I pray every day that she will see that I am doing my Duty by her motherless baby and sorrowing Husband.

The life here is very fast and loud, and Mr Salter is obliged to be away a good deal on account of his Business, but I am resolved, Eliza, that Homesickness shall not be my Downfall. I sought out the nearest Church, as Father did instruct, as soon as I got here, and was Gathered In to the Fold by a very nice Vicar. So I have Friends, but do still miss the sweet green fields of Buckland and our own Church Bells on a Sunday evening.

By the time this letter gets across the Atlantic, you will be married, Eliza, to our cousin Philip, and settled down on Larksleve Farm, which was the Birthplace of my own dear mother. I think of you very often in your new situation and do wonder how you are *Getting On*. I keep very busy, the housekeeping being very different here, and no Fresh produce such as we had in Buckland. Sussanah's child is known as Eddie, and have took to me and do already call me Mama, which is a Blessing. I find myself with child, which should, God Willing, be born in January 1858.

Please write to me, dear cousin, when you have the time.

Your affecshunat cousin, Rhoda.

It had hardly been an argument, much less a quarrel. Luke was so slow to anger that the high point of Meri's temper had usually been passed before harm could be done. He was learning, however, to be wary of domestic upsets; the rows between husband and wife in the tan were spectacular. The damage done to valuable possessions by gypsy women in rage had appalled him. Jealousy was the most frequent cause of conflict, followed closely by a husband's failure to hand over his profits from dealing. Luke had seen a young rawnie chop her husband's set of flash new harness into a hundred pieces. He had witnessed the burning of a tent, the breaking of china, and the smashing of a drunken rai's nose with a kettle-tripod.

Meri complained of the unfair division of labour between them.

'I can't make clothes-pegs,' he told her, ' 'tis lowering, so 'tis! I be a mason – trained for seven years – whyfor should I bide yer to home, whittling they liddle bits o' stick?'

'But I told 'ee, Luke. You makes the pegs, I sells 'em. Thass how it got to be.'

'I can't do it, no I can't! I do build churches. I do work in stone, I handles chisel and mallet.' He held out his thickened fingers, his rough-grained palms. 'I earns thirteen shillings a week wi' my hands. Whyfor shall I make clothes-pegs?'

' 'Cause you'm still sending most of your money to your Ma.'

'I earns enough. Do 'ee know how much farm labourers is gettin'? Six shillings – an' a drop o' sour milk if they's lucky.'

Her voice became shrill. 'Us don't count up in wages.' She lifted up her pinna' and pointed at her money-belt. 'Woman got to mind the fam'ly gold. Men do only go boozin' in the kitchima.'

'Not me, Meri. I do bide alongside you. Every hour when I idden workin' we two be together.'

He spoke the truth. He was not like her father, her brothers and uncles. But clothes-pegs would have to be made and sold. The whole rhythm of her soul's life depended upon it.

He came back to the tan on the following evening, to find her surrounded by a pile of rind and a stack of ready peeled willows. She paused long enough to drop the knife upon the grass, ladle stew from the pot on the tripod, and fetch bread for him from the cratch.

'What you doin'?'

'You can see what I doin'.' She picked up a willow and measured it against a piece of ready cut hazel. Satisfied as to size, she cut off the hand's length of willow and threw it to dry with a stack of others. Nearer to the fire, he could see a heap of tin strips.

'Where's your supper?'

'I'll eat later. I got to get this lot finished.'

Not wishing to appear interested, he gave his attention to the food; he watched her when all her attention was on the knife. Her deftness surprised him.

'You done that before now?'

''Tis man's work.'

'What do 'ee have to do next then, wi' they liddle sticks?'

'They's too wet to show 'ee proper.'

'Go on then, Meri – show I.'

She snatched a piece of cut willow and split it for two-thirds of its length. Then she pared the split to widen the fork. She picked up a strip of the tin and hammered it around the peg to prevent the slit from widening.

'There you are,' she mocked him, 'thass how you makes a clothes-peg. 'Tis easy, idden it?'

The names of the months meant nothing to her. Their chavvie, she told him, 'would be born roun' about black-thorn blossom.' Meri, who had always been lithe and active, was suddenly peaky and quite unlike herself.

Luke cleared the last of the medieval blocks from the base of the bell tower and recalled the prediction that to disturb old church stones would bring ill-luck down upon the masons. Increasingly, he felt like a Biblical Samson beset on every hand by temptation and evil. He longed for a sight of the Somerset Levels, for the flatness of Montacute lanes. Here in Buckland St Mary there were byways so steep and narrow, so littered with loose stones, that no carriage or waggon could ever travel down them. In these places he had seen the harvest carried in on crooks by farm labourers mounted on ploughhorses. It was, Luke believed, in these wild and secluded hamlets that Satan carried on his work undisturbed. He gave little credit to the efforts of the Reverend Soames, who rode daily up and down the parish on his fine horse. Visiting the needy in their leaky hovels, pouring water on the heads of gypsy chavvies were not, thought Luke, practices that were likely to vanquish the Buckland Devil. What was needed here was a man of thunder, a giant of a preacher, like the man in the little blue waggon who had eased Luke's conscience in the town of Bridgwater.

He was learning to read weather signals. The blue

smoke hovered just lately, it hung about on the September drizzle before curling upwards; his bare feet often slipped these days on sodden grass as he crossed from vardo to fireside. There was an ominous bustle within the tan. The peeled hazel stick of the Council had been uprooted, and the evening talk was all about horse-fairs and profitable chops to be made in far off places. Meri was restless. He had recently found her wandering in a copse of larches and oaks beyond which the road divided. One road led out towards the Somerset Levels, the other wound downhill into Taunton.

Norton Fitzwarren, she told him, was where they were bound for. She had already wrapped the precious china in his spare Sunday shirt and in between her best petticoats and blouses. She had dismantled the bender in his absence, and arranged for the loan of a steady mare to pull the waggon. Norton Fitzwarren, she explained, lay closer in to Taunton, to the autumn fairs and markets. The common-land grazing for the grais had all been used up. To stay longer in the Blackdowns would only antagonise the local farmers. For a moment or two her excitement, the fierce quickness of her gestures, had almost seduced him into believing that to move on was his only option, which was strange because he had believed her to be so content that she would remain in Dommett Wood with him forever.

Her anger, when she finally accepted the truth of his refusal, was so destructive that he could only believe her to be possessed. He laid hands on her head and shoulders and commanded the Demon to depart. But she writhed away from his touch and this time her Devil was bigger than his Devil. She dragged the kettle-iron from the ground and whirled it about her head. He ducked just in time as it flew past his head and crashed through the vardo window. She could not, he reflected, chop up the harness, since they did not own a horse, but he was too slow to prevent the blanket from singeing on the fire, and too nervous of the knife to stop her from slicing up her best green velvet skirt and embroidered jacket. Between her paroxysms of weeping and vituperation, Luke tried to point out the stupidity of her actions. Her quick reply was to set fire to the bender.

'You got no decent clothes – you poor, poxy mason! If you had I'd rip 'em to pieces. Go home to your Ma – take your thirteen shillings! Go an' live in they nasty liddle houses what is stinking of the leather. Take your bloody Bible an' get out from yer! I don't never believe your Pa was a Rom. 'Twas a lie you told I!'

'But I never said it, Meri. 'Twas your tale – remember?'

She hammered her fists upon his chest, clawed at his eyes. 'Beat me then! Go on – if you's a man – floor I.'

He gripped her wrists and set her firmly away. 'Only one you is damaging is yourself – and the child you carry.'

She would not come into the vardo with him, but sat up all night weeping and cursing on the step. He was surprised that no member of her family came across to reproach him. The rest of the Rom went about their business as if the commotion between the Carews was none of their business. In the morning, the company ate breakfast, doused their fires, and stowed their belongings without a glance in Luke's direction. Whatever the outcome, it would have to be his sole decision, or hers. He tucked the Bible inside his shirt and took it with him for safe keeping. He walked out of Dommett Wood that morning without once looking back. He knew her now. She was unstable, unreliable, changeable as the sky. She must go where she pleased. He would not say one word to dissuade her.

He stood on the site of the new bell tower. He measured depth and width with the master-mason. Luke believed in his right to stand fast. To do only what his conscience ordered. But all day the memory of her was wrapped around him, flitting in between his eyelids, dancing a heathen Tarantella. Smiling at him.

Habit set his feet on the familiar road. He went slowly, past the School House, the duck-pond, out beyond Kymer's Farm, and into the forbidden lane which had first led him to Meri.

Their vardo had been pitched in a spot so well chosen that, until it reached the breeze, smoke from their fire would spiral several feet upwards without deviation. He lifted his head towards the yellowing crowns of the elm trees; he saw a wisp of blue, smelled bacon frying, heard a dog growl.

She was sitting hunched up beside the fire. The beauty of her, seen in profile, made his heart ache. She did not look up at his approach. Her father's lurcher lay beside her. The green vardo was in its usual position among the holly thicket. All that was new was the silence and the empty spaces within the clearing.

He stood beside her, slack-jawed and tongue-tied. He curled and uncurled his fingers. 'Didden reckon as I'd find 'ee still yer,' he muttered.

'Whyfor have 'ee come back, then?'

'I got nowhere else to go now – have I, Meri?'

Blackthorn hedges were dark with the ripening of a million sloes. Rosehip and hawthorn berries were scarlet and crimson. The gathered cider-apples lay in heaps beside the press. There was a nip in the morning air, a closing down of evenings. Hannah's grandmother had been buried by the parish, and John Greypaull, Overseer of the Poor, had noted her passing in his Account Book. 'Paid for a Shroud and Coffin and Grave for Betsy Cooper 11s.6d.'

Daniel Greypaull brought rye-straw across to the Larksleve stackyard and used it to thatch the ricks of his son Philip. Rachel brought apples and plums to Eliza, to be dried and bottled and made into jam. John Greypaull presented his son-in-law with a set of flails, and a deal of instruction.

'Now don' 'ee be tempted to thresh out too much grain at one go. 'Tis better to flail as is needed, that way 'twill keep better.'

Eliza's mother viewed her daughter's burgeoning figure with some satisfaction. Her doubts about Philip's virility had been confounded.

The halter that was Larksleve chafed upon Philip's neck. He had been led on a long rein through haysel and harvest. He had sweated and burned in the fields like a labourer, and without complaint. He had been his father's obedient son, Eliza's good husband. He had surprised himself.

He knew that the men in his family despised him, that his father's labourers whispered about him behind cupped hands. Superiority was a matter of conviction, and Philip's truth lay in the mirror. As his mother had so often told him, he was a chime-child, born in the magic hours between Friday's sunset and Saturday's dawn. Such a child, it was said, was bound to be gifted, but no one in Buckland St Mary had ever appreciated this, especially Eliza.

She would have him a farmer. Her dedication to his conversion was stronger than that of his parents. Eliza was a drover, the keeper of his irregular conscience, a force before which he could feel himself bending. Her gentle manner, her deference to his opinions could not quite conceal the iron within the velvet.

The land trembled on the brink of winter. There were blue-white days of keen wind and high cloud when cold bit at the heels. The fortunate ones, those who had earned extra shillings at haysel and harvest, were able to buy new boots and warm clothing. The others, and there were many of them, sewed patch onto patch, darn onto darn; they lined their leaky boots with brown paper, and prayed for an easy winter.

John Greypaull's labourers stuffed rags into their broken windows, spread rushes across their earthen floors for warmth, and waited for the autumn gales that would bring the dead wood crashing. This was the season when the blue devils claimed their own, when the failed farmer took a strong rope out to his stable and hung himself from a beam, when mothers counted up their children and wondered how many would still be alive when the swallows returned.

The first of the hiring fairs was held in Bridgwater, and men who were hoping that a new master would be more generous than the old one stood in line with the sign of their skill pinned onto their jacket lapel. The shepherd sported a lamb's tail, the thatcher a badge of woven straw. The fair occupied a great space on the edge of town. Amusement booths and refreshment tents formed an outer ring inside of which stood the cattle and sheep pens, and the lines of tethered horses.

For the space of the day Philip Greypaull played farmer. He could almost take pleasure in the equality of his new status as yeoman. He saw his two dry cows go up for slaughter, his pigs auctioned, and his butter sold.

The exodus started in mid-afternoon. As the light began to fade, farmers left the fair, anxious for their own safety and that of the money they carried. The rails of the empty pens were cleared away, and all that remained unsold was a line of broken-winded horses. Among the owners of this rejected horseflesh, Philip recognised, with satisfaction, a few of those gypsies who had lately been pitched in Dommett Wood. The fall of dark added a new dimension to the fairground, and all at once the blare of organs was louder, the flare of naphtha was brighter, the gingerbread stalls and gin-booths more inviting. Philip breathed in the smoky air and jingled the new gold in his breeches' pocket, it was the first profit from his season as master of Larksleve, and for a moment he knew how it felt to be his father or his uncle John. He became aware of the cutpurses and pick-pockets, and kept both fists tightly bunched around the money. He was already anticipating Eliza's disapproving face, heeding Daniel's warning. He gambled and lost with the thimble-rigger; visited the Fat Lady and the Mermaid. He laughed for a good five minutes at the antics of Mr Punchinello. It was as he made to leave the fair and start for home that he saw Blanche Sablon for the first time.

The Sablons were a troupe of acrobats. In their own country they were street-performers, but a winter in England had forced them to buy a booth and a green and yellow showman's waggon. They travelled from fair to fair. When the weather became too severe they performed in the upper rooms of inns and taverns. All it took now to under-mine Philip Greypaull's good intentions was a pair of spangled tights and the call of pan-pipes.

Blanche Sablon walked the rope. She placed one slender foot in front of the other and crossed the width of the booth. The other Sablons were grouped underneath her; they followed her progress with assumed attitudes and exclamations of terror. Each time the drums rolled out for the next performance, Philip was the first to be in line handing over his money.

In December the cold became intense. Snow began to fall, the separate flakes whirling white against a dull sky. The stock was safely gathered into the fold-yards, the cows kept in the shippon. Loveday and Eliza drew water in every

94

available bowl and bucket in case the pump froze over. Wherever a true woman came, said Philip's mother, she at once created a home. Through a curtain of snow the Larksleve farmhouse shone, lighted and secure.

Survival, warned Eliza's mother, was what you must aim for. Later on there would be bacon and hams to cure, cider to be brewed, and soap to be made. A supply of all these items had been provided by both sets of parents, but, like the store of new linen, the good boots and clothing, these gifts would not last forever. Next year – warned Elizabeth – next year, my girl, you won't have life so easy! Generosity, she insisted, was all right for the gentry, and ministers of the cloth, and everybody knew that the Soameses were well-connected. They had a parlour-maid who waited at table: a jumped-up girl from the village who fancied herself in an outfit of brown mousseline, with a frilly white cap and a little lace apron. Yes, warned Elizabeth, alms to the poor was best left to Parson. That warm dress, that wool cloak, seams let out and passed on to Loveday, might well be the very clothes you would need for yourself next winter, Eliza, should your harvest be a bad one.

Larksleve Farm.

Dear cousin Rhoda,

At last I find time to pick up the pen and answer your letter. Have missed your dear company of a Sunday evening, but glad to heare that you arrived safe across the Atlantic and settled in your marriage with Mr Salter. To be so content with a Husband is not given to us all, Rhoda. This letter, I am sorry to say, is writ in heaviness of Spirit. I sit here alone in my new Parlour that is all done out in Blue, and Elegant, if I do say so, in this house which have been Home to many Greypaull brides, and was the birthplace of your own dear mother, my Aunt Harriet. My marriage to cousin Philip took place on May

1st, and I could wish as you could have been present. All was done in great style, silk gown, and big dowry, and my hopes of happiness *quite raised*. I could wish that you was here now, dear Rhoda, having no sister what I can talk to, and Mother being so devoted to the four Boys as not to notice that I am downcast. I regret to inform you that all is Not Well between me and Philip. It was my wish that us should be all-in-all to each other, but Taunton do still have the strongest pull on him, and do take him away from home *very often*. I think I may be with child, what could turn out to be a Blessing if it be a Son.

My first Haysel was a good one. After that come weeding and stone-picking, what is hard on the back, but nice to see my fields looking clean and in good order. My harvest is all carried, and my cheese-house have already got many cheeses shelved, what is a Blessing, for this Philip is not, nor ever will be A Farmer. He is overfond of *his bed*, and that is no good in a Yeoman. He don't never shout at me. He is Pleasant but Idle.

I write all this to you dear cousin, in the trust that you will keep it all confidenshul. It have eased my heart to set down on paper all that do grieve me, for I do not know what to do *Next*.

Please give my kind regards to Mr Salter, and a kiss from me for dear little Eddie. Keep up your spirits, Rhoda, and place yourself in the hands of our Redeemer, especially with regard to your present *Condition* what is a dangerous and uncertain travail for us women in this Vale of Tears.

Please write again when you have time, and inform of all what befalls in Charlotte, N. York.

Your affectshunat cousin, Eliza.

Meri came to Larksleve on a gloomy afternoon that was frozen into silence. Luke had purchased new boots, had insisted that because she was with child it was vital for her to wear them. She put on the boots, too sad to argue, and heard with surprise her own footfall ring hard on the frozen earth.

She found Eliza newly-bathed and wrapped in a towel, the hip-bath set on rush matting before the inglenook fire. Meri, scandalised, blushed fiercely.

'You don't never take all your clothes off at one go?'

'Course I do. Why shudden I? What do you do?'

'Us washes a bit at a time, starting at the top and working down.' She pointed at the hip-bath. 'Anyway, us cudden carry thik gurt pot around the country. O' course, in summer us goes in the river.'

'Wi' all your clothes on?'

'Mos'ly.'

Eliza giggled. 'You be a funny lot, I mus' say.'

Meri bridled. 'Us is cleaner'n you gorgios! Us don't peel taters in the same bowl as us washes the dishes. I've seen gorgio women wash their clothes, throw out the water, then soak the cabbage in the same bowl. Dirty cats!'

'You mean – you got diff'rent bowls for everything?'

'O' course!'

'That must take a lot of bowls.'

' 'Tis mokardi if we don't do that. I broke my washin' bowl t'other day. I cud chop 'ee something for a new one.'

Eliza said slowly, 'I wants a token against trouble. For nex' year. For the baby.' She pointed to the coral pendant on the silver chain. 'I wants that one.'

'Well – I dunno, Liza – '

Eliza put on her clothes, clumsy with haste. She left the kitchen, and returned with a china bowl in her arms. She set it in front of the gypsy.

'I bet you never had one as fine as that. Thass a weddin' present. Us had four o' they altogether.'

Meri slipped the pendant across her braids, and put it around Eliza's neck.

'Thass for nex' year,' she crooned, sing-song, 'an' for a safe birthing.'

The china bowl was blue, wide and shallow. It had a design of flowers painted on its rim and inner surface: a red rose, a yellow chrysanthemum, a small white daisy and green, wreathing leaves. When she filled the bowl with water the flowers seemed to float on the surface. She would keep it always. She had never owned so fine a bowl, or one so pretty.

Outside, the grey smoke rose; it lay heavy on the freezing air, and then plumed up into the leafless branches. There had been a finality about that exchange of gifts between her and Eliza. Something valuable had ended.

The Devil was said to be active again in the village. Strange marks were found in the first snow, dead crows on door-steps. John Greypaull's horses suffered from an outbreak of coughing, and his brother Daniel broke his ankle while walking on level ground. The black hound of legend was heard, baying among pine trees in the high hills, and Walter Greypaull, who was not a drinker, was said to have seen its shadow lurking in the larch copse beside the crossroads.

A lone gypsy was as conspicuous as a tropical bird among house-sparrows. She was also vulnerable. Without the protective colouring of her own kind, Meri was obliged to bear with angry mutterings and closed cottage doors.

Eliza spread word about the village that the gypsy girl could cure ringworm and croup in children. That she possessed that rare gift of one who can 'bless for bleeding'. The rumour prevented a threatened stoning, and the possible firing of the plain green vardo. Eliza left a bowl of milk overnight in the shippon to placate the fairies. 'Seems as we'm all pixie-led,' muttered Meri, 'one way or another.'

There was a week of gales when the huge trees crashed together. Meri gathered firewood; the owl crept for shelter; the mole burrowed deeper. Cattle were found staring perplexed beside icy ponds. The fieldfares pined in the leafless hedges. Down in Norton Fitzwarren Meri's people were out in the orchards, bargaining with farmers for the mistletoe and holly. The plan that she should join them for a few weeks at Christmas had to be abandoned; she was not well enough to travel. The sight and smell of food made her nauseous, and her restlessness was pitiful to see. A severe frost came down on Christmas Eve and oil froze in the lamps.

It had been made clear to Luke Carew that his curious insistence on remaining a mason would be tolerated by the Rom only up to and including the birth of the child. As a family man he would then be expected to pack up his vardo and join with the rest of them 'on the drom'. The child, he was told, would be born in their tents in Norton Fitzwarren at the end of March.

It did not occur to Luke, or to anybody else, that Meri might give birth prematurely, in Dommett Wood. When she went into labour the February snows were lying in twenty-foot drifts in the Blackdowns. People were walking on the tops of hedges. Norton Fitzwarren and its gypsy encampment was as distant and inaccessible as the moon.

There were no swaddling clothes, no preparations. No provision had 'been made for a confinement in the Blackdowns. Luke had been present at the births of several brothers and sisters; he had fetched the midwife, boiled water, taken care of the younger children. He had tried to forget the moans and screams that had issued from that upper room in Wash Lane. But in the face of Meri he read disaster. All initiative left him. He stroked her forehead, held her hand.

'What'll I do for 'ee?' he groaned. 'I mun go fetch a woman up yer. Us can't never manage this sort o' business on our own.'

'No,' she ground out, 'no gorgio woman gonna touch me. I knows what I mus' do, I seen plenty of birthings. Only trouble is – I be still in the waggon. I got to be down on the ground, Luke. I got to be in a bender. I can't give birth in the vardo – 'tis mokardi.'

'We got no bender, Meri. You burned 'un. Remember?'

'Then you's'll have to make one.'

'I can't. There's deep snow outside.'

'Then you got to put I underneath the vardo on clean straw. Thass the way birthings got to be for a traveller-woman.'

He fed wood into the little black stove, increased the heat in the already stiffling vardo.

'Us got no straw,' he said calmly, and then suddenly his fear made him angry. 'You shan't set foot outside,' he raged, 'you better forget about all they daft gypsy notions.' He bent over her and stared into her face. 'Do you want it born dead? Is that the truth o' it?'

She rolled her head towards the window, to the falling snowflakes. 'It might be better,' she whispered. 'I knows somethin' what you can't know.'

It had been a season in which the framework of the vardo had twanged with the bitter cold. The stove had gone out in the early hours, and they had awakened in the mornings to find the blankets frozen. Two inches of ice had needed to be broken before he could fill the kettle from the water-jack. The winter had stripped Luke down, made him humble. He had become a hulk of shivering flesh, incapable of coherent thought. Whatever there might be of Rom blood in him it had not been sufficient.

Now he stepped out into moonlight made brilliant by frost. The snow was hard packed, so that he could walk along the drifts, see the tops of trees poking up between them like hedges. He was temporarily disorientated by the whiteness. Without the landmark of the bell tower, he was no longer certain of the exact location of the village.

He talked to himself out loud for reassurance. 'Her'll be all right. Her's on'y seventeen, an' healthy. Nothin's ever ailed her, so far. My Ma birthed nine. No trouble. 'Tis nature – so 'tis! God is good. He won't turn His Countenance from we 'cause her bain't proper Christian. Us was married by Parson in Bridgwater. Our Father, which are in Heaven, hallowed be Thy Name – '

He came sobbing into Buckland St Mary, out of breath and incoherent. He made for the carpenter's house and blurted out his story. A child was despatched in haste to fetch Mother Tavender.

'Her's a tidy body,' William Greypaull reassured Luke, 'her's had plenty of experience wi' child-bed and death-bed.'

Clutching the tools of her trade – a bundle of clean rags and a pair of scissors – the woman agreed to go with him.

The struggle, it appeared, would not be so much to achieve the birth, as to settle the taboos that surrounded it. The mood in the waggon had changed in his absence; Meridiana

101

had grown angry. A set of crockery, she instructed, must be set aside for her sole use. He was not to touch anything which was used in her confinement. To do so would make him 'unclean' and weaken his manhood. He must, most of all, be certain not to touch the child. A young baby, it seemed, had a dangerous and debilitating effect upon a male Rom.

Mother Tavender, busying herself about the vardo, snorted and shook her head. 'Well, I never did! Such talk! I never come 'pon such ways in all my life.' She paused. 'O' course, if you was to have a red-headed baby - now there's a diff'rent story - '

Meri repeated that the birth could not possibly take place inside the vardo. Confinements must be limited to benders or underneath waggons. No matter what the weather! There was some precedent for a gorgio midwife, but only in exceptional cases. If they had been living in Norton Fitz-warren, the necessity would never have arisen.

'Too late, my gel,' said the midwife, 'you be too far gone now for us to shift 'ee.'

In the end he was thankful to be banished. He took shelter with the lurcher dog in the little lean-to which held their dry firewood. He could not be still; he walked between the vardo and the lean-to, making a narrow path in the falling snow.

There was silence where no silence should be. Birth was a noisy business, full of yelling and high drama. When the door was finally opened he saw dread in the midwife's face.

He cried out, 'What is it? Is she - ?'

'She's all right, son. 'Tis the babies. They be - '

'Babies?'

'Aye. Two boys. They bain't - '

He climbed the steps and pushed the woman aside. A mewling sound down beside the stove spun him around on

102

his heel. The hawking basket was serving as a temporary cradle. He sat down on a bunk and lifted them carefully together. He laid them across his knees, and slowly and very gently he unwound the wrappings. They were so tiny that they could lie quite easily side by side in the crook of his arm. At first he could see no deformity in them, and then he turned them over.

There was a pronounced curve in each tiny spine, an ugly twist in each small shoulder. Their little faces were preternaturally aged, as if they had lived through a previous existence.

'Why?' he whispered. 'Dear Lord in Heaven, why?'

The village woman crept to his side. 'They's weakly,' she muttered, 'They's not likely to last long.'

'No!' He could feel such a love for these two surging through him; he folded them close together; baby birds, fallen too soon from the nest and broken. He looked sternly at her.

'I hopes you don' mean what I think you mean, Mother? These be mine – mine an' my wife's. God-given. They is to be fed an' kep' warm. You understand what I tells 'ee. No accidents. No mishaps. Should anythin' happen to these two – you'll have me to account to.'

She had not known there could be so many ways of feeling guilty. For Meri to want was to have; the distance between all and nothing had never existed for her. She had no need now to question her conscience. The pointing fingers were all her own.

His first action towards mending disaster had been characteristic. He had fetched water and the Bible. He had prayed, the tears splashing onto his fingers as he traced a cross on each small wrinkled forehead. Without her permission he had mumbled urgently, 'I baptise thee both, Charles and

Henry, in the name of the Father . . .' He had given them gorgio names, made them his Christian own. Meri ceased to listen.

She began to watch him attentively now, aware of a need to know the spread of this man who was neither gorgio nor Rom, but a bewildering and awesome blend of both. She lay helpless on the rear bed, underneath the window, too weak to tend to her own needs and shamingly dependent upon him. At every turn she was mortified to see how flagrantly the rules of her people were broken, their customs flouted. It was some consolation that a woman had assisted at the actual birthing. But since Mother Tavender's departure all had been silent anguish and recrimination, an unvoiced condemnation which held Meri and Luke apart, preventing each from giving comfort to the other.

The proper observance of Rom taboos was, she now realised, dependent upon their habits of communal living. Within the safety of the tan, close to grandmother, mother, aunts and cousins, there would have been a bender made ready for her confinement, her own separate crockery and blankets, and Luke promptly banished from all unclean contact with mother and children for the obligatory four weeks. Every pulse in her blood raged against his involvement with the new-born, but weakness and a new sense of caution kept her silent and unnaturally acquiescent.

Fascinated and yet fearful, she saw how his thick rough fingers became gentle as he cleaned the babies and wrapped them together in her best petticoats and shawls. She wondered at the tender voice he used to quiet their mewling, felt a bitter pang that was jealousy at his utter dedication to the weakly pair who lay side by side in the hawking basket.

Every day since the birth she had waited to feel the mother-love leap within her, for the flint stone of her indifference to splinter and gush forth tears. But, after the first

few days, the rebellion had been complete and even her own body had denied them nurture.

Work on the new bell tower had been temporarily suspended. With all the lanes between Montacute and Buckland St Mary still blocked with snow, it was likely to be several days, if not weeks, before the cartloads of golden Ham stone came rumbling back up to the village.

Within the confines of the vardo, Luke laboured night and day to keep life alight in his wife and babies; the little ewe-goat his only ally. He began to treasure the goat; he made her as comfortable as he could inside the lean-to, and became anxious about the dwindling stock of hay. His insistence on the need to store firewood had ensured them warmth, but feeding the babies was his greatest problem. Meri, still weak and clouded from the long labour, had removed her soul from all involvement with them. He no longer attempted to place them in her arms, instead he set pots full of snow to melt upon the stove and used the boiled water to dilute and warm the goat's milk. He made several attempts to pour milk into the babies mouths with a small spoon, but they only choked and spluttered, and most of the precious liquid was wasted. At the end of their first week of life, Luke's sons were so far sunken that they no longer cried.

There was a morning, he thought it might have been a Sunday, when he went down on his knees beside the hawking basket and prayed aloud to the Lord to show him what he must do. Luke opened his Bible at a random page; the text that lay underneath his finger said, 'and in grief the people rent their garments'.

He did not understand it. He knelt, perplexed, and looked first at his sleeping wife and then at his dying children. A memory came back to his mind of Meri, in Bridgwater town, tearing strips from her cotton petticoat to bind his feet; that same garment still lay in a drawer. He fetched it, and in his grief he rent it from end to end. Even as he did so, the sun came through from behind the clouds and the snow on the vardo roof began to thaw and drip.

Meri had woken at the sound of tearing cotton. 'Luke – what you doin'?' Thass my last petticoat you'm rippin'. Now you's hev took all o' my good clothes to wrap up they babies!' A thread of alarm pulled her muscles taut. He had become so strange since her milk had failed; she knew that he blamed her. He was always muttering now, busy at the stove or praying, up and down beside the hawking basket, his great shoulders hunched together in the small space, his beautiful face dark with anguish.

Now Luke stood straight, the white cotton shift bunched up in both fists.

'They 'ont drink from the spoon, but I knows now how I must feed 'em. The Lord just came down to I, an' revealed it in a vision.' He held the thin cotton out towards her.

'I mus' soak these bits o' rag in the warm milk. I mus' let it drip gentle in their mouths, so as they don't choke. They's sure to live now, Meri. Us got the goat, an' enough hay to last till the thaw.'

She turned herself away from him towards the window. She heard a wind spring up among the snowy trees, and knew that it came from the south. She could hear him talking to the babies, could guess at his actions: the warmed goat's milk, the dipped rag, the small twisted bodies in the crook of his arm, and he, features melted with love, dripping back into them the life her body had denied. As she watched, the first runnels of the thawed snow began to pour down the vardo window.

The silence of the deep snows had broken, and the Blackdowns were filled with the sounds of rushing water. The thaw had been rapid and complete; colours of earth reappeared; life stirred again and moved. Small creatures rustled tentatively in hedgerows seeking food; but the lurcher, weakened by his long fast, failed to catch a single rabbit.

They were all growing weak. The day came when their eked-out provisions were finally exhausted and the cratch empty. The stock of hay was diminished, and the goat's dwindling milk sufficient only to sustain the babies. Luke had not worked for five weeks. He had paid Mother Tavender for her services, bought in supplies of food and hay, now the canvas money bag held only coppers. Enough for a loaf or two, a few days' fodder.

'They's got plenty of everything down to Kymer's.' She had propped herself up on a pointy elbow; the blanket had fallen away to reveal the thin sticks of her arms.

'Us got no money to buy with.'

'I never buys things.'

'If you do mean thievin' – well I can't do that.'

'You's'll hev to.'

'Stone'll be comin' in on the cart any day now. I'll be earnin' again by Monday.'

'You'm too weakly.'

'No I idden.'

'Thass good then!' Her head fell back onto the pillow, her fingers plucked the blanket. 'Reckons as I'll be the first to go, bein' as I be the weakest. You's can make I a grave underneath a blackthorn. 'Tis good to hear as you'm feelin' strong – gypsy graves hev got to be dug deep.' She paused and looked towards the hawking basket. 'As for they chavvies, I got a fancy to have they two planted together. But not alongside I. Lay 'em underneath the hazel, 'twill be nice for 'ee to visit our graves every springtime.'

'Do 'ee stop that Meri! 'Tis more than I can bear.'

'You'm soft, Luke Carew. You'm not man enough to

107

keep the hearts beatin' in your wife and children.'

'I won't steal.'

'Thass not stealin'. They old farmers is dirt-mean. Down-along to church they be every Sunday morning, Bible-thumpin' an' praying. But jus' let a hungry traveller knock on their door an' they straightway lets their dogs loose.'

'Farmer Kymer's a good man. I can't rob 'un. Anyway – I bain't no poacher. I'll be bound to get caught an' then they'll transport I.'

'Not if you'm careful. Roms don' get caught – well, not often. If my legs 'ud on'y bear me I'd hev bin down to Kymer's long since.' She gave him that old sly glance from beneath her eyelids. 'I cud tell 'ee what to do, Luke. Where to go. How to do it.'

Once again her insidious power lapped his senses; the opiate of her voice numbed his Baptist conscience.

'There's an empty bee-skep back o' Kymer's barn. There's a liddle brown hen what lays away from the coop. Do you jus' put your gurt hand in there, very gentle; they eggs won't sting 'ee.'

He saw her smile for the first time in weeks, saw her lips curve and stretch the thin skin across the proud bones, and he felt his heart break.

'You's hev bought stuff from Kymer many a time, Luke. All his dogs do know 'ee, so there'll be no barkin'. The farm wife leaves milk in the shippon for the pixies. You's'll find it in a yellow bowl down beside the milk pails. There's a heap o' loose hay far side o' the yard. Bring back as much as you can carry.'

'Us'll still be wi'out bread.'

'Taters,' she said briefly, 'kep' in tidy liddle sacks in a shed down near the stables.' She looked at him, sharply. ''Tis all layin' down there, Luke. On'y waitin' for the fetchin'.'

'I dunno what my Ma 'ud say if she ever found out. We

bin hungry many a time, but us never went out pinch-in'.'

'More fool you then! Takin' from them as hev got too much idden pinchin'. Thass spreadin' things around a bit more equal.' Her voice became impatient. 'Now do 'ee get on down to Kymer's while 'tis still dark.'

The dogs had rattled their chains at his footfall, but then they had caught his familiar scent, heard his urgent whisper, and lain quiet. He had filled a sack with loose hay, helped himself to the potatoes. He had cushioned the eggs in hay and stowed them away in his jacket pockets. He had found the pixie-milk, exactly as she had predicted, in the shippon. He had poured the liquid into Meri's little covered can, and gripped the carrying handle firmly between his front teeth. Once away from Kymer's he had needed to rest many times. It was almost morning when Luke came back to Dommett Wood.

They ate cautiously after their long fast.

'I can pay Kymer back when I got some money. I can leave it underneath the pixie-bowl in the shippon.'

Meri grinned. 'They'm daft enough to think 'tis fairy-gold.'

With the warm food inside her, and Luke restored in her estimation as a reasonable provider, Meri's spirit began to lift. She watched him drape the washed clothing to dry across the hawthorn bushes. He chopped wood and peeled potatoes, and Meri hardly remembered any more that these were the risky tasks, unsafe, and likely to destroy the manhood of a male Rom.

Thin March sunlight fell into the clearing. It touched the vardo window and found the hawking basket. The babies, warm and fed, stirred in sleep and shook their bony fists against the world. At their brave signal she felt the womb contract within her, the pain so searing that she cried aloud. For the first time since their birth, Meri lifted her children; she laid them face downwards across her knees and unwound their wrappings. She flexed her fingers and began to massage each crooked spine, each twisted shoulder. She knew that she would never wake again on any morning without the cloud of these two on her mind's horizon. She would never again walk the drom with a singing heart, stride out unconcerned on a wild March day to touch the barbed gold of blossoming furze, never laugh aloud to see the nut-trees hung with catkins.

When Luke came in she was smiling. 'Come you here, young man,' she said, 'an' do some sortin' out. I amn't sure which one o' these is Charles an' which one's Henry.'

News had been thin in the village that winter. The story of misshapen twin boys born in Dommett Wood to the stone-mason and the gypsy had made Mother Tavender a visitor to be seated nearer to the fire, fed and treasured. She told of the young father's anguish, the mother's strange indifference.

'Her wudden even touch 'em, ''They's a judgement'', her whispered to me, '' 'tis my own wickedness what has made 'em grow crooked''.' The listeners, ever avid for drama, had nodded their agreement. Hadn't the gypsy's continued presence in the district caused bad things to happen?

'Now him,' Mother Tavender continued, 'now him took it very diff'rent. He straightway took up water on his finger an' baptised 'em.' She rubbed her hands together at the memory of a job well done. ' 'Twas no fault o' mine. I birthed 'em safe enough. She can never blame me for what happened – they was already growed crooked.' She shivered. 'They'll be all dead by this time. Nothin' human could ever

110

live long up there, not in this cold. You shudden never have pulled the bell tower down, I told 'un.'

News of her friend's misfortune reached Eliza through the village carter on his last call before the final storm; that snowfall which was to close in the only clear path that was left up to Larksleve.

Eliza welcomed the blizzards, came closer to happiness in those days of deep snow than she had ever been. With Larksleve now inaccessible to both sets of parents, she and Philip had sampled briefly the delights of first freedom. ' 'Tis nice,' Eliza confessed, 'not to have mother comin' up yer and findin' fault every day.' Philip had given his lower lip a judicious tweak. ' 'Tis about time my father kep' to his own place. Him and Samuel be always across yer, spyin' on me.' Isolation created an illusion of adventure: they planned rebellion together. But Eliza would always associate happiness with guilt. She believed, secretly, that the pleasurable moments must always be paid for with tears before bedtime.

Together, they laboured through the short hours of daylight, and Eliza, her body awkward with the child she carried, now shamed Philip Greypaull into making that extra effort he would otherwise have shirked. In the evenings he helped her to set their soaked clothing to dry before the inglenook fire, and, seated on facing settles, they had eaten supper, already nodding to sleep in the sudden warmth. His face, seen dimly through rising steam, was more youthful than ever. Nothing ever dimmed or touched him, unlike the other Greypaull men whose dull skins furrowed early.

Sometimes Eliza thought about Meri and the crippled babies, and she remembered the coral necklace and touched it for luck. Perhaps they should never have chopped for the blue china bowl? Perhaps she had stolen away Meri's only good fortune?

Relieved of her mother's frequent and inhibiting visits, Eliza's mind began to move outwards and discover its own thoughts. Her confession to Philip had surprised her; she had not known until the snows came just how deeply she resented her mother's presence. She was ashamed of this new desire for independence which grew inside her as strongly and inevitably as the coming child.

Overnight, the familiar contours of Larksleve had vanished under snow; Eliza's world had been coloured white and empty. Uneasy thoughts beat about her like flocks of seagulls swooping inland, crying in the night, demanding shelter. As a child, she had loved and feared her mother, had never been able to bear Elizabeth's displeasure. Just a hint of that ominous crease between her mother's eyebrows had sent the terror shafting through Eliza. There had been propitiation, learned early: the pink glass bowl bought with hoarded pennies, the embroidered hanky, the sampler worked with sweating fingers; and none of it valued one half as much as her brothers' smiles. She longed to confide in the man who slept beside her, but knew that Philip, dearly beloved son of his mother, Rachel, would never comprehend; and no one had ever asked her if she loved him.

Love, between Greypaulls, had to be deserved. Warmth was bestowed where it had been properly earned, and gratitude was obligatory. Heart never reached out to heart without some reservation. They were a tight, contained tribe, closely intermarried; a people who hoarded the memory of every handshake given, every gesture of kindness. Greypaulls kept inventory against the day when it should be time to claim back, with interest, whatever they had loaned to one another of their time and affection.

Whenever Philip thought about Eliza, it was to wonder

112

what demon drove her, what need nagged inside her that could only be met by keen and daily toil. She never laughed. Even her smiles were rare. He remembered Eliza as a child, prim and obedient, her small face grave, her freckled hands folded. Her confessed resentment towards her mother had surprised him, had made Eliza seem more approachable, less worthy. He longed to confide in her but knew that she would never comprehend.

It had always been made clear to Philip that his father's goodness towards him was undeserved. Marriage to Eliza should have set straight the record, but somehow it had not; and no one had ever asked him if he loved her.

Philip woke in the night to hear the sound of dripping water, and he knew that the thaw had reached up to Larksleve. In a day or two his father and Sam would ride over, cast a critical eye, and volunteer the good advice that they had not been asked for.

After snow there was mud with all its attendant problems; cattle bogged down in wet fields and needing to be rescued, damp firewood made for a smoky kitchen, and Eliza, who had not once lost her balance in icy conditions, now fell heavily while carrying milk pails across greasy cobbles.

Elizabeth was the first to come, bearing gifts for which she would have to be thanked. Eliza's mother was a fine sight, she came wheeling into the farmyard in a spanking new dog cart, pulled by a chestnut pony, the colour high in her face, her confidence, as always, unbridled.

'Why - whatever's bin goin' on yer! Leave you two to yourselves for a few days an' just look what happens.' She rushed about opening doors and windows and complaining about the smoky kitchen. She exclaimed at the bruise on Eliza's forehead and demanded an explanation of it. She referred to Philip, using her usual derogatory epithet of 'he'.

'I passed he down in Old Meadow as I came up yer. Got a cow stuck fast, he had. "Serves 'ee right," I told 'un. "You shud a' had more sense than to turn they beasts out in field so quick after thaw." ' Her dark brows drew together and Eliza felt the sword of her mother's displeasure run through her. 'Whatever was you thinkin' of, maid; surely you knows better, even if he don't?'

'I tries to put 'un right, Mother. But I can't always be nagging. We was runnin' short o' fodder – '

'You only got to ask your father, Liza. You knows that, already.'

Her mother was unpacking a hamper; she had brought a ham, two freshly-baked pies, and sufficient bread to last a week.

'I was planning to do my own baking tomorrow – '

'What? With the wood soaking wet, an' the fire smokin'?'

From a leather bag Elizabeth withdrew a number of woolly garments. 'I bin knittin' for 'ee all through the blizzards. Six of everything is what us'll need to begin with. I be starting tonight on the stitching of the flannel petticoats an' binders. Everythin' in plain white, mind you! Remember that now, Liza. You mustn't never dress a baby in colours for the first twelve months.'

Eliza felt tears prick behind her eyelids. She longed to go down to Old Meadow where Philip wrestled alone with the bogged-down cow. She remembered her recent confession to him. ' 'Tis nice not to have Mother comin' up yer and findin' fault every day.' She should have known that her wicked pleasure in Elizabeth's absence would have to be paid for.

'Well – Liza?'

All her life she had been thanking her mother for something. Today the words would not come at once. The rebellious voices inside her shouted, 'Whose farm is it? Whose husband? Whose baby?' But the teachings of five-and-twenty years were not so easily overridden. Fear of her parents' authority, a trained disinclination to cause trouble, forced Eliza into obeying the very command she hated. She cast her eyes downwards, made her voice meek, her air submissive. 'Thank you, Mother,' she murmured, ''tis so good of 'ee to take all this trouble – ' She risked a glance upwards, and saw that Elizabeth still waited. 'Us don't deserve such kindness – I really don't know what us 'ud do without you an' Father.'

The performance had been enacted, the ritual gone through. Tension eased in the kitchen, Elizabeth sighed. 'Well, thass all right then!'

Philip sweated in Old Meadow; every move he made saw the cow more firmly entrenched, and the pulling ropes had left weals in both his palms. It was almost a relief to see Sam and his father breast the rise and ride out towards him. Sam looked grim, but Daniel chortled. 'Now then – wass all this? 'Tis withies what you do plant in mud, bor! Not cattle.'

'Us run short o' fodder, so I thought – '

'Too soon, you gurt dummy! Din' you never learn nothin' when you was to home, alongside I? No, o' course you didden.' The colour rose in Daniel's face. 'Where was you then, when us was sweatin' in field an' shed? I'll tell thee! You was off whorin' and boozin' down to Taunton. You was wastin' your Mother's egg-money on filthy trollops. Now you be landed on that poor liddle Liza, may God help her! Us see'd her about the shippon as us rode up yer. Gurt black bruise on her forehead, bor! Now what you done that for?'

His father's unreasonable switch from laughter to anger did not surprise him, even so, it never failed to turn Philip's stomach.

115

'Her slipped an' fell, Father. They cobbles is greasy after snow. She was carryin' the milk in – '

Sam said, 'An' you still in bed, eh? 'Tis where you usually be when there's work waitin'.' Samuel's face was tight with anger. His words spurted out from between clenched teeth. For the first time in his life, Philip feared his brother.

'I warn 'ee, Philip! Our Liza bain't your usual pub-trash. I've see'd the sort o' woman you fancy. Remember the Turk's Head? Our Liza's a lady. She got a long head on her shoulders. She's cleverer than you an' me put together.' Samuel's body slumped; anger all spent, he pleaded, 'Do 'ee treat her right, Pip. She's your wife; she's carryin' your child.'

His brother's use of the old childish nickname salved the hurt a little, but Philip still fought a thickness in his throat. He looked from one Greypaull face to the other.

'I gonna lose this cow before much longer. Do 'ee bide yer an' help me! Father – Samuel?'

Nobody had counted her cheeses, made in exceptional weather, or her butter-pats, stamped with the Larksleve rose, packed in ice and ready for next Friday's market.

Nobody had allowed for his inexperience of coping with shed-housed stock in blizzard conditions.

Across the supper-table, each one still smarting from secret hurts, Philip and Eliza faced one another, as do strangers.

Charlotte, New York.

Dear Cousin Eliza,

It is my great pleasure to tell you that a son was born to me and Mr Salter on January 15th of this year. His name

116

is George Hodder Salter, and he is a strong and handsome infant, if I do say so. My travail was long, and no woman of my family beside me in that time. But Mr Salter never left my side, what was a Great Comfort to me. He is a Good Man, and this first child of mine have bound us closer than I could have hoped for. I have come to Love my Husband, and tho' I do still weep for home when I am by myself, still I do know that my place is beside Mr Salter here in Charlotte, N. York.

Do not be downcast, dear Eliza. You will have your Mother with you in your confinement, and to be a Father will be *good* for Philip. I well recall him as Idle in school and later on, but feel sure that you are the Right Partner for such as him. A true woman must keep many sorrows *hid*, Eliza. Mr Salter do also spend time away from home, his business being very early morning in the Meat Market, but I do keep myself busy with both children, what do make much washing and sewing, as you will soon find out.

Your news of Haysel and Harvest do pull my heart towards Larksleve. To have a Farm one day is my secret wish, and in this great Land of America all things are Possible. But Mr Salter is a butcher, and do seem devoted to the Meat Business, so I have said *Nothing* about it. The snow is very deep here and I have not left the house since being confined, many steps leading down from our house to the sidewalk, and a baby carriage what holds *two* infants heavy to push. All food brought in for me by friends of the Church and Mr Salter.

Please give my regards to cousin Philip. Do *not* show him this letter. Write as soon as you can after your delivery. I shall be worried to know all that befalls. Put your trust in the Lord, dear Eliza. You was ever Devout, and He will not Abandon you in your Houre of Need.

Your affectshunat cousin, Rhoda.

Candace was born at Whitsuntide, neat and compact, with thick dark hair and sallow skin, a respectable Greypaull. John confided to his brother Daniel, 'I was half afeared to look in the cradle, bor. But, thanks be to God, the proper strain have run true again. Us'll have no trouble wi' this one.'

Elizabeth moved into Larksleve on the day of Eliza's confinement and was not to be shifted. She made every corner of the house her own. Philip had been banished at once to the cupboard-bed beside the fire.

' 'Twill be easier for 'ee, gettin' up in the mornings,' she assured him, 'you mus' get to the milkin' early, so that Loveday an' me can get on wi' the cheese an' butter-work in the dairy.'

He never saw the Taunton markets. 'No sense you traipsin' down there wi' your bits of goods. Your father'll take stuff for 'ee; I already asked 'un. You got your hands full up yer, wi' Liza laid-up, an' the haysel late-comin'.'

Elizabeth arranged the baptism. 'Us can't have a proper do in Buckland church,' she decided. 'They masons be still tearin' walls down. Us'll have it all fine an' showy down to Combe St Nicholas.'

'Reverend Soames won't like that,' Eliza ventured.

'Then 'un must lump it! There was nothin' wrong wi' our old church that a bit of elbow-grease wudden of mended. Greypaulls bin christened and wed there for hundreds of years.'

'But me an' Philip was married at Buckland – '

'That was diff'rent. They got the new transept an' chancel finished. Now, they've tore down the bell tower, so us got no bells; an' the Lord only knows where the font be resting!'

Eliza insisted on naming her baby for the gentle girl who

had sewn her wedding slippers and, since the tailor was her nephew, Elizabeth could not easily disagree. Walter Greypaull and his young wife, Candace, stood as godparents to this first, and most satisfactory, issue of Philip and Eliza.

As the water was poured on the baby's head, a beam of sunlight touched the red of Eliza's hair, the yellow curls of Philip. John Greypaull sighed and looked at the child. Dressed in the embroidered christening-robe that had served for so many of them, Candace lay, dark and contained, in her sponsor's arms. John had purchased a silver cup in Taunton, had her name engraved on it. A fresh start, he thought, a new generation, and, God willing, all the rest of them would be boys.

Philip's mother, Rachel, was also considering the future. She was a silent, almost morose woman, whose opinions were never sought. Rachel hoarded her own thoughts. Elizabeth would always forestall her in such matters as the baptism of Candace, and the proper management of Larksleve. She listened, without comment, to the criticisms of Philip from Daniel and Samuel. Carpings which were familiar to her and no more than old words sung to a new tune. But in a crisis it would always be she to whom Philip turned. Only Rachel understood him, knew the pain of the child's heart that beat in his man's body. To be born a Greypaull, but not of their nature, had been Philip's misfortune. Rachel saw her eldest son as a shorn lamb cast between wolves.

Greypaull aunts and uncles had always looked sideways at Philip. His reputation had caused the fathers to fear his proximity to their daughters, the mothers his possible corruption of their sons. But the ownership of Larksleve, and the arrival of Candace had given Philip family status. Philip and Eliza now had their own Sunday evening callers.

119

Cousins came up from distant farmsteads to sip parsnip wine in the dim blue parlour. For a year or two there were to be visitors to Larksleve. Philip always sang on those Sunday evenings, accompanied by Eliza on the rosewood piano. Cousin Walter would recite his latest poem, and the women would chat about recipes and babies; the men would bemoan the effects of the repealed Corn Laws, and the state of the weather. For a year or two, Eliza was to be almost happy.

Meri had always known in some dark place of the soul that these children would be less than perfect. That grey shadow, perceived so often about the shoulders of others, had hovered about herself and Luke from the hour of the twins' conception. She dared not weep; once begun there would be no end to tears, and weeping served her no purpose.

Instead, she pinned a fleecy blanket crossways, from hip to shoulder, and nestled the babies, side by side, within its folds. She walked with them sleeping safely against her body about the lanes and hills of Buckland St Mary; and the people of the village saw her, head proud, chin tilted, and were confounded.

She did not visit Larksleve. She had heard tell of the perfect daughter born to plain and scrappy Eliza, weak and foolish Philip. Meri had looked at herself and Luke, and could hardly bear the contrast. She avoided all Greypaulls. This desperate need to save face must mean, Luke said, that Meri had been guilty of having too much false pride in the first place.

'I shudden never have chopped my coral for her blue bowl,' she muttered, 'now her's bound to have proper babies, always.'

' 'Tis the Lord's Will,' Luke told her, 'they liddle 'uns is our cross, an' us got to bear it.'

She did not blame Eliza for their misfortune, the chop had been a fair one. She longed to return to the tents of her people, but a message brought in March by the village carter had warned her of sickness in the tan. 'Your Pa says to stop away,' Tom Every told her. 'Smallpox is raging down to Norton Fitzwarren.'

Luke never tired of watching Charles and Henry. On warm summer evenings he would set them down in the clearing, near to the tethered goat, and watch their attempts to scuttle crabwise towards her across the cropped grass. They had Meri's dark and penetrating gaze, her straight and heavy hair. They were still thin and scrawny, but healthy and alert. They paused to look wide-eyed at flowers, laughed unexpectedly at birds on branches. They showed resource; already they assembled their awkward limbs to achieve unsteady crawling movement. Luke felt an aching pride to see that neither child could bear to be parted for more than a second from the sight of his brother.

Greater than her sorrow at the crippled babies, who might yet, with regular coaxing and a certain magic, be persuaded to grow straight, was Meri's need to be with her people. Her days were spent in the hills, walking without purpose, the lurcher at her heels, the twins slung across her hips inside the blanket. Her present situation was unnatural. No Rom was ever alone from choice. Continued existence as a race apart depended on close family ties, and Meri had seen enough of gorgio ways to know that she could not live among them. To be Rom was to be aggressive, to argue and shout, to dominate an opponent. Luke's gospel of meekness was that of the gorgio, learned from his mealy-mouthed Baptist mother. One vardo, pitched beside a solitary fire, did not make for a home. Already, the silence of Dommett Wood had changed her; the empty cathedral of trees had reduced Meri's spirit, made her wary. She trod softly where only last year she had skipped and run. But the building-up of the bell tower was under way, and Luke, in whom trust had been placed, was earning good money and was not to be moved.

It was an accidental fall of stone, which resulted in a badly lacerated hand, that finally caused Luke to spend some time around the vardo. Reluctantly, he said, 'The carter do go down to Taunton on Friday. I cud ask 'un to take 'ee to Norton Fitzwarren. But on'y for a day, mind! Smallpox shud be all over an' done wi' by this time.'

Meri washed and ironed her remaining plaid, braided a few tattered ribbons in her hair, and mourned the silks and velvets which had been sliced in temper, or taken by Luke to clothe the babies. The twins, fed on broth and bread soaked in sweetened goat's-milk, could be left safely with their father. Hadn't Luke, from the very beginning, outstripped her in maternal matters?

Meri travelled with the carter to a high point on the road from which she could see her family's waggons. They were pitched, as usual, in Badger's Lane, pulled up in a long line, one behind the other, with a vardo set sideways-on at either end to contain the horses.

She came down slowly, through fields, towards the tan, and the months of her separation from it were like a dream and this the day of her awakening. No one came out to meet her, but she had not expected a reception. They could not have known that she was coming; even so, the deserted tan, the absence of noisy chavvies alarmed her. The skin of her forehead tingled and then beaded with perspiration. Grief waited; she could smell and taste it.

A great fire, banked safely with oak, smouldered in the clearing, but no kettle or stewpot hung from the crane. She came up to her father's bow-top and found it stripped, all his furniture and clothing stacked in a neat pile on the ground. She began to run, knowing already what must have happened, but not yet willing to believe.

A bender tent stood at the far end of the lane, well beyond the last waggon. Inside it two coffins rested on trestles. A single candle burned at each head, and Meri's brothers kept vigil. An uncle put his arm about her shoulders and guided her in. The coffins had been made wide enough to contain her mother's best dresses and trinkets, her father's whip and fiddle. The lids had not yet been closed, and she looked upon her parents' faces and found them greatly changed.

' 'Twas the smallpox,' her uncle whispered, 'they seemed like they was over it, an' then all to once Jesse took worse an' died. When your mother see'd what had happened, her said as her wudden go on wi'out him. Her followed Jesse a few hours later.'

It was not permitted that gypsies should bury their dead in the daylight and, in fact, they had no desire so to do. But word had spread around Norton Fitzwarren, and the watching gorgios had left their beds and their houses for the spectacle of a double Rom funeral at midnight.

The fasting mourners said their last farewells; the coffins were closed, and they moved out of the tan towards Norton churchyard, the long procession lit only by a single lantern. A corner of the churchyard had been set aside for gypsy burials, and many fresh mounds bore witness to the scourge of smallpox.

Jesse Loveridge and Helena, his wife, were buried reverently and in silence. No graveside tears were allowed to disturb their committal; grief was a private matter, and death, that unnatural occurrence, was denied recognition while the gorgios were watching.

Lamentation would come later, and grief be severe and of long duration. Meanwhile, the ritual of burning had to be observed. Meri watched as flames consumed the bow-top, the flash harness which had been Jesse's pride, the Spanish shawl, the velvet cushion, the green and yellow striped rug.

Meri sat among the mourners. She faced-to around a separate fire, and knew this gathering to be a female Council, a cabal of sisters. Grandmother Loveridge looked keenly at her.

'You's hev had many troubles since us last see'd 'ee.'

'I birthed twins. Both boys, born afore time, an' weakly.' Meri paused. 'They'm growed crooked in back an' shoulder.'

'You's hev had no smallpox?'

'No.'

'You'm still pitched in Dommett?'

'Aye.'

'Your man won't shift from that place. He'm gorgio.'

'No Granny! He'm Rom, more gypsy than the ribs o' God. My Pa said so.'

Grandmother Loveridge reached for Meri's hand, and held it. ' 'Tis time us spoke straight, together. Your Pa 'ud of tore the moon out the sky to see you smile. But when Rom lies to Rom – thass a bad thing. No good never come of it – never! Jesse made it right with Council for you to marry, an' your man Luke be at least half-an-half, that I do believe. But he idden no traveller! Him got his feet planted in ground. In his true heart Luke Carew be a gorgie – now do you admit that, Meri!'

'He'm learnin', Granny. He "fetched" stuff from Kymer's when us was starvin'. I can change 'un. I know I can.'

'But will 'un travel? Thass what us got to know. Will 'un go on the drom wi' the rest of the family?'

Meri was silent.

124

'We'm movin' out from yer, in the mornin'. This be a sad place, now. 'Tis all full o' sickness, an' restless spirits. Too many Rom hev took bad an' died yer. Us dassn't bide no longer, Meri. Now do you give we answer, girl. Can you speak for your man? You's can take a quiet mare back up to Buckland an', if you so wishes, you can join up wi' us on the Glastonbury road. We'm makin' for the Holy Wells an' the Tor. Us needs a blessin' after so much sickness.'

She would have to trust her safety to the gorgios' superstitious terror of a gypsy woman met by moonlight. Meri left the tan, on foot and in darkness, to walk the eleven miles back to Buckland. She left the road and moved across country, and no man dared to accost her, even in the summer dawn when Blackdown farmers rose early.

She came into Dommett Wood in sunshine to find Luke dressed and busy at the fire. The twins, curled together like puppies, were still asleep in the hawking basket. At the sight of her face Luke cried out, 'Where hev you bin all this time? What's happened to 'ee?'

She ran to his arms and he held her close. Her head, heavy with grief, rested on his shoulder; and Luke knew in that moment of touching how Meri had changed. How the wild heart had finally broken within her.

The King of the Gypsies came to Dommett Wood that evening. He rode in on a coloured mare, a fine sight in his broad black hat and the dark green suit with its many pockets and shillings for buttons. He sat down at the fire and ate supper with Luke and Meri. When the meal was finished, James Boswell said, 'Us needs to know what is in your mind, brother.' He nodded towards Meri. 'This yer's my dead sister's daughter. Since the sickness her is without parents. Will you join wi' us on the drom, brother? Shall us travel together? Us can do wi' a strong chal like yourself, an' your Meri's a fine money-spinner. Her'll make you your fortune in a few years. Us moves outwards from Norton in the morning. Now – what says you, brother?'

Meri waited, and now, for the first time, she was to see Luke aggressive, his gaze more penetrating and bitter than that of James Boswell.

'I thank you for your offer, sir. No doubt you means well, but I got other plans made what do not call for travelling.' Luke waved a hand towards the vardo. 'Us got two hindered children what will never stand up to a winter in the open. An' there's more. They be both boys, an' as like unto one another as a face what sees itself in a looking-glass. I bin in carnivals an' fairs. I seen liddle creatures like my two set up in booths for the ignorant to make mock of. 'Tis often the only way the crippled can earn their livin'.' Luke stood up and squared his shoulders. 'I comes from Montacute, sir, where there is a Baptist chapel, an' the Word of God is heard on a Sunday. I got a mind that my children shall grow up safe there – hid away from all evil.'

She had never heard him speak at such length, or with so much passion. Meri looked at her uncle and saw a respect for Luke flash behind his eyes. James Boswell was silent for some moments, and then he said, 'I cannot argue wi' what you say, brother. Although I mus' tell 'ee that us 'ud never see harm come to Meri's chavvies. But 'twill be a torment for your wife to live in one place. Her is pure Rom, wi'out taint. To travel is her nature. You's'll never change that.'

Luke turned to Meri. 'Then 'tis all up to you, maid! You is free to go wi' your uncle if you so minds. But they babies stops in my hands. If you should bide alongside I – then 'twill be in my house, an' my village, for always.'

To live in a house, for always, and between gorgios was a plan so repellent to her that she could not at first answer.

But a life without Luke was equally impossible to believe in. Her long isolation in Dommett Wood, the sorrow of the babies, her first experience of close bereavement had so mangled her spirit that she could only whisper, ' 'Tis for thee to say, Luke.'

Luke had already spoken to the quarry-master. He had pleaded to be allowed to return home for the sake of his children. The owner, himself a Particular Baptist who believed that compassion and business belonged together, had asked casually, 'How much do 'ee reckon thik big green waggon be worth then?'

'A hundred an' fifty, maybe more, an' my missus bin left a bit o' money by her father. Us won't be in need.'

'It jus' so happens,' said the quarry-master, 'as I got a cottage comin' vacant. I be askin' two hundred an' thirty for 'un, but bein' as 'tis you, I'd take a straight two hundred.'

'Buy a house? Thass only for rich folks an' farmers.'

'You think it over, boy. 'Tis a good Ham stone house, middle o' the village. Four rooms an' a strip o' back garden.' The man grinned. 'That 'ud set your Ma up proper. Her might even come to like the gypsy if you was to land home a property owner.'

James Boswell was willing to pay a good price for the vardo. Together with Meri's inheritance there would be enough gold to buy the cottage and a few sovereigns to spare. The gypsy-king came back to Dommett Wood in the morning bringing with him more money than the stone-mason had ever dreamed of; he had also provided a steady mare to pull the waggon. They were to travel down to Montacute, together.

All was made fast before moving. The sooty kettle and cauldron were placed inside the pan-box, underneath the waggon. The steps were unfastened and suspended from hooks beneath the cratch. The fire was doused, and a final patteran of twigs and grasses was left at the end of the lane.

It was one of those luminous mornings when the earth seemed to touch the sky. Flying clouds sent shadows racing down the ripened grain, and Meri remembered last year's harvest, and knew that she rode into bondage. They came up to that haunted copse of larches and oaks where the road divided, where one path led down into Taunton, and the other turned out, towards the Somerset Levels. Thoughts, so painful that they were hardly thoughts but more like sad ghosts, slipped in and out of her mind and were lost beneath the turning wheels. Never again to see the blue smoke rising, to face-to around the evening fire, to hear her mother's voice, her father's laughter. Never again would she walk where the road was steepest, or ride on level ground. Never block the wheels to spare the grai, or lie with Luke in a bender-tent underneath the moon, or waken in the night to hear the great trees talking.

As they came into Montacute, James Boswell said, 'Keep to your own religion. Avoid what is mokardi. Pass on what is Rom to your children, an' their children. We is a proud people, an' special. Remember that, Meri, when you is trapped between gorgios!'

Larksleve Farm.

My dear cousin Rhoda,

Was delivered safe of a healthy daughter at Whitsun. The baby named Candace for cousin Walter's wife. My strength come back quick, which is a Blessing. Mother bided here for six weeks. Her and Philip do not *Get On* together. I am *not* ungrateful but feel that you are in a good Posishun in Charlotte, N.York with no Mother to look over your Shoulder, like mine do, and meddle all the time. My Mother and Philip's Father do treat we like children which we is *not*, having now a child of our Own.

Loveday is here with me all the time now, Father having sent her to live in, which is a Blessing since Philip still not pulling his *Weight* with the work.

How is the Life in Charlotte, N.York? I do not have a baby carriage there being no place to push it on Larksleve. How is dear Mr Salter? I recall him as very handsome with Black Hair and a Noble Brow. You was right about the baby making washing, but it is summer and all dries very quickly.

My haysel was late this year after big snows and wet spring, but a good crop. I will give this letter to the Carter next time he comes up. You are in my thoughts and Prayers, dear Rhoda.

Please write and tell all that befalls. My kind regards to dear Mr Salter, and a kiss for your two boys.

Your affectshunat cousin, Eliza.

Eliza Greypaull watched the gypsies' descent of Buckland Hill. She heard the clatter of the dragshoe upon the flinty road and, from the concealment of the blackthorn hedge, she saw Meridiana Carew, seated high beside her uncle, riding for the last time through Buckland St Mary. The proud face, crowned with coiled braids, looked more beautiful than ever. They had not spoken together since that day when Meri had chopped her coral necklace for the blue bowl.

Eliza remembered the love-charm, the amber necklace, Meri striding barefoot and triumphant up to Larksleve to tell about her marriage to Luke Carew. She recalled the awful intensity of Meri's gaze, the old wisdom of her girl's mind. Eliza had heard tell of the sale of the vardo, and the purchase in Montacute of a Ham stone cottage.

She watched until the green roof with its squat black chimney dipped beneath the rise and out of sight. She turned back to face Larksleve – and the rest of her life – and felt old. Older than her own mother.

Meri came into Montacute head down, feathers laid close; a wild bird who already felt the shadow of cage-bars. Luke carried the babies, she held the blue bowl, led the goat on a long rope. She walked meekly, took small steps, followed one pace behind him. She did not look at the house, or the sugar-cone Hill which rose up beyond it. Meri looked into the face of Charity Carew and felt a lurch of satisfaction. Luke's mother stood, clean-aproned, beside his front door, and Meri, whose business it was to read faces, knew, in that first exchange of glances, that the altered balance between them was already understood. Charity might boast to her neighbours of the solid house owned from footing to roof-tree by her son, but the knowledge that it had been bought with gypsy money would always curdle her pleasure and make sure that she kept to her own house.

Meri stepped barefoot across the threshold and felt trapped. That heaviness of spirit which always fell on her within walls was so strong in this house that she could hardly breathe. She moved through the rooms, opened doors and casements, heard Luke's deep voice pulse with pride.

'Look-see Meri! All the old feller's furniture hev bin left in yer. Us'll hardly need to buy a thing.'

There was a wooden bedstead, a chest of drawers, a cupboard, a table, a few chairs, an oaken settle. The previous owner had been a widower, without issue. Everything in the house was dulled with dust and stank of gorgio.

' 'Tiv all got to be burned,' she cried, 'I won't use dead man's leavings. That old mush be still in yer amongst his chairs an' stuff. I won't live wi' gorgio ghosties!'

He made promises to quieten her. 'Us'll buy new. Us'll

give all this old stuff to Mother in the morning. On'y now us got to sleep. We be all wore out from the journey.'

To be weary from so little travelling marked him down as gorgio. That night she lay alone on the bedroom floor, wrapped in her plaid, and wakeful underneath an open window. Moonshine doused the golden village in silver; it touched the conical Hill and she recognised its shape but could not have told the source of that recognition.

She wondered if Luke would be allowed to bury her within the boundary walls of the churchyard. Meri did not expect to make old bones.

There were to be a few uncomfortable weeks of readjustment in which Meri would strip the house of its furnishings, refuse to close doors and windows, and to wear boots. Montacute had looked sideways at her, had avoided direct confrontation, had paid her the respect due to an owner of property, but feared her reputation as a chovihanis. The children of the village were frankly curious and stared. Women smiled nervously at her; men crossed the road when they saw her coming. Those shopkeepers to whom she had once sold clothes-pegs were polite, but uneasy. The landlord of the King's Arms Tavern prayed nightly that Meridiana Carew would never again set foot inside his taproom.

There were September mornings when a sight of the white road winding was to be a torment to her; days when she would crouch at the hearth of her cottage and rock her body to and fro in an agony of longing to be gone from that place, that prison. On such days she would pin the blanket crossways from hip to shoulder, snatch up the twins, and with Charles on her back and Henry tight against her heart, she would walk until their hungry crying drove her back into the cottage.

131

All her life she had roamed where the fancy took her, spent her time prodigally, and without censure. She had seen the Montacute women herded within their houses, away from light and air, heads bent against sun or towards candle-shine, fingers plying needles through the stinking leather.

Luke said hesitantly, 'Mother was thinkin' that p'raps you 'ud like to learn the glovin' – you havin' so much time all day, an' nothin' to do.'

'You's can go an' tell your Mother to leave the thinkin' to the horses. They got bigger heads.'

'There's Chapel,' he persisted, 'you cud come an' sit alongside I on a Sunday night. That 'ud please I proper, Meri!' He had looked so sad and eager, like a chavvie who feared a blow and yet hoped for a kiss.

He bought her a pair of new boots, a long dark dress and a sober shawl to cover her braided hair. She walked beside him, head bent, to the whitewashed chapel, and the congregation, remembering her in plaids and amber with the flying ribbons about her head, peeped from behind their prayer-books, and congratulated each other upon their Christian toleration.

Luke dug and manured his garden, took cuttings from the damask rosebush, promised her vegetables in the springtime, fruits in the autumn.

'Nex' year – nex' year,' cried Meri, 'you'm like that Liza Greypaull up to Buckland, always worritin' about what's comin'. You'm like they daft gorgie maidens what wants to know what is writ' in their hands!'

'You bain't fortune-tellin' no more? Pastor 'udden like that, Meri.'

' 'Course I idden.' But she lied, and he knew it. There were girls who waylaid Meridiana in secluded lanes beyond the village; women who would pay as much as twopence for a hint about the future. Meri wore the money-belt about her

132

waist again, and the weight of it lightened her spirit. Luke prayed for an extra five minutes in chapel on a Sunday morning and tried to believe that, given time, she would settle down.

Religion had ebbed and flowed in Montacute. It had always come into the village on strong tides, which had then receded. Certain legends had been washed-up, a church beached, a population left stranded with an embarrassment of faiths.

The eleventh century had brought them Tofig, Lord of the Parish and standard-bearer of King Canute. At this time, a great crucifix of black flint was dug out of the Hill and carried by Tofig into Essex. This relic was known as the Holy Cross and it led to the raising of the great Abbey at Waltham.

One hundred years later came Robert, Earl of Mortain, who had imported a French prior and his monks from Cluny, and built them a Cluniac priory on the skirts of the Hill. This alien house of worship was dissolved in 1539, and the villagers at once built a parish church in its shadow, which they dedicated to St Catherine, who was female and English, and sounded altogether safer.

The seventeenth century brought the Nonconformists. First to come were the Congregationalists, clustered around their pastor, Thomas Willis. At the same time, the Presbyterians were meeting in the house of one William Hooper. By the year 1733 Quakers had arrived in the village, and their leader, a certain William Isaac, was allowed to use his house for Meetings.

In 1758 came the Anabaptists, who met at first in the house of Samuel Geard, a weaver, and later on in the house of John Harris, a mason.

The Wesleyan Methodists made a failed bid for souls in

1822, but would not be bested, and still lingered on in the village in dwindling numbers. But it was to be the Particular Baptists, meeting first in a private house and then in a barn, who eventually obtained 'a spot of ground' on which to establish their faith and build their chapel.

This spot of ground, obtained by Jesse Geard, in 1824, was leasehold and determinable upon three lives. This gamble with posterity was not quite as reckless as it might at first appear, since the trustees so named were all young children. But a careful watch was kept, quite naturally, upon the health of these three young men upon whom the continued leasehold of the Particular Baptist chapel depended.

Montacute was very old, its Hill even older. In the Domesday Book the village was listed as Bishopston, and the street which housed Luke and Meri still bore that name. Luke's house did not stand by itself, but was joined in a long row of dwellings which lay close beside the King's Arms Tavern. Built of the golden local stone, with an iron-studded door of oak and mullioned windows, even Meri, who was no judge of buildings, had seen at once that this was a strong house. Its solidity weighed her down. She had hoped for a flimsy construction, a tumbledown hovel, raised in haste, which a few winter gales might easily demolish. But Number Three, Bishopston, was a house rooted firmly in earth. It had grown out of the Hill and would never crumble. There was to be no pulling-out from this tan, no moving-on in rain or sunshine, never mind how sweetly the drom beckoned, or the birds sang.

Luke brought her solid chairs and tables, beds and cupboards, all brand new and untainted, made by his younger brother, George, who was a carpenter's apprentice. Luke's joy in the house, his delight at the ownership of these four rooms and strip of garden was so overwhelming that she had recently heard him groan and pray out loud for a deliverance from sinful pride.

Meri feared the risky indoor spaces, those shadows which lurked in stairwell and passage, that unavoidable movement at night from one room to another. When a family was gathered together, all underneath one constricted roof or canvas, there could never be a chink or gap which allowed Beng to enter and make his mischief. In this house of separate rooms they seemed rarely to be together. She would begin to speak, only to discover that he had gone out to the kitchen, or further, up into the chilly bedroom. Even her chavvies would escape her, crawl laughing from parlour to kitchen, and sometimes up several stairs.

She had once suggested that it might be homelier if they should all eat, sleep and live in the one room. He had reasoned with her, pointed out that it was for that very reason that he had brought her to Montacute, so that she and the children might know the benefits of privacy and space. In Dommett Wood she and Luke had faced-to around the fire, and eaten their meals in the proper manner with fingers. In Montacute he insisted on sitting at the table made by George, on cutting bread and meat with a knife. He had taken her to Number One, Wash Lane. For the first time, she had entered the two small rooms in which lived the nine members of his family. She had seen the drabness of their hours, all the daylight minutes spent within walls, the magical night-time only spied behind windows.

She had looked at Charity Carew, seated at the gloving, had seen Luke's two tiny sisters lashed tightly with rope to their mother's knees, so that they might remain standing upright at their stitching whenever weariness and sleep should overcome them. She had breathed in the stench of newly-cured leather, seen the piles of gloves still waiting to be stitched. 'They be workin' late,' Luke explained, 'the factory-master do collect the work on a Friday morning, an' it better be ready, or there's trouble.'

'How old is they chavvies?' Meri asked.

'Louisa's four, an' Mary-Ann is six.'

'Thass wicked!' she told Charity. 'Thass cruel to strap they liddle maidens upright to your knees to sew gloves. Us 'ud never do a thing like that to our chavvies!'

'No,' said Luke's mother, 'but you do send 'em out pinchin'. You do train 'em up in wickedness an' evil. Be better for you my girl, if you was to sit yer alongside we an' do your share o' the work, 'stead o' gallivanting about the lanes wi' they two poor crippled creatures tied up in a blanket.'

'Crippled they might be,' flared Meri, 'but they is never to be lashed upright to my knees. No! they never shall be. My chavvies shall know the smell o' meadows – not leather.'

'Fine words don't fill bellies,' said Charity, 'unless you be a thief o' course, and takes your bread out o' decent bodies' purses.' She raised her strained gaze from the glove she held and aimed an unfocused, almost blind, stare in her daughter-in-law's direction. 'I had a husband once what talked like you. Now look how he left me! I got eight children still to home, an' no man. My eldest son have lately got himself a proud wife an' a big house.' She waved her hand at the five daughters who were sewing, at the three boys, dead-asleep in the cupboard bed. 'Everyone o' they must earn their keep, one way an' another. But honest, mind you! They knows that. Nothin' comes across my doorstep what is not proper paid for. I can say wi' my hand on the Bible, that not one o' mine have ever stole so much as a breadcrust.'

Meri glanced at Luke and saw the dull flush that rose beneath his brown skin. She felt the laughter bubble up inside her. It filled her mouth and curved her lips upwards. She remembered Kymer's and the blizzard, and guilty Luke leaving shillings underneath the pixie bowl in the farmer's shippon. 'Aye,' she told Charity Carew, 'you'm right, there. You's is all a bunch o' holy creeturs. All bound to go to Heaven. But I hev got to tell you about my religion. I be Rom, an' my heaven is yer, wi' your Luke, in his bed, an' in the fields an' woods, an' anywhere else he happens to want me.' Meri wagged her chin at Luke's astonished mother, 'You is a poor pinched-mouthed woman what could never have pleasured your man. Never mind about all they nine children!'

*PART TWO*

The pulling down of St Mary's medieval church had always been seen by the people of Buckland as a blasphemy that might well set loose the Devil. Old Stones, like old bones, were best left undisturbed, and in the years of the rebuilding tragedy had come upon many families. John Hill of Meanwood had been killed while hauling stone for the church from the Ham Hill quarries. Winters had been more severe than was usual; hay had rotted; harvests had been lighter. Two cottages had been struck by lightning and totally destroyed in the ensuing fire. Even John Edwin Soames, vicar of the parish, had himself only narrowly escaped retribution. He had been watching the final winching into position of the stones which would crown the bell tower when a massive block fell from a great height onto the very spot where he had recently been standing.

People still remembered Luke Carew, whose dismantling of the old bell tower had resulted in his ensnarement by a gypsy, and the birth to her of crippled twin boys. Eliza had also suffered failures. Her second child had been a daughter, and Philip, who had found a safe way to annoy his mother-in-law, named the new baby Madelina for his favourite sister. Once again, the good strain had run true; Madelina was as silent and dark as her older sister.

His father-in-law had clapped Philip on the shoulder. 'Well, bor! 'Tis a shame 'twer another maiden. Us is still waitin' for our first grandson, remember, so better luck next time.'

Although she filled every hour with effort, Eliza could never achieve the weightiness of Castle Farm. She wanted the safety of grain stored in barns, of stock housed in sheds. On Larksleve the corn that was gathered up in August had already to be milled by November. Calves and weaner pigs were sold in the market before they had reached their full growth and value. Larksleve teetered constantly on the tip of disaster. There were always the bills which Philip had neglected to pay, the fences he had not mended, the beast whose sickness he had failed to notice, the lurch from one crisis into another.

The purple velvet bag was empty. Her dowry, which should have been their security in years of hardship, had been squandered in the taverns of Taunton. He had concealed the bag, as ineptly as he did most things, underneath a pile of shirts in a linen-press where she was sure to find it. Perhaps he wanted her to know? He was good at the veiled indiscretion, the suspicion planted, the hint dropped. Once, when he returned very late from market and stumbled to the canopied bed to lie dead-drunk beside her, she had lit the lamp and studied his face in sleep. She had gazed for a long time at the smooth young features, at the faint down of gold on his cheekbones, the dimpled chin, the curved irresolute mouth. She had turned out the light, and out of the dark had come the face of Samuel, a Greypaull face with a wide strong mouth and the thin cheeks ploughed with worry. She had wept then, not knowing for whom her tears fell.

Philip's recent anxiety that she should conceive had coincided with yet another financial crisis. Eliza knew quite well what it was that prompted his constant attentions, his solicitude towards her. His romantic insistence on taking her early to bed, and his wish that she should lie late with him in the mornings had much to do with the money that was owing and nothing at all with desire or affection. 'There's work to be done,' she taunted him, 'bread to be baked, cheeses to be made. It might well be another maiden – that do sometimes get to be habit wi' some women – you could be unlucky for a third time, an' your Pa more disappointed than ever, an' not willin' to part with a single shillin'.'

Eliza did not want another child. With Candace turned four, and Madelina almost two, she had achieved a little freedom. But Eliza usually did what people expected of her. The stigma of red hair and freckles was sufficient to harness any surge of rebellion she might otherwise have shown, and she was by nature a gentle girl, whose only desire was to please. The intimacy of marriage had turned out, as her mother had warned her, to be a short and brutal experience. If there was any tenderness in Philip, it was not likely to be wasted on Eliza. But she knew her duty.

Conception had previously altered her view of the world, changes within her body had brought on a peculiar state of mind, and so it was this time. In those few months before her step slowed and her body became unwieldy, Eliza indulged in strange fancies. She wrestled a garden from the rough ground and brambles which surrounded the farmhouse. She coaxed a patch of cultivated grass, and on a bank of raised earth beside the front porch, she spelled out the name of LARKSLEVE in flowers. She dusted the keys of the rosewood piano, looked out her neglected sheets of music, and played for an hour every evening in the stuffy blue parlour. In those treacherous weeks of her transformation culture suddenly became important; she planned refinement for her children. Sons who could read and write. Daughters who behaved like ladies.

She remembered Madelina's baptism, and the Greypaulls gathered together in the Larksleve parlour; Candace, a solemn two-year-old, in a white dress with a pink sash, the new baby asleep in her father's arms. Philip's mother had wept at the little tableau, had compared her son and his little family with that other, more illustrious brood in London. Philip's likeness to Albert, Beloved Consort, grew, she declared, more striking with every year that passed. Rachel was a Royalist, she hoarded an album of cuttings and photo-gravures of the First Family; she shared Queen Victoria's belief in the sanctity of the home, and its role as a place of refuge and peace for a toil-worn husband. Mothers, thought Eliza, rarely saw their sons with the eyes of truth.

Culture had always been patchy among the Greypaulls. It selected some and rejected others. There had been scholars, like great-uncle Philip, poet and soothsayer, whose inter-minable verses had been published in little calf-bound volumes and church magazines. Then there were the farmers, like Daniel and John, who signed their names shakily on parish documents, and sang memorised hymns on a Sunday from inverted hymn-books. A long haysel and harvest could empty the schoolroom for weeks, even months; education in a farming community was dependent upon the release of children from agricultural labour. It had been the Reverend Soames who had finally persuaded Eliza's father that a little bit of book-learning might be an invest-ment in the family's future. A boy who could add and subtract and form his letters was less likely to be swindled by the knowledgeable in the fairs and markets.

What John Greypaull had really feared was a son who might one day consider himself to be cleverer than his own father. 'I'll give 'em a couple o' years in school, Reverend. That'll be enough.' Eliza's enrolment in the little church school had been incidental. 'Her 'ud be more use biding to home,' Elizabeth had grumbled, 'but her cousin Philip an' our four boys is already signed up wi' teacher, an' paid for. Us can't look mean afore the whole village.'

At the age of six Eliza could read her brothers and cousins off the page; her writing was neat and without blots. She was a grave and quiet child, and especially beloved of the rector's lady. Mrs Angelina Soames, who knew nothing about the contamination of the red-haired, had taken the clever little girl into the Rectory and taught her the first principles of music. There had been many raised eyebrows in Buckland St Mary when this latest bid for superiority by the Greypaulls became known. 'I minds a time before Land Enclosure,' said an old man, 'when they Greypaulls was not so high an' mighty.'

'After all,' said the baker's wife, 'when farmers' daughters is showed how to play piano, however could a body be expected to know who was common-folk, an' who was gentry?'

The power that is wielded by the very weak against the strong is a subtle force that depends wholly upon coercion. Eliza, knowing herself to be manipulated by Philip, would grow angry and resentful, and say bitter words. Sometimes she would hear herself and pause and think: Whatever's happenin' to me? I be gettin' to sound just like Mother.

Elizabeth visited Larksleve most mornings; the dog-cart always loaded up with the sort of gifts which would call into question her daughter's abilities as a housewife and mother. Elizabeth, who no longer milked cows every day, found time for the sewing and knitting, the fancy baking. She also brought gossip to the Larksleve kitchen.

'Your aunt Annis be expectin' again, an' her over forty. Disgustin' I call it.' Elizabeth poured tea from the big brown pot and began to eat the oatcakes she herself had baked.

'You be lookin' peaky, our Liza. You wants to kick that idle lummock out o' bed in the mornings, 'specially now you be in a certain condition. An' that meadowland over by Dommett should have already bin put down to corn last season. Father was only sayin' this morning that us could lend 'ee our breast-plough to strip the grass off. Francis can bring it across tomorrow. 'Tis about time your brother had a word or two wi' gen'leman Philip; him needs telling about several things, besides crop-rotation.'

There are ways of suppressing understanding, of stifling love at source. The slow drip of Elizabeth's poison had paralysed that first weak stir of affection, that faint tenderness Eliza had once felt for Philip. In those early days, before the children came and the dowry money was squandered, they had worked together. She remembered the blizzards of that first winter at Larksleve, and she and Philip digging sheep from the frozen hillside, elated because for a week or two they were freed from the domination of their parents. It was easier these days to feel resentment towards him, to abhor his evasiveness, his cheating, his lies.

'Your uncle Robert called in last night,' said Elizabeth. 'Asked how you was doin'. Said as how you two mus' be makin' your fortune.' Eliza spooned porridge into Madelina, and wiped the little girl's chin with a shaky hand.

'Oh? What made 'un think that, then?'

Elizabeth assumed a knowledge of worldly ways she did not actually possess. She said off-handedly, 'Farmers what is doin' well sometimes rents a room when they goes down to Taunton. To do business in – you understands me – in an inn or tavern. 'Tis more dignified, your uncle said, than shouting an' swearing in the open market.' Eliza fastened Candace into a clean starched pinna', and began to brush the child's black hair with unnecessary force.

'So what has all that got to do wi' me an' Philip?'

'Now don' you take that tone wi' me, Miss! Us have only got your best interests at heart? Your uncle thought as you ought to know where your money's goin'. "Him" has bin rentin' a room in the Turk's Head for this past twelve month, according to your uncle Robert, an' wi' no more business to settle than a barefoot gypo'.'

'But he cudden,' cried Eliza, 'us got no spare money – '

'Your dowry?'

Eliza, who could never lie, especially to her mother, hung her head and began to weep. Elizabeth spoke sharply to her. 'Don' 'ee start that, now. You knows I can't abide tears. Stop it, now, Liza. You'll only upset me.'

Eliza sobbed on an indrawn breath. 'Whatever would 'un want with a private room? Us owes money at the smithy and at the mill. 'Tis on'y the cheese an' butter what is keepin' us going, and now, with another baby – '

Elizabeth stood up abruptly. 'I know'd as that dowry money was all gone! I said so to Father. Well, there's no help for it now, our Liza, Daniel Greypaull'll have to be told all about this.' She paused, savouring the drama. 'Your brothers'll be comin' across for a word wi' Master Philip. You bide quiet in house, mind! No sense in your interferin'. Him idden worth a hair o' your head, maid! Even if 'tis red hair. 'Tis Samuel you shud of married. Didden I always say so?'

They brought the breast-plough to Larksleve on a farm-cart. James and Francis, both together, rumbling across the yard in mid-morning just as she had set her cheeses to drain beneath the press. Eliza had felt the new child quicken inside her at the sight of their bitter faces. Francis never wasted words, 'Him still in bed?' She nodded, and the two men marched through the porch and across the hallway. She watched their mud-caked boots and gaitered legs as they mounted the spiral staircase. She heard a door creak open and Francis say, 'Well – well! So 'tis true what we've yeard about 'ee, cousin. You truly be an afternoon farmer.'

She heard a thump and a whimper, a loud crash and then a high-pitched scream. She heard her brother James say mildly, 'Us have brought 'ee the breast-plough, cousin. Thik parcel o' land out by Dommett bin left far too long under grass. That field wants strippin' an' burnin', right away. Us'll be back to check-up in a day or two. Jus' to make sure you be out o' your bed – an' hard grafting.'

Her brothers nodded briefly as they passed through the kitchen. Candace and Madelina trembled, and hid in the folds of Eliza's skirts. Francis grinned. 'Him'll need a bit of help to pull on his britches. Don't reckon thy man'll be standin' upright for the next few days.'

She soaked towels in hot water and applied them to his aching body. 'They shudden never have done that,' she said. It was hardly the moment to ask him about the rented room in the Turk's Head tavern.

The breast-plough was made of wrought-iron and fixed to a long shaft, which was angled so that the blade would lie flat and pare the meadow turf into strips. The cut turf was then left to dry, and later burned. The ashes were scattered across ground as a vital source of fertilizer. Philip loathed the breast-plough. He would rather leave land under grass for ever than have to use it. To walk all day pushing the wooden shaft before him was a torment which almost broke his back. He could hardly bear the pressure of the protective boards against his thighs, especially since the beating. But the number of his tormentors had widened lately. It must now include James and Francis Greypaull who had sworn to watch every move he made. 'Us reckons,' said Francis, 'that a proper man – a farmer you minds – should be able to cut a quarter-acre of turf in a day. Better get a move on, hadden you, cousin! Because when you've stripped this meadow you can start to plough 'un.'

The beating, although it had humiliated him, had hardly counted. What had alarmed him was his father's visit. Daniel had come alone, had taken his son into the chilly parlour, and spoken softly, but with such menace as turned blood to ice.

'Now, bor, let we understand one another. I be a God-fearing man what hopes to meet my Saviour when the last trump is sounded. When my time is come I means to stand on the right hand of God the Father, an' no snivellin', snot-nose idler of a son is goin' to upset that. I bin Church-warden these many-a-years. I kneels down every night an' every mornin', I hev prayed for 'ee, Philip, but you is possessed of a Devil. You thinks you is clever, bor! You indulges in the sins of the flesh in Taunton, and you thinks that we poor clodhoppers up in Buckland don't know nuthin' about it.' Daniel's voice became a whisper, he glanced towards the closed parlour door. 'Us knows all about it: private room in Turk's Head tavern. Money lost gamblin'. Drunk on a Friday an' never sobered-up till church on Sunday. I prayed that a son o' mine should come back to Larksleve. I want my grandson to be born an' grow-up yer. I want 'un to love every stone of this house, every field an' tree.' Daniel looked at Philip, 'You don't know what I be talkin' about, do 'ee bor? You didden never feel it. You never picked up a fistful of this good earth an' know'd how the Lord God had blessed you.' Daniel's shoulders slumped. 'You is ridin' hard towards ruin, Philip. You keeps bad company in Taunton. You hev squandered all Eliza's dowry money, an' you got debts enough to finish you off. Your uncle John hev said that he won't help you, that 'tis only throwing good money after bad. When's the child due?'

'In a month.'

'Better start prayin' for a son, bor! Thass all what's gonna save you.'

&#10087;

Charlotte, New York.

Dear cousin Eliza,

I have not written to you for a long time, altho' your news do come to me in Father's letters. Our second child was born in April last year, a girl, for which I was thankful. Her name is Rhoda Rosalind, names chose by Mr Salter. There have not been much time for letter writing what with Eddie 4 yrs. old, and Georgie only 2 yrs, and the new baby. Mr Salter's brother James also living with us at present, and a Mr Powell, both butchers and lately come out from England. I have some help in the house, an Irish woman name of Bridget Reilly. A good and willing servant but *Untrained*, which do make for double work when I must *Instruct* her in everything. But she is devoted to the children.

Mr Salter's business is *thriving*. He is early up, and early to bed, the Meat Business being heavy and tiring. We attend Church on Sundays. Much of my time spent in cooking and mending, the men being Very Heavy on their clothes and of good appetite. Ready-made clothes are very dear and poor quality, so I make for us all. Mr Salter bought me a length of Pure Silk in blue to make-up a dress for myself for Rosalind's Baptism. My looks not much changed, which is a Blessing, and looked very Smart in the Blue dress.

The children stay in good health, but for Eddie, who I

now think of as my own son, and do worry about in winter. His chest is weak, and suffers very bad with croup, which is terrible to watch. Mr Salter is very good at such times. Sits up at night, and how many men are that nice and thoughtful?

I heare no good of Philip in Father's letters. What is to be done with him, Eliza? You wrote about your Mother's meddling, but I think this is done for your own good, your Mother knowing of Philip's *Weakness* and wishing to *Protect* you. Father writes that you have a second daughter, Madelina. Do not lose *Heart*, dear cousin, a son is bound to follow, the men having always outnumbered the women in the Greypaull family.

Please write if you have the time and inform of all that befalls on Larksleve.

Your affectshunat cousin, Rhoda.

The ploughshare whispered sweetly through the moist earth and steam from the flanks of the oxen rose into the thin air. For a week he had worked from dawn until nightfall. He had stripped the grass from the Dommett meadow, burned the turves and then scattered the ashes. Now he must put the exposed ground to the plough. Philip stumbled behind the oxen, leading reins in his right hand, foot in the furrow, and could not turn back.

A ploughman must walk ten miles to turn over one acre, and the very nature of the task imposes isolation. He was hardly aware of the flaming beechwoods, the lavender tint of October skies. More than anything else, Philip feared to be alone, for these were the dangerous days at the year's close, when the heart turned inwards, when the soul brooded and grew bitter on slights and hurts, both real and imagined. To brood was in his nature. To preserve pain in the vinegar of hatred.

He hated Daniel Greypaull, loathed that pious face and its flowing whiskers, that wide-lipped sneer which always grew broader at the sight of Philip. His father had spied upon him, had hoarded the knowledge gained until it could be used to best advantage. Only Mother understood, recognised that shyness, induced by a fear of being found wanting, which made Philip malleable and suggestible in the company of wills stronger than his own. To sing was his greatest pleasure – and yet he could find courage to step forward only when the drink was powerful in him.

He turned the oxen on a tight rein, negotiated the headland, and relaxed into the familiar misery of cutting the next furrow.

The singing birds had left the Blackdowns, and now came the leafless season. November shifted the balance between daylight and darkness; working hours on the land grew unalterably shorter, the long nights colder and without comfort. Elizabeth had moved in to Larksleve, bringing Loveday with her. The house filled up with womens' business, and Philip was more than ever redundant. He had always preferred to drink in company, or in the stimulating atmosphere of Taunton, and to drink was all that was left to him to do. He saddled the mare and rode down into Buckland village. He sat in a corner of the Lamb and Flag taproom and drank rough cider with the farmers and their men.

'Us don' often have the pleasure of your company, Mr Greypaull.' The landlord's respectful words held a note of insult. There was laughter among the old men who sat close to the fire.

'Better serve his cider in a stemmed glass, landlord! Un's used to finer company than what lives up yer to Buckland!'

The talk was all about cattle and weather, about the

152

importation of Yankee corn which had lowered their profits. 'Corn Laws never shud a' bin repealed,' said the landlord, 'business never bin the same since, an' 'twill get worse yet. You mark my words!' They began to talk about a farmer called Gardner, who lived in Combe St Nicholas, a man who had fallen on hard times and had negotiated a loan 'jus' to tide 'un over'. The time for repayment had come and gone at Michaelmas, and Will Gardner, still unable to meet his debt, was now about to be sold-up by his debtor. The innkeeper looked to the corner where Philip was sitting. 'They Greypaulls is goin' to take every last stick from Will Gardner – they'll ruin that man for a hundred pounds.'

The man had said Greypaulls, but not which Greypaulls. Philip left the taproom and rode across country to Warren's Farm. A legal injunction was spread out on his mother's kitchen table; Philip pointed towards the parchment. 'Whass all this then, Father?'

Daniel grinned and rubbed his hands together. 'I done Will Gardner a good turn, bor, I lent 'un gold when 'un was strapped. Time come for payin' back – an' not one penny offered. Time! That was what 'un asked for. Time is what landlord calls in the pub, I told 'un, an' if you had spent less time in boozin', you wudden never have had to borrow off I in the first place. Money back, I told 'un. Money or goods – 'twill amount to the same thing in the long run.'

Slowly, Philip read the words aloud: 'Made this eighth day of November in the Year of our Lord 1862. The said William Gardner is indebted to the said Daniel Greypaull – the said William Gardner being unable to pay is requested to assign to the said Daniel Greypaull all his Corn in Ground, Farming Stock, Implements in Husbandry, Household Goods and Furniture, and all other Effects in the Schedule hereunder written. To Have and to Hold:

153

| | |
|---|---|
| Two Hayricks | Two Carts |
| Nine Acres of Wheat | One Plough |
| Eight Dairy Cows | One Pair of Drags |
| Eight Yearlings | One Pair of Harrows |
| Five Horses and Colts | Four Feather Beds |
| Six Mahogany Chairs | One Mahogany Bureau |
| Six Other Chairs | Two Mahogany Tables |
| One Piano | Two Other Tables |

When's the sale, Father?'

'Nex' Monday.'

'You can't do that! The man got six children, an' another one due any time now. What'll become of 'em? They'll end up in the Poorhouse.' Philip squared his inadequate shoulders. 'What about your Christian charity then, Father? You be always preachin' about it. Anyway - you don't need that hundred pounds right away!'

Daniel spoke softly. 'No bor, I don't need it. But you do. An' as for my Christian charity, well, I reckons as how charity should begin at home - don't you, bor?' Daniel paused, and grinned. 'Let we wait and see what the stork brings across to Larksleve. Now, a grandson for me 'ud be worth a hundred pounds of anybody's money.'

The Implements in Husbandry were ranged around Will Gardner's farmyard. Philip walked between the rows of worn-out equipment. There were riddles with broken meshes, flails on which the handstaff had become detached from the swingle, broken baskets and shovels, blunt scythes and sickles, hay knives with badly split handles. The dairy utensils were in equally poor condition and insufficient for the making of saleable cheeses and butter.

How this man and his wife must have struggled! Philip reached out a hand to the scarred elm of their milking stools, to the worn willow wood of their shoulder-yokes. There was something pathetic and very personal about these last items, even to call a bid towards their possession would have seemed indecent. Several broken tines had devalued the harrow; the wooden plough had rotted, its iron share and coulter thick with red rust.

The bidding for the Corn in Ground was brisker, and the auctioneer moved straight away to the sale of the farming stock, the carts and the two hayricks. Household Goods and Effects were the last to fall under the hammer. The mahogany table and six matching chairs, the bureau and the upright piano, all bore the gloss of love that comes only from a woman's hand. The four feather beds fetched a high price; Will Gardner and his family would sleep on straw pallets in the future.

Philip followed the crowd through the rooms of the farm-house. He studied the eager faces, saw the flicker of old spite, heard the gloat of satisfaction thicken bidding voices. Next Sunday morning these same sanctimonious farmers and their wives would be present in Buckland church praying for their own deliverance from evil.

Will Gardner, it seemed, had found one supporter. A farmer from Combe St Nicholas had offered him a labourer's job and the hovel which went with it. The sale raised one hundred and twenty-five pounds and fifteen shillings. The repayment of Daniel Greypaull's loan was ensured.

James John Daniel Greypaull was born that same evening. Eliza held her son in her arms, touched his dark downy head, matched his neat pale features against those of his sisters. She felt the curious detachment of a mother who has produced an overly-significant child.

Elizabeth wept; her husband, John, dabbed his eyes and found speech hard to come by. Rachel gazed at the dark male Greypaull baby and said nothing at all. The hundred sovereigns, raised that day by the sale of Will Gardner's living, were passed jubilantly over to Philip by his father Daniel. 'Promise is a promise, bor. But all your debts paid up right away mind! No more idling in bed in the mornings – no need, eh bor? Us got what we wanted. Us got us a grandson to take on Larksleve.'

The blacksmith was paid, the miller's bill settled; stock was replenished, a dozen sheep purchased, a colt, a pair of oxen. Philip bought-in corn surreptitiously to conceal the shortfall in his own harvest. He visited Taunton and brought back a cloak and bonnet, rich green in colour and trimmed with fur. Nothing was too good for Eliza, mother of his son. Philip smiled and smiled, his usually agreeable features more pleasing than ever. Eliza wrote a letter to Charlotte, New York.

Larksleve Farm.

Dear cousin Rhoda,

This letter long overdue, but I find myself with time for the pen and ink being laid-up in bed with my third child, *A Son*. My parents and Philip overjoyed, which makes me feel for once I have done *Something Right*. Mother have moved in, as usual, but Philip not complaining this time. Mother planning a big Baptism with all the Family invited. Your dear presence will be sadly missed, Rhoda. This lying-in is very irksome, things *going on* downstairs which I am not told about, and feel that the Reins are *not* in my Hands. But Philip very cheerful about a Son, and he have brought me a beautiful green cloak and bonnet from Taunton, fur-trimmed with muff to match. For my girls he brought cloaks and bonnets of scarlet which do suit their dark looks. I do feel, dear Rhoda, that the birth of a son is a Good Omen for me and for Larksleve. Baby's name to be James John Daniel, already chose by my father and Philip's, and us, as usual, *not even asked* about it.

I hope things still go well in Charlotte, N.York. News

comes to us from your Father when they visits on a Sunday, your Father having a High Regard for Mr Salter who is a *Worker*, and not like some I could mention, but will not. Have resolved to be more *Charitable* towards my husband, him having been spoiled by his Mother when a child, but do not intend to make same mistake with my own children.

We had a good haysel and harvest, but do not seem able to put anything away for a Rainy Day which is a great worry to me. Will have to start thinking about School soon for my girls, and all costs *Money*. I think of you often, and our Schooldays together, and your great Courage in sailing the Atlantic and marrying Mr Salter to bring up poor Sussanah's motherless child.

'I keep up my piano practise, and already my two girls do sit alongside me and learn their first notes. Your brother Walter is writing a Book about the rebuilding of our Church, and several Poems which is *Uplifting* and do raise our Minds and Hearts above everyday matters.

Please write when you find time. My regards to dear Mr Salter and your three children.

Your affectshunat cousin, Eliza.

It was to be a memorable baptism. The new church was not altogether finished, but the font was back in position, and the bells hung. As Elizabeth said, 'Us have traipsed down to Combe St Nicholas for two baptisms already. 'Tis about time us had the convenience of using our own church.'

Many candles had been lit against the grey December. The church was crowded to the doors and porches. Elizabeth had organised a social occasion, a celebration in which noses could be put out of joint, detractors confounded and eyes swiped. The birth of their grandson had knitted Greypaulls together. James John Daniel was to be the compensation for all their past disappointments, for their own younger sons and daughters who still clung stubbornly to home and showed no inclination towards marriage.

Philip stood up at the font, elegant in new dark broadcloth; Eliza was demure in her new green outfit, and the little girls bright as holly berries in scarlet cloaks and caps. The precious old christening robe had never looked so splendid.

'I baptise thee – James John Daniel – ' chanted the Reverend Soames. Eliza's worries flew up between the burning candles; her wild thoughts tangled in the flames and became scorched around their edges. The birth of a son had steadied Larksleve. They were suddenly solvent, affluent even. She knew that the money had come from Daniel, but there was some mystery surrounding it, something significant and awful. When questioned, her parents had become evasive. She now sensed a new and more terrifying anger towards Philip from her four brothers and from Samuel Greypaull.

The service ended, and the child was returned, blessed and baptised to his mother's arms. Knowing how keenly the parish watched her, Eliza walked out of the church with a light step. She trod carefully where the path sloped downwards, smiled at the gathered people as she negotiated the lychgate. Her father waited beside his carriage, the door held open. She had just set her foot upon the step when the shout of an approaching man made her turn back and look down the road.

The man was wearing a tattered smock and filthy breeches. His eyes were bloodshot and his hair uncombed. He pushed a handcart, the burden of which was covered with a strip of green sailcloth. In spite of John Greypaull's attempts to prevent him, he came up swiftly to the carriage and wedged his handcart tight across its door.

'Don't 'ee know me then, Liza?'

158

She looked at him, tried to imagine him shaven and washed, his brown hair in order. ' 'Tis Will Gardner, idden it, from Combe? Us went to school together.'

Tears trickled down his grimy face. Eliza reached out a hand towards him. 'Why, what is it then, Will? Be you in some sort o' trouble?'

Will Gardner looked around at the dumbstruck people. 'So you didden tell her?' He turned to Philip. 'You never told her how your bills was paid? Whose farm was sold-up to buy her a new green cloak an' bonnet?'

Eliza began to tremble. She pulled the woollen shawl tight around the baby. 'As you can see, Will, I bin lately confined. I bin laid-up fast to home for the past six weeks. If you needs help then you best see my father about it. He's Churchwarden,' Eliza faltered, 'us'll have to be going, Will, 'tis getting chilly an' the baby might take cold – '

Will Gardner leaned across the handcart. He dragged back the sailcloth cover with a violent gesture. 'My missus is already cold, Eliza Greypaull! No – don't turn your head away. Do 'ee take a long look, so as you'll never forget what you saw this day.'

The dead face of Mary Gardner stared up at Eliza. An infant, much smaller than her own James, lay across the woman's breast. They were both as waxen and still as dowsed church candles. A shocked murmur rippled out from the gathered crowd.

'Oh, Will,' cried Eliza, 'whatever have happened?'

'So they never told 'ee? I thought not. Your father-in-law sold me up to get the money to pay off your debts.'

'I don't believe it.'

' 'Tis true. How else cud your Philip had paid off the money-lenders? Last night, my Mary gave birth on a heap o' straw in a freezin' hovel. Her'd slipped away afore I know'd it. Didden want to live no more, I reckon. Now I be left on my own wi' six children to see to.'

159

'Us'll help, Will.'

'I want nothin' from you, Eliza!' He stared hard at Daniel. 'Better get your big book out, Churchwarden. You got seven extra poor souls to oversee now in your parish.' Will Gardner covered his wife and child with the green tarpaulin. 'I trust as you'll give 'em a pauper's burial.' He pushed the handcart away towards the little tin shed which stood behind the fine new church of St Mary's in Buckland.

Four years in Montacute had seen no difference in Meri. She treated the cottage as a broken-wheeled vardo, incapable of movement, from which she must emerge each morning to go about her secret business. She still gathered hazel and willow-wood, herbs and wild flowers. She squatted, cross-legged, upon the hearthstone and whittled at clothes-pegs. She told fortunes whenever the price was right and the client to be trusted. The hawking basket stood in a corner of the bedroom, the Scotch plaids and coloured ribbons folded tidily inside it. Luke's absence for fourteen hours of each day, except Sunday, left her time and to spare for her own inclinations.

The twins had confounded all of Charity Carew's predictions. They had walked early: a loping, uneven gait, always hand-in-hand and inseparable, each child an astounding repetition of his brother. They were sharp and alert, compensated for their crippled state by an extra awareness in all five senses. They always seemed to know long before their mother where the rarest herbs grew, when the nuts were heaviest, the wild fruits thickest. Meri believed that her Henry and Charles could hear the grass grow.

But they were solitary children, content in the company of one another. Meri, who had grown up in a tan full of shouting chavvies, could not bear to see her children's

160

isolation. ' 'Tis p'raps better so,' Luke comforted her, 'they idden never strong enough for rough an' tumble. They be strange liddle mommets.' He laughed indulgently, 'Already they be copying you an' whittlin' out their funny liddle clothes-pegs. They do make a stab at carvin' out horses' heads too.' But Meri worried. There had been another baby, last year. A girl, still-born and with that same old wicked curvature in spine and shoulder. Luke and she had wept, and wrapped the little body in a length of linen; and young George Carew had made a wooden box to hold her. Luke had baptised her and called her Annie, although she had never breathed. The Montacute sexton had buried the little box up against the church wall with only Luke's prayer and Meri's silent curse on the gorgio God for a service.

The blue china bowl with the wreathing leaves and coloured flowers was kept for her personal use: her own ablutions, her private laundry. There were many bowls in Meri's cottage, each one with its separate and particular purpose. She heeded the warnings of James Boswell. She remembered who and what she was; her ways would always be Rom ways.

Use of the blue bowl always brought Buckland St Mary to mind. She would remember the tiny red-haired Eliza, present owner of the coral pendant. Meri knew, without doubt, that Eliza was bearing healthy children. What else could she be doing while in possession of the coral? Meri's longing for a child was urgent; and although she feared the outcome, she used all her herbal skills to aid her own conception, but without success.

She longed for a sight of her own people, but she could never quite pin them down. She would come upon a circle of still-warm ashes, glimpse a wisp of smoke in the lanes, catch a sight of the painted waggons and coloured horses as they wound out of sight around the Hill. She ached for the look of things that were not hemmed about by stone walls. It was only the proximity of the Hill, rising up behind her cottage, that had made it possible, desirable even, for her to stay in this place. Her love for Luke, wild and sweet though it was, would not have survived long amongst these gorgios. She had needed a secret refuge and the magic Hill was her antidote to village morality, to the religion which bred complacency and stricken conscience.

The Particular Baptists saw virtue as its own reward. To be usefully employed, industrious and disciplined was supposed to lead them towards higher thinking and cosier living. Why then, asked Meri, were these women still condemned to the slave-labour of the gloving? Their God, argued Meri, smiled only on the gloving masters, who lived in fine houses and rode out with their families in carriages on Sundays.

The turf of the Hill was a carpet to her bare feet. She would pick her way among abandoned quarries, towards the chink and ring of mallet on chisel, towards the place where Luke worked. She would lie, with the twins beside her, on the lip of the quarry. She would point to those little tin-roofed huts, pitched in among the steep cliffs of the Ham stone, to those inadequate shelters which housed the men who sawed and carved the sandstone. Jackdaws rose from their nesting-places; she saw butterflies asleep in the sunshine; heard the lark rise on a long note, and vanish into the dark blue heaven. The Hill had become her religion, her salvation, her chapel.

The moneybelt had filled up, at first with silver, and then with gold. Meri looked now to the future, to a time when Henry and Charles must stand alone in a world of gorgios. Mockery and ridicule could not be prevented, but to own enough ground to uphold an opinion would, one day, be important to them. The gorgio, she noticed, respected the man who controlled his own freehold-acre.

Clothes-pegs and woodshaving-flowers no longer brought in a sufficient income. There was a limit to the number of houses she could cover each day on foot and hampered by two crippled children. The alternative arrived, unsought and unplanned. A solution that was safer than petty pilfering, kinder than fortune-telling. It came with a request from a village woman, a glover whose sight was failing and who said she could not afford the doctor's fee for a consultation.

The woman came calling late at night and in secret, at that time when Luke and the twins were already sleeping, and Meri still crouched by her kitchen door to watch the moon climb across the Hill.

'Missus Carew?'

'Aye.'

'Can I have a word?'

'If you wants to.'

They had come to her before, but only in times of minor trouble, when their babies choked with the croup, or their warts had plagued them. She had helped where she could, for pennies. This woman offered gold.

'A sovereign, Missus Carew, if you can help I.' The woman was past her childbearing years and Meri thought it was probably safe enough for her to answer.

'Tell I first what 'tis, then.'

'I don't see proper any more. 'Tis my eyes what do plague me. I had to give up the glovin' long since, but it didden make no difference. 'Tis like a cloud in each eye what do stop I from seein' clear. I can't afford no doctor – but I got a sovereign for you, if you wants to help I.'

'Why come to me, then? Give your sovereign to doctor.'

'I don' believe in doctors.'

'You believes in gypsies?'

'You eased my daughter's child from croup las' winter.'

'Eyes is diff'rent.'

'Please, Missus Carew! If'n your spell don't work I won't tell nobody.'

' 'Tidden spells what'll cure 'ee. If I do try to help 'ee, 'twill be proper medicine. You understands that?' Meri's tone was sharp.

'Anythin' at all,' said the woman. 'Anythin' you say. On'y help me, will 'ee? I be so frightened of this darkness.'

'Come back in the mornin'. I got to have a look in daylight. But if I can't do nothin' for 'ee, then I's'll hev to say so.'

The woman returned the next morning. Meri looked in each eye and, as she had feared, found a creamy-white caul, that disease which she had heard her grandmother describe as 'webb-eye'.

As Luke had predicted long ago, in Dommett Wood, the twin boys were always to be sickly. It was only her skill and knowledge of herbs which pulled them through every dangerous winter. George Carew had made her a cupboard. In it she kept all her ointments and potions, all her essences and distillations.

The Hill was a treasure-house of plants and flowers. There was a certain rock-cress which, when beaten into a poultice of rancid hog's-grease, made a powerful remedy for sciatica and gout in the hands and feet. There was hawk-weed which she decocted and mixed with hyssop and honey to help her children's winter-long coughing. There were the brilliant green leaves of the hoary plantain which, when bruised and applied, healed fresh cuts and old stubborn ulcers. But to treat the eye for blindness was a dangerous and difficult task; a mistake made in this devout village would most certainly see her driven out, or burned alive for practising witchcraft. Meri had once seen the damage done

164

to an eye by a gorgio doctor who had aggravated the very condition he proposed to cure.

'You's hev got a white webb growing down your eye,' she told the woman, ' 'tis a tricky matter, an' I don't care to meddle.'

'Do somethin' for I, Missus Carew. Anythin' at all – I won't never tell nobody.' Tears fell down from the woman's milky eyes and Meri felt a growing pity for her. To have lived all her life in a stinking cottage, to have stitched the hours away by candle and rushlight, to have never known time for the sweet winds on the Hill, to have never watched the sunset, the moonrise.

'How much can 'ee still see?'

'I can find my way along the road, an' back to my own house.'

'''Twill hev to be a secret matter 'twixt thee an' me. Otherwise 'twon't work. You understands what I be sayin'?'

'I understands. Here – take the gold – then I'll know you means it.'

'No gold. Not yet. I got to think how best to go about things.'

'Come over to my house, Missus Carew, when you be decided. I lives alone these days. Come wi' your hawking basket an' clothes-pegs. That way, nobody'll know what you be really up to.'

As a young girl, living in the tan close to mother and grandmother, Meri had noticed how often a sickness and its possible cure would appear close together. This Montacute woman had come to her in the springtime when the wild yellow wallflowers sprang from the old church walls. The yellow wallflower, ruled by the moon, was more powerful than any other of its species. It had many uses, one of them being the cleansing of film and mistiness from the eye. Meri made a lotion from the sweet-smelling flowers and, for a

165

summer's span, the woman experienced a marked improvement. She returned on a dark November morning, feeling her way along the village street to Meri's cottage.

' 'Tidden workin' no more, Missus Carew.'

Meri examined the toughening membrane which shut the light from the woman's eyes. 'You needs somethin' stronger.'

'Then give it to I.'

' 'Tis a secret thing, know'd only to my grandmother. I never yet used it myself, not on nobody.'

'You can't make I no worse than I already be. You might even make I better. Try it, Missus Carew. I do beg 'ee to try it.'

She would need a pot of clarified honey and the gall of a freshly slaughtered hare. The honey, collected from her own bees, stood ready on a kitchen shelf. To obtain a newly-killed hare's gall would not be quite so easy.

The poacher, Noboth Rugg, owed her a favour. She had always treated his sprains and cuts for payment in kind.

'I needs a fresh hare, Naboth. Quick as you can, mind.' He brought her the hare still warm, concealed in the pocket of his special jacket, and passed it to her from behind a furze-bush in a fold of the Hill where people rarely walked. She mixed the gall with the clarified honey, prepared a thick cotton bandage, and placed the whole risky lot underneath clothes-pegs in the bottom of her hawking basket.

' 'Tis your own wish that I shud do this?'

' 'Tis so, Missus Carew.'

'It might be hurtful.'

'Nothin' so bad as this awful darkness!'

'You mun bide still, wi' this stuff bandaged to your eyes, from nightfall to sunrise. I shall come back tomorrow mornin', an' then us'll see what hev happened.'

If the gorgio woman had no sleep that night, then neither did Meri. She gazed at Luke's sleeping face, smooth and untroubled in the creeping dawnlight, at her children, curled together in their separate bed. She remembered her uncle, James Boswell, the King of the Gypsies.

'Keep to your own religion - pass on what is Rom to your children. We is a proud people - remember that when you is trapped between gorgios.'

She went back, fearfully, the next morning to the woman's cottage. She removed the bandage, saw the brown water flow from the swollen eyelids, felt the woman's sightless stare, knew a brief twist of panic. Gently, she wiped the mess of gall and honey from the wrinkled face, and felt the curving of a smile grow beneath her fingers.

'Why! You be wearin' your best plaid, Meridiana! The one wi' the red an' yeller checks an' the green thread runnin' through 'un. You got on your best silk apron, an' they lovely amber ropes is hangin' from your neck. Dear God, girl! You be still as beautiful as you was at seventeen. You idden never changed a bit!'

For a moment or two they wept together, gorgio and gypsy. But almost at once the old relationship between them was re-established.

'That'll be a sovereign, then,' said Meridiana.

'Worth every penny of it,' said the Montacute woman.

It had never been known as a safe place, but some parts of Taunton were more dangerous than others. A well-dressed man never dared to walk alone in Bath Place or Blackboy's Lane, both of which were narrow and unlit, and inhabited by brothel-house keepers, prostitutes and sedan-chair carriers. Silver Street, with its open drains and filthy courts, was another thoroughfare to be avoided by respectable people. The theatre stood in this street, and the comedians and players were lodged in the unsavoury courts and alleyways of East Reach. Philip Greypaull loved every aspect of

Taunton. He revelled in the noise and smells of Fore Street, in the butchers' shambles strung out all along the Parade, and the screaming fighting fishwives who positioned themselves directly underneath the Guildhall windows. Oystersellers called from Castle Green, and sedan-chair men flapped and swished about their business. He ached to be a part of this squalid teeming life. He yearned to spend his time among the dissolute and degenerate. Philip had recognised lately that he was as a sounding brass, a clashing cymbal, as a green bay tree which could only flourish among evil and temptation.

Eliza ran a tidy household, a productive dairy and cheesehouse. Washday was on Monday; she ironed on a Thursday; Wednesday and Saturday were set aside for baking; the house was polished and scrubbed every Friday. On Tuesdays she carded wool and spun it. Sundays were taken up with church, and visits from both sets of parents. Her father's cowman had recently married Loveday, and it had been John's suggestion that Jed Hayes should move across to work on Larksleve. Eliza's brothers had repaired the leaky labourer's hovel which stood in Cherry Furlong, and Loveday now went home every evening to be with her new husband.

Eliza watched Loveday's dreaming face, heard her sing as they worked together in dairy and kitchen, saw her come alive at the sight of Jed. Eliza drew her children close around her; she kissed the small pale faces, gently brushed the fine dark hair which was so unlike her own or Philip's. Sometimes she woke in the night and went to their bedsides to convince herself that all was well.

Her husband was rarely at home these days, but his absence was a relief. Although she knew that such prayers were wicked, she often prayed to God that there would be no more babies. Philip had made no demands upon her since the birth of their son. The clench of fear that lived inside Eliza relaxed a little and she began once again to lean out towards refinement and culture.

There had been Greypaulls at the court of Elizabeth: poets and musicians, barristers and architects. Great-uncle Philip, long-dead eccentric, still had a reputation in the parish for the sanctity and length of his religious verses. Cousin Walter, the village tailor, was presently engaged upon the writing of a book about the rebuilding of Buckland church. Eliza practised her music; she encouraged Candace and Mina to sit with her at the piano. Education, she believed, improved the quality of life. Philip was persuaded to buy a governess-cart and a small black pony. Eliza's egg-money provided the necessary fee, and the two little girls were driven to the village school every morning by Loveday Hayes.

There were still important questions to be asked, but it seemed easier and less disruptive to say nothing. Since the gift of one hundred pounds from Daniel, Philip's pockets had been filled with gold. More money was coming into Larksleve than could ever be explained away by his keen pricing of her butter and cheeses. ' 'Un's up to somethin','' said Elizabeth, 'new governess-cart and pony, payin' Jed Hayes a reg'lar wage – which I never expected to see. Hiring odd-job men to do the work 'un should be doin' hisself.'

The memory of Mary Gardner's dead face had stayed with Eliza. Loveday brought her the village gossip. 'They be still blamin' Master for what happened over to Gardners. They do say that if us hadden of owed so much money that Will Gardner never wud a' bin sold up.'

'But that idden fair, Loveday! You knows how my father-in-law do love litigation. He be always off to Chard, altering his Will and takin' out summonses on poachers.'

Eliza wondered what it was about Philip that made him his father's butt and scapegoat. She suspected that other men resented the elegant figure which never thickened, the grace with which he sat his horse; they disliked him for his disdainful air, despised the ineptitude of him.

James John Daniel was not, after all, a typical Greypaull. Unlike the secretive Candace, the timorous Madelina, he was turning out to be a merry baby. To hear his laughter in the house moved Eliza. From the earliest days of his life, he had come alert at the sound of horses, had lifted his head at a whinny from the stables, at the ring of hooves on the cobbled yard. He was the darling of his sisters, the secret joy of his mother's heart. In spite of protests from Daniel and John, Eliza began to call her first son Jackie.

There was a certain sophistication, a kind of elegance and style which would have been ridiculed and condemned in the parish of Buckland St Mary. Philip had recently been obliged to rent a lock-up cupboard in the Turk's Head tavern; in it he concealed the fine feathers that could only be worn on his visits to Taunton.

He had purchased a waistcoat of canary-yellow plush, fine woollen breeches of a pale cream colour. He had been measured for a pair of patent-leather shoes with shiny buckles; he sported a cravat of emerald silk, and carried a silver-topped cane. The fashionable barber in North Street had exclaimed at the shortness of his flaxen curls and encouraged him to allow such attractive hair to grow low on his neck. It was only the state of his hands that revealed Philip's natural occupation. He bought a pair of chamois-leather gloves and began to wear them on every possible occasion.

Philip also thought about the Gardners; but the selling-up of the farmer and the birth of his own first son, Jackie, had become juxtaposed in Philip's mind with the amazing

170

upturn in his financial standing. His success at the gaming-tables and on the racetracks of Taunton had recently earned him the nickname of 'Lucky' Greypaull. He had always suspected that his father and uncles were mistaken in their chosen religion. He longed to tell those smug hypocrites, John and Daniel, that the joy of life was in the living of it and not in some uncertain promise of a glorious hereafter.

He travelled to the assize fair, carried Eliza's butter and cheeses into market, and then successfully wagered the proceeds on a single turn of the cards. He noticed an advertising poster, and learned that the famous and talented Sablon family, who, it was said, had performed before all the crowned heads of Europe, were to give a one-night-only performance in the Silver Street Theatre.

The theatre obliged all tastes, and classes of people. Charles and Edmund Kean had once walked its boards in the roles of Richard III and Othello. Comic singers appeared on the bill along with high-wire acts and jugglers. Bouts of wrestling were often followed by a performance of some tearful melodrama of the day. It was a palace of chipped gilt and dusty velvet. Its bar-room, and carpeted promenade were notorious venues for ladies of easy virtue, and Philip was one of the theatre's most devoted patrons.

Taunton was full of characters, men who lived by their wits, who had never milked a cow or strained behind a breast-plough. There were men of business whose hands were never soiled. There were the wine-merchants and druggists, the mercers and hatters. Lower in the scale, came the artisans: the saddlers and harness-makers, the silver-smiths and gunsmiths, the coopers and blacksmiths. There were men of vast importance: surgeons and physicians, inn-keepers, and the guards and coachmen who manned the Bridport Mail and the Tam o' Shanter.

It was while he was standing in Fore Street, observing the arrival of the North Devon Mail, that Philip saw Miss

Blanche Sablon and her family of acrobats and tumblers as they stepped down from the coach and were welcomed into the warmth of the London Hotel.

The Sablons no longer performed under fairground canvas or on street-corners. The green and yellow showman's van had been abandoned long since. Over the years, their high-wire and balancing feats had become more spectacular and dangerous, but the main attraction was still Miss Blanche Sablon. Since that visit made long ago by Philip to the hiring fair in Bridgwater, the thin pretty child had grown into a beautiful and voluptuous woman.

Philip approached the theatre manager. 'I got to meet this one, Bob! Arrange it for me.'

'Well – I don't know Phil – '

'You've fixed me up with plenty of others.'

'This one's different.'

'How d'ye mean?'

Bob Watson looked uneasy. 'She's a top-class filly. A high-stepper. I don't quite know how to say this – '

'You don't need to,' Philip pulled out a handful of silver.

'Money talks, Bob. Arrange it for me and I'll make it worth your trouble.'

'Come backstage then, after the performance. I'll see what I can do.'

The theatre was full that night, every seat sold, the promenade and walk-ways crowded. As Philip edged towards his seat close beside the stage he found a wall-mirror. The smock and gaiters he had worn that day in the market had been exchanged for the outfit he kept in the Turk's Head cupboard. Now he paused to adjust the curls which grew down to his shoulder, to admire the emerald cravat and yellow waistcoat. He could hardly endure the minutes in which Blanche Sablon dangled from ropes and balanced on high-wires. He observed the quality of her family's costumes, the silk-lined velvet cloaks, trimmed

172

with ermine, the jewelled headbands, the embroidery and spangles.

The performance had lasted for a full thirty minutes; Philip followed Bob Watson down a poorly lit passage and waited while the manager tapped on a locked door. 'Visitor for you, Mam'selle. The gentleman I mentioned. Will you see him?' She was seated before a mirror and still wore the revealing blue costume in which she had defied death. Philip stared at the glory of her auburn hair, her alabaster skin, the incredible length of her legs in the spangled tights. All pretence at sophistication left him. He mumbled, 'I be so proud to meet 'ee Miss Sablon. I reckon that I see'd 'ee perform once before, long time ago. You was walkin' the tightrope at the hiring fair, in Bridgwater. But you was no more than a child, then.'

Blanche Sablon looked angry; she frowned and turned to face Bob Watson. 'Who ees theese person – am I supposed to know heem?'

'He's a farmer, Mam'selle. Name of Philip Greypaull. Comes from a very old yeoman family, well respected around Taunton.'

The tightrope walker stood up and walked towards them; she stood very close to Philip. He could feel the warmth that emanated from her skin, smell her exotic perfume. He had a view of her remarkable cleavage and was suddenly tempted to reach out and touch the coils of burnished hair that wound about her head, but dared not. Bob Watson was right. This was a top-class filly, a high-stepper.

Blanche Sablon smiled. 'You are a pretty fellow, Phil-eep Greypaull,' she held out her hand, 'now don't be shy. Geeve me your right 'and, won't you?'

Philip held out his hand, palm downwards, but Blanche Sablon unexpectedly reversed it. She ran her long white fingers across his calloused palm, touched the half-healed gashes and the broken fingernails. She turned upon Bob Watson, her face tight and ugly with anger. 'What ees theese you bring me? What 'ave I always tell you? I 'ave say bring only gentleman to me, n'est ce pas?' She flung Philip's hand away. 'Why, 'ave you breeng me theese – theese ploughboy! Theese – lumpkin! Theese Johnny Raw!'

The shock in Philip's face seemed to amuse her; she returned to the mirror and began to remove the greasepaint from her face. Her laughter was that of a complacent woman, confident in her own beauty. 'Go back to the promenade, Mistair Greypaull. That ees where the women of the town walk. Do not be too ambitious, eh? Keep to your class.'

She spoke to Bob Watson. 'Do not waste my time in the future, Mistair Watson. Only gentlemen – remember!' She waved contemptuously at Philip. 'Take heem away now – I do not weesh to know heem.'

He had obviously ridden hard from Taunton, uphill and in teeming rain. Philip's inability to stable the mare, his lack of concern for the animal's distressed condition was nothing new to Eliza. She led the horse into a loosebox, rubbed her down with a handful of straw and calmed her.

Philip had never been troublesome when drunk, only muddled and incoherent, wishing merely to lie down and sleep. She came back into the kitchen expecting a trail of wet and muddy garments to be strewn across the flagstones and Philip already gone to his bed. But he was slumped into the inglenook settle, as close to the fire as it was possible for him to be. She moved the lamp, the better to observe him, but his head was bowed and she could not read his features.

He still wore the ankle-length cloak in which he rode horseback in winter. The heavy tweed had begun to steam.

'You'd best get they wet clothes off. You'll take a chill if you sits there much longer.' She returned to her pile of ironing; she lifted the flat-iron from the trivet, wiped it clean, and began to press one of Mina's dresses. Philip bent down and fumbled among the fire-irons; he selected a long brass poker and thrust it into the heart of the fire.

'Fetch me some cider, Liza.'

'Don't you think you've had enough for one night?'

'Cider, Eliza!'

'All right, then. No need to shout, you'll wake the baby. Perhaps a pot o' mulled cider 'ud do some good – help to ward a chill off.'

He had rarely spoken harshly to her, but now he snarled. 'Hold your prattle, woman. Don't talk to me as if I was one of your children.'

She answered him softly, a note of satisfaction in her voice. 'Whass happened then, Philip. Did somebody upset 'ee down to Taunton?'

He lifted his head and looked straight at her, and suddenly she feared him. 'Don' rile me, Liza. 'Tis the wrong time an' place for your clever tongue to start waggin'.'

She brought him a pewter mug filled with cider; he withdrew the poker from the fire and thrust its glowing tip deep into the liquid. The cider hissed and foamed, spilling a little across the hearthstone. Eliza fetched a rag and bucket, and began to rub at the stain. 'Leave it!' he shouted.

'But cider do mark so – specially on those bluestone flags.'

'God damn it, Liza. Can't you never talk 'bout anythin' but housework an' farmwork? I be sick o' hearin' 'bout how many cheeses you got ripenin', how many pots o' jam is in the pantry, how much longer the hams is likely last.'

'But thass all I ever got to talk about, Philip.' Her voice took on a sad note. 'I s'pose I cud talk to 'ee about the

175

children – but I don't somehow think you ever wants to hear about them.'

He began to laugh. 'They three dollies? They proper liddle Greypaulls. What cud 'ee find to tell about them? They be just like you, Eliza. No spirit in 'em. 'Tis always "Yes, Papa", an' "No, Papa". Candace don't often speak to me at all, and Madelina, who I named for my own baby-sister, why, she cries the minute I go near her. You've made sure that they liddle maids won't love me. As for the boy – he's all yours.'

The surprise in her voice was unfeigned. 'Why, Philip – I didden know you felt like that about 'em. You never said – '

'You always did reckon yourself too clever. Remember school? Top o' the class, wasn't you, cousin? But you never did see what was under your nose. Too busy hobnob-bin' with the Soameses. Learnin' piano with the Vicar's lady! 'Tiv all got to be ladylike wi' you, eh Eliza? But you is still deficient in a lot o' ways. Never did learn from Vicar's wife how to go about pleasurin' your husband.'

Eliza flushed. 'You can save your coarse talk for the Taunton harlots! 'Tis a rare enough thing for you an' me to be talkin' to each other, Philip. Let we keep it polite, then.'

He drank deeply from the mug of cider and wiped his hand across his mouth. 'Coarse talk? You wudden recognise coarse talk if you heard it. Let we talk all polite then, cousin. Let we talk about love betwixt a man and a woman.'

She snatched up the pile of ironed garments and began to hang them across the airing-line which hung above the fire. He reached out and grabbed at her arm, but she pulled sharply away, almost unseating him from the settle.

He began to laugh, 'Always busy, eh, Liza? Too busy to be troubled wi' a husband. There's bin precious liddle love between we two, Eliza. Only a bit of a scuffle now and again underneath your flannel nightgown.'

Her face flamed scarlet. 'Don't you dare to talk to me like that, Philip Greypaull. 'Tis disgustin', so 'tis! I always done my duty.'

He laughed. 'But 'twas never romantic for 'ee, was it? Not like in they books you read. Come on now, Liza. Tell the truth. Don' pretend that you didden dream sometimes of how nice it cud be with somebody else – our Samuel, for instance?'

The colour drained away from her face. He was entering her mind with a subtle and twisted understanding of what went on there.

'I never ever looked at your Samuel – not in the way you mean.'

Philip shook his head. 'Did 'ee really think I never noticed? Even in church, on our weddin'-mornin', who was it that you smiled at?'

'But you never wanted me! You took me to please your father; everybody know'd it. 'Twas a joke all over Buckland.'

He ignored her outburst; he said reflectively, 'I thought at first that perhaps you had some kindness in you. But then you began to scold and chide, you never put your arms around me. All you talked about was work an' money.'

'I don' understand you,' cried Eliza, 'you never did behave like a grown man. You is like a child – an' I already got three children! What time do I ever get to put my arms around you? Keepin' Larksleve goin' is my main job – an' never any help from you.'

'Thass masterly, Liza. But you was always clever, wasn't you? I shud a' known that you'd turn it all around to make out that I be the one at fault.'

'I don't know what you mean! 'Tis the drink talkin' in you.' She looked at his face, at his petulant mouth, his eyes dark with disappointment. 'Somethin' happened didden it, tonight in Taunton, some girl upset you?' She saw the anger flood his face and she grew reckless. 'Did your harlot refuse you then Philip? Did your fancy-woman see through you? You ought to be ashamed o' yourself. You is the father o' three children an' still you goes runnin' down to Taunton like some callow boy.'

'Who says I got three children? I only got your word for that, cousin.' He pointed to the ceiling. 'Didden 'ee ever notice, Liza, how all three of them children is the livin' image of our Samuel.'

'Thass wicked,' she whispered, 'thass not true an' you knows it. Your brother is a decent man – '

Philip laughed. 'But 'tis still in the heart an' mind, eh Eliza? They do say that red-haired women be witches. Did you make a spell, then? Did you wish for children that would look like our Samuel?'

He was accusing her of those sins which he knew full well she had never found the courage to commit; he had even grudged her the comfort of an exchanged smile with Samuel. Suspicion was his only weapon, but it was Philip's ability to gauge her mind, guess at her dreams which disturbed her. She had not thought him so sensitive or so perceptive.

Eliza put both hands to her burning face. 'The Reverend Soames did say that cousin shud never marry cousin. Your family an' mine be all blood related. That do lead to madness – '

'I bain't mad, cousin. I knows you an' your fancy ways. Children sent to school as if we was gentry. Piano-playin' on Sundays in the parlour. The name o' Larksleve writ in flowers. My God! Do our Sam ride over of an evenin' an' read cousin Walter's poetry to 'ee?' He pulled the tweed cloak tighter around him. 'I got no time for genteel ladies, Eliza. Nor do I think much o' maidens what hangs around gypsies.' He pointed to the coral necklace. 'You always wears that gypo's rubbish. What is it then? A love-charm to tempt our Samuel?' He laughed. ' 'Tis our ugly liddle Samuel what do need a love-charm. No woman, save you, have ever give him a second look!'

She felt sick. That he should have had so much poison in him, borne so many grudges and all of them false and undeserved. She put her hand to the coral necklace. ' 'Twas all for your sake,' she whispered, 'all the wishes an' the love-charms, I wanted so bad for 'ee to love me, Philip. But you never didden.'

'So you looked to my brother?'

'No, cousin! Thass where you be quite wrong. First of all I loves my children. After that, I loves Larksleve, this house, this land. I fills every minute of my life wi' work o' some sort. I got no love left over for any man.'

'So thass how matters do stand between us?'

' 'Tis your own fault, Philip. You can't expect to get love back, when you never gives it. Why, you'd even smirch the name of Sam what do love you dearly an' have always done – '

'Sam have took to preachin' at me lately. He gets 'xactly like Father.'

The petulance was back in his voice and Eliza took courage from his altered mood. 'P'raps you shud lissen to 'em.'

'What do that mean?'

'Other farmers come straight home from market. You often bides all night in Taunton. Since Jackie was born you got plenty o' money. More money than we is ever makin' on Larksleve.'

He smiled. 'So that's what really nags you. You don't like it that I shud have gold in my pocket what don't come from grafting in harvestin' or haysel.' He raised his head, and the passion in his face drove her back towards the table. 'I got friends now, Eliza. Good friends what'll never let me down. I took a long look at poor Will Gardner. I see'd where honesty and sweat will put a Buckland farmer. I thought about it for a long time, an' then I found out the one thing that I was good at. They do call me "Lucky Greypaull" down to Macey's.'

'Macey's? Why, Philip - thass a gamblin'-den. Father do say thass the wickedest place in Taunton; 'tis full o' thieves an' robbers.'

'You shudden say that. Oh no! 'Tis Macey's money what do pay Jed an' Loveday's wages.' He stood up abruptly; he allowed the long tweed cloak to fall down from his shoulders. She could see the fine cream breeches, the yellow waistcoat, the emerald cravat, his feet, elegant in buckled shoes. He hooked his thumbs into his waistcoat pockets and stood with his back to the fire, legs astraddle. 'Take a good look at me, Liza. This is how gen'l'men go dressed in Taunton. Smock an' gaiters won't do for the ladies I visit.' His voice had begun to slur a little. 'They tells me that I pays for dressin'.'

There was something about him now that alarmed her. He was no longer the wayward child to be scolded and sent supperless to bed. He swayed forward, reached out an arm and grabbed her, and all at once she became aware of his intent.

'No, Philip! You be drunk. I won't have you near me. I won't allow it.'

He pressed his hands hard upon her shoulders until she was down on her knees before him.

'I met a woman in Taunton,' he said thickly, 'mos' beautiful woman I was ever that close to. She was quality, Eliza. Fine pale skin, an' eyes like vi'lets. She had red hair - masses of it, but dark-red, like beech leaves. She was tall, wi' a body like I've only see'd in paintings. My God! how I wanted that woman!'

Eliza, afraid that movement might set off the violence in him, knelt immobile upon the hearthstone. He swayed, almost fell, then recovered his balance. She looked up and saw the unshed tears in his eyes. 'I wanted her, Liza. I was ready to pay any sum she asked for. Do you know what she called me? She called me a ploughboy, a lumpkin, a Johnny Raw!'

Eliza, no longer afraid, said quietly, 'An' so you be, cousin. Thass exactly what you be. Why don't you face the truth an' stop all your play-actin'? You sneer at me because I read books an' play piano. You say that school is on'y for the children of gentry. But you – you think that fine clothes can make a gentleman of you! All the family do know what you are. Why, there's hardly a Greypaull that'll visit this house any more! They all knows you for a drunkard, for a gambler an' womaniser.' She looked up at his contorted face. 'Better think it over, eh cousin?' She taunted, 'When harlots do refuse you, 'tis a poor look-out, indeed!'

He regarded her in terrifying silence. 'So,' he said at last, 'you got more spirit than I thought. Now that do please me very much, Eliza. But you got this ploughboy, this lumpkin, for a husband, an' you is in no position to refuse me – eh cousin?' He knelt down before her, his eyes level with hers, his hands tearing at her clothes. 'Harlots do refuse me – but you can't, can you? You had all your own way up to now; you got your tidy liddle Greypaull children wi' their black hair an' green eyes. You do like to give orders, like that mother of yours.' He flung her shawl and dress across the kitchen, and stared insultingly at her thin, half-clad body. 'You idden no prize, Eliza. My God! You be hardly worth the trouble. But there'll be no more Greypaulls born in this house, no more children what do look like my brother Samuel.' Philip kicked the shiny, elegant shoes from his feet and began to unbuckle his belt; then he threw her backwards violently upon the hearthstone. 'A daughter this time – eh Eliza? A daughter wi' dark-red hair an' eyes like vi'lets. An' she shall be called Blanche. Blanche Greypaull.'

Summer came to Buckland St Mary, and the sun shone upon the just and the unjust. In Eliza's garden the name of Larksleve bloomed in pink, and white and yellow. The haysel fell heavy, and corn stood high in the fields. Blossom had set firm on fruit-trees, the herd was milking well and young things thrived. Loveday Hayes had announced that she was in an 'interesting condition', and then she miscarried, as was her habit. Jed blamed the heavy work in shippon and dairy for his wife's inability to carry full-term but, as Loveday pointed out, her mistress Eliza, who was scarcely larger than a well-grown pixie, had borne three strong children without mishap while making cheese and butter on the very day of her confinement.

Some problems were beyond resolution, and Eliza, who had never, until now, found the devil she could not outface, found it hard to reconcile herself to the bearing of a child conceived upon a hearthstone and fathered by a drunkard. She had always believed Christian goodness to be its own reward. Her revulsion withered all his attempts at a reconciliation. Philip, when sober, was a contrite child who demanded forgiveness, but, as she had told him, she already had three children and there was no place on Larksleve for callow boys.

Eliza had not known about the vengeance in her, had never guessed herself capable of such bitterness, such vindictiveness towards him. No day ever passed without a re-enactment in her mind of that scene in the kitchen. She recalled every word of that improbable conversation in which she had been accused of infidelity with Samuel. The alien child grew within her, taking from her blood and bones all it needed for an independent existence, never knowing itself to be nurtured by her implacable anger.

Meri's need to wander had never lessened. From the top of Ham Hill she could see the Poldens, the Quantocks, and the march of Mendip. Approaching rain would bring the far hills closer; on a day of broken cloud, if she was careful to concentrate her gaze and the light allowed it, she could see the finger that was Glastonbury Tor beckoning to her on the far horizon.

Meri was again with child. The knowledge had delighted and alarmed her. She intended that this child should be hers, straightbacked and strong. 'We must say extra prayers in chapel,' Luke told her, ''tis on'y the Lord God what can help us.' Meri knew better. If this was to be a child without blemish, then different gods would need to be appeased.

Luke could not be expected to understand her anguish. He had his garden, his moss and damask roses, the mason's craft, the chapel of the Particular Baptists. Charles and Henry had each other; there was no place for her long bare-foot stride in their hindered world, and they had grown too heavy for the fleecy blanket. Meri began to watch for smoke in the lanes, for still-warm ashes, for the patteran which would tell her that her family had lately passed that way.

She found them in June, on a fine warm evening. She watched from the Hill as the waggons and carts drew into a sheltered lane just below the quarries. The horses were taken from the shafts and left to graze along the lane's edge; she heard the jingle of brass as the harness was pulled from their backs and thrown across a thornbush. Soon, the flames leapt up from an ash stick fire; water was fetched from a spinny, and the tea-kettle hung from the tripod. She saw the benders assembled, smelled the bacon frying. She crouched low in the lee of a furze bush and waited until the lurchers had been fastened to the axles and the company seated at their ease around the fire. The last time she had walked into a tan it had been to find both of her parents dead of the smallpox in Norton Fitzwarren.

Wreathed smoke rose high in the summer evening. She moved downhill, drawn by the sight of the painted waggons, the coloured horses, the murmur of voices. She was unsure of her reception, dreaded a rebuff, or an outright request to leave the tan. Meri halted at the lane's end and studied the group that faced-to around the fire. An old brown couple sat close together; a dark young man and a pretty chavvie argued amiably about the division of the last strip of bacon; a good-looking young woman held a baby in her arms. As she came closer to the fire, Meri recognised her cousin, Lavinia Loveridge.

She crept down the length of the hedge to find a gap through which she might see them more clearly. The lurchers growled and shifted their position underneath the waggons. The dark young man leapt up and cried, 'Who's there? Who is it?' Meri stepped through the gap in the hedge, and Lavinia recognised her. For a moment they clung and wept together.

They counted up the years since their last meeting. The dark young man was Lavinia's husband, the elderly couple his mother and father. 'This is the Lock fam'ly,' Lavinia said. 'We'm making for Glastonbury and Queen's Sedgemoor.'

The chavvies fell asleep and were put to bed inside the vardo. Meri studied the straight limbed children and began to weep. She told about Charles and Henry, and Annie who had never breathed. ''Tis a curse on I,' she told the company. 'I do cure village women o' their sickness, but I can't help myself.'

'When's the chavvie due?' asked old Mrs Lock.

''Bout Christmas, I reckon.'

'Then 'tidden too late, yet. If you'd a-bin livin' among your own kind this wudden never hev happened. There's ways an' means o' makin' sure of healthy chavvies.'

'Then do 'ee tell I, Mother!'

'That do call for travellin', my girl, an' from what I hears your gorgie husband won't budge from this village.'

'But I can travel. On'y tell me what I must do, an' I shall do it.'

Luke tried to dissuade her. Prayer, he insisted, was the only answer. Prayer, constant and sincere. Chapel twice on Sundays, faith in the Almighty. 'I knows,' he said gently, 'how much you do grieve for a strong child. But if 'tis the Lord's will then us got to abide by it. What diff'rence can it make if you fetches water-violets from Sedgemoor, or picks tansy leaves on the Poldens. You told me that you had come to believe in the Lord Jesus. Now that got to make things turn out better!'

But it won't, she thought. How could he know that her Lord had never seen the chapel, that salvation for her was in the hills and meadows, by the rivers, and in the tall trees? But six years of village propriety had shown Meri that there was more than one way of professing a faith. She lowered her gaze, pleated a fold of her sober skirt, and tried to look humble, pious even.

'I got a longing to go to Glastonbury, Luke. To bathe in the Holy Well – to drink the blessed waters. I feels a need to say prayers in a holy place. I wants to kneel down in they Abbey ruins.'

'A pilgrimage?' There was awe in his voice. 'You wants to make a pilgrimage to Glastonbury? Well – who'd athought it.' He considered. 'You'll come back, though? You won't bide long? I cudden bear to live if you was to – '

She ran to him then, and held him in her arms, smoothed his rough curls with tender fingers. 'Course I'll come back, you gurt ninny. What ever 'ud I do without 'ee? On'y let me do this one journey,' she pleaded, 'an' I'll bide yer alongside 'ee for ever after.'

185

Meri packed the hawking basket with a supply of food, a clean dress and several pinna's. She buckled the money-belt around her waist and braided a yellow ribbon in her hair. She instructed Luke's sister Susan in the proper care of Charles and Henry. 'I's 'll be gone for a week,' she told the girl, 'you do as I say, an' I'll give 'ee a sovereign.'

The Locks moved out of Montacute the next morning, and the women of the village, seeing Luke Carew's wife seated high on the leading vardo, told one another that this was no more than they had expected. Wonder was, that the gypsy had bided in among them for a full five years.

The circuitous route followed by generations of Loveridges and Locks was to take them into Sedgemoor by way of the Blackdown Hills. It was explained to Meri that the birth of Lavinia's second child had caused them to miss the Council held yearly in Dommett Wood.

'We was held fast in Dorset,' said old Mrs Lock. 'That was a hard birth; us had to fetch out a gorgie doctor come the finish. Two long months we bided in that cursed Bradford Abbas, while 'Vinia got her strength back; and us fearing every footfall lest it should be the landowner or the gavvers come to shift us on.'

'Aye,' said Meri, ''twas never safe to stop long in Dorset. To murder the Rom was always good sport for the gorgio in they parts.' Meri fingered the yellow ribbon that secured her thick braids. 'Where is you hoping to pitch then?' she asked softly.

'As close into Ilminster as us can get,' said Lavinia's husband. 'I got business down there what'll take two days to settle. After that, us can follow the Isle river up to Langport.'

'Don't you fret, maid,' said old Mrs Lock, 'us'll bring 'ee to Sedgemoor in time for the water-violets and tansy.'

'I'll be glad to go first into Ilminster,' Meri murmured, 'I got some business of my own up in Buckland.' They glanced curiously at her, but asked no questions. She lifted a hand to her smooth brown throat. 'I done a foolish thing, once. I chopped my coral pendant for a china bowl.'

Lavinia drew breath, sharply, 'Oh Meri! You never didden! That coral was old. It was brung from a far land by great-grandmother Loveridge. No wonder they poor twins o' yourn was born crooked.'

'Who did you chop with?' asked Taiso Lock.

'Mrs Liza Greypaull, up to Larksleve. Her what married Philip Greypaull from Warren's Farm.'

'You'll never get that pendant back,' said Taiso. 'They Greypaulls is a mean lot – even each to each they won't give much.'

'Liza'll give it to me. She's bound to when I tell her how much it matters.'

Mrs Lock shook her head. 'O dordi, dordi!' she wailed, 'you is always such a headstrong woman, Meri!'

It had felt strange at first to be out again upon the Queen's highway, to see the thick dust eddy and settle beneath her bare feet. Her ear, attuned for so long to the twins' continual whining, to Luke's deep tones, must adjust now to the Rom speech, must be prepared for the inevitable questions.

They travelled all day through green and pleasant country and, when night approached, they pitched in a dingle close to a stream. Lavinia and Meri filled the jacks with water, while the men attended to the livestock and cut wands for the extra bender which would have to be erected. Meri collected wood and built a quick fire to boil the kettle, while Lavinia and her mother-in-law prepared the evening meal. The familiar tasks stirred memories in Meri of other times and other places. Lavinia's daughter was named Helena; her limbs were straight, her movements unhindered. Meri reached out a hand to stroke the rough uncombed curls and was rewarded with the flashing smile that came easily to a child who had never known pain. When the meal had been eaten and the children carried sleeping to their beds, Lavinia asked the expected question.

'How is it then, cousin, living atwixt gorgies?'

Meri stared at the red heart of the fire. ''Twas my own choice. I is not complaining. I got a good man what never beats me or goes boozin' in the kitchima. I makes a tidy bit o' money, one way and another. My children is kept safe, and as well as they ever can be. I wants for nothing.'

Lavinia said, 'But that idden quite true, is it, Meri? – you wants for the company of your own kind. Us hev spied 'ee walking in the hills. You is never a settled woman. You is mis-contented.'

'I thought once,' said Meri, 'that I could have anything I wanted, all easy-come, like pulling dead wood from a hedge, or snaring a rabbit.'

'You was ever a proud one,' said Mrs Lock, 'I minds well the way your eyes did flash, your savage temper. The gorgie husband hev brought you low, my lovely! Now how did that ever come about when he don't drink, or beat you?'

Meri's gaze moved from face to face around that circle. She studied the old brown couple who sat so close together, Lavinia who had been almost a sister, and the pure-blooded Taiso Lock who was her wedded husband. 'You can't understand,' she told them, 'because you only meets the gorgie on the doorstep. 'Tis all chapel and gloving in that village. Everybody watching everybody else to see who the Lord'll punish next. They be very keen on the punishments of the Lord in Luke's village.'

'Us heard as how you goes to chapel.'

'I got a foot in both camps, Mother!' Meri cried, 'and

thass a tricky way to be standing. Straddle a bit too far in any direction – and you falls flat on your face.'

'Thy gorgie man must be a living wonder,' said Lavinia gently.

Meri said, 'He is my heart's joy – and my heart's sorrow. I would lie me down on the ground and die for him. But he don't know that.'

'You wants a strong child for his sake – not your own.' The sudden comprehension in the old woman's eyes made Meri cry aloud. 'Yes. Oh yes! My Luke is like an oak tree what have growed two crooked branches, and I can't bear to see that. 'Twas my wicked pride what made the mischief. I got to get back my coral pendant.'

'And if you don't?'

'Then us'll try other ways, Mother. Rom spells or gorgie prayers, there's not much difference.'

Meri left the dingle early next morning, and began the long climb up to Buckland St Mary. The Blackdowns were locked into early summer, and she had forgotten the charm of these high places: how the blackthorn leaned together to make a shade, how the dog-rose climbed and starred the hedges, how the steep lanes dipped and twisted between the rich fields. The season of haysel, almost over in the low-lands, was about to begin in Buckland. Men stood in line at the smithy and waited to get sickles sharpened and scythes adjusted. Haycarts rumbled out of carthouses; rabbits and field-mice sniffed approaching danger and fled the standing grass. In Dommett Wood the foxgloves and forget-me-nots would be flowering in shady places. On Larksleve Farm there would be honeysuckle climbing the peaked porch and nodding in at bedroom windows. The low white house with its reeded thatch and pale blue casements must, by this time, be housing a brood of healthy chavvies, and Eliza surely willing to relinquish possession of the coral pendant.

The sun was already high when she came up to Larksleve and, as Meri had expected, the farmhouse was deserted. She looked upwards to the steep fields which rose behind the house and there was no mistaking Eliza Greypaull. The tiny figure in the blue dress, red curls escaping from beneath a white cap, had not changed in the past six years. A short climb, and Meri was standing in blackthorn shadow, unobserved by the toilers in the hayfield. She recognised Jed Hayes, who had once worked as cowman on Castle Farm. Samuel Greypaull, sallow and insignificant as ever, worked silently beside him. The two men wore smock and gaiters, and hats of plaited straw, but it was the tall, slim man who claimed Meri's close attention. Six years of marriage to Eliza had not made Philip a farmer. He lagged at some distance from his brother and cowman. He used the scythe awkwardly, and paused too frequently to hone the blade. He wore boots and moleskin trousers and a fine lawn shirt, open at the throat, with lace-trimmed cuffs rolled daintily back across his forearms. The sun had bleached his yellow curls to flaxen, and tanned the fine skin of his face. Meri had seen gentlemen who lived in fine houses exhibit that same air of bored distaste when faced with some uncongenial task.

The buxom red-cheeked woman must be Loveday, grown heavier and, in spite of the wedding band, still obviously childless. The chavvies who played around her were so clearly Eliza's. Three dark-haired, green-eyed Greypaulls, with the same pale skins and neat features as most of their kin. The two women tossed the cut hay with long-pronged forks and turned it to dry in the sunshine on the far side of the field. But for the rustle made by the scythes and the laughter of the children, a brooding silence lay across the little group.

Meri settled down to wait and, as she had expected, it was

190

Eliza who was the first to lay down her hayfork; she picked up the empty wicker basket and began to make her way downhill towards the house. Meri moved silently along the hedge, keeping pace with Eliza but, as yet, unseen. They came face-to-face in their old meeting place, in the Home meadow. Eliza nodded her head very slowly, as if in answer to questions not yet asked. Meri said, 'I thought as p'raps you'd be surprised to see I?' She smiled uncertainly.

Eliza, unsmiling, said, 'I've bin expecting you for a long time. I knew you'd be sure to come back yer, sooner or later.'

Meri became still and cautious. This was not the welcome she had expected. The pliant girl had grown into a bitter woman, and Meri, whose business it was to read faces, fell back before the fierce green gaze.

'Why - whatever have happened to 'ee, Liza? You is so much changed I hardly knows 'ee.'

They walked on together through the porch and into the shade of the Larksleve kitchen. Eliza cut cheese and bread, set the food upon a board, poured buttermilk into a blue cup, and pushed the meal across the table.

'Sit down. You must have had a wearying trip.' Meri hesitated. 'Sit!' rapped Eliza, 'you've bin living in a house these past six years. You must have got used to chairs and tables by this time.'

Meri sat down. Eliza moved briskly from table to pantry and back again. She lined the wicker basket with a clean white cloth, in it she packed cheese and bread, pasties and oatcakes. Meri crumbled bread awkwardly between her fingers, but did not eat. 'You got three good chavvies, Eliza.'

Eliza nodded.

'The twins is quite growed since you last seen 'em. They walks by theirselves, but not steady.' Meri paused. 'I had another baby - a girl - Luke called her Annie. Her had that

191

same wicked twist in back and shoulder. Her never drew breath, which was a blessing.'

'I be sorry to hear that, Meri.'

'You don't sound sorry!'

Eliza leaned across the table. 'I know what brings you here,' she said, 'I know what you've come back for.' She raised a hand to her neck and pulled the coral pendant from beneath the high neck of her dress. ''Tis the necklace, idden it, Meri, what brings you so far from home?'

'I got to have it, Liza. I be with child again – so you got to give it to me. All I want is one chavvie, straight and strong. You got three already.' Her voice grew eager, she pulled the length of yellow-green amber across her braids and held it out towards Eliza. 'A fair chop this time,' she wheedled, 'take it, Liza! My amber made Philip Greypaull love you, once. Remember! I know how you wants him to love you – you always did, though you never showed it.'

Eliza grew very pale. The freckles stood out, liver-coloured and ugly against her white skin. 'Well,' she whispered, 'you be wrong there, Meri. Things have changed since you last come here. You is not the only one to be with child. But mine was forced upon me by that drunkard I call husband. I don't need your string of amber. All I want is the pendant. It protects my children. I believes on it, same as you do.'

Meridiana tipped her head sideways and considered Eliza. 'You know 'tis against your religion to trust in witchcraft?' Her voice was gruff and uncompromising. ''Tis a wonder you dares to step inside your church when you'm wearing my pendant.' She looked at Eliza's throat, at the heavy silver chain from which hung the fashioned half-circle of silver flowers, each one inset with petals of coral. 'I wants it back! I got to have it! You bain't Rom. It got no meaning for you. You can do just as well wi'out it.'

'No I can't.' The passionate words cut across the gypsy's

192

whine. Eliza clutched at the pendant with both hands. 'Take anything else in this house. But to get this from round my throat you'll have to kill me first!'

Meri stood up. Her compelling gaze transfixed Eliza. ''Tis a bad thing to refuse a gypsy – 'specially one what is offering you a fair chop. But I'll not need to kill you, Eliza Greypaull. The shadows is already thick around your shoulders. You got so many sorrows coming that no pendant of mine can ever save you.'

'So her wudden part wi' it,' muttered Mrs Lock.

Meri feigned an unconcern she did not feel. ''Tis no great matter,' she said. 'Truth to tell – I don't fancy that pendant no more. Seven years around a gorgie neck have probably weakened the power.' She looked thoughtful. 'Thass a troubled family. 'Tis my belief that one o' they women is dealing wi' the Devil. That got to be the servant, Loveday. I knows Eliza; her is too religious for outright witchcraft.'

'Her kept your pendant.'

'Aye. Much good may it do her! Poor Liza's ill-luck is tied up in that fancy-dan of a husband. That man have quite changed her spirit. Poor Liza!'

The Somerset Levels were strange and atmospheric, and rarely ventured into by gypsies. It was a landscape of pollard willow, of withy beds and low hills. The water-violets flowered briefly in the month of June, and were to be found only in the deepest rhynes. These rhynes were deep ditches filled with water, they separated the withy beds from the pasture and the fields from the moorland. It needed a whole day of careful searching to fill one small basket with the purple-streaked flower heads.

The wild tansy grew in high places. They found it

blowing bright and yellow on the slopes of Polden. According to old Mrs Lock, a decoction of water-violet flowers would cool Meri's troubled head and spirit. The leaves of the tansy had been created for the sole purpose of aiding those women who found themselves with child. Of all the plants and herbs which grew around Sedgemoor, the tansy, said old Mrs Lock, was the most effective in staying miscarriage and ensuring that a chavvie would be strong and carried to its full term. There was also the other magic.

Meri went into Glastonbury town alone and on foot. She knelt and prayed among the Abbey ruins, sought and found the Holy Spring, cupped her hands and drank the tangy waters; and all the time her gaze turned back towards the Tor. She recognised its shape, felt its power. She watched the sun go down behind the Hill, saw her own shadows lengthen and, even though she felt fear at the approach of darkness, still she was drawn irresistibly towards the narrow path that led up to the Tor.

The Lock family had pitched in a valley-field close beside the Hill. To begin with Meri caught the smell of bacon frying; for a time she could see the smoke from their fire and hear their voices, and then a bend in the track robbed her of this reassurance, and she stood, quite alone, on the high point of the Tor. She remembered her grandmother's story about the young boy Jesus who had walked long ago in this place with his uncle Joseph. She knelt down and placed her hands together, as Luke had taught her. The moon rose, full and white, edging clouds with silver; she was aware of the moss beneath her knees and the wild wind which caught at her yellow ribbons. She knelt for a long time and no prayer came into her mind; and then slowly a certain energy flowed into her body. She saw visions: she ascended to a great height and looked down upon a Tor lying white under winter snow and streaked with lilac shadows. She saw it green and blown with blossom under blue May skies. She

194

saw it black and silvered with moonlight, and knew that she was restored again and safe within her own body. No prayer had come into her mind; she had not asked for a straight-backed child, or a safe birthing. She had knelt on the summit of Glastonbury Tor and felt the earth move; and Meri knew that all would be well within her.

Winter had come down on Larksleve; a dry crackling season with hoar frost night and morning, and such a brooding coldness over the fields and hills that it had reached into the souls of people. Eliza's kitchen was the heart of Larksleve, the place from which came all warmth and comfort. The presence of a child, curled quiet in the inglenook in the high-backed settle by the fire, was too frequently forgotten, and self-containment had come naturally to Candace. At first she had listened to them, absorbed, but not compre-hending. Lately, she had understood, and with that under-standing had come the withdrawal of spirit which was to shape her life.

There was to be another baby. Grandma had said, ''Tis about time they two maidens was give reg'lar tasks, our Liza. With another baby comin' you'll need all the help you can get. They spends too much time lolling round, doin' nothing. Laziness is inbred, an' us don't want them turnin' out like their father.'

Mother talked all the time to Candace and Mina; some-times she would pretend to be a horse to make Jackie laugh. But Mother never talked to Father. At first, the silence had felt like a finger cold on her heart. The children in school had said that her father was a rascal and a rogue, and Candace supposed that he must be. She had never yet heard a good word spoken about him.

Grandma Rachel had come to see them just before Christ-mas. She had said, 'I heard how the poor departed Prince

Consort did use to have a live fir-tree brung into the palace every Christmas. He did light it wi' candles, an' tie ribbons on it. 'Tis such a pretty notion, Philip – don' you think so, Eliza.' Then Father had gone straight away to Pickett's Copse, and cut down a little fir tree, and set it in a barrel of earth on the parlour carpet. He had asked Mother for coloured ribbons to decorate it, but she had rushed out of the parlour and left him alone on his knees beside the tree. Father's face had looked funny, just like Jackie's when he was about to cry. Candace had wanted to cry too; she had run to the kitchen and pushed her face into the settle cushions. After a while she had heard the door slam, and Father ride fast away down the lane. Grandma Elizabeth had said, 'You must help your mother now, Candace. Poor maid, her do on'y have me an' you to rely on these days. What time did that father of yours come back from Taunton?' And Candace had told her, and seen the anger flare in her grandmother's face. It was not easy to know whom you were supposed to love. There was Mother who never smiled any more, but whose gentle fingers brushed your long hair, and who left the rush-light burning in your bedroom when you were frightened of the dark. There was Father, with his smiling face and pretty curls, who rarely noticed Candace or Mina, or Jackie. Perhaps it was safer to love only herself.

Candace woke early that morning. She slipped from the bed she shared with Mina and drew back the window curtains. The moon was still high in the sky, it shone on the frosty fields and showed her the horse and its rider as they approached the gates of Larksleve. Her father was coming home; it was Monday morning. He had been in Taunton since Friday. She went down to the kitchen, expecting to find her mother with the fire already lit and the kettle boiling, but she found Eliza crouched upon the hearthstone, her face grey and old with pain. 'Is that your father?' she whispered, and Candace nodded. 'Tell him, quick, before he dismounts – tell him to fetch Grandma Elizabeth an' Loveday.'

The little sisters clung together in the inglenook corner while Loveday boiled pans of water and attempted to comfort an inconsolable Jackie. Candace concluded that it was easier after all to decide whom she did not love. She wrapped her arms about the terrified Mina.

'Don' 'ee cry now, maid, that'll only upset me. 'Tis that new baby what is making Mama scream so. Thass a wicked child what does that, Mina. Us idden never gonna' love it!'

'So her's gone, then,' Charity Carew had said, 'back to her own sort?'

'No, Mother. Her is with child, an' has gone to Glastonbury with her cousin to pray that all goes well this time.'

'An' you believes that? More like her's gone off pickin' they daft bits o' grasses an' flowers. Whass wrong wi' prayin' in our own Baptist chapel?'

'Her had a mind to go to the Holy Well, an' when Meri is of a mind then I got to lissen to her.'

Charity had sniffed. 'Round her liddle finger you be Luke Carew, an' you the size of two men put together. I'll be surprised if us sees her ever again.'

But Meri had returned, as promised. She had decocted the flower heads of the water-violets, boiled up the leaves of the wild tansy; and Luke had watched her grow quiet and contemplative, had seen her bloom like a rose.

'Tell about Glastonbury, then!' he had pleaded; she was the traveller lately returned from far away places. So she told him about the winding drom through Somerton and Street, and how it had brought back sad memories of her mother and father. She told about the Holy Well and its bitter-tasting waters 'all hid away in the dark under low trees'. There was the strange grey Abbey where she 'had felt frightened a bit in amongst they funny gurt stones'. But when he asked her about the Tor she fell silent.

'But you must of see'd it, Meri. Why, I often sees it myself from the Hill on a clear day.'

'If I tell 'ee, you won't like it.'

'Us shudden have no secrets – 'tis my child same as yours.'

She clasped both her hands across her stomach. ''Tis the Tor,' she confessed, 'what do give the Blessing.' She glanced fearfully at him, expecting a rebuke. 'Our women hev always said so, an' now I knows 'tis true. I felt it, Luke. 'Tiv got a strong pull what draws the soul from a body. They do say that when Jesus Christ was a chavvie he walked upon the Tor wi' his uncle, Joseph.'

Luke stared at her, saw the faith in her dark eyes, and was humbled. So she had finally arrived at the place he had wished her to be, but in her own time, and by her own route.

'Then you believes?' he whispered, 'you truly believes on the same Lord as I do?'

'If Jesus walked on the Tor,' she said simply, 'then us is bound to have a straight-backed chavvie this time.'

Eliza's new daughter showed no sign of her reluctance to achieve life; she was quite unwrinkled, a miracle of alabaster skin, violet eyes, and copper-coloured hair. 'That bain't no ordinary infant,' muttered Daniel to John, 'us got we another changeling yer, bor! This one'll give us trouble. As sure as old leaves fall.'

Philip was the last to come; he had waited until all the women were busy in kitchen and dairy, and Eliza left white and unattended in the canopied bed. She heard his footfall on the staircase and felt the hatred bloom inside her. She looked towards the frosty window, concentrated her mind upon frozen ponds and leafless hedges. She tried not to watch his face as he bent over the cradle. She heard him gasp and then moan. 'My God – whatever have you done here, Eliza?'

''Tis what you ordered idden it? A daughter wi' violet eyes an' copper-coloured hair. I was only obeying you, cousin Philip.' Her voice was no longer gentle, but hard and drum-tight. 'You likes women what obey you – like that soft creature, your mother. You called me a witch. You accused me of consorting with your brother Samuel. You hinted that any dark-haired child I bore could never be one of yours. Well, now you got your proof. Even you could never suspect that what lies there, in that cradle, was fathered by Samuel Greypaull.'

He turned back to the bed and faced her; shock had driven the high colour from his cheekbones. 'I never meant it, Liza. 'Twas the cider talkin'. You must of knowed that?'

'I know you for an evil man, Philip Greypaull. 'Tis a devil-child what you give me upon the hearthstone.' Eliza lay back among the pillows, and tears filled her green eyes. 'You is my shame, cousin Philip, the burden God has put upon me. What have I ever done wrong in my life to deserve such as you?'

He went down on his knees beside the bed and reached for her hand, but Eliza thrust both her arms beneath the bed-clothes.

'Don't touch me,' she warned him, 'God's curse is on you.' He went back to the cradle.

'Why, 'tis your hair, Eliza, only several shades darker. My eyes, only bluer and bigger.' He laughed uneasily. 'We was bound to have a red-haired baby, sooner or later. 'Tis the law o' nature.'

Eliza did not answer.

She was slow to recover from this confinement, troubled in heart and spirit. Eliza had only wanted safety: grain in her barns, stock in her sheds, gold in reserve against hard times. The birth of the alien child had convinced her that certain problems were quite beyond her resolution. She began to wrestle with acceptance. She prayed, 'Thy will be done', but did not really mean it. She resolved that there would be no more children, but could not imagine how this was to be achieved. Her mother had advised her. 'You wants to keep your bedroom door locked, our Liza. Never let "him" in when you knows un's drunk. You be too much given to breedin' maidens. Now I had my four boys long afore you was ever thought of.'

There were only two ways of doing anything; her mother's way and the wrong way. 'You be right, o' course, Mother,' said Eliza, wryly. It would never occur to Elizabeth Greypaull that a child might as easily be conceived upon a hearthstone as in a marriage bed.

This time the baptism was to be a quiet affair. 'Immediate family only,' said Elizabeth. After all, one maiden was very like another and she was not anxious to have it known around Buckland that the Greypaulls had bred another unlucky red-head. 'Us'll call her Rachel,' she declared. There was more than a touch of malice in her voice. ''Tis about time a child was named for "his" side of the family.'

'No, Mother!' Eliza wrapped both hands tight together and made her voice firm. 'The name for this child was chose long ago, by her father. Her given name is Blanche. 'Tiv all been decided.'

Meri had done all that she could in the way of repairing ill-fortune. Christmas had passed and the child not yet born, but she took heart from the unusual quietness of her emotions, the strength of her body. She had used tansy leaves and water-violets; she had seen visions on the Tor and prayed in the Baptist chapel; drunk holy water from the Glastonbury Well and recited a certain incantation known only to Rom women.

Jye Carew was born on the same January morning which first saw that beautiful child, Blanche Greypaull, but, unlike her, his beauty caused no consternation. Even Charity rejoiced to see the straight limbs of him, the fine large head crowned with black curls, to hear the strong loud crying in the house.

To feel maternal love for the first time made Meri aware that she had never loved Charles and Henry. She held Jye close to her heart and knew that her reluctant pity was not enough; she resolved that in future she would try to do better by them.

To be warm, to be fed and sheltered, to have a few shillings put by against hard times was the most that Luke Carew had ever hoped for. For Meri, to be left unmolested by the gavvers, to find a constable or farmer who did not object to her presence was a kind of contentment. But the coming of Jye brought a peace upon the household. Charles and Henry felt it and were less fretful. Meri would never be reconciled to a life within walls. She would always need to walk the Hill, to search for smoke in the lanes, always need to study the patteran which indicated the path taken by her people. But now there was Jye, the symbol of her love for Luke, the vindication of her defection from her own kind. She consented at last to Chapel baptisms, and on the first day of March Luke Carew's three sons were immersed, together.

The felled copse-wood was stacked in neat piles where Jed

Hayes had left it. The cutting and drawing of logs was a punishing occupation, and Philip tired easily these days. Jed tended to set up the kind of cracking pace which the master of Larksleve found it impossible to match. 'You cut – I'll draw,' Philip had said. The hired man had grinned and touched his forelock, 'Yes, zur, an' what'll I do when that's finished?'

'You'd best ask the missus.'

Eliza's authority within the house was unquestioned; for the sake of Philip's pride she deferred to him in public, but concealment of the true situation was no longer possible before the servants. It was to Eliza that they looked these days for their daily orders, and it was Eliza who commanded their loyalty and respect.

The woods were quiet in winter, the glades solitary and dim, coloured brown and silver. Philip came up to Pickett's Copse, turned the oxen to face towards Larksleve, halted them in their yokes, and allowed the hauling chains to lie empty upon the ground. From this high place he could look down on the reeded thatch of Larksleve; he could evaluate his roof-tree, his prison. He sat down on a log just inside the glade, and began to smoke the expensive tobacco to which he had recently become addicted.

The need to invade and possess the hearts of their loved ones was a characteristic of the Greypaull women, he thought. It was a subtle witchcraft, seeming to be blameless and overlaid with good intentions. He had only once dared to accuse Eliza of its practice. 'You've already made sure that they liddle maidens won't love me,' he had said, 'as for the boy – he's all yours.'

He would come back to the house in the evenings, and stand in the darkened yard and watch her through the kitchen window. She would sit, mending-basket on the table, the sleeping Blanche in a cradle at her feet, the older children gathered about her. He would see her stroke their hair, touch their faces, make them her very own. He would burst into the kitchen, deliberately disruptive, and snatch up the baby from her cradle. He would rock her in his arms, and feel love for her rise and break inside him. 'And who is my beautiful girl,' he would cry, 'who is my copper-haired lovely? Blanche is her father's darling, and'll always be so.'

They would turn round to face him, fix their strange green gaze upon him, but never smile. He would feel foolish then and thrust the baby at her mother. 'Bedtime,' Eliza would murmur, and at her word of quiet command they would begin to undress before the kitchen fire. They would stand obediently before him in their flannel nightgowns, not wishing to be kissed. They would chant, 'Goodnight – God bless, Papa,' but never look directly at him. He would watch them climb the spiral staircase, those neat, dark children: Candace, his first-born; Madelina, whom he had named for his little sister; and James John Daniel, who was to have been his pride and joy, his true companion. But James, whom Eliza called Jackie, did not need his father. He was the darling of his older sisters, appropriated by his mother, petted and indulged by all four grandparents.

Philip stood up, kicked at the log, and watched the wood-lice scuttle. It was cold in the clearing. He pulled on his chamois gloves and began to haul at the piled logs, securing the chains with which he was to drag them downhill to Larksleve. He still believed that, given the opportunity and some encouragement from his family, he might yet become a famous singer. He had seen others, less talented than himself, graduate in one night from taproom entertainer to top of the bill in a London theatre. The fortuitous presence of an impresario in the Turk's Head tavern could still see him launched on a brilliant career. Philip dreamed of packed theatres, appreciative audiences, adoring women, while the oxen, yoked and chained to their burden of logs, plodded downhill before him towards Larksleve.

John Greypaull's oldest son Francis had finally found a wife: a landowner's daughter from Devon, older than Francis, but wealthy in her own right and with comfortable expectations. She was no beauty, but, as Elizabeth said, 'Our Fran won't need to worry about the price of corn, or what beef is fetchin' on the hoof. Property, our Liza, thass the thing! My word now – look at this place!'

They had travelled the few miles to the wedding across the border of Somerset into Devon; Philip and Eliza, with their three oldest children, had shared a carriage with her mother and father. They drove in past a gate-house, up a winding drive, to arrive at the door of a pillared and porticoed mansion. 'If I catches you gettin' even half-way drunk in this place,' John warned Philip, 'then I'll horsewhip you wi' my own hand.'

Francis Greypaull had met Selina Hammett-James in the home of a professional matchmaker. Such matters were often arranged, for a fee, by those parents who wished to ensure a profitable marriage for an unprepossessing son or daughter. Francis had not quite fulfilled the Hammett-James's expectations, but he came from an old and respected family of yeomen, and was known in his own parish to be industrious, religious and sober.

'Be you quite sure, Fran?' Eliza had asked him. Francis had looked at her and she had guessed his mind.

'Money,' he had said briefly, 'I've seen what the lack of it can do. I got no wish to end up mean and grasping like father, an' our uncles; or like you an' Philip, with your whole living depending on weather, an', in your case, on Philip biding sober enough to drive a plough.' He had touched her shoulder. 'If you ever feels the need,' he said awkwardly, 'if it so happens that you wants help – '

Eliza said, 'Thank you, Fran. I be grateful for the offer.

But, while I got my health an' strength, it won't never come to that.'

Harvest Supper was still held at Castle Farm. Eliza had helped her mother to set up the tables and prepare the feast. Elizabeth had said, 'Whass up wi' your Loveday? Her looks proper down in the mouth. Is her carryin' again?'

'I don't think so, Mother.' It was true, Loveday Hayes had been unnaturally quiet, almost sullen. 'Come to think about it,' said Eliza, 'Jed haven't bin his usual self, lately. He've hardly had a word to say this past fortnight.'

It was not until Loveday was fortified with good food, and Jed had strong drink taken, that the couple found courage sufficient to face Eliza. They asked her to step outside the barn for a quiet word, and the grim set of Jed's young face warned of coming trouble.

'Us don' like to put more burden on 'ee, Missus. You always bin so good to we - but things got to be said. Us have had no pay from Master for some weeks - an' that hev bin hard graftin' in haysel an' harvest.'

Loveday said, ''Tis on'y 'cause us got no children, an' had a few shillings put by that us hev managed so long wi'out sayin' something - '

'Don't worry,' said Eliza, 'I'll speak to him about it - right away.'

But when she had gone to search for Philip her mother had waylaid her. Elizabeth had whispered, 'Your father'll drive you home, Eliza. Let "him" bide yer - 'uns dead-drunk as usual, an' us don't want no more mishaps.'

Philip came back to Larksleve in the early morning; he had been roused from sleep by John Greypaull's herdsman, who had come to Castle Farm barn to collect dry fodder. He was unwashed, unshaven, wisps of hay still stuck to his hair and clothing. It was to be the wrong question, at the wrong hour. But Eliza was angry. Before he could soak his head at the pump, or change into a fresh smock, she had pounced upon him.

'Did you pay the harvest gang off?'

'Course I did. They was a rough lot this year. No pay and I'd have had a riot on my hands.'

'So you took advantage of Jed and Loveday, who be quiet an' docile, an' not likely to make trouble?'

'I dunno' what you mean.'

'Oh yes you do, Philip! They two be good an' faithful servants, an' you hev let them work like a couple of oxen all summer, wi'out a penny-piece paid between 'em.'

'They eats yer, in the kitchen. You be always givin' Loveday bits an' pieces. I've seen 'ee do it.'

'Thass no reason not to pay 'em. I won't – '

'Don'ee go on so, Liza. I got a bad head. I got to lie down for a bit. Let me be!'

'An' leave Jed to do the field-work? 'Tis time for ploughing, or didden you know that? Perhaps,' Eliza whispered, 'perhaps you 'ud sooner I fetched my brothers up yer. You seems to pay more keen attention to James an' Robert. Another good hiding might make a power o' difference to 'ee.'

'You'd do that to me?'

'Yes, I would! I got four children to think on. I got a farm what is goin' to fail if you don't pull yourself together. What sort o' man are you? What sort o' husband an' father? How much more money do you owe?'

'No more. 'Twas on'y the wages. I'll settle up wi' 'em on Friday.'

'Now, Philip!'

'I can't, Liza.' He attempted to smile. 'What about your egg-money, then? You always got a bit put by.'

'Thass for the schooling, an' for Mina's music lessons.'

'I think you better forget all that. You'd best pay Jed an'

Loveday. They'll leave, else.'

She counted up her egg-money and found that it was barely sufficient to pay what was owed to Jed and Loveday Hayes. Her children did not return to the village school that autumn. When the first of the hiring fairs was held in November, Jed Hayes stood in line, the badge of his craft pinned upon his lapel to inform a new master of his availability and skill.

Blanche was more forward than the other children. She spoke her first words at ten months, walked on her first birthday. She was inquisitive and demanding, screamed if she was not the recipient of somebody's instant attention, and quite wore out all those who came into her orbit. Eliza had tried to love her, but she felt no impulsion to touch the heavy auburn hair, to stroke the fine, alabaster cheek. The child defied all classification; she was singular, of herself, and her mother could not begin to like her.

Mina loved Jackie with the heart-whole devotion that is given by the timid child to the one who is utterly fearless. Her brother, at the age of four, would already climb the tallest trees, jump the flooded ditches; and once, when nobody was looking, he had ridden bareback on his father's bay mare. Mina had wanted to love Candace, but her older sister did not like affection; she always pushed away the encircling arm, avoided the proffered kiss. They had all three decided long ago that they would never love the baby, Blanche.

Grandma Elizabeth had said, 'An' why is they three children not at school, Eliza?'

'Because us can't afford it, Mother.' Grandma had offered to pay, but Mama had said 'no'. Mina was glad. She was teased at school by the other children. 'Your mother is a witch,' they taunted, 'an' your father is a gambler.' She had asked her mother what the word meant, and her mother had said that a man who gambled was a fool, that he wasted his time and money playing cards and betting on horses, that such a man would lose all that was good and dear in life, and deserved to burn in Hell-fire for all Eternity.

The significant card-schools were to be found in certain inns and taverns. Macey's, frequented by visiting bishops, famous actors, and the local gentry, was considered to be the most exclusive. The Winchester Arms, kept by an ex-army sergeant called Bidgood, came next in the order of importance. The smaller, less particular schools had their quarters in the upper rooms of inns like the Four Alls or the New Angel. Philip aspired to the tables at Macey's, played occasionally at the Winchester Arms, but was more usually to be found sitting-in among the blood-and-dust atmosphere of the Four Alls.

His cronies considered him to be something of a dandy for, although he could drink and swear and roister with the best, his elegance had never deserted him completely. The fact that he was unusually literate for a farmer had also endeared him to tavern landlords, who relied on him for the making up of their accounts, and the reading and writing of their letters. He performed similar favours for army men who were stationed at the barracks. He wrote letters of apology to the mothers of young sailors who had berthed in Lyme Bay and, on travelling inland, had found themselves ensnared by the delights of Taunton.

The Four Alls yard was both extensive and private. A high wall concealed the many brutal and degrading pastimes which were enjoyed by all classes. Cock-fighting was a favourite sport; badger-drawing and bull-baiting involved the use of dogs bred especially for the purpose of biting and tormenting their helpless victims. Fights between men were commonplace and roused little interest, but a fight between women drew excited crowds and was always an occasion for heavy betting.

The acquisition of money meaht little to Philip. A heap of sovereigns, a banknote represented just so many chances to sit-in at gaming-tables, or the lurch in the gut which came when he placed his bet on a fighting-cock or a battling woman. He had his ups and downs, the good times when the cards fell out in his favour, the bad times when the captive bull or badger would forget its role and kill the attacking, biting bulldogs.

It was Jeremiah Jones, pawnbroker and moneylender of North Street, Taunton, who knew just how strongly the gambling habit had gripped Philip Greypaull. The loans had been small to begin with: one pound, two pounds, and always repaid with interest on the appointed date. The name of Greypaull, painted on farmcarts and waggons, on milk-churns, and stamped on cheeses, was all the collateral he was likely to need, or so he had thought. But the word in Taunton said that Philip had begun to visit Macey's. The loans from Jeremiah had increased accordingly. It was five pounds now on a Friday morning, sometimes ten. Jeremiah, who had no wish to turn away business, began, nevertheless, to worry a little. He faced his best customer in the little back room of the pawnshop and said casually, 'I hears as how you be sitting-in at Macey's these days, Mr Greypaull?'

Philip smiled. 'You hears right, Mr Jones. I got weary of all that rough stuff at the Four Alls. 'Tis more of a man's game what they plays at Macey's.'

Jeremiah said quietly, 'And it takes a man's money to keep upsides with the wealthy customers who patronise that place?'

Philip bridled. 'Be you hinting-on at something, Mr Jones?'

Jeremiah spread placating fingers across the desk. 'Why no, Mr Greypaull. I don't never have no worries in your case. I just wanted to make clear between us just how the land lies.'

'The land,' grinned Philip, 'lies in Buckland St Mary. It goes by the name of Larksleve, and 'tis my land; I got the documents to prove it. You'd better remember who you're dealing with when you talks to me. I bain't one of your snivellin' labourers what can't write his own name. I don't come yer to pawn my boots every Monday morning. I can cover with land and livestock any sum that I care to borrow. Why! I could buy and sell you, Jeremiah – no question about it!'

The moneylender nodded. 'Well now! You can't imagine how relieved I be to hear all that, Mr Greypaull.' He twisted the heavy gold ring on his knuckle, and rapped with it smartly upon the top of his desk. He opened an account book at a page which bore many entries. 'Your debt stands at fifty pounds as of this morning,' he said coldly, 'not a penny-piece have been repaid for this last six weeks. That means no more credit. You've reached your limit.'

'But why? Old Moggridge, the surgeon, owes you two hundred. He told me that himself. Why should his standing be higher than mine?'

Jeremiah Jones closed his account book. ''Tis for your own good, Mr Greypaull. You got a wife and children dependent on you. I also,' he said softly, 'hears other stories about you. Rumour reckons that you is pretty deep in debt to other people. A hundred pounds owed up at Macey's, and Macey himself fetched in to issue you with a final warning. Be warned by me. Nathan Macey don't believe in talking. He uses cut-throats and bullies to reclaim his money. There's a mighty persuasion in a well-stropped razor.' Jeremiah smiled. 'Now me, I'm a reasonable fella. Something on account each week and we shall bide friends.

210

But if you got any sense at all, Mr Greypaull, you'll stop well away from Taunton town in future.'

Churchwardens and Overseers of the Poor were invariably chosen from those yeoman of substance who farmed in the parish. Family pride could not allow it to be known that Daniel's oldest son, Philip, was, once again, cutting close to ruin. Although, in a tight community where everyone knew everybody's business, such knowledge was difficult to conceal.

John Greypaull began to make surreptitious gifts to his daughter and her children. New cloaks and bonnets, hand-made boots and gloves were sent up to Larksleve from Taunton. As Elizabeth said, 'Us can at least see to it that our poor Liza and her children do look prosperous an' content when they walks into church on a Sunday morning.'

Appearances counted. To arrive for Sunday service in a governess-cart or carriage, to go well shod, to be suitably but soberly garbed, to have a child or two receiving instruction in the village school, to have Parson and his lady call in a social capacity: these were the signals which proved the respectable, the God-fearing family.

Respectable men did not get drunk, at least not in the presence of those whom they considered to be inferior in class and station. Respectable men did not gamble or frequent low taverns and halls of dubious entertainment; they observed the Lord's Day. They conformed.

Respectable women deferred to their husbands, at least in public. The good wife was unselfish, religious, concerned only with raising her children to walk in godly ways; she kept a good table, clean beds, thick lace curtains at her windows, and an aspidistra on the what-not in the parlour.

Jed Hayes found employment with a yeoman who farmed in Broadway, and reckoned a three mile walk, night and morning, to be worth the security of six shillings placed regularly in his hand every Friday evening. Loveday remained with Eliza; she had come, at the age of nine, from the Bridgwater Poorhouse to be John Greypaull's bonded servant. The Greypaulls were all she had ever known of family, and she loved Eliza. 'You bide alongside me,' Eliza had said, 'an' I'll see to it that you an' Jed can stay on in the cottage.'

The absence of Jed set the burden of work squarely back onto Philip's shoulders. It was not like the old days when Eliza and he had worked side by side on Larksleve. The proper care of her home and the four children, a desperate need to maintain her production of cheeses for the market now meant a working day of at least eighteen hours for Eliza.

Her father had found her that autumn, skirts hitched up, walking behind the oxen in the high fields, harrowing-over the newly ploughed earth. John had sought out his son-in-law and backed him up against a stone wall. 'Whass your game, bor?' he had whispered. 'Be you of a mind to kill my daughter? Because if you is, I must warn 'ee, Churchwarden or not Churchwarden, I will, by myself, cut 'ee up into liddle pieces an' feed 'ee to the pigs.' It had been no idle threat.

'Whass your game, then?' Philip demanded of Eliza. 'Tryin' to shame me again, was you? Showin' your fam'ly that you got to do the field-work these days?'

Self-righteousness came easily to her. 'An' so I must,' she told him, 'being as we don't seem to have any men about the place to do what must be done.'

He lifted his hand and would have struck her, but he recalled John's threat just in time and thought better of it. Whenever Philip was sober, when a hard fourteen hours of

212

ploughing and dragging had sweated the cider from his body and cleared his mind, he would perceive his own folly and feel shame. If he could only maintain a balance between the drudgery of Larksleve and the delights of Taunton; if the benefits of having been born a Greypaull were not constantly being undermined by the ungodly lusting of his flesh and his vacillating nature.

For Philip love equated to need. Once, he had dreamed of a clinging, devoted wife, children who would adore him. He had imagined their warm arms about his neck, their infant kisses, and himself standing foursquare upon the hearth: their rock, their souls' foundation.

But it was little Eliza of the steady green gaze, Eliza of the thin indomitable aspect, who was loved to distraction by her children. She had them respectful, obedient, well-mannered; her miniature gentleman and ladies. People said that they did her credit, except perhaps for Blanche, who, at the age of two, was already exhibiting certain disturbing characteristics.

Christmas was almost upon them, and a vague, romantic yearning for better things had made him, once again, uproot a fir tree and carry it, planted in a barrel, into the Larksleve parlour.

Eliza said, 'What's that tree doing on my carpet?'

''Tis the custom,' he said, ''tis what they do in Germany at Christmas, the Prince Consort introduced it in the palace. My mother said so.'

'How knowledgeable you be,' she mocked, 'you an' your dear mother. But there – you goes about the world a good deal more than I do. 'Tis on'y you what got the time an' money.'

It was late in the evening and, for once, there was no child in her arms or clinging to her apron. He pointed towards the rocking-chair. 'Sit down, Eliza. 'Tis time us tried to sort this lot out. Us have had three long years of coldness between us, an' your sharp tongue don't make things any better.'

'You got a short memory,' she told him, 'but I still recall the things that was done and said the last time we talked together. No good ever come of talkin'. 'Tis actions what is called for.'

'Thass right, Eliza.' He sat down on the settle, and sounded penitent, even humble. 'I bin doing some thinkin' lately. I be getting older. 'Tis time I give more thought to Larksleve, to you an' the children. I know I've never bin exactly what you hoped for – '

'Hoped for? I never hoped for nothin'. I knowed that you wasn't no farmer. Everybody said so.' She looked at him across the hearthstone. 'What I never bargained for, never dreamed of, was a drunken sot of a husband who would force me against my will.'

He hung his head. 'I know, Eliza. I shud o' begged your forgiveness long since, but I bin too ashamed to say so. The things I said about our Sam – I never meant 'em. I jus' cudden bear it when you smiled at him and not at me. I get jealous: I can't help it.'

She shook her head. 'What a child you still be! You should have bided to home, alongside your mother.' For the first time in years he could hear a faint thaw in her voice. 'P'raps tidden all your fault,' she murmured, 'you was a spoiled and ruined child.'

'Not by my father. He beat me till his arm ached, always said as I was a lazy, good-fer-nuthin'.'

'An' so you be, Philip. Too idle to get out o' your own way. Oh, I knows that 'tis your nature, but that do make the life hard for me an' the children.'

The ready tears sprang to his eyes. 'I means to do better in the year what's comin'. I made a resolution. I got five good

214

reasons to pull myself together – you, Eliza, an' they four children. An' then, there's Larksleve.' Suddenly, he was on his knees beside the rocking-chair, his head in her lap, his tears wet upon her fingers. She looked down on the yellow curls and saw, for the first time, that they were already streaked heavily with grey. She rested a tentative hand on his shoulder, and he raised his head. She perceived a face that was no longer boyish. He had made the transition from youth to age without the intervening stage of manhood. 'Don' turn away from me, Eliza,' he pleaded, 'I'll give it all up – but you'll have to help me.' He paused, 'You never have helped me, have you? You only blames an' criticises, like my father.'

'' 'Tis all a bit sudden, idden it,' she said, 'this change of heart? Be you in some kind of trouble?'

He drew back. 'Well, idden that jus' what I shud have expected. I goes down on my bended knees – an' what do you give me? Accusations an' suspicion. You is a proper Greypaull, Eliza. Bible in your hand – an' hatred in your heart.'

'No!' she cried. 'Thass not true, Philip. But 'tis hard to believe that you really mean what you say.'

'Have I ever said it before?'

'No, you haven't.'

'Have I ever broke a promise to 'ee?'

'You never made one!'

'There you are, then – '

Charlotte, New York.

Dear cousin Eliza,

No letter have passed between us for five long years, and this I do truly regret, but can only say that my house is always filled with friends and relations lately come to America to seek their Fortunes, and not much time left over for the letter writing habit. You will be surprised to heare that after a gap of *seven* years I find myself confined to bed with my third child, a son called John James. Hence this letter.

Things *Go Well* with us in America, tho' Mr Salter works much too hard, and will not *Rest*. It is only the birth of our third child which has hindered our moving westwards to a city called Chicago, where he plans to set up a Big Meat-Market. We shall move as soon as I can get back my strength. This last birth having quite wore me out, and the air of New York not good for Eddie's chest, I shall be glad to leave here with our littel family, this last baby also delicate, I fear.

I hear from Father's letters that your Brother Francis have at last got married, and *To Money* which could be a Blessing with prices being low in England, and farming, so Father says, in *Dire Straits*. I also heare that you have had your fourth child, and a baby girl more beautiful, says Father, have never been seen around Buckland.

Please answer this letter, dear cousin, a hard birth this time have quite lowered my spirits, and I find myself longing to walk the lanes of Buckland like we did as girls. My regards to cousin Philip, and a kiss for your dear children.

Your affectshunat cousin, Rhoda.

Larksleve Farm.

My dear cousin Rhoda,

Your letter came up with the carter this morning and I cannot lay myself down to sleep without answering it. To hear from you after all this time was such a pleasure. Pleased to heare that you were delivered safe of another son, and hope that you are improved in health and spirits by the time this letter comes to hand.

News from Larksleve is both good and bad. My four

children do grow every day in health and goodness, and are obedient and easy to govern, except sometimes the baby Blanche, who is Beautiful but needs much *Attenshun*, which she gets too much of from Loveday, who is still childless herself, and much attached to my littel Brood.

This summer of 1867 have been a bad one. Hay rotted on the trestles, and Corn blighted before it was gathered. Price of Corn have fallen to fifty-two shillings a quarter, and is likely to fall further. Importation of grain and *Foreign Meat* is the ruinashun of our Home-Bred cattle. We are still the richest country in the world, so Father says, but I ask myself, why do our Poor get Poorer, and our farmers struggle. Situashun of some labourers' families pitiful to see. Have myself needed to go *Gleaning* this year, and not leave the fallen grain for the village women, which did *not* please them, they always having had this priviledge in other years.

But, dear cousin, money is needed for my children's schooling, which must be paid for from my egg-money, Philip being a *Total Loss* in that department. Went with Loveday and the children into the Harvest fields on every evening, gleaned over a Bushel, and all our hands much scratched and bleeding from the stubbles, but children happy to run in the fields. Took a bottle of cold tea and pasties for our supper and was not too weary to sing a Hymn as we gleaned.

Do not worry too much about Mr Salter's working *Hard.* To have a husband what do *not* work is the greater Evil. I tell you this, Rhoda, out of Despair, and trusting it will go *No* Further, but I know myself to be Deceived by Philip with *Other Women*, which he would not have time for if he was to do his fair *Share* here on Larksleve. Yes, you have a good man in Mr Salter, even if marriage to him have meant you living your life in America. God have rewarded you for your unselfish act in leaving Buckland to bring up poor Sussanah's motherless boy. Your story is a beautiful one, dear Rhoda, and an example to us all. Would that I could be like you. Please write your new address from Chicago. Regards to the children and dear Mr Salter.

Your affectshunat cousin, Eliza.

Mina was happy. She sat, warm and secure, on the cushioned settle, with Candace and Jackie beside her and tried to tell them how she felt. ''Tis nicer this Christmas,' she confided. 'My stomach have stopped churning every time Papa comes in the door. He bided home this time, an' carved the goose, an' Mama tied ribbons on the fir tree.'

'An' Mama laughed,' said Jackie, 'her don' often do that.'

''Twas like a pain,' said Mina, 'what went away in the night.'

Candace, who was nine years old and loved nobody, said, 'That won't last long. Jus' you wait till he gets drunk again. They'll be shoutin' and snappin' like they always do.'

The predictable outcome of the reconciliation was a fifth pregnancy for Eliza. 'Didden I tell 'ee to keep the doors locked?' Elizabeth raged.

'He was sober all Christmas,' said Eliza. 'He've promised to go on diff'rent in the future. He've already done all the winter field work, an' he milks an' mucks-out night an' mornin'.'

'An' so I shud hope! He got a mind to kill you, our Liza! If you was to die, Master Philip 'ud have another woman up yer on Larksleve before you was cold. Him's nuthin' but a liar an' a cheat, an' well you knows it. Never mind – the truth will out. Us'll know soon enough what him's bin up to.'

''Tis months since he went down to Taunton, Mother.

His father do take our stuff to market. Give 'un some credit. He's tryin' to keep out o' the way of temptation.'

'There's some other reason,' said Elizabeth, 'his sort don' ever change. I don't like it, our Liza. Him's got a shifty look about 'un lately.'

If ever Eliza felt happy, a visit from her mother would set her back, would undermine her. She had thought of the child she carried as being the first to be born of love. To believe this had been important to her; it had almost cancelled out the misery and coldness of the past ten years. She truly believed that Philip had changed. He no longer dissembled; he was frank and charming. He toiled alone in field and shippon, and the sag of dissipation left his face and he was handsome and boyish again, considerate with her, tender with the children.

The baby was born in early October; a pretty child, with her father's yellow curls, blue eyes, and tea-rose complexion. To placate her mother's anger, Eliza allowed Elizabeth to choose the name. 'Annis,' she decided, ''Tis a good old family name what do go back for generations.' The baptisms had become less ostentatious with each successive birth. The family christening robe was on loan to a cousin, and the baby Annis was obliged to make do with a robe borrowed from the Vicar's lady. Eliza's strength returned, and she toiled again, never seeming to know when she was weary.

The strangers rode up to Larksleve on New Year's Eve, two heavy-set men in dark broadcloth and bowler hats. Eliza and Loveday were at work in the dairy; Philip was cutting and drawing wood; Elizabeth was in the kitchen with the children. The men had walked in at the open front door and gone straight to the parlour.

'Come out of there,' Elizabeth had screamed, and Eliza,

hearing the commotion, had come running. She unracked the shotgun from the chimney-breast and levelled it at the intruders. 'Out,' she commanded, 'out in the yard, or I'll shoot 'ee.'

'No need for that, ma'am. We are here on sheriff's orders. We've got a signed Note of – '

'What sheriff? What orders? If you think you can walk in my door an' rob defenceless women, then you be quite wrong. Out, I said – '

'Where is your husband, Mrs Greypaull? He is the one we wish to deal with. We have no business with you.'

At the mention of Philip she lowered the shotgun. 'My husband? What business have you got wi' Philip?'

'Money owed,' the man said briefly. 'Money owed at Macey's. A gambling debt incurred by Philip Greypaull. There is also a sum of fifty pounds, owed to Jeremiah Jones, moneylender of North Street, Taunton. We are empowered to seize goods and chattels to the value of one hundred and fifty pounds. We have here a Note, signed by – '

'How long has this money been owed by my husband?'

'Since November of last year, ma'am.'

Elizabeth said, 'There now! What did I tell 'ee, Eliza? You shudden never have trusted 'un. Just you wait till your father and brothers do hear about this lot!'

The baby Annis began to cry, and Elizabeth lifted her out of the cradle. Blanche, who could never bear to be overlooked, screamed and rolled about on the pegged-rug; the three older children, at sight of the shotgun in their mother's hand, had retreated to their haven in the inglenook settle. The men walked around the parlour; they stroked the rosewood piano, prodded the horsehair sofa, expressed satisfaction at the sight of so much fine silver.

'You can't touch that,' cried Eliza, 'thass wedding-presents! Thass my daughters' christening cups, my little boy's silver knife an' fork set, what was given him by his

220

grandfather. This is my piano, I got the bill to prove it - '

'Sorry, ma'am. The law says that nothing is yours. This house and its contents belong to Philip Greypaull, and Philip Greypaull owes one hundred and fifty pounds to his creditors in Taunton.'

Elizabeth stood up. She placed herself between the two bailiffs and Eliza. 'My husband is John Greypaull of Castle Farm. This yer is my daughter. Come with me to see my husband, touch nothing in this house. This is a matter soon dealt with!'

She turned to Eliza. 'Now don't you cry, maid. You knows how that on'y upsets me. Your father'll set this lot to rights. You sit down quiet by the fire, an' drink a cup o' tea wi' Loveday.'

News of the bailiffs' visit soon spread around the village; the two men had gossiped in the Lamb and Flag inn. They had taken a drink with the landlord and asked for directions to Larksleve. Tongues wagged; heads nodded. People recalled Will Gardner and Mary, his wife, who had died in child-birth. Some chickens, it was said, were at last coming home to roost for the Greypaulls, and not before time.

The name of Larksleve continued to spell itself in flowers: crocus in the springtime, candytuft and stocks in the summer. The name grew and flowered without any help from Eliza, not quite as neatly as in that first season, but recognisable, and still dear to her.

John had spoken to the bailiffs; he had paid off the Taunton moneylender, and settled Philip's gambling debt. High words had been exchanged between John and Daniel. Positions had been stated, lines drawn and intentions made clear.

''Tidden no good talkin' to 'un,' Daniel had said, ''tis actions what is called for.'

'Thass easier said than done, bor,' John had sighed, 'us is gettin' too old for such worry. It do break my heart to see my maid go on bearing children what her can't provide for. Us have paid-up this time, but never no more. Times is hard. Even labourers be gettin' up on their hind-legs an' demanding more wages! I still got three sons to home what do need consideration. One hundred and fifty pounds have made a tidy hole in my pocket.'

'I give 'un a hundred pounds,' said Daniel, 'when I sold-up Will Gardner. 'Tis pouring good money after bad. You be right. Us is gettin' too old for such worry, bor! Much more o' this sort of thing an' I'll bury my missus.'

James and Robert rode across to Larksleve. They spent twenty energetic minutes with their cousin Philip. They left him bruised and bleeding, but sufficiently undamaged to walk behind the plough.

It was Philip's deception that enraged Eliza.

'You lied,' she accused him, 'you lied from the minute you went down on your knees and begged my forgiveness. You already knowed then that you was deep in trouble.'

He slumped at the kitchen table, head bowed, and tried to excuse himself through split and swollen lips.

'I meant it, Liza, I was tryin' to make amends. Why, you know that I never bin near to Taunton for a whole year.'

'O' course you haven't. You didden dare to! They must have bin waitin' for 'ee with knives, they must have bin demanding their money. How you ever managed to keep it so quiet for so long, I don't know.'

'I sent a token payment now and again. The carter delivered it for me. But that money only covered the interest, I never could have paid off a hundred an' fifty pounds.'

'Don't you never stop and think?' she asked, 'Don't you never consider what'll be the outcome?' She looked at him, at the blankness of his eyes, his uncomprehending stare. 'No. You never consider anything beyond your own gratification. 'Tis only the pleasure of the moment wi' you Philip. Never mind your wife an' children. Never mind tomorrow.'

'You worries too much, Eliza. 'Tiv all bin squared away an' settled. Forget it.'

'Well – somebody got to worry. I warn 'ee, Philip, your father an' mine have had enough of your antics. They won't pay up next time. 'Twill be the Poorhouse, an' no mistake.'

Philip laughed. 'They'll never let that happen. They cudden stand the shame. Let 'em pay, Eliza!'

Respectability for Luke had meant his promotion to the position of banker-mason. It had been confirmed by his elevation to sidesman in the chapel of the Particular Baptists. The four-roomed house of which he held the Deed of Ownership, the well-stocked garden, the three small sons who walked before him to the Chapel on a Sunday morning: these were his silent answer to any eyebrows which might still be raised.

Respectability for Meri had been a matter of conforming, but the whitened doorstep, the clean starched apron, the thick lace curtain at her cottage window was as far as she was prepared to go. There were still those wild March mornings of high cloud and keen wind when the blood tingled and the drom beckoned. Her growing reputation as a chovihanis was whispered about behind closed doors, but it was conceded that she was probably a witch of the 'white' persuasion and therefore harmed no one.

Sometimes, in busy seasons, she would seek work in the fields and orchards. Every day must be made to yield a coin or two to fill the money-belt. Luke disapproved of her turnip-singling, her apple-picking, but had more sense than to say so. Meri's fears were all for her children. Jye, who was straight and strong, would be able to fend for himself; but Henry and Charles would need to own property sufficient to support an opinion in the community. She saw gorgio respectability as a curse. Poverty for the twins would mean banishment to the Poorhouse, and an early death. They must never be subjected to a gorgie master. She had seen how employers treated their hirelings, had seen whole families evicted into the village street and left to seek shelter in tumbledown hovels and derelict sheds. She had worked alongside the inmates of the Poorhouse, observed their condition and listened to their stories.

'An' they calls my people dirty hedge-crawlers,' she had said to Luke, 'us what lives free in our own benders and waggons, what looks after our sick, an' them what is fell on hard times. Us could show the gorgie what is true religion.'

'Thass not fair, Meri. There's many a poor ragged gypsy trailing round this kingdom, an' well you knows it. Why, I often sees travellers in the lanes an' dingles what is near to starvin'. You come from a well-off family; your uncle Boswell is King o' the Gypsies.'

'They still got their freedom,' she insisted. 'They is not tied to a cottage or a glovin'-master. 'Tis better to die of hunger underneath the sky, than to take your last breath in a stinking Poorhouse. An' if a gypsy is close to starvin', then 'tis the fault o' the gorgio what do harry an' chivvy him, an' lock him up for catchin' a hare or rabbit, or diggin' a turnip and a few potatoes.'

Meri would always keep to her own mind and, as far as she was able, to her Rom beliefs and taboos. She was prepared to adapt where adaptation came out in her favour, but she would always be aggressive, domineering, loving the profitable chop, the crafty bargain. She had already marked down the isolated cottage and its spot of ground which she intended to buy when it next became vacant. Meridiana, who was 'pure Rom, wi'out taint', had been forced by the respectable gorgios into planning a safer future for her crippled twins.

Luke, on his thirtieth birthday, had counted up his blessings and found that there were more than he had even hoped for. There was Meri, who was passionate and loving, and still beautiful to look at. Meri, who worked to secure a future for her children. Meri, who loved him with a truth and intensity that he found gratifying, but frightening.

There were the twins, who, in spite of his fears, had walked and talked early. They were not as other children: the need to wander was urgent in their blood, and deformity had forced them to seek isolation. They had absconded from the village dame-school, had proved so disruptive and unwilling to learn that Luke had been asked to remove them. Unlettered and untutored, they roamed the Hill, gathered herbs and grasses for their mother's potions, snared an illegal rabbit for the pot. Luke had seen them deep in conversation with gypsy families who pitched close to the village. Charles and Henry had inherited Meri's blood and longings. Luke had admitted to this, long ago. He had taken them to his chapel and offered them to the Lord. He trusted that with Meri's assistance the good Lord would see fit to do the right thing by them.

The recent promotion to banker-mason had confirmed his standing in the village. Luke's banker was made of seasoned oak, sturdy and four-legged, braced to receive the heaviest stone block, and set at the required height for a very tall man to wield mallet and chisel. He no longer dressed stone, or prepared blocks for older masons. He was allowed to work on church crosses, to do delicate carving in mullioned windows; his thick fingers loved the sandstone.

Caution brought him last of all to Jye, who was straight and handsome and beloved of his mother, Meri. The boy, so everybody said, was Luke's living image: a quiet child, regular at his lessons, always respectful. Sometimes the Lord

would take the good child before its time. Smallpox and
typhoid often raged in the village. Luke prayed, for Meri's
sake, that Jye would be spared to grow up into manhood.

So many lies, evasions, half-truths; so many deliberate
deceits. To even guess at Philip's dirty little life in Taunton
disgusted Eliza. 'Smock and gaiters,' he had once boasted,
'won't do for the ladies I visit. They tells me I pays for
dressin'.' Except for that one year when terror of his debtors
had kept him close to Larksleve, he had become an absentee
husband, a negligent father, a truant farmer.

There was nowhere for her to turn but to church. To
confide in her mother would be a dangerous submission of
will and purpose. Eliza held fast to that rock of the virtuous
woman: a belief in all-powerful, all-seeing God, who would,
when He saw fit, punish and destroy the transgressor. Her
feet took the narrow track from shippon to dairy, from
wash-tub to clothes-line, from kitchen table to baking oven,
and, every Sunday morning, from house to church.

Larksleve was her beloved place; inside it, Eliza laboured
to create the security of routine and custom for her children.
Stability could only be achieved by a strict adherence to
duty; each child had the daily tasks which could not be
shirked. All her children were skilled gatherers; of firewood,
fallen apples, cob-nuts. Waste was wicked, taught Eliza.
Every day, every month must yield an estimated harvest.
There were rows of preserves in the Larksleve pantry: jams
and jellies, pickles and chutneys. All the days at Larksleve
Farm were labelled according to their yield, every season had
its haul, its bounty. Eliza was always at least two seasons
ahead, nothing escaped her zeal. Every scrap utilised, every
gap breached. Hard times had made her careful. Prices were
falling, and Philip Greypaull had failed her. Providence and

good husbandry, taught Eliza. Never an acorn or an apple, never a son or a daughter wasted.

There was a part of her mind in which lived those thoughts that she could not acknowledge. But some sorrows had to be faced. There was Samuel, at whom she no longer dared to smile. He had never married, and hardly ever came to Larksleve. When he did ride across it was never to see Eliza and the children; these visits always ended with high words and recriminations between Philip and his brother.

Eliza had once planned for culture and refinement, for her children's attendance at the village school, for music lessons, books on shelves in the parlour, for selected readings from cousin Walter's poems. But in this household where every penny must be made to count the lessons were held now at the kitchen table, if and when Eliza had time to spare. Music was no more than a laboured ten minutes at the rosewood piano; tunes played with stiff and swollen fingers to please a sick child or celebrate a birthday.

Eliza did what she could; her children were polite, she taught them to welcome the rare visitors who came to Larksleve, but it was their isolation which concerned her and their increasing dependence upon one another.

Candace and Madelina worked at opposite ends of the kitchen table; it was a wide, long table with one half kept clean and scrubbed satin-smooth for cooking. The other end was used for the dirty jobs, like the cutting and salting down of a freshly slaughtered pig, the dressing of poultry, and the cleaning of lamps. Candace was responsible for the maintenance of rush-lights. The fat skimmed from cooking-pots was kept in the long, cast-iron greasepan, and the rushes were laid to soak in the fat and then dried. Mutton fat burned the brightest, and it was always up to her to see that the rush-light holders were safely fitted with well-dipped tapers. Charred lamp-wicks were also scrubbed clean by Candace, and their glass-funnels wiped clear and made sparkling before replacement. She had her favourites among the lamps; there was one with a rose-tinted funnel and pretty china base, which belonged in Mama's bedroom. The parlour lamps had funnels of pale-blue glass which gave off a sad light, and were rarely used. The kitchen lamps were tall, with bases of solid brass which she also polished every Friday morning.

Candace, at the age of twelve, was a small thin child who never ailed. She had inherited the Greypaull toughness of body and spirit, her mother's ability to take on those unpleasant tasks which others shirked. It was Candace who ran out to the pump in sheeting rain or in darkness to fill water buckets for the kitchen. Candace who gutted rabbits and chickens, who helped Eliza with the gory business of putting away the slaughtered pig. Candace who listened, tense and unobserved from the haven of the high-backed settle, to the sharp words exchanged between her mother and father, and the anger of grandparents, aunts and uncles.

Almost everything on Larksleve frightened Mina; she could not abide the crow of the rooster, the squeal of pigs, the dangerous lumbering of cows and oxen. She never went into the stables, the shippon, the far fields and lanes unless in the company of her sisters and brother. Mina at the age of ten was a tiny girl, as dark and neat featured as her sister Candace, but gentler. Her chosen place was at the smooth end of the kitchen table; her bread, her pies and puddings were already as good as her mother's or Loveday's. She loved her brother Jackie; it was Mina who sponged and mended his torn clothing, who bathed his frequent cuts and bruises, who wiped away his rare tears. Grandpa John had given Jackie a pony for his seventh birthday, and, without the safety of saddle and bridle, her brother was putting the tough little Exmoor to jump every fence and hedge on Larksleve. Whenever his mother's voice took on that sharp tone that was reserved for her father, Mina would cover her ears and cower close to Jackie.

Annis was the child whose looks most favoured Philip; she was doted upon by her grandmother Rachel, who described her fair curls and blue eyes as being 'sweetly pretty'. Annis cried a good deal. She clung to any arms that were prepared to hold her. With Eliza and Loveday so often absent from the house, the care of the little girl was left mostly to Candace and Madelina.

Blanche cared for herself. At the age of five she was as tall as her two older sisters; ungovernable and violent in temper, she refused all attempts by her mother and Mina to teach her to read and pen her letters. Blanche was beautiful, and she knew it. Her auburn hair hung thick and shining to her waist; it changed colour according to the light, smouldered on dull days, caught fire in sunshine. Her eyes had retained their deep shade of violet; her skin was the dazzling white hardly ever found on a farm child; unlike her mother, Blanche never freckled.

Rachel Greypaull collapsed across the churn while butter-making; she slid down to die alone on the earthen floor of her own dairy. When Daniel, her husband, found her some hours later he was heard to complain that since it was a hot day, and she had failed to 'turn' the butter, a whole churn-ful of milk had 'gone off' and would have to be fed to the pigs.

Propriety required of him that he should pin on an arm-band of black crêpe, and follow on foot behind the farmcart and two black horses which transported Rachel's coffin down to Buckland churchyard. As he walked, he thought about Rachel. A foolish woman. She had lacked stamina, had been sentimental and inclined to make unwise attach-ments. But she had raised six children, and kept a good table. He would miss her.

Philip had been told of his mother's death by Eliza, bluntly and without concern for his feelings. 'Your mother's dead. Your Samuel came across to tell you – but, as usual, you was not to be found.'

'Dead? Mother? But her can't be. Why, I was across to Warren's on'y yesterday – '

Eliza set the washing-basket on the table and began to fold linen. 'Cadging was you? Telling your Ma how bad your wife treats you?'

Tears began to roll down his face. 'Yes,' he shouted, 'yes, if you must know, thass exactly what I said. My mother is the on'y one who'll lissen. Her knows what I got to put up with. She knows you for the hard woman what you be, Eliza Greypaull!'

Eliza folded the white sheet very neatly and laid it away with a heap of others. 'An' now her's dead,' she said softly, 'an' just what'll you do without her, I wonder? Who is you going to tell all they lies to in the future, Philip? Who'll keep you provided wi' your cider-money?'

It was a question he had never asked himself. His mother had never really looked old; there had been something almost girlish about her, even her attachment to the Royal Family had been innocent and childlike. He looked closely at Eliza. 'I don't believe it,' he cried. ''Tis another of your tricks, done to mortify me.'

Eliza spoke in the calm voice she used when Blanche was in a tantrum, 'I don' never tell lies. 'Tidden worth it. Liars always gets found out. Get yourself across to Warren's. They'll have fetched Mother Taverner across there by this time to do the layin'-out of the body.'

Philip walked behind his mother's coffin, saw her buried in the Greypaull corner of Buckland churchyard, and still he could not believe that he had been abandoned. Even when Sam stood beside him at the graveside and muttered, ''Tidden no use you blubbering now, bor! 'Tis your high-jinks what have helped to kill her. Jus' you bear that in mind, bor, when you is next in Taunton.' Even then, he had still believed it all to be some monstrous jest played upon him by his unkind family.

Rachel had not left a formal Will, but the sealed envelope, found by Daniel inside the family Bible when he had entered up the date of his wife's death, contained a statement as legal and binding as any solicitor's document and a good deal more poignant. In a shaky, unpractised hand Rachel Greypaull had written: 'On my death. All that what is mine is to be given to my most beloved son, Philip.'

It was to be the old tin trunk, a military heirloom of some long-dead Greypaull, packed in anger and delivered in silence by his brother Samuel, which finally confirmed for Philip the fact of his mother's passing. It stood, for days untouched and skirted around, in the Larksleve hallway. In the end it was Eliza who said, 'Either open it – or dig a hole in the midden and bury it deep! I can't do wi' it standing there. 'Tis in my way!'

He had opened the trunk late at night, when the house was silent and the children sleeping. He had thrown back the lid and the first thing to touch his fingers had been his mother's old leather money-purse crammed full and bulging with sovereigns. He hefted it in his hand and estimated its contents: seventy pounds, perhaps eighty. He had not, after all, been abandoned. Even from beyond the grave Philip's mother had provided. He rose early on the following morning. It was high summer, fine and warm; the haysel was behind him and harvest yet to come. He stood in the porch of the house and watched the sun come up behind the slopes of Larksleve, and he remembered the bitter days and months of his banishment from Taunton. To have entered

231

Macey's while owing so much money would have been to risk a slashed face and a thorough beating. When Eliza and Loveday returned from their milking in the Home meadow, Philip was seated, washed and shaved, and already eating the breakfast prepared for him by Mina.

They no longer quarrelled discreetly or late at night when the children were sleeping and Loveday was at home in her own house. With her servant and the five children all seated at the breakfast table, Eliza said sharply, 'Your mother left you some money.'

For a moment, the certainty in her voice nonplussed him. 'No – no,' he stammered, ''twas on'y a heap of old frocks an' trinkets. Nothing of any value.'

Eliza said, 'Her wudden of bothered to pen a Will for a few old frocks, there was a purse full o' gold in that trunk. No use you shaking your head to deny it. I see'd it for myself.'

'You looked?'

'O' course I looked! You was bound to lie about it. You tells so many lies you never knows what truth is, any more.'

'You shudden have opened that trunk, Eliza. You had no right.'

'I had the best right of all, cousin! That purse might be said to be yours – on paper, but that is really family money, and, as such, it shud be spent on Larksleve.'

He laid down his knife and fork and pushed his plate from him. 'Thass my own money, willed to me by my mother, for my personal use. That gold is private, an' none o' your business.'

'Private is it? Have you looked lately at your five children? Have you seen the state o' their boots an' clothing? Why, 'tis patch set over patch in this household. Darn stitched over darn! 'Tis a mercy that they don't go to the village any more; they looks like poor labourers' children.'

Philip looked around the table. He tried to gauge reactions to Eliza's scolding words. Five heads were bent carefully to bowls of porridge. Loveday Hayes was staring at the fire as if it were a new invention. He laughed: 'Get your mother to provide. She always has done. Why, I can mind the time when her was always in this kitchen, bringing food and clothes, an' interferin'.'

'Mother's gettin' old. Times is hard for everybody, an' with Robert gettin' married after harvest there'll be others for her to see to.'

He stood up. 'Then want must be your master, Eliza. I'm off to Taunton. Don't wait up, will you?'

Philip had ridden down to Taunton in early January only to find that he was no longer worthy of credit. 'You shows us the colour o' gold before you sits-in,' he was told by the card-schools.

'Sorry, Mister Greypaull,' said Jeremiah Jones, 'I waited a year for that last loan to be repaid – and then had to put the bailiffs on 'ee come the finish!'

This time it would be all smiles and handshakes. He had let it be known in Buckland St Mary that his mother had willed a small fortune to her beloved elder son. The news had spread around the markets, reached the inns and taverns, and filtered through to Macey's. This time, he found a dozen hands outstretched to shake his, a place made free for him at the table of his choosing. Mr Macey himself set the drinks at Philip's elbow, and invited the prodigal to inspect and select from the exclusive girls who lolled against the plush-lined walls.

Philip looked around him, sniffed excitement in the room, saw the greed in people's faces, felt the tension, and knew this to be his most beloved place in all the world.

He had gone into Macey's on a Friday morning; he did not emerge until the evening of the following Wednesday. In that time he had become drunk, and then sober, and drunk again. He had slept in a number of beds, with a variety of women, and trebled the stake-money he had brought with him into Taunton.

Philip's failure to return had, at first, annoyed and then alarmed Eliza. She knew that he had carried the whole seventy pounds into Taunton. She had waited up on the second evening, had watched the empty lane that led up to Larksleve, and imagined him lying robbed and bleeding on the Taunton road. By the night of Wednesday, she was so exhausted by the extra work and the worry caused by his absence that she was dead asleep and quite unaware of his return. Her first knowledge of his presence in the bedroom was to feel his weight across her body and his hands tearing at her flannel nightgown, but long before she could object or struggle the damage had been done.

Of all the household, it had been only Blanche who was still awake and heard her father stumble across the kitchen and up the spiral staircase. It was only Blanche who heard Eliza scream, 'You filth! You evil creature!' and her father's laughter, and the chink of coins across the bedroom lino. 'Here you are,' he had shouted. 'Here's a couple o' sovereigns to buy your children's boots. But, I tell 'ee, 'tis an overpayment,' he had laughed again, 'you idden never worth that much money, Eliza!'

Elizabeth Greypaull stayed away from Larksleve. ''Tis better not to see what goes on over there,' she told her husband, ''tiv all gone beyond our power to cure. They do say that "him" spends half the week in Macey's an' the Turk's Head. Rachel shudden never have left him all that money.' She glanced sideways at John, 'I do hear that our Eliza be expectin' again. If 'tis true, then that child must have bin forced upon her.'

John looked old and very tired. 'Us shudden never have

married her to Philip. But I thought, an' so did Daniel, that our Liza could be master of him.'

'No woman can be master over the Devil, an' thass what he is, John!'

John Greypaull nodded. 'I'll drop the word to James an' Robert. They can wait at the crossroads. Catch 'un on his way home from Taunton. That won't matter no more if Master Philip gets damaged – 'tis on'y Liza an' Loveday what works these days up on Larksleve.'

Loveday Hayes, who had longed for children but never borne a live child, could not envy Eliza. 'Oh, Missus,' she cried, 'not another baby! 'Tis too much for 'ee with all the work, an' him not comin' home four nights in seven.' Loveday attended church on Eliza's command, but the hem of her dress swung heavy with charms and she carried a dried hare's heart in her apron pocket.

There were many in Buckland St Mary who bore grudges against Philip Greypaull, and it was easy enough to pay off a debt in these dark hills. Loveday bought two wax candles, melted them down and moulded them into the image of a tall and slender man. She saw Jed safely away from the cottage and on his way to the Lamb and Flag, and then she withdrew the hatpin from her Sunday bonnet and plunged the metal many times into the waxen limbs of her employer.

Philip lay drunk across the neck of his bay mare; he saw the two riders who waited at the crossroads, but did not recognise Eliza's brothers and was therefore unafraid. But before his cousins could seize and beat him, pain had already gripped Philip's body. He fell from his horse, writhed and screamed in the ditch and cried to God in Heaven for mercy.

James looked at Robert. 'Bloody little coward! 'Un's yelling for help before us have even touched 'un!' James bent down and yanked Philip upright. 'Stop play-actin' cousin,' he said quietly, 'you is not performin' for the ladies of Taunton now. You is on home-ground, an' we is about to pay back for all the harm what you hev done to our liddle sister.'

Loveday went across to Larksleve before sunrise. She found Eliza soaking bread in boiling water to make a poultice. 'Master's very ill. He've bin ravin' half the night. He swears that the Devil come upon him at the crossroads. He got terrible pains in his arms an' legs, an' he's bruised all over.'

'Well, I never,' said Loveday, 'well, there's a thing, now! 'Tis a long time since the Devil got loose up to Buckland. Not since that gypsy lived up yer in Dommett Wood, an' that Montacute mason started pullin' down the bell tower.' Loveday smiled. 'You bide in house, an' do what you can for Master. I'll be down in meadow seein' to the milkin'.'

Blanche, at the age of six, was far too clever for her own good, everybody said so. Unable to read or write a single figure or letter, she had a biting answer for every question, was adept at the cutting remark, found it simple to ridicule the dour Candace, the tenderhearted Mina, the rash and reckless Jackie. Annis, who was a crybaby and only four years old, was not yet worthy of her notice.

Blanche had become Loveday's confidante and shadow. The child was usually to be found around the cheese-house and dairy. Loveday allowed her to stamp the butterpats with the Larksleve rose, and to wrap the muslin around the finished cheeses. Unloved as she was by her sisters and brother, Blanche had become attached to her mother's servant; and the childless woman had found herself drawn irresistibly to the beautiful but dangerous child.

When the house-pig was slaughtered that autumn, Loveday begged to be allowed the animal's heart, and Eliza, who was barely able to find her servant's wages, was glad enough to hand over the gift. Blanche, running in and out of Loveday's cottage, had already come upon the tall wax figure, full of holes, and the wicked hatpin which lay beside it. 'Thass my Papa, idden it?' she had asked, and Loveday had flushed but had not denied it. ''Tis all right. I won't tell nobody. I don't like him neither.' Blanche had curled a confiding hand into Loveday's fingers. 'Let I stick the pin in him, Loveday!' she wheedled. 'Just once, for all the times he shouts at Mama.'

Now Blanche was asking other questions. 'What you want wi' the pig's heart, then?'

'It's for Jed's an' my supper.'

'No 'tidden. I can tell. You wants it to make some magic. Show I, Loveday. Show I how 'tis done!'

So the servant showed Blanche how to carve the initials of her victim in the centre of the pig's heart. How to stick the heart with pins and thorns to direct the evil towards the intended victim and prevent it from harming the rest of the household. Together, and in secret, they placed the heart on a high ledge inside the inglenook of the Larksleve chimney. 'That'll settle his bones,' said Loveday, 'that'll put paid to Master Greypaull.'

Annis was ill but only Candace had noticed. Eliza and Loveday, needing to harvest the root crops before the onset of heavy frost, had been absent from the house for every daylight hour. Responsibility for the feeding of stock was already weighing heavily on Candace, the added burden of a sickly Annis was more than she could bear.

'I can't get her out of bed in the morning, Mama. She do complain all the time of feeling tired. She lays on the settle close to the fire and cries out with the pains in her legs.'

'Laziness,' snapped Loveday, 'that's her only problem.

Why, when I was in the Bridgwater Poorhouse I was already scrubbing floors at her age.'

Mina's sense of fairness overcame her natural reluctance to cause trouble. ''Tis a pity you don't say the same about Blanche! You never scolds her, do you Loveday?'

'Blanche helps me in the dairy an' cheese-house. Her got a wish to learn and I do teach her.'

'But who does all the work,' blazed Mina, 'and who sits on a milking stool and eats apples?'

'Blanche is only six years old,' said Loveday, 'her idden big enough yet to do real work.'

'And neither is Annis! She's only four. You got no call to say she's lazy.' Mina outfaced her mother's servant. 'You favours Blanche. If she was the sick one, then you'd be the first to notice.'

Loveday's broad face flushed crimson. 'Well, 'tis high time that somebody in this house loved Blanche. There's not one of you got a kind word to say for that child.' She glanced sideways at Eliza. ''Tidden that liddle maid's fault if she was not exactly welcome. Why, that pretty liddle dear do keep me company as if she was my own child.'

Jackie said, 'Take her home with you, why don't you? We don't want her.'

Loveday ignored this observation; she turned back to Mina, 'As for you, miss, holy is as holy does.'

'Well at least I don't put spells on people – '

'That's enough,' said Eliza. 'I won't have you children answering back to Loveday. Any more sauciness and you'll go straight to bed. A good dose of salts is all that Annis needs. Remind me about it at bedtime, Candace.'

The fact that her children ailed so rarely had made Eliza less watchful than she might otherwise have been. Isolation from village contact had prevented the spread of epidemic to Larksleve. The few homely remedies that stood on a back shelf of the pantry were all she had ever needed to keep her family in health. The pallor of Annis, the child's habit of whining and lying about on the settle instead of romping with the others had been noticed and then forgotten among the many tasks that demanded her attention. Eliza recalled the recent complaint by Annis of a sore throat, and in fact for a week or two the child had been quite unable to speak. She lifted the little girl to her lap, and was shocked by the light weight of her.

'Have you been feeding her properly?' she asked Mina.

'Her won't eat, Mama. I make her special treats, but she don't touch 'em.'

'Where does it hurt you then, Annis?' asked Eliza.

The little girl rubbed her legs and murmured; she was already nodding to sleep in her mother's arms. Eliza made to rise from the chair.

'Better get her to bed,' she told Candace, but it was Loveday who sprang to take the child from Eliza's arms. 'You shudden be lifting her, Missus. Not in your condition.'

'I be lifting turnips by the ton, Loveday. This child weighs next to nothing.'

She turned to Mina. 'Candace got her hands full with the yard work. I want you to keep a special look-out for Annis. I got to get the turnips up before the hard frost, so I shall put her in your special care. Keep her warm by the fire, and try to make her eat. I'll take a look through the physic bottles in the pantry and see if there's something what might fit the picture.'

Annis was dosed with a variety of medicines but nothing seemed to fit the picture. The day came when the thin little legs would no longer hold her upright. That night she developed a sudden fever and her incoherent ravings roused the household. A note was despatched with the carter to be delivered to Dr Priddy in Whitestaunton. The doctor came; he examined the child, asked questions and looked grave on hearing Eliza's answers.

'I'm afraid, Mrs Greypaull, that your little girl has got rheumatic fever.'

Eliza asked the only question that mattered. 'Will she live, Doctor?'

'A lot will depend on the nursing you can give her. She'll need careful watching for the next few weeks. Rheumatic fever is like a bad dog. It only licks the joints, but it bites the heart. She must not leave her bed or make any effort whatsoever. Complete rest is what is needed.' He paused. 'I might advise the same treatment in your own case, Mrs Greypaull, but that would be a waste of breath, I suppose?'

Eliza nodded. 'I'm well enough, Doctor. But Annis – ?'

Dr Priddy placed a hand upon her shoulder. 'She has the best chance in the world of a complete recovery. Conditions are better up here than in the villages and towns. You have good food, no damp, no overcrowding. But take care of yourself, my dear. From what I'm told, your family would be in a poor way without you.'

It was Mina, aged eleven, who volunteered for the task of nursing her little sister. Mina alone seemed to know instinctively what must be done to secure a little ease from pain for Annis. The low pillows placed underneath the swollen knee-joints and ankles, the sponging of the small feverish body with warm water, the junket and fruit jelly fed slowly by careful spoonsful were all the work of Madelina. Eliza and Loveday took turns at night to sit up with the restless patient; her nightgown and sheets, soaked with perspiration, needed to be changed frequently in that first week.

Blanche volunteered her opinion on the striking-down of Annis. ''Tis my belief that her is bewitched,' she said firmly.

'If she is,' said Jackie, 'then 'tis some of your Loveday's magic what have gone wrong.'

Dr Priddy had left instructions that a bottle of physic was to be collected from his surgery in Whitestaunton. Eliza waited for Philip's return from Taunton, but he did not come; and the carter would not be returning to Larksleve for at least a week. Jackie volunteered to make the journey on his pony, but her son's compulsion to jump every ditch and hedge made this a risky offer. In the end it was decided that Candace, Mina and Jackie should walk together to fetch the medicine from Whitestaunton.

They set out at midday, wrapped warmly against the cold December. The girls wore their capes and bonnets, and Jackie wore thick breeches, his cap and reefer jacket, and a long woollen muffler wound several times around his neck. Eliza issued several instructions. They were to walk briskly, to collect the physic, and return home well before the fall of dark. They were not to be tempted into leaving the road and cutting across country. 'There's but one narrow lane leading up to Whitestaunton. 'Tis a rough track, but you'll find Dr Priddy's house close beside the church.'

They had rarely travelled further than their grandparents' farms, and those trips had been made in the governess-cart and accompanied by adults. To go as far as Whitestaunton, on foot, and on such an errand of mercy was high adventure for them, the kind of experience that would never be forgotten. A tale to be told a hundred times on future winter evenings around various firesides.

Mina had filled a small basket with bread and cheese and three apples. The picnic was to be eaten on the outskirts of Whitestaunton. The white cloth which covered the food could be used later on to wrap the physic bottle. Eliza watched from the porch as they set off down the misty lane. 'I don't like to send them so far,' she told Loveday.

'You got no choice, maid.' Loveday pulled the shawl tighter about her shoulders, 'I'll be off up in field, now. There's one more row of turnips to be lifted, and then we be finished wi' they dratted things. Don' 'ee worry, maid. They won't come to no harm. They be sensible children.'

They had skipped and run to begin with. It was like a holiday to be away from the dreary tasks which usually took up their daylight hours. Later on, they settled to a steadier pace. Candace said abruptly, 'This is how Pa must feel when he gets away from the farm and rides down to Taunton.'

Mina glanced curiously at her older sister. Candace, who hardly ever displayed emotion, had spoken in a voice that trembled.

'He don't want to be a farmer,' Jackie said thoughtfully.

'Well, he got small choice.' Mina's tone was sharp and self-consciously pious. 'We all got to fit ourselves to the station in life where the good Lord has seen right to put us.'

'You needn't try to sound so clever,' said Candace, 'you pinched all that from the Reverend Soames' sermon.'

''Tis true though!'

'Why should it be?' argued Jackie. 'I don't mean to be a farmer.'

'You got to be,' said Mina, 'you're the son, and it's always the oldest son what takes on the farm. You know very well what Grandpa Daniel says – '

'The Devil take Grandpa Daniel!'

'Oh Jack.' Mina halted in the middle of the lane. 'May the Lord forgive you!'

But, shocked as they were by this heresy from Jackie, his sisters had found pleasure in the daring statement. One word soon led to many others, and suddenly the temptation to push back the boundaries of what was normally permitted became too much for them. It was easy, out here in the winter landscape with home already hidden in a fold of hillside, to make a space between themselves and the sinister conflicts which divided Larksleve.

'Loveday Hayes makes magic against Papa.'

'I know. She always begs for the hearts and lungs when I guts a hare or rabbit.'

'She does other things against him. She sets toads in his path to ill-wish him.'

Jackie laughed uncertainly. 'They old spells is all rubbish! Anyway, Loveday always gets it wrong. She magics the wrong person – that's why our Annis is gone down with the rheumatic fever.'

'Loveday acts a bit crazy,' said Mina, 'She thinks that Blanche belongs to her.'

Candace nodded wisely. 'That comes of her losing so many of her own babies.'

'I shan't never have babies,' said Mina.

'No more shall I,' agreed Candace.

'I shan't never be a farmer,' shouted Jackie, 'no matter what Grandpa says.'

'I don't like Blanche,' ventured Mina softly.

'Thass an evil child,' said Candace, ''tis my belief that her come straight to Larksleve from the Devil!'

'Oh, Can!' The two younger children paused to gaze admiringly at Candace. The shocking statements were growing more uninhibited by the minute.

'Well, I hate Blanche,' boasted Jackie, 'and I hate Grandpa Daniel, and all they miserable aunts and uncles.' He halted to adjust his loosened scarf with a mighty swing. 'I hate the Reverend Soames and all his soppy angels.' He swallowed hard and looked frightened. 'Most of all though – I hate Papa.'

'Oh Jack.' Mina's voice was half-fearful, half-admiring, 'I don't think you ought to go as far as that.'

'Why not?' There were tears in Jackie's eyes. 'If you two really loved Mama then you'd do something to help her.'

'Like what?'

'I don't know, you're bigger than I am. You could think of something.'

Candace said, 'The new baby'll be born soon. Mama looks wore-out, what with Annis being sick and Papa never home.'

'We could appeal to his better nature,' said Mina, 'we could ask him not to go so often to Taunton.'

'He got no better nature.' Jackie sounded savage. He began to kick a stone along the roadway.

'Papa might go away one day and never come back.' Mina sounded unhopeful.

'He might fall off his horse. He's always drunk.'

'That mare knows its own way home from Taunton,' said Jack gloomily. 'It always brings him back no matter what state he's in.'

Ridding themselves of Papa was an insoluble problem. Even Candace, who had experienced a fleeting insight into her father's dislike of the farming way of life, was bound to agree that things would be easier without him. 'P'raps us had better leave it up to Loveday,' she concluded.

For their feelings to have found expression was unusual and not likely to be repeated. Nothing had been decided; they were not normally articulate children. They linked arms and walked on together, strangely united by this revelation of their secret thoughts. They came into White-staunton, halted at the hedgeside, and ate the bread and cheese and apples.

They collected the physic from Dr Priddy, wrapped the bottle in the clean cloth, and placed it in the wicker basket. They began the long walk home, but the adventurous mood of the early morning had been replaced by weariness and a curious reluctance to return to Larksleve.

'I know a short cut,' said Jackie.

'How can you? You're not allowed to come this far from home.'

'I rode over here once on Blossom. I followed some gypsies. There's a bridle-path that runs down beside the combe. It goes into some woods and comes out close to Larksleve.'

'Oh Jack,' cried Mina, 'you shudden never follow gypsies.'

'Is it really a short-cut?' Candace paused to consider the matter.

'It's only half the distance.' Jackie had already begun to scramble across the deep lip of the combe. 'Come on girls, Mama said to be sure and get home before dark falls.'

Mina hesitated and twittered. 'Mam said on no account was we to go across country.'

'Oh do shut up!' shouted Candace, 'if you want to go home by the road, you can go by yourself.'

They followed the bridle-path for an hour; they came to the woods as Jackie had promised. But already it was growing dark, and the two girls needed some persuasion before they would step onto the woodland path and walk between the tall firs. They held hands and sang hymns for comfort.

'We should have kept to the road,' moaned Mina, 'we should have done what Mama told us.'

They were almost through the woods and in sight of Larksleve, when a huge pale object reared up suddenly before them. The apparition seemed to materialise from beneath the bracken; it made no sound, but swayed menacingly before them in the awful darkness. Too terrified to scream, too frightened to look backwards, they began to run. It was only when they were safe inside the Larksleve kitchen that Mina began to weep. Somewhere, in their headlong flight, they had dropped the wicker basket which held the medicine bottle.

Annis recovered very slowly from her rheumatic fever, and without the help of Dr Priddy's physic. Disobedience, said Loveday, was bound to bring punishment with it. The ghost, said Eliza, had most probably been a straying cow or goat.

Taunton had changed; it was no longer the dangerous and ill-lit place that had excited the young Philip Greypaull in those early days when he had ridden down from Buckland St Mary with his father and Samuel. The coming of gaslight had cast illumination onto several illicit occupations. Many of those dark lanes and shadowy passages, which had once housed the brothels and gaming-houses, had been transformed into wide and well-lit thoroughfares. New churches had been built and old ones refurbished. Silver Street, that colourful home of comedians and singers, had been widened, and the Taunton theatre closed down.

People no longer depended for transport on the North Devon Mail, or the Tam o' Shanter; they travelled in comfort, and at great speed, on the steam-locomotive railway. The old Turk's Head had been pulled down, and a new, slate-roofed inn erected on its site.

Some things had not changed. The taverns of the town were still as cheerful. The people drank and smoked and sang bawdy songs to one another. Men were still carried home in the small hours, much the worse for drink, on the shoulders of their womenfolk; people still swore and gambled. Debauchery and fornication still flourished away from the invasive gaslight. The inhabitants of the little courts still pawned their shabby boots for the necessary coppers to buy bread on a Monday morning. New delights swam up to replace the old ones, and there were a hundred ways in which a fool might yet be parted from his money.

There was a kind of boldness in Philip that might almost have been mistaken for courage. To have antagonised so many people, to have risked so much to gain nothing, had required a dedication to foolhardiness that had sometimes surprised himself. He no longer walked where the path was darkest, or risked the hazards of Bath Place. Young women were no longer attracted to him; he had retained his slim and elegant figure, but that bright colour which had once flushed his cheekbones had changed to a mottled, ugly purple, and the long curls lay grey upon his collar. Excitement was more necessary to him now that it had ever been. That regular ache in the gut from cider drinking, the first hour of giddiness and nausea experienced on rising, could almost be disregarded among the green baize and chandeliers of Macey's, or strolling among the race-track crowds at Bloomhays.

Larksleve had become the place to which he returned when his body was exhausted; Eliza was the woman he used when he had no other. Of all his children, he loved only Blanche. He had once made use of the child's extraordinary looks to taunt Eliza. 'There's not many people,' he had said, 'who 'ud ever believe that she was your child. Which is truly a blessing, eh Eliza? They ugly green eyes an' ginger hair is a gift o' the Devil. Her got no freckles, either! Have 'ee noticed that, Liza? Her never gets a single one, no matter how hot the sun is.'

He had lifted a strand of the heavy auburn hair, touched the alabaster skin, and felt the child flinch, and saw her move away to stand beside her mother. He had cried out, 'Come to Papa, Blanche. Do 'ee come yer, my liddle maid, an' kiss your Papa!'

But Blanche had narrowed her violet eyes, 'I hate you; you're nuthin' but a drunken swine, an' I won't come near you. You better look out, 'cause one day I's gonna stab you right through the heart with the hatpin. Then you'll fall down dead, an' my Mama won't have no more babies!'

The changes in Montacute were less spectacular than those in Taunton. The village had been served by a steam-train since 1853; now there were a few allotment gardens, and

247

better wages for the stonemasons and glovers. Disturbance was coming from agricultural labourers, who were no longer prepared to bow the knee and pull the forelock, to be called 'Johnny Raws', and exist on a diet of kettle-broth and boiled potatoes, or to bury two children out of every three in the Montacute churchyard.

A man called Joseph Arch was travelling the country. His magnetism and fiery words had already roused the farm labourers of Oxfordshire and Dorset to riot and burn their masters' hayricks. Joseph Arch had formed a Union, he was demanding fair wages, and organising strikes against recalcitrant farmers. At his meeting in Yeovil, the Montacute fife and drum band had accompanied him onto the platform, and it was at that meeting that Arch had called for a great, open-air gathering on Ham Hill, on June 17th, to discuss the conditions of Somerset labourers.

Joseph Arch was a man of the people, a Primitive Methodist and Nonconformist, who had started work at the age of nine, who had first been employed as a bird-scarer, then a ploughboy, and had eventually risen to the position of stable hand. He spoke a language that Somerset men understood; he had also been flogged by an overseer, had gone hungry to work, and cold to bed.

News of the Ham Hill meeting had run at a great rate from village to village. Arch had promised to address the gathering at half-past seven on that Sunday evening, but the quiet streets of Montacute had been noisy since early morning with the click of pattened feet and the laughter of excited men and women.

Luke watched the invasion from behind the thick lace curtains at his cottage window. The sight of so many light-hearted people alarmed him. 'I don' like the look of it, Meri, 'tis all bound to lead to trouble. Us had sooner bide yer in house until 'tis all over.'

'You can do as you please, Luke, but I wudden miss this

for the world. Thass a good man what is comin' to speak! He do talk out bold against the gavvers and magistrates. He'm on'y sayin' what we Rom hev always held to – wild beasts an' birds was put on the earth for every man to catch an' eat. 'Tis all very fine for you masons, you got your Guilds an' such. But what about they poor farm lads? I've worked alongside 'em, remember. I've see'd 'em locked up for catchin' a rabbit, or takin' a handful of master's wood for their own fire; I knows all about they stingy farmers. Any man as'll stand up against 'em shall get my cheer!'

When evening came, the twins, reluctant as ever to go among strangers, stayed at home and tended to their caged-birds; Meri took Jye by the hand and began the long climb to the top of Ham Hill. Luke followed, several paces behind them.

The meeting called by Joseph Arch was to be held on that part of the Hill where the Roman gladiators had once fought and played their games; that hollow which local people now called 'Frying Pan', a tiny amphitheatre, with a floor of green turf, angled sides and a single narrow entrance.

Luke had never seen so many people. They had come at first in their hundreds and then in their thousands: men and women who had, for the first time in their lives, shown defiance, laid down scythe and hayfork and left their master's field without asking his permission. Even the most subservient and timid of farm labourers had caught the growing urgency and fever and climbed up to Hamdon Hill to hear Arch speak.

He came into the green area, a bearded, heavy-set man dressed in moleskins and a billycock hat. The Montacute drum-and-fife band marched before him, and a group of Arch supporters sang the Union song. The evening sun shone into the packed amphitheatre. It could not, thought Luke, have held so many people since the Romans had dwelt there. When Arch began to speak there was a rustle of excitement, and then silence.

He told them that he too had been an agricultural labourer; that he had also suffered poverty and indignity, that he had been down-trodden, had felt grief and despair at his situation. Their only salvation, said Arch, lay with the Union, and the Union message was that wherever a farmer refused to increase the weekly wage to sixteen shillings, and reduce the working day to eleven hours, then the workers should withdraw their labour. Arch spoke about the unfair laws; the Poaching Prevention Act by which hungry widows were being searched by Constables as they left their master's fields and fined heavily if they should be found in possession of a single turnip. He spoke about housing: about the mud-walled hovels in which three generations of a labourer's family were forced to sleep all together in one room. A recent census, Arch told them, had recorded an instance of twenty-nine people who were living and sleeping in a Somerset cottage. The plight of farm workers, said Joseph Arch, was greater in the counties of Somerset and Devon than in any other part of the country.

The magnetic voice reached to every ear in the amphi-theatre, every ear except that of Jye Carew. The boy felt the emotion that radiated out from speaker to listener, but was too far away to follow the essential movement of Arch's lips. Jye had been sitting with his parents, but now he began to move down through the crowd; he edged closer until he was among the group who sat nearest to the speaker.

It was that magical hour of the evening when the sun shone level with the hillside before dipping out of sight beyond the Quantocks. Luke followed his son and watched as the walls of the surrounding quarries turned to gold. A shaft of light illuminated Jye's head as he strained forward, a hand cupped behind each ear to catch the sound. Luke remembered the boy's recent inattention when seated in the rear seats of the chapel, the way he had strained towards voices, watched faces. The way he had failed to come when called. The truth could no longer be avoided.

Jye was deaf, and his deafness was increasing. Luke tried to imagine the isolation of the non-hearing. To lose bird-song, the comfort of familiar voices, the sweet ring of chisel on stone, the singing in the chapel.

The Montacute drum-and-fife band played the speaker from the Frying Pan; and the uplifted labourers began to move downhill towards the village, singing hymns and praising Joseph Arch. They had found a champion and, although they might risk dismissal from job and cottage, hundreds joined the Union that night and more were to sign with their mark in the weeks that followed.

Meri had no charm, no herb or flower, no incantation that could halt deafness. She could only watch while Jye, her perfect boy, moved out alone into the silence.

People, said Elizabeth Greypaull, usually deserved the misfortunes that befell them. Eliza could not agree. Her life was lived in anticipation of disaster. That old nightmare had returned, in which she was up behind a bolting horse, the broken traces in her hand and the road running steep down-hill all the way. The shadows which had followed her down the years now began to race before her. She had not asked for Philip's love or devotion and she had not received it. All she had wanted was gentility, and a little kindness. Only the coral necklace, chopped all those years ago with Meri for the blue bowl, had remained true to its promise. Once again, and for the sixth time, Eliza was delivered of a healthy infant.

There was to be no rejoicing at the arrival of Simeon.

Even his name was chosen absentmindedly from a hurried roll-call of long-dead Greypaulls. Once again, the christening-robe was to be provided by the Vicar's lady, and the birth of a second son to Philip and Eliza meant no more than another child to feed and clothe.

One day, just before the child was due, they had sorted through the baby clothes, she and Loveday. They had counted up the flannel binders, all felted and thick from too much washing. They had mourned the heap of shrunken woollens, and sighed at the dozens of yellowed, embroidered petticoats and dresses.

Eliza said, 'I mind the time when I had Candace, an' Mother brought six of everything that was needed. All white an' new.'

'Your mother's ageing fast,' said Loveday, 'her's gone downhill very quick since Mrs Rachel died.'

It was true. It had been an age since Elizabeth cantered up to Larksleve with the governess-cart piled up with gifts for Eliza and her children. Her mother's desertion of her did not surprise Eliza. She had known for a long time that Elizabeth's strength was a myth, that her thunder was borrowed from others in the family. Faced with an insoluble problem, Elizabeth had turned her face away from her daughter, had denied help when it was most needed.

The management of Larksleve was slipping away from Eliza. There had been a time when she marched in step with the season, when she had been aware of the state of each crop, the height and condition of meadow-grass, the health of trees.

Now, the field-work was done without proper supervision, and only when Philip could afford it, by a succession of casual labourers, who came from surrounding parishes. Eliza wept to see the crooked furrows in the ploughed fields, the ditches blocked and the stones and weeds that choked the good earth. The shelves of her cheese-house were almost

252

bare. Several cows had died or gone dry that winter, and Philip, more uninterested than ever, had refused to replace them. Her ambition had been narrowed down to the payment of essential bills and the provision of sufficient food for her six children.

The day came when she could no longer pay Loveday Hayes, not even with milk or butter, not with eggs or flour. "'Tidden fair that you shud stay here wi' me,' said Eliza, 'when you could be earning yourself good money elsewhere.'

'Oh, Missus,' cried Loveday, 'you an' me have knowed one another since we was children. I growed up in your father's house. I never had no other family!' Her broad face creased into lines of pain. 'I can't bear to see 'ee do without me! That proud 'ooman across to Castle Farm – beggin' your pardon – I means your mother – her don' never come – and wi' Mrs Rachel dead an' gone, well, you on'y got me to rely on.'

Eliza nodded. 'My mother do only go visitin' where she can be powerful. Her always did like to tell people what they shud do an' how they shud do it. 'Tis a lost cause yer on Larksleve, Loveday! Never mind, us'll manage somehow. Don' 'ee cry now, girl. That'll only upset me.'

Loveday stayed; and on wet afternoons she sat down with Eliza at the kitchen table, and helped to make-over the dresses left by Philip's mother into garments for the four growing girls. Eliza's green cloak was sacrificed to make trousers and a jacket for Jackie.

"'Tis boots they need,' complained Eliza. 'I never thought to see the day when they wore pattens – but 'tis either that or they go barefoot.'

John Greypaull paid a rare and embarrassed visit. 'Us don' see you an' the children in church of a Sunday, Eliza?'

'I got no churchgoing outfit, Father. I wudden care to disgrace the family pew wi' darns an' patches. As for the children – they do all wear pattens these days, an' that wood do click shamefully on church flooring.'

'I done all I cud, girl! But times is hard as you must know. There's a lot of unrest in the district. There's talk of labourers striking for more money. Your mother says you shud be firmer wi' Philip.'

'I can't keep 'un out of Taunton – an' that's where the mischief happens.'

'My brother Daniel don' acknowledge his son no more; he turns his head when us comes face to face wi' Philip in the market.' John walked slowly across the yard and remounted his horse. He bent down to Eliza and placed a hand upon her shoulder. 'Anything's bothering you, maid, you just let me know,' he said vaguely, 'us'll have to have another stern word wi' Philip Greypaull.'

The streets of Taunton stood empty on race-days. The entire population, it seemed to Philip, abandoned whatever they happened to be doing and either walked or drove out to Bloomhays. He had been accepted only lately into the fraternity of racing sportsmen. It had taken several weeks of freeloading at Philip's expense before the clique had been prepared to admit the farmer from Buckland into their select and wealthy circle. The rumour that he had inherited a fortune from his mother was, of course, exaggerated, but his luck at chemin-de-fer in Macey's had been witnessed by them and noted.

The nobility and the wealthy merchants sat up in the grandstand, while the common folk and punters pushed and shouted against the flimsy rails which lined the racecourse. It was the kind of scene which set his blood tingling. He had invested in a pair of cream breeches and knee-high, shiny boots. He wore a pale-grey frock coat and matching topper, and carried his silver-topped stick. He strolled around the perimeter of the course and was reminded of his visits to the hiring fair at Bridgwater. Nostalgia gripped him, and a vague regret for days past. He visited the thimble-riggers and Mr Punchinello, and the booths which contained the tightrope-walkers and the Bearded Lady. He walked as close as he dared up to the line of gypsy tents and waggons, and, at once, a group of ragged children gathered about his feet, their hands outstretched. He smiled and tossed them a half-dozen coins, and nodded his gracious acceptance of the gypsy-mother's blessing. Ah! Taunton was the hub of the turning world and he belonged in it; it was here that people knew how to live, when to work and when to indulge their pleasure. The first race was announced, and he chuckled softly at the sight of the pickpockets and cutpurses, who were busy relieving excited men of those valuables which still happened to be about their persons. He walked past the lines of carriages and gigs, bought a copy of *Bradshaw's Correct List of Horses and their Riders*, and then looked up at the sound of his own name being shouted from the grandstand.

'Philip – Philip Greypaull! Come on up, man. We've got a red-hot tip for you. The three-thirty – '

The bill at Keat's had not been paid for over a year, and Eliza, ashamed to be seen driving into Buckland, had sent Loveday down with the sack of grain to be milled. Loveday returned, her face and temper flaming. 'They shut the door on me, Missus! They said that they had see'd Master going about in Taunton dressed like a lord.' She dragged the sack from the dog-cart and let it drop on the ground between them. 'I can't help 'ee, maid. I wud if I cud – but we got no savings.'

'How could you have savings,' cried Eliza, 'when I never pays you a single farthin'?'

The two women walked slowly into the kitchen where Mina waited at her end of the kitchen table, bowls and bread-tins ready. 'Where's the flour then, Loveday?'

'There won't be none, child. First pay your bill – thass what miller said.'

'But I got to have flour, Ma! I can't make bread wi'out it!'

Mina's cries reached out to the stables and the shippon where her sisters and brother scraped and broomed. The children came running to their mother, and Simeon, sleeping in his cradle, was wakened by all the turmoil and began to cry.

Eliza picked up her year-old son; 'Now do 'ee all stop this crying. We got potatoes enough to last the week out, so nobody'll go hungry.' She turned to Loveday. 'There's that one cheese left on the shelf. I was countin' on the money from that to get – but no matter. Us'll have to eat 'un.' She spoke to Candace. 'I have never left you alone in your lives, but you is old enough and well able to mind the others. I got to make a journey into Devon. I got to see my brother Francis.'

Eliza, in forty-one years of life, had never travelled further than Taunton, and then only once, to have a tooth pulled. She had seen the train, of course, rattling alarmingly across the distant landscape, whistle screaming, shedding clouds of steam. She knew that the train came to Buckland Halt at six o'clock every morning, to pick up milk, that it travelled southwards, across the border and into Devon. But exactly where it stopped she did not know.

Eliza did what she could about her appearance. She put on the only blue gingham dress that was still without patches, scraped her red hair out of sight beneath her starched white bonnet, and pulled a thick woollen shawl about her shoulders. Candace and Mina waved goodbye from the front porch. Mina wept: 'P'raps us'll never see her again. P'raps her'll get lost down to Devon, an' never find her way back.'

'Don' be so silly,' snapped Candace, 'Father's always goin' to Taunton, an' he never gets lost. Why – even when he's dead-drunk, the horse knows its own way home an' brings him back. I shud say that Mama's got a lot more sense than Father's horse.'

Asked about her destination Eliza said, 'As far as I can go for sixpence,' and the man on the station laughed, and gave her a ticket. She had parted with her last coin but one in all the world, but she knew that she could rely on her brother Francis. She remembered his awkward touch on her shoulder on the day of his wedding. 'If you ever feels the need – if it so happens that you want help – ' Now the day had come and she had no one else to turn to; Eliza forced her trembling legs towards the snorting monster, and prayed to God that she might yet be spared to return to Larksleve.

The compartment was filled by a mother and her brood of noisy children. Eliza sat stiffly in her corner, knees pressed tightly together, spine rigid. She watched the flying fields and hedges, and could hardly believe her temerity in making this journey. Steam streamed past the carriage window, blotting out the view, and Eliza turned in panic towards the harassed mother. 'Cud you tell me,' she stammered, 'cud you p'raps direct me to Fallon's Court, near Tavistock?'

The woman frowned, and considered. 'Why – you wants the next stop after this one, my dear! But 'tis a tidy walk out to Fallon's.'

'How far would you say?'

'Cud be ten mile, maybe twelve. Goin' there for a job, be you?' The woman shook her head. 'He've got a proper name in the village, I can tell 'ee! Married her for her money so we yeard, an' he don't mean to part wi' a single penny of it. I shud be careful my dear, if I was you. You don' look very strong, an' they say that thik Francis Greypaull do treat his servants somethin' wicked!'

Anxiety had made her forget the directions given by the woman on the train. Eliza had walked all day, taking first one lane, and then another until she was thoroughly lost. It was evening when she came to Fallon's Court, a cold spring evening. She pulled her shawl tight about her and turned into the driveway, passing between the imposing wrought-iron gates, and recalling the morning of Francis' wedding. She had worn her green cloak and bonnet then, and her girls had been smart in their scarlet outfits, Jackie had looked handsome in his sailor-suit. As she walked, several carriages rattled past her; she turned the bend in the drive and the house was revealed, lit brilliantly in every window and looking like a great ship braving a dark ocean. Eliza drew back into the bushes, and watched as the carved double doors were opened up to admit the elegant men and women who were descending from carriages and broughams. It began to rain, a heavy shower that had soaked her through long before she could reach her brother's front door.

Eliza tapped, timidly at first and then loudly. The man who opened the door looked down at her from his great height. He grabbed her by the elbow; 'Round the back,' he snapped, giving her a hard push. But Eliza had caught a sight of Francis as he passed with his guests across the hall; she twisted away from the man's grip and ran forwards. 'Fran,' she cried, 'Fran – do 'ee spare me a few minutes.'

The embarrassment of her brother Francis was as unexpected as the sudden rain shower. She lifted a hand to her limp white bonnet and looked down at her muddied skirts and soaked shawl.

'I'm sorry,' she murmured, 'I see you got visitors; but I bin lookin' for this place since early mornin' – '

Francis opened the library door. 'For God's sake come in here,' he muttered. He closed the door and turned to face her. 'How could you, Eliza? Tonight of all nights. Couldn't you see that we were entertaining? The most influential men in the country are here with their wives, and then you come running towards me looking like a – '

'Yes, Fran – what do I look like?'

He rubbed a hand across his forehead. 'I wasn't expecting to see you. It was a shock.'

''Tis a shock for me too, Fran. I never expected unkindness from you. But I didden mean to shame you.'

He sighed. 'Sit down, I'll get you a brandy.'

'I don't drink spirits.'

'You'd better have something, you look half dead.'

Francis moved to a cupboard filled with bottles and glasses, and Eliza edged a little nearer to the fire, half afraid to tread upon the thick pale carpet; she looked around her at the booklined walls and leather chairs.

''Tis a fine house, Fran,' she murmured, 'you do live in some style these days.'

He handed her a glass. 'Drink it up, Eliza. I don't have much time. Why have you come here – I suppose you want money?'

Francis Greypaull put a hand into his pocket and carefully counted out five sovereigns. 'Now drink up that brandy, Liza, and put that gold away safe in your purse. I really must be getting back to my guests.' He hesitated, took a step towards her and then retreated. 'You'd better not show yourself in the hall again, the butler can take you out the back way.' Eliza looked down at the gold on her outstretched palm, and then up at her brother's face, then she bunched her fist around the five sovereigns and threw them at him.

The last coin in her purse brought her back, late that night, to Larksleve only to find that the miller's bill had been paid in her absence. 'A note,' explained Loveday, 'it come wi' the carter just after you had left. Candace read it for us.

It said to take the grain back to the mill. That everythin' was straight an' settled.'

Eliza thought about it. 'That'll have bin Samuel,' she said at last, 'nobody else 'ud do that much for me.'

'There was no name on the note, Ma. 'Twas written in big letters.'

'Your uncle Sam is a good man,' explained Eliza, 'what do help God in working out His purpose.'

'What happened down to Devon?' Loveday asked.

'He left me to walk to the station on my own. He offered me five sovereigns.'

'Oh maid! Whatever have happened to your Francis?'

Eliza's eyes filled with tears and she could not answer. Loveday moved the rocking-chair closer to the fire, and pulled off Eliza's patched boots. 'Don' you fret, maid. Us got soup warmin' ready for 'ee, an' tomorrow I'll be off to miller, an' by teatime we'll have bread to eat.'

'My brother was ashamed of me, Loveday.'

'That don't surprise me. They be all a proud lot in your family – savin' you, Missus.' Loveday poured soup into a bowl and stood over Eliza while she drank it. 'From what I heard, your Francis hev got hisself wedded to a woman wi' a face like an old boot – jus' so he cud live in a fine house, an' use her money.'

'I don't blame them,' Eliza said quietly, 'they helped us out so many times one way an' another. But it never made no difference, did it? When I think about Larksleve, and the way it was when I came as a bride, an' look at it now, Loveday! Anyway, farming is in a bad fix. Prices keep fallin'. Times is bad all over.'

'Times is always bad if you lissens to farmers. Your Francis cud of spared you more than five sovereigns. When I think of how he left you, to walk in Devon by yourself in the dark, why, you cud of bin attacked an' left for dead in they strange places!'

'God was with me,' said Eliza. 'But this I will say, I'll die before I ever ask for help again.'

Philip's need to lie had diminished since the death of his mother; her opinion of him was the only one he had ever valued and, as Eliza had told him, the truth always paid in the end. He came riding back, after two weeks' absence, to find that his wife and daughters were attempting the haysel without the hand of a solitary man upon the scythe. He announced at the supper-table, 'You can expect the bailiffs up yer again in the morning, Liza. 'Tis only a temporary set-back, but a certain bill has got to be paid right away, an' I find myself temporarily embarrassed.'

'You mean you're spent-up? That all your mother's hard-earned money have gone on cards an' horses?' She covered her face with her hands. 'Oh Philip – whatever's to become of us all?'

He laughed. 'Go an' say a few more prayers,' he advised her, 'or consult wi' your mother. Her always did know what was best for everybody.' He turned to the silent children. 'I want you lot up an' dressed before light tomorrow morning. Feather-beds are to be hidden under straw in the barn, cooking-pots an' kettles likewise. Lamps must be put where the bailiffs can't find 'em.' He paused and grinned at their astonished faces. 'Unless you wants to sleep on the floor, in the dark, an' have nothin' to eat, you had all better do what your father tells you, this time.'

The bailiffs, who also knew a trick or two, came riding into the yard before daybreak, and Eliza, legs trembling, was uncomfortably aware that feather-beds were at that moment being thrust from back bedroom windows and hidden in straw, by her three eldest children.

'You can make it hard for yourself, ma'am, or you can make it easy. 'Tis a sizeable debt again – 'twill take some covering, an' no mistake. If you got valuables, then our advice is to hand 'em over. 'Twill be easier all around, in the long run.'

Eliza moved from kitchen to parlour and back again, until the long wide table was covered from end to end with all her treasures. She gave them the beautiful green and gold dinner and tea services, which had been a wedding-present, the monogrammed cutlery of solid silver, the lamps with the blue-tinted funnels. She looked questioningly at them, and returned to the parlour to fetch Jackie's little knife and fork set, and the engraved christening cups that her father had given to Candace and Madelina, and still it was not sufficient.

'Any personal property, ma'am?' They asked her. 'Any rings or jewellery?'

She lifted a hand to the coral pendant. 'There's this,' she faltered, ''tis worth quite a lot, I believe. That's a heavy chain, made of solid silver, and the stones is coral.'

The bailiff wound the necklace around his fingers and tested it for the weight. 'That'll do nicely,' he told her, ''tis an ugly lookin' piece though. I reckon as how you'll never miss it.'

Chicago.

Dear cousin Eliza,

It is with a heavy heart that I put pen to paper to tell you of all that has befallen since we left New York in the year of 1867. I understand from my brother's letters that the Family no longer visit you on Larksleve due to the *Vicisitudes* and *Bad Behaviour* of cousin Philip, which is hard on you, dear Eliza, none of it being *Your Fault*. So I will inform you.

We made the move to Chicago, it being the Centre of the Meat Business at this time, and full of Opportunity.

262

Mr Salter purchased a Business which thrived and Did Well. For five years he worked night and day, and owned a Seat on the Chicago Board of Trade. But in 1872, on October 3rd, tragedy struck us in the death of dear Eddie, aged seventeen, who went down with pneumonia and could not be saved in spite of all the doctor's efforts. My only consolashun at this time was that poor Sussanah was again re-united with her son. Mr Salter went into a sad depression after Eddie's death, from which nothing could rouse him. His health having been undermined by hard work and worry over business, he declined at a great rate, the flesh dropping from him in a matter of weeks. In spite of all efforts, my dear Husband passed Away, Safe in the Lord, on September 23rd of this year, having survived poor Eddie by ten months. I am left with my three children, George aged fifteen, Rosalind aged fourteen, and John aged seven. There is plenty of money, and as you know I have always longed to return to the farming way of life, but great courage needed at this time for such a Venture by a woman without a Husband; money being easily lost as you well know, Eliza. People here are moving West into Wisconsin and Minnesota, everybody wanting a better *Life* after the end of the Civil War. There is talk of a Machine which can Reap, Bind and Thresh, and do the work of five men. I am truly tempted to move West, and leave this city of Chicago in which I have already buried two of my Loved Ones.

My brother's letters inform that you have two more children, a daughter, Annis, and a son, Simeon, making *Six* altogether. Please write and tell of all that has befallen. I sometimes have a dream about Larksleve Farm, and visiting my grandparents when I was a child. Do your girls sit with their mending in the inglenook settle on a winter's evening? Kind regards to all.

Your affectshunat cousin, Rhoda.

Dear cousin Rhoda,

I take up the pen at once to answer your sad letter, which came up by the carter at noon today. I cannot tell you how grieved I am to hear of the deaths of your two loved Ones, and pray that Our Saviour will give you the strength to bear this double blow. How comforting it must be for you to have George and Rosalind to lean on, and the company of little John. I am glad to heare that you are not *Short* of *Money*, being so far away from England and only Strangers to rely on.

You write, dear Rhoda, of returning to the Farming way of life, and I can understand this, you not being, nor ever could be, truly settled down in a City. You was ever one for the fields and hedgerows, and I well remember the Haysels and Harvest Homes when we children played all together. That do seem like it happened in another life, dear cousin, so much pain and sorrow have come to both of us in the meantime. Do *not* think of going in for farming by *Yourself*. Without a man by your side it is not possible to *Manage*. I speak as one who have had bitter experience of this *Lack* of a husband's support. I will not burden you with all my troubles, you having more than enough of your own to Bear at this time. I will only say that Larksleve is in a State what do break my heart, and all for the want of a good husband and father.

My two oldest girls have growed up and are young ladies, Jackie a keen horseman, and Blanche beautiful to look at, but very wilful. Annis and Simeon still babies. My children are the only reason I have left to feel Proud and hold my Head Up. We no longer go down to Church, lacking proper clothes and boots, and not wishing to Shame the Family, but I will say a Family Prayer for the Souls of Mr Salter and poor Eddie. Keep up your Spirit, dear Rhoda. A woman's lot is Hard to Bear, but

God is with you. Do *Nothing* on your own. The World is very hard for a Woman without a Man, as I well know.

Please write and inform of Future Plans.

Your affectshunat cousin, Eliza.

Her prediction as to Charles and Henry's future had been proved to be only too correct. Meri's twins, at the age of sixteen, were quite unable to support themselves or even begin to make a living. Their lungs, cramped by deformity and delicate from birth, were barely sufficient to take them through each autumn and winter. In summer and springtime, they hoed and singled, and gathered in the cider-apples alongside their mother. But Meri had seen how an hour of unremitting labour, the constant bending of their twisted spines, the pressure on weak legs would leave them exhausted. Meri, more than ever convinced just lately that she would never make old bones, had said to Luke, 'Us got to see they two proper settled, in a place of their own. That can't be left a minute longer. I wants to see them dependent on no man.'

The isolated cottage with its 'spot of ground' had just become vacant. Meri emptied the money-belt upon the table, counted up her savings, and found that she had enough and a little to spare. She paid for the cottage, filled the rooms with all the furniture they could ever need, hung thick lace curtains at the windows, and handed them the key. Luke saw to it that there was a breeding-sow in the sty, a house-cow in the meadow, and enough wood to last a bitter winter placed in the little shed. He gave them a sackful of seed-potatoes. 'You must always have 'tiddies in the garden,' he told them, 'if you got a tiddy to roast or boil, then you always got a meal.'

He gave them some cuttings from his moss and damask roses. ''Tis nice to have a flower or two,' he confided, 'even if they do take up too much space. The Lord God made the roses to be enjoyed just as much as the 'tiddies.'

Jye, grown tall and straight, could only watch and smile from his new world of silence. His isolation had become as severe as that of his two crippled brothers.

She had hoped that with Charles and Henry settled the uneasiness that plagued her would at least grow less, if not disappear altogether. But that old presentiment of gathering shadows was becoming so strong that Meri, sometimes waking in the early hours, would see the white moon swim above the conical Hill, and she would know it for an omen, and rock her body to and fro in an ecstasy of terror. Luke, half-waking, would hold her close. ''Tis on'y the moon, my dear,' he would whisper, 'there idden nothin' that can harm 'ee. I won't let it.'

She had risen, slow and heavy-eyed that morning. She had packed crusty bread, a wedge of cheese, an onion and an apple. She had said, as she always did, 'Your nammet's ready, Luke. Will it be enough until Jye comes up wi' your dinner?' She had lifted a corner of the curtain and watched him stride away towards the lane that led to the Hill. In her mind, she went with him as she always did; her spirit moving one step before him, willing him safe.

She had come to know every inch of the Hill, had trodden the fine soft turf in every season and in every kind of weather. She was familiar with the movements of shepherds and their flocks, could sit motionless behind a furze bush, and catch a rabbit with her bare hands. Those frequent expeditions when she went in search of a rare herb or flower would take her out beyond the old workings, past those hollows of no more than twenty feet where an ancient people, using crude tools, had once delved and dug. She would take the twisty road that led upwards to the deeper

266

quarries, hear the chink and clink of chisel on stone, and be eased in her soul just to know that Luke was close by.

Meri had thought that this year of 1874 would see no end to winter. The snows of January and February had given way to rain: a daylong, nightlong downpour, that had brought Luke home each night, cold and drenched to his skin. Even he, who rarely grumbled, had said, 'I never see'd such rain, Meri. 'Tis enough to move thik old Hill on his foundations!' His words had brought a sudden picture to her mind of the conical Hill, so innocent and beautiful in summer, moving malevolently, depriving her of all she held dear. 'Don' say that,' she had cried, 'I can't bear it!' He had laughed then, he was used to her fanciful nature, her dramatic outcrys.

She watched as Jye pulled on his new boots and laced them. In a school of more than sixty children, Luke Carew's son was one of the few boys to go shod in leather. Meri tapped his cheek to gain his attention; moved her lips carefully and slowly to form the words. 'Hurry home, Jye. Watch the church clock, careful. You muss be yer by twelve, to take up your father's dinner.'

The rain had stopped. A finger of sunlight pierced the bruised sky. From her kitchen window Meri saw blackthorn blossom shaking brave against a drying wind and the Hill rising dark and smooth behind it. There was a time, but he had been much younger then, when Jye had heard the clock strike from the church tower. He could still remember lying warm in his bed on a cold night and counting the strokes as they fell on the frosty air.

Now, he heard nothing. Now, he must always be watchful. It had come upon him very slowly, this silence. His losses had been gradual, little sounds to begin with. The patter of rain, parts of certain words, the wind in the treetops. Later on, he had lost birdsong, the ring of his father's spiked boots on the flint road, the voices of his two brothers as they had whispered together, his mother's rare laughter, and her stern instructions.

Jye watched the big hand as it crept upwards to join the small one. When the hands were about to join at the very top of the clock, he left his books and his bench and approached the teacher. 'Beg to be excused, please.' His speech was clear, but toneless. The teacher nodded his permission. Most people only nodded or shook their heads at Jye. He ran the few yards from school to where his mother waited at her front door. He took the bag, heavy with the stone-jar which held soup and the half-loaf wrapped in a white cloth, and set off towards the lane that led to the Hill. Meri called out, 'Quick now, Jye, or that soup'll be cold,' and then she remembered that he could no longer hear her.

Jye walked quickly, his long strong legs covering the distance between the village and the spot where his father waited; he moved the bag at intervals from one hand to the other. He passed a shepherd who was turning his flock to another part of the Hill. He slipped and almost fell among the yellow-stone brash which the recent rains had washed up from beneath an ancient cutting. He came into the working quarry, to the little tin-roofed hut perched high among the steep sides where Luke would be standing at his banker.

Any other boy but Jye would have been warned by the silence, by the absence of men's voices, the rattling of chains, the chugging of the steam-crane. He left the empty hut, bag still in hand, and walked to the edge of the precipice. He looked down into the floor of the working and saw a huddle of men gathered around the still form of a very tall man: a man with a head of thick black curls who was lying face downwards. Even from a great height, Jye could see the yellow stain across his father's clean white shirt where the boulder had struck him, squarely and fatally, between his shoulders.

Meri shook her son so violently that his head rocked back and forth upon his shoulders. 'You'm wrong,' she cried, 'you don' hear proper no more, Jye. 'Twas somebody else's name what they told you.'

'I see'd 'un, Ma. He was lyin' on a flat stone. All the men was standin' round 'un. They had took their caps off.' Jye caught his breath and his top lip trembled. 'I climbed down. They had turned 'un over, an' I cud see 'twer Pa.' He indicated the uncovered half-loaf still lying in the bag. 'I covered his face, Ma. I covered his face up wi' the breadcloth.'

She only believed it when she saw them coming: a dozen men, carrying their workmate down the hillside; the little procession slipping and sliding on ground made dangerous by the recent rains. They carried him upstairs, laid him on the bed, and covered him. They closed the curtains. They tried to tell her, to explain how it had happened. But she was stone; she was granite.

The rain, swore the master mason, it must have dislodged the whole bloody rock-face. There had been a fall of stone, unexpected; he paused and blew his nose. Luke never should have been down there - not his place - he was no labourer - no sawyer. His job was on his banker - he was a craftsman - but Luke was too good-natured. They took advantage of him. It had been a morning of disasters. They'd had trouble with the steam-crane, and then a wedge had slipped and old Jacob had suffered a crushed foot. Luke had gone down to see what he could do - he was the biggest and strongest of all that two hundred.

The rock had struck him square between the shoulders; it had pinned him to the ground, had crushed his rib-cage. There was nothing to be done for him, said the master mason. He had died within minutes.

Meri of the violent mood, the dramatic gesture, so

quickly roused to anger or to laughter, was seen to be silent and calm in the face of death. She kept her mind fixed upon the need for ritual. Whatever there had been of Rom in her husband must be properly served now in the manner of his going.

The woman who saw to such matters came in from the village; she washed Luke's body, dressed him in his black, chapel-going suit, combed his rough curls into neatness, and placed the Bible between his folded hands.

He didn't look dead. Meri approached the bed, lit the single candle which began the vigil, and looked down on the beloved face, quite unmarked by pain, still handsome. He had died quickly, they told her. Could hardly have known what was happening to him. She was glad to see his face undamaged, his head intact. The black curls lay about his ears and upon his forehead. She reached out a hand, as she had done so often in his lifetime, and then, remembering her grandmother's teachings, she rapidly withdrew it. Not even for Luke could she break 'taboo', and touch the dead.

Together with her three sons, Meri began her fasting vigil. The strangers came in a long procession, tapping at the open front door, tiptoeing up the staircase, shuffling up to the bedside and muttering their condolences, then creeping, uneasy, away. They had not come in his lifetime, these men and women who had accepted her into their chapel, but had never quite swallowed the fact of Luke's Rom wife.

''Tidden natural, no 'tidden!' wept Charity Carew, 'the way her jus' sits there beside 'un, wi' that candle burning at his head, an' never a kind word to say to me, his poor mother.'

Meri had gone to a cupboard just before the funeral. She had taken out her hawking basket, knelt down beside it, and lifted out her old plaid dress and the knot of flying ribbons. She had looked up to find Jye standing beside her. 'No, Ma,' he had said, 'you didden ought to wear that. That wudden be proper.' She had felt her old anger spurt, briefly. But Jye, his tone suddenly grown deeper, had pushed the black curls from his forehead and spoken to her with Luke's voice, and she had laid away the plaid and ribbons, and put on sober black.

Luke was buried in the Montacute churchyard on an afternoon in March. It was a day of keen wind and high cloud when the great trees crashed together, and the Hill, having moved once to claim its victim, stood four square again, as it had done since the world began.

Charity had offered hospitality, had invited Meri and her sons back into her cottage along with the rest of the mourners. But Jye had declined; he had gone with Charles and Henry to the little stone house, with its 'spot of ground', just beyond the village. Meri had gone, as she had longed to, quite alone into her own house.

Luke had been a simple man. His few books, his workclothes and boots, the Bible, the stone soup-jar, the dinnerplate and cutlery which had been his made an unimpressive mound on Meri's hearthstone.

She made quick fire with ash-sticks; on it she placed his clothes and boots, and the Bible ripped from end to end. She took up a hammer and smashed the plate and soup-jar. She dug a hole beside the damask rose bush, and buried the cutlery and shards together.

Her grief could not have been displayed before gorgios, but now her lamentation would be severe and of long duration. Those shadows meant, as she had thought, for herself or her children had instead claimed the first and only love in all her life. He had gone out that morning, intact and strong, and he had been brought to her six hours later, his body smashed, his heart broken, and he had been thirty-six years old.

If she could only have done what her instinct ordered, he would never have been buried in the Montacute churchyard.

271

She would have taken him, with Jye's help, secretly to where the blackthorn blossomed. Luke would have lain beneath the Hill that had claimed him, open to the snows of winter, covered by the flowers of springtime.

The significance of a sixteenth birthday was the lengthening of a young girl's skirts and the putting-up of her long hair. Candace stood before the looking-glass in the hall, tilted her head and patted the dark, bouffant curls.

'What do 'ee think?' she asked Mina.

'Oh, 'tis very elegant, Can'. It do quite change you. An' they long skirts is a great improvement, they do make you look fuller – an' taller.'

Blanche and Annis were washing dishes at the kitchen table. Blanche began to giggle. 'Nothin' ever goin' to improve your looks,' she called out to Candace, 'you be still liddle an' skinny, an' your fingernails is always dirty.'

Candace went into the kitchen; she grabbed Blanche by the shoulder raised a hand and left the marks of all her four fingers across the smooth white cheek. Blanche never cried. She continued to wash dishes as if nothing had happened. 'Your fingernails 'ud be dirty too,' Candace shouted, 'if you had to work in the shippon an' stable, like I do. I don' hang around wi' Loveday pretending to help her. You is nothin' but a leech, Blanche Greypaull. A lazy, good-fer-nothin' leech – jus' like your father!'

Blanche screamed; she beat both hands into the bowl and sent the water flying. 'I bain't then! I bain't nothin' like him.' She turned upon her little sister, Annis, who was drying dishes. 'Her's like him. Her even looks like him. Her got they same liddle yellow curls an' blue eyes, an' hers always whining an' crying. Don' you never dare to say that I be anything like Father. I do hate an' detest that man somethin' awful, I tells 'ee!'

272

Candace spoke loftily to Mina. 'Somethin' will have to be done about this child. Her is keepin' company too much wi' Loveday Hayes. 'Tis my belief that they is practising witchcraft together.'

Blanche began to shout. 'Don' you tell tales on me, Candace Greypaull. You can fancy yourself a lady, wi' your long skirts an' your hair up on top of your head, but jus' you wait. I's goin' to show you what a real lady looks like.' Blanche caught at her own heavy mane of hair and swept it, with a single gesture, upwards and around her head. The transformation in the child was startling. Eliza, halted in the open doorway, could only stand and stare. Unaware of her mother's presence, Blanche pirouetted. She dipped her coiffed head towards her astonished sisters. 'One day, you three will be fighting to know me. I's goin' to have a carriage, an' a house wi' servants, and more money than you Greypaulls ever dreamed of.'

Candace laughed uneasily. 'Why, you be already nine years old, goin' on ten, an' you can't write your own name, yet. What kind of lady 'ud you make?'

Blanche smiled and rolled her violet eyes, 'I shan't need readin' an' writin'. I shall be rich enough so that I can pay somebody else to do all that for me.'

Eliza came forward. 'Did I hear some mention of witchcraft among you?' Blanche let her hair fall upon her shoulders; she looked mutinous, her lips folded into a thin line.

Eliza turned to her eldest daughter, 'Candace?'

''Twas nothin' much, Ma.'

'I want to know! If the Devil's mischief is bein' practised in my house, then you had better tell me about it.'

Candace looked at Mina, and then at Blanche. ''Twas that kitten what died last Christmas. Don't 'ee remember, Ma? I found 'un frozen in the shippon.' Eliza nodded. 'Well, Blanche an' Loveday took the corpse, an' put it on a

273

ledge in the inglenook-chimney. I just happened to be passin' the kitchen window. I saw 'em do it.' Candace shivered. 'You know what that do mean, Ma. That do mean harm to somebody in this house.'

Eliza's hands flew upwards to cover her face. 'Why - that's terrible,' she whispered, 'I can hardly believe it. 'Tis all my own fault. I shudden never have stopped you girls from goin' to church on Sundays. My pride wudden let you go in pattens and patched clothes - and now the Devil have found a chink, an' got in yer among you.'

Eliza turned to face the child she could not love. 'Blanche?'

'All right, then! Trust Miss Sneaky-Drawers to be watchin'!' Blanche laced her fingers tight together and looked straight into her mother's face. 'I found the kitten. It was dead, an' Can' had thrown it on the dung-heap. Loveday see'd it too. It was a black one. Loveday said what a pity it 'ud be to waste 'un.'

'Waste?'

The child's lovely face flushed with pleasure at the memory. 'Oh yes, Ma. 'Tis a certain powerful magic what do come from a kitten's corpse. Most 'specially a black one. Loveday was mad because the pig's heart didden work.' Blanche nodded. 'Don' you worry, Ma. That kitten up the chimney is all us'll need to finish Pa off.'

'Why, that's wicked! That's so evil I can hardly believe it. To do such a thing, Blanche. To do such a thing against your own father.'

Blanche looked surprised. 'But you hates him too, Ma. I heard you say so. Don' you remember? You once said that he was filth - that he was evil. I minds the night he threw the money at you. I minds what he said. He said, "You idden worth that much, Eliza." '

Eliza also remembered and was ashamed. She wondered what other damage had been done to these children. 'But that don't mean that you shud use witchcraft – ' she faltered.

'But I loves you, Ma!' cried Blanche, 'I loves you more than any of the others. I on'y done it for your sake.' She paused. 'Do you know what Loveday says? "Better for all of you if he were dead an' buried." That's what Loveday says. "Your poor Ma hev got a big enough family to feed already." '

Blanche began to sob, and Eliza for the first time put her arms around this daughter; she pushed the hair back from Blanche's forehead and did not flinch at the touch. 'Don' 'ee cry, maid. 'Twill be all right. Us'll say an extra prayer together. Don' 'ee cry now, maid. That'll only upset me.'

Philip came into the house and found them praying together, all of them down on their knees upon the pegged rug. Even Simeon, who was only two years old and could hardly balance, had his hands pressed together, his eyes screwed tight shut. 'You can get up off your knees,' shouted Philip, 'your prayers is answered.' He laughed at the way their eyes flew open, at the way they looked up at him, fearful and without joy. 'What a miserable bunch your mother hev turned you into. Well now, you can get your heads up! Take a look outside – see what Papa's brought you!' He had been drinking, just enough to make him expansive, flamboyant.

Eliza said, 'What's this then? What trouble is you bringing me now?'

'No trouble.' He pushed her towards the window. A smart black pony fidgeted between the shafts of a high-sided phaeton from the seats of which the children were already unloading a number of packages and boxes and bringing them into the kitchen. Eliza watched them tear paper and lift lids, saw them happy and excited. He had brought new cloaks and dresses, boots and bonnets. A sailor-suit and a coloured-silk jockey cap for Jackie. A shawl of crimson wool for Loveday.

'An' where did all the money come from?' asked Eliza.

'None o' your business.'

'Us needs new stock,' she murmured, 'the cows is old an' almost dry; us got no followers to take their place. The harrows an' drags is in a pitiful state an' do need urgent attention by the smithy. Barn roof is leaking – '

He held up his hand. 'You can forget all that, Eliza. Us is all finished wi' grubbing a living from stock an' soil.' He began to empty his pockets onto the kitchen table, and gradually his shoulders straightened as he was relieved of the weight of gold. More sovereigns than had ever been contained in her dowry spun across and heaped up on the kitchen table.

'How?' she whispered.

He separated a small pile of coins and pushed them towards her.

'That's yours,' he said, 'to do with as you like.' He fetched the velvet bag which had once held her dowry. 'This is not to be touched,' he warned her, 'this is my stake-money.'

'Stake for what?'

He swaggered a little, hooked his thumbs into his waistcoat pockets and grinned. 'You sees before you, Eliza, a racing gentleman of some keen judgement.'

'You've bin away a whole fortnight – '

'Travellin', Eliza – to any place what boasts a decent race-course. I got friends now; good friends what'll never let me down.'

'I seem to have heard that once before.'

'This is diff'rent. I is in wi' a crowd of the quality these days. No more smock an' gaiters! No more walkin' behind the breast-plough or sweatin' over haysel an' harvest. I shall

276

make ladies out o' my daughters; Taunton folk's'll touch their caps to me an' my sons.'

'Money don't make ladies – nor gentlemen, either. 'Tis schoolin' they be short of, an' the company of other children.'

'Send 'em to school then!' He lurched towards the spiral staircase, 'Do anything you bloody well want to. I shud of known that nothin' I ever do cud please you.'

Sin was a universal reality for Eliza. It was as tangible as her own red hair. Even though she had never travelled further than Taunton and Fallon's Court, and the number of souls known to her was small, most of the wickedness and shame contained in the world must, she felt, be present here in Buckland St Mary, and more particularly on Larksleve. Acceptance of Philip's gifts was a fresh dilemma. In the past she had been able to believe that such presents had been paid for, at least in part, with Larksleve money. But not now. Gambling, for him, had become a way of living. He no longer concealed his compulsion. 'No more sweatin' over haysel an' harvest,' he had said, 'Taunton folk's'll touch their caps to me an' my sons.'

Eliza's girls accepted their father's gifts, while still reserving their right to detest the donor. Candace, practical as ever, said, 'They cloaks is all too long. But us can make muffs with the strips cut off the bottom. Muffs is bein' worn these days, according to the *Courier*.'

Mina said, 'I s'pose 'tis all right? That money do come from racetracks, but proper clothes an' boots do mean church on Sundays.'

Blanche preened up and down the kitchen in her purple cloak and lavender bonnet. 'Course 'tis all right! Us shud take as much from Pa as us can get. Us got to grab an' grab, maids – while the silly old fool still got some money!'

She was in two minds now about the efficacy of the pig's heart and the dead kitten in the chimney. She talked it over with Loveday. 'That man is in league wi' the Devil,' Loveday said bluntly. ''Un do only seem to thrive, an' wax rich on overlookin' an ill-wishin'.'

'Pa's very rich,' Blanche confided, 'I see'd the kitchen table all covered wi' sovereigns.'

'An' I'll bet not much o' that gold'll come your Ma's way.'

'He bought her a carriage wi' side-lights and leather cushions.'

'Thass on'y to drive his strumpets about in when he's in Taunton.'

'What's a strumpet?'

'A girl what's no better than she should be – a painted hussy.'

'I think I'll be a strumpet. I fancy painting my face an' ridin' in a carriage.'

Loveday laughed. 'I can just see you, my lovely! You'd make the wickedest woman what Taunton ever saw.' Loveday looked thoughtful. 'P'raps us had better leave your Pa in peace for the time being. Us had better not kill the golden goose just yet – eh maid?'

Eliza, who knew little or nothing about such matters, thought vaguely that her child-bearing years would be over after forty. There had been her aunt Annis who had died in child-birth at the age of forty-one. 'Disgustin',' had been Elizabeth Greypaull's judgement upon her sister, at the time. But Eliza had seen hard work and exhaustion as the cause of the stillborn daughter and the mother's death.

Philip's absences in Taunton, those nights when she slept alone and unmolested, had become a reprieve for Eliza. The years had coarsened him; there had never been much gentleness in him, but he used her lately as he used his horse, mercilessly and without care. Blackdown farmers rarely locked their houses, but Eliza had taken to drawing the bolts across the main doors, barring all entry to Larksleve after dark. She who abhorred the lie direct had invented a prowler, had insisted on this excuse as a need to protect her growing daughters.

She would waken on nights of storm and sleeting rain and hear the mare's hooves clop into the yard. She would hear Philip's footsteps as he stumbled to the porch, hear the smashing of his fist against a panel and his curses when he discovered that she had barred the house doors against him. Four heads: two dark, one fair, one auburn, would nod wisely together. Eliza's daughters would watch from their bedroom window as their father made his uncertain way towards the stables. He would come back to the front porch many times before morning, to assault the front door. He would appear at the breakfast table unwashed, unshaven, the straw still clinging to his hair and clothing. It was not difficult to hate him.

Her seventh pregnancy was so unexpected that she believed herself to be suffering from a tumour, and, in fact, Eliza, who had never ailed in her life, seemed to fail and sicken now even unto death. It had taken a consultation with the doctor in Whitestaunton, to convince her of her condition. 'I be too old for all this,' she sobbed to Loveday, 'an' I be fair wore-out what with one thing an' another. I shall die this time, Loveday, I knows it. An' whatever will happen to my children?'

The baby was due in November, and Eliza, so nauseous and dizzy that she could barely walk upright, allowed herself to be persuaded by her girls and Loveday that she should reserve her strength and spend part of each day in bed. This year the blossom on Larksleve nodded in the hedgerows, but remained ungathered. Jams and jellies were made if and when the girls found time. Eliza had trained them well, but the burden of the younger children fell on Candace and Madelina; Blanche, slothful and crafty, shadowed Loveday; and Jackie, who was a boy and therefore superior, did just as he pleased.

The fact that Larksleve was solvent for the first time in years gave Eliza no pleasure. Tainted gold had bought the food they ate, paid Loveday's wages, and clothed and shod her children. Of all the precious herd, only one beast remained in the meadow to serve them as house-cow. Her dairy was unused; all her beautiful marble dishes and slabs lay as white and still as Eliza herself. The butter-churn was turned once weekly by a reluctant Blanche to supply their own table. The cheese-house was closed, its troughs polished and unused, all its shelves bare. The Larksleve fields lay fallow, choked with weeds and stones. Samuel Greypaull gathered in their scanty hay-crop and deposited it, without a word, behind the barn by moonlight.

Eliza lay on heaped-up pillows and remembered Meri; she raised a hand to touch the coral pendant and found that her throat was bare. She recalled the bailiff who had wound the silver chain around his fingers. ''Tis an ugly lookin' piece,' he had said, 'Reckon as how you'll never miss it.'

She walked in the late October sunshine, weak and unsteady, certain in her heart that she was seeing Larksleve for the last time. This year the cider-apples had gone ungathered. They lay where they had fallen in red and yellow heaps, rotting among the long grass in the orchard.

Philip was hardly aware of events at Larksleve. Eliza's pregnancy, his six children, the house, the farm occupied the closed places in his mind where depression lived, and a certainty of his own failure. If he thought of Eliza at all it was when he had reached the maudlin stage of the evening.

'I shud never have married, you know,' he would tell his companion of the night. 'I wed wi' my cousin – a mean, red-haired woman. She tried to make a farmer of me!'

The room in the Turk's Head tavern was reserved now on a permanent basis. The snug little room at the top of the staircase, with its wood-fire burning, and the racing-prints around the walls, was more home to him than Larksleve had ever been. In it he kept his fine clothes, entertained his 'ladies', and spent hours considering 'form' and 'runners' with his new and aristocratic friends of the Taunton racecourse. Dissipation of one sort and another had limited his judgement; instant gratifications and ease of mind and body were more necessary to him than ever. He still visited Macey's, but it was his skill at judging horseflesh, his ability to assess and then back a winner, that had caught the attention of the 'quality' who sat high in the exclusive grandstands.

Racing had always attracted the highest and the lowest; on racedays a royal prince might rub shoulders with tramps and vagrants and not feel demeaned. But, at first, Philip Greypaull had been nervous among the nobility, he had tried to adapt his speech, to be deferential, obsequious even. He had recognised his own value only when Toby Hoare-Leggatt began to consult him before placing a single bet.

Self-deception had never been difficult for Philip. To be taken-up by the likes of Hoare-Leggatt reaffirmed his old conviction that as a chime-child he was still one to whom great and glorious things were bound to happen. He began to travel with his new companions; he visited Newmarket, Epsom and Goodwood, riding in the first-class compartments of railway-trains, transported by phaeton to the racecourse; and, to begin with, Philip had been astonished at the scope and luxury of the arrangements for a single day's racing. Hoare-Leggatt always travelled with his 'man', a silent, broad-shouldered servant, who carried one hamper filled with china, cutlery and linen, and another which was crammed with food and wine. Philip soon became familiar with cold game pie and lobster salad, strawberries and cream, and champagne. His instinct for the corrupt and dishonest, his knowledge of the villanies perpetrated by welshing bookmakers, bribable trainers and jockeys, ensured that his high-born companions avoided many pitfalls; and they were not ungrateful.

Toby Hoare-Leggatt was the son of an old and illustrious Somerset family, a young man who would one day inherit a landed estate. He was a pleasant easy-going youth, disliked by his father and indulged by his mother. His involvement with Philip Greypaull, profitable to begin with, was now leading him to speculate more heavily than he could afford. Some of the Buckland farmer's obsession with gambling had transferred itself to Toby; he lived for that moment when, with all bets placed, the horses saddled and cantering to the start, the flag would go down and the race begin. But the partnership with Philip was not always successful: a horse, suddenly and inexplicably gone lame, an early faller in a big race, and Hoare-Leggatt suddenly found himself in the kind of trouble which could force a man to flee the country, or blow his brains out.

They were riding in Hoare-Leggatt's phaeton on their way back to Taunton. The driver had been instructed to go by way of Ilminster and Chard so that Philip might be set down as close as possible to Larksleve. The losses of that disastrous day had been submerged beneath a quantity of whisky by all but Toby Hoare-Leggatt. He had not uttered a single word since leaving the racecourse.

They drove through Chard and began the long climb uphill towards Buckland St Mary. The phaeton halted just outside the village. 'Well,' said Philip awkwardly, 'that's it then. See you next weekend, in Macey's.'

'Not me. I'm finished.' Hoare-Leggatt covered his face with both hands and began to weep.

'For God's sake, man!' Philip shouted, 'things bain't that bad. Us on'y lost a couple o' races. You got to expect a few setbacks.'

'I was in too deep, Phil. Those races were intended to recoup my earlier losses. I - I wasn't betting with my own money - I only get a paltry allowance. I hocked some stuff with Jeremiah Jones - got him to stand me a sizeable loan. He'll go straight to my father.' Toby lowered his hands and looked straight at Philip. 'It's not the first time I've been in trouble. The old man threatened to transport me if it happened again.' He paused, 'I don't like to ask you, but I'm desperate this time, I - I don't suppose you could see your way clear - a pledge, perhaps?'

The whisky fumes were strong in Philip's brain. The reversal of roles in which a young blood like Hoare-Leggatt was reduced to appealing for money from a Buckland farmer made him reckless. He hooked his thumbs into his waistcoat pockets. 'Anything, my boy! Anything what I can do to oblige you. You only got to say the word.'

'I'm talking about a lot of money, Phil. More straight cash than you could possibly lay hands on. You see - I'm in pretty deep to Jeremiah - '

'Don't you never worry, Toby old man!' Philip reached over to pat Hoare-Leggatt's shoulder. He pointed upwards, towards the hills that rolled out towards Exmoor. 'See that farmhouse - the white one, wi' the steep rise goin' up behind it? That's Larksleve. That's all my property, free-hold an' unencumbered.' He paused to drink deeply from the young man's proffered hip-flask. He wiped his mouth with the back of his hand. 'Tell 'ee what I'll do - but on'y for my very good friend, mind! I'll pledge that whole issue: farmhouse an' outbuildings, barn an' dairy, land an' livestock. I'll cover your debt to Jeremiah! That'll keep the old devil off our backs until us can recoup our losses.' He gazed blearily at Hoare-Leggatt. 'How's that, then, for a proof of friendship?'

Hoare-Leggatt wept again, with gratitude this time. His display of emotion would have been embarrassing to anyone less drunk than Philip. That the young man carried pen, ink and paper so conveniently inside the picnic hamper also failed to surprise him.

The pledge, written rapidly in a form of words with which his friend seemed only too familiar, was signed by Philip Greypaull, and witnessed by the manservant Joseph Oates. It was dated November 1st, 1875.

Philip left the phaeton and began the steep climb up to Larksleve. Evening was coming down; dry leaves rustled beneath his feet, and the smells of wood-smoke and bracken mingled strong on the quiet air. He paused at a twist in the lane, took breath, and felt his head clear a little. He had an unusual view of the farmhouse, its whiteness blurred between tall trees, its windows lit and secure between blue shutters.

He knew every inch of the house which lay behind those windows: the children's bedrooms, Jackie's birds' egg collection set out on an oak chest, the samplers on every wall, stitched by his four daughters, the room he shared with Eliza, the canopied bed, the mahogany closets, the flowered wash-stand china, the rose-tinted glass of the oil-lamp's funnel. He recalled the parlour: the piano, the horsehair sofa, the aspidistra drooping on the what-not, all that cold blue gloom preserved behind close drawn blinds.

He was reluctant to think about the kitchen, that woman's domain, its bluestone flags worn smooth by the feet of many Greypaull wives. He remembered the shotgun racked above the fireplace, the hearthstone upon which he had once violated Eliza. He thought about his children, touched them fearfully, one by one, with his mind's finger, and was afraid.

He remembered the pledge given to Hoare-Leggatt, and witnessed by the servant, Joseph Oates, and Philip was suddenly down on his knees, cold-sober and retching helplessly among the dead leaves.

Eliza was sick, sick enough to need a doctor. Loveday had taken advantage of Philip's rare presence on Larksleve to say as much. 'Her never bin like this before. Not in all the years what I've know'd her. I see'd her safe through six deliveries, but her bain't right wi' this one. Jus' you look at her, Master!'

The baby was due at the end of November. Philip looked at Eliza and felt his soul cringe away from the sight of her thin face and freckled hands, her swollen body, and the hair, still red and defiant, that curled from beneath her white cap. He remembered how Will Gardner had once pushed his dead wife and stillborn infant on a handcart towards a pauper's funeral. He counted up the sovereigns that remained in the velvet bag. 'Us'll go over to Whitesaunton,' he told Eliza, 'Loveday reckons as how you need a doctor.'

They drove to Whitestaunton that same evening, and Eliza, seated high on the phaeton and wrapped in a thick cloak, seemed to him to be an unlikely passenger for this particular vehicle. As if she had read his thoughts, Eliza said, ''Tis a long time since we two rode out together, Philip. That must seem strange to you, to have your wedded wife sitting up beside you.'

The remark made him angry. He had been drinking steadily since midday, as was his habit. Now, he pulled out a silver hip-flask and took a long swig at the whisky. He whipped up the horses, and the high-sprung vehicle leapt forward; it bounced across the uneven surface, and swayed around corners in the twisty lanes, until Eliza cried out, 'Oh, Philip! Do 'ee slow down, I beg you. The candles in the sidelights is guttering, an' likely to blow out.'

The whisky had touched his brain; he laughed, then shouted, ''Tis what you needs, Eliza! Too much lyin' about have made you sluggish. A good shakin'-up is what you wants – ' As he negotiated the sharp corner into White-staunton village, the phaeton tilted, ran for a few yards on two wheels, and then slowly turned over.

She would never forget the tilting of the phaeton, or those moments of terror when she had clung to the side-rails and willed the vehicle to remain upright. There had been a swift descent across a hedge, and down into a stackyard. She had heard the shattering of glass, felt pain, and seen the candles fall out of their holders to land among the loose straw and set fire to the stack. Eliza had known agony then; first in her head and eyes, and then low down across her body. Someone had lifted the weight from her legs and dragged her away from the flames. Her vision had blurred until all she had seen was a point of light which whirled her away and down into darkness.

The first sound she heard was the crying of an infant; the first face she saw was that of Dr Priddy. Eliza laid both hands upon her stomach and found it flat and empty. She began to laugh. This, she thought, must surely be the only birth that she was never to recall with horror. Her laughter alarmed the doctor, he was an old man who feared hysterical women.

'You're all right now, Mrs Greypaull. You're tucked up

safe in your own bed, and a fine son is in the cradle here beside you.' He took her hand and stroked it. 'You've had a bad time. Now tell me where you feel the pain.'

Eliza stopped laughing. 'My head,' she said slowly, 'my head feels heavy, and I can only see with one eye.' She tried to sit up. 'Be I blinded, Doctor? Do 'ee tell the truth – is my sight gone?'

'Lie still, now! Of course you're not blind – you can see me, can't you?' Eliza touched the bandages on her head, and traced them downwards towards her left eye. ' 'Tis on'y the bandage,' she said relieved. 'I was frightened, just for the minute.'

Dr Priddy turned swiftly away towards the cradle. 'Don't you want to see your son? He's a beauty.'

'He's the on'y one I never screamed for,' smiled Eliza. 'Imagine that, doctor. A bang on the head – and when I wake up – 'tis all over.' She gazed at the child in the doctor's arms. 'That don't seem right somehow, that I never suffered for him.'

'What do you intend to call him?'

'I don't know. After the first four babies, the names don't seem to be quite so important.'

'I'd be honoured if you would call him Louis. It was my father's name, and it is my name – and since I don't have a son – '

'Why, o' course, Dr Priddy. 'Tis a lovely name, though a strange one. That'll make the Greypaulls sit up an' take notice. We be all Williams an' Walters an' Johns.'

'Ah – family tradition, I hadn't considered that. Perhaps you should call him after his father?'

'Philip?' Eliza shuddered. 'Philip is a bad name to have if your name is Greypaull. There'll never be another one – never! Not in my family.'

'Then Louis it shall be, and you may be sure, Mrs Greypaull, that he'll be remembered in my Will.'

287

The baby, so Loveday informed her, was already two days old.

'Two days,' cried Eliza, 'I can't have bin knocked-out for that long!'

'Oh yes, you was, Missus. I thought that you was dead when they brought you home.' Loveday began to sob. 'I never meant it to harm you, maid. 'Twas him I wanted to finish, an' there 'un sits, rockin' hisself to an' fro in my kitchen, just as right as ninepence, and that useless kitten's corpse still resting up the chimney!'

'Is he sober?'

'Bin sober these two days.'

'Send 'un up yer.'

'You be supposed to lie quiet, doctor said so, no rowin' or shoutin'.'

'I cudden shout at this moment.'

''Un won't come up. Doctor tried to force 'un, but 'tweren't no use.'

'Then let 'un bide. Send my girls – send all my children.'

They came to her bedside: Candace frowning to hide emotion, Mina weeping at the sight of her bandages and bruises, Jackie scuffing boots embarrassedly across the bedroom lino, Blanche, remembering the kitten in the chimney, looked guilty but defiant. Loveday brought Simeon and Annis and showed them their new brother.

Eliza counted them, all six strong and healthy, and with no taint of that madness which was said to result when cousin married cousin. She reached for the coral pendant at her throat, and then remembered that she no longer wore it. She looked down at the new child in her arms, and a tiny lamp of fear lit up inside her.

She lay in her bed and could not remember if it had been a day or a week since she had fallen from the phaeton. After

288

that first hour of lucidity, and wonder at the baby born without her knowledge, Eliza slipped back into a time of confusion. She had nightmares in which candles toppled over slowly into strawricks, and it was always Philip who screamed and burned in the flames. She tried to tear the bandage from her left eye and had to be restrained. She believed that a herd of cows stood unmilked in the Home meadow, that hay stood uncut in the high fields, and a whole grain harvest waited to be gathered upon Larksleve.

The Greypaulls had heard the news from the carter: about the accident in Whitestaunton, about the son that had been born to Eliza on that same night. They did not come. John and Elizabeth rocked beside their own fire, kept their feet firmly planted on their own hearthstone. 'Us be too old for so much trouble,' said Elizabeth, 'an' her got Loveday alongside her, an' all her own maidens.'

Samuel Greypaull said to Daniel, his father, 'Us shud visit in time o' trouble. 'Tidden Christian not to do so.' Daniel said, 'I wudden breathe the same air as Philip Greypaull. I won't have his name mentioned in this house no more.'

A month passed; Christmas came and went. The baby, Louis, took a fever and was baptised in haste by the Reverend Soames across a bowl of water in the Larksleve kitchen; and still Eliza lay upon her pillows and would not stir. ''Tis as if the will hev gone out of her,' said Loveday to Candace. 'Doctor reckons that her is recovered in body. That eye do still trouble her some, but doctor won't let her take off the bandage. Her bain't ready for that, yet, so he says.'

People, Elizabeth Greypaull had said, usually deserved the misfortunes that befell them, and that old nightmare of the bolting horse had come true in a way that Eliza had not expected. But still, her anticipation of disaster was as powerful as ever. It lived with her now like a demanding child, draining her of strength, enervating her spirit. Not even the removal of the bandage, the revelation of the scorched cheek and eyelid, badly healed and inevitably scarred, could lessen her terror of the blow that was yet to fall. Not even the knowledge that she now lacked all vision in her left eye could satisfy Eliza's premonition that the greatest sorrow of all had not yet come upon her.

There had been some talk of school for Blanche and Annis, and perhaps for Jackie, but it had come to nothing. The sovereigns that remained in the velvet bag were diminishing with every week that Philip stayed close to Larksleve. Jackie, who could read a little and write his own name, was relieved when the threat of lessons was lifted from him, and, as Mina said, he was needed now to bring home the firewood, feed and milk the cow, and do errands in the village.

Jackie loved his mother, feared his father, and trusted Mina. His life was lived mainly among horses, his own, and those of other people. He was known and welcomed in every gypsy encampment from the Blackdowns up to the fringe of Exmoor. He scorned the use of a saddle and rode, like a Romani chie, with no more than a bit and bridle to aid him. He had courage of the reckless kind that will set a horse at a high hedge at the risk of a broken neck. Sometimes he met his grandfather Daniel, riding along the lanes or in the high woods. 'Remember, boy,' he would say to Jackie, 'remember that all this is yours in the years to come. All what has bin done, for good or ill, was done for your sake. Us wudden never have wedded your mother to your father, but for the need to keep Larksleve in the family.'

One day, greatly daring, he had looked up at the proud old man seated high on his chestnut hunter, at the stern face and flowing whiskers, and said, 'Supposin' as how I don't want it, Grandfather?'

His grandfather had raised his riding crop, and then

lowered it again. He had studied Jackie for a long time, had looked down from the superior height of his own mare to where Jackie sat, small and skinny on his Exmoor pony. 'You got guts, boy. But whether they be of the right kind I'll take leave to question.' He paused and stroked his snowy whiskers. 'Whass your name, then? Your full name?'

'Why – 'tis James John Daniel Greypaull – but you knows that!'

'Thass exactly what I thought 'twas. Now you lissen careful, an' I'll tell 'ee somethin'. This James John Daniel Greypaull is an important feller. He was made especially by the livin' God of Abraham an' Moses to live yer on Larksleve. He was born to plough this land an' bring forth crops in their rotation. To plant striplings, an' lay down plantations so that generations yet to come shall in their turn call down blessings upon his name. Do 'ee understand, boy, what I be saying?'

His grandfather had pointed a finger towards the farmhouse. 'I was born in that house, boy. Just like you was. But I had a conniving brother what curried favour wi' our uncle and got me cheated o' my birthright. But nobody'll ever cheat you, James Greypaull! 'Specially not that evil creature what you do call father.'

It was some weeks later, soon after the birth of Louis, when Jackie came upon that evil creature, his father. He was seated on a fallen log in Pickett's Copse. In one hand he held a half empty whisky bottle, in the other he clutched the shotgun. Jackie had watched him from a thicket, had seen his father tip his head back, take a long swig from the bottle, and then open his mouth once more and insert the barrel of the shotgun between his lips. Jackie had waited to hear the gun's report, to see the blood and brains spill out across the dead leaves, to see the pigeons fly upwards into the beech boughs. He had waited for a long time, but in the end his father had laid down the shotgun and picked up the

291

bottle. Jackie had moved away, silently, along the ride-way. He told no one, not even Mina, of what he had seen that day. It was a pity, he thought, that his father had lacked the necessary courage to pull the trigger.

The bolting horse of Eliza's nightmare was to come to rest at last on a sweet spring morning. Warm sunshine had lured her outdoors; she went slowly into her garden, leaned upon the gate, and saw primrose and violet already in bloom along the steep banks of the lane.

The name of Larksleve had spelled itself out again in late snowdrop and early crocus. 'See there,' she said to Annis, 'see how the letters is writ in flowers. Do 'ee always remember that pretty sight, maid, in the years to come. 'Tis the name of your home spelled in white an' yellow.' She turned at the sound of hooves, and saw two men riding down the lane. She recognised the bowler hats, the sober suiting. For a moment she clung to the garden gate, she spoke calmly. ''Tis the bailiff's men come back again,' she said to Annis, 'you had better go up, maid, an' wake your father.'

Philip came into the kitchen, and this morning he had put on the flannel shirt and moleskin trousers of a working farmer. As if, thought Eliza, by the wearing of suitable clothes he could possibly persuade these men that he was, in fact, an industrious and sober yeoman.

The children had come running from their morning tasks; they gathered around her sensing, as they had always done, that this was yet another of those times of trouble in which she would need support. They seated themselves in the inglenook settles; Candace held Simeon in her arms, while Loveday rocked the baby Louis. All were now present.

'Sit down, Mr Greypaull,' the Court Officer looked stern but sad, as if he was not enjoying this particular mission. 'I think you know who and what we are?'

'I know it.'

'I also think you know what brings us here?'

'No,' said Philip, 'I don't know. Why should I?'

'You are acquainted with the Honourable Toby Hoare-Leggatt?'

'I am.'

'In fact, he could be described as a friend – a very close friend?'

'Not close. I on'y met him a few months ago.'

'But close enough, Mr Greypaull. Close enough to cover a gambling debt for him.'

Eliza looked at Philip's face and read disaster in it, and suddenly the wild horse inside her reared up and fell back in terror. She knew that this was the point towards which she had hurtled for so many years. The headlong flight had ended, her nightmare horse would bolt no more.

The Court Officer was repeating his question. 'A gambling debt, Mr Greypaull, of a size which involved you in pledging your entire estate?'

'I was drunk. We both were.'

The men held up a sheet of paper. 'It's a legible statement, properly signed by you, and witnessed by one Joseph Oates. I'll read it to you. It says, "I, Philip Greypaull, yeoman, of Larksleve Farm in the County of Somerset, do pledge my entire estate for the means of covering all debts and monies owed by Tobias Miles Hoare-Leggatt." That's clear enough, Mr Greypaull. Look here – do you deny your signature?'

'I signed it,' said Philip, 'but I was drunk. He talked me into it – he cried – he said he'd bin in trouble, that his father 'ud transport him.'

'And so he has, Mr Greypaull! Young Hoare-Leggatt is at this moment on board a cattle-boat bound for Australia. But the debt remains, and the debt is yours.'

'You wudden take all I got? You cudden – I got seven children and a wife.'

'You should have considered that a long time ago.' The Court Officer looked angry. 'The pledge is a legal document properly signed by you in the presence of a witness. The excuse that you were drunk at the time won't be of help if you decide to enter upon litigation.'

'Litigation? How could I go to litigation. That costs money.'

'Then I have to serve Notice of Quittal upon you, Mr Greypaull. I think you probably know the procedure. There will have to be a sale, held here, of course, on Larksleve – '

'I know – I know.' Philip stood up suddenly. 'Leave your damned Notice and get out!' he shouted. 'You've said what you came to say, now leave me alone!'

Loveday beckoned to the children and they followed her in silence out of the kitchen. Eliza was left alone with Philip. 'Well,' she said, 'so you did it in the end. You rid yourself of Larksleve.'

He opened his lips to speak, but no words came. Eliza sat down to face him across the table, one hand lifted to hide her scarred and sightless eye, as was her habit. She said softly, 'Nothing much left that you cud do to harm me was there, except to take away my home.'

''Twas never like that, Eliza.'

'Oh, I think it was. You've bin punishing me, one way and another, since the day us got wed. You know what this means – it means the Poorhouse for us all.'

'Greypaulls 'ud never let that happen. Can you see an Overseer of the Poor committing his own family?'

She shook her head. 'Greypaulls hev abandoned us, long since. I went once to my brother Francis and he showed me the door. Your father and mine be old men now, they got other, more deservin' children to look out for. Don't you ever pin your faith in the family.'

'They won't never put us in the Poorhouse,' he insisted, 'they cudden stand the shame.'

'They've had plenty of practice in standing shame wi' you, Philip. We all have.'

'Don't turn against me, Liza. Us got to stand together now in our hour of need.'

She removed her hand from the sightless eye and pointed at the burned and puckered flesh of her left cheek. 'You blinded me in one eye,' she whispered, 'but I got sight enough left in the other. I hev forgiven you so many times, but you hev used me shamefully Philip. I see you very clearly and, God forgive me, but I do loathe an' detest what I see.'

Eliza, who had rarely been without a child in her arms or about her skirts, now had an unusual and passionate wish to walk by herself.

'I'm going to Castle Farm,' she told Loveday.

'Be you fit to go alone, Missus?'

'I'll be all right.'

But she had no intention of visiting her mother, instead she made for the lane that led into Dommett Wood. She walked down slowly across meadow grass, and the morning air was bright and full of birdsong. Already, the violets were massing in the shady places, the primroses full and pale in the hedgerows. There was green along the hawthorns and in the crowns of trees. She thought briefly forwards, towards haysel, and then remembered that it no longer concerned her.

Eliza came back to that dim green place, narrowed in its beginnings by hedges of untrimmed blackthorn which still grew inwards and shut out the daylight. She stood at that gate which hung between the blackthorns, and looked into the secretive shuttered clearing from which Meridiana had once come running.

The lane still drew Eliza. She moved as near to her father's gate as she could without actually touching it. For a moment she saw the painted waggons drawn into a circle, smelled the bacon frying, heard the chavvies crying. She seemed to hear Meri's urgent whisper, 'You'm not wedded then?' and her own reply, 'Next month, on the first day of May. To my cousin Philip.'

To remember, like this, was painful and self-indulgent. There would always be the Spartan inside her which rejected memories and regrets. She had never been the one to cry for the moon – and yet how was she to go on with her life while Buckland and Larksleve still filled her heart and mind?

She thought about the week that had just passed: the arrival of the Court Officers, the first shock of knowing that Larksleve had been pledged away, the agony that followed. To begin with she had doubted the God who could punish her like this without cause or reason. The Reverend Soames had come; they had knelt in the parlour and prayed together for understanding. The prayers had calmed her. As the Reverend Soames had pointed out, she still had her seven children, all strong and healthy, and devoted to Eliza. If she would hold on to Faith, believe in God's divine purpose, in His wisdom, then she would come through this Vale of Tears and emerge, strong and triumphant, into eternal glory.

There had been other visitors that week: all their Greypaull aunts and cousins, their uncles and brothers. Even the parents who had abandoned them in time of need had hauled their bones into carriage and dog-cart, and come to survey the wreckage that was Larksleve. Oh, they could come now! To remonstrate, upbraid, to have their say and give advise about the uncertain future which lay before Eliza and her doomed children.

No choice in life had ever been allowed her. She remembered Meri asking, 'You'm still feared o' your mother?' and her own reply, 'Aren't you?' 'I's seventeen,' Meri had told her, 'I do's what I wants to.'

Once again, it was the Greypaulls who had decided upon the future of Philip and Eliza. They had sat, last night, around her kitchen table, all those proud bewhiskered yeomen, their plump complacent wives. They had decided upon Taunton as a suitable place of banishment, eleven tortuous miles from Larksleve and set down in the anonymity of the crowded town, the shame of the Philip Greypaulls would, they trusted, soon be forgotten by the people of Buckland.

It had not surprised her to learn that Daniel owned property in Taunton. ''Tidden no palace,' he had warned them. 'Number Two, Hunter's Court is a one-up two-down cottage, just off East Reach.' He had cleared his throat noisily to gain maximum attention. 'I won't charge 'ee no rent, though 'tis a sacrifice to me. I was gettin' three and sixpence a week from the previous tenant.'

'One-up two-down,' Eliza had cried, 'but there's nine of us, uncle!' The family had all glanced sideways, one towards the other. 'What is it?' she had demanded, 'Tell me quick what you got in mind!'

John, her father, had said, 'Now you got to be sensible, maid. It do stand to reason that you can't provide food for nine mouths – 'specially in the town.' He had looked uneasily around the table. 'Us have talked it over, very careful. There is only one answer to be found. They three oldest children must be sent from home to work away. Candace is seventeen, Mina is fifteen; us reckons that domestic service in London 'ull be the best chance for them. As for James – well he's a natural horseman. There's a stable what breeds steeplechasers down to Bishop's Hull. The master there is willing to take the boy – no wages – but live-in, all found. That'll leave you to manage with the four youngest.' John had waved a hand at the assembled Greypaulls. 'Everybody here have chipped-in with money. There's enough to buy an annuity – but in your name on'y, Eliza! That'll give you a reg'lar sum every week. Enough for you to live on.'

Philip had not been consulted. He had stayed in a corner of the kitchen, silent in the shadows. It had been, she thought, as if he were already dead, and not one of his kin prepared or anxious decently to bury his body.

Eliza walked back to Larksleve along the sunken lane, and it was like the aisle in church on a Sunday morning; like the hush that comes between the ceasing of bells and the intoning of first prayers, that time when God is very close and faith comes easy. She stood at the entrances to her fields, numbered them in her heart, and recalled the haysels and harvests when she was a young wife, still filled with hope and plans for a barn filled with grain, sheds with stock. She wept at last, unable to hold back the agonies which wracked her. She knelt down on the rutted track and let the dust trickle through her fingers. She raised a hand and touched the scarred skin of her left cheek, the sightless eye. Well, she told herself, you did try, maid. You tried, an' it never made no diff'rence. Now you must set your foot on another path, turn your face towards Taunton. There's three children to get ready for a life out in the wide world, four young ones still to rear, and a husband, a poor broken creature, destroyed by his own hand, in body and spirit.

The selling-up of Larksleve had been fixed for the first day of April. Notices had gone up all around the district. Assessors had come out from Taunton to value the place. They had cast a speculative eye. 'Rundown,' they had said, 'but good farmland. Nice house, in neat order.' The whole lot together should just about cover the debts owed by Tobias Hoare-Leggatt. They spoke kindly to Eliza; they advised her to pack up her family's personal effects. Nothing much left but the rubbish, they had said, when farmers have bid in a final sale.

The day of the sale marked an end for Eliza. Her mind could not reach towards the cottage in a Court off Each Reach, Taunton; it was quite unimaginable to her. Even the practicalities of life after Larksleve, the fact that they would be without furniture and beds, cooking utensils and linen had not yet impinged upon the misery that gripped her. She rose early, aware that every smallest task was to be performed for the last time in this house. She stood in the front porch, and in the half-light she could see all the Implements in Husbandry ranged around the farmyard. She stepped out into the chill of early April and walked between the rows of worn-out equipment. The auctioneer's men were setting out riddles with broken meshes, flails on which the hand-staff had become detached from the swingle, broken baskets and shovels, blunt scythes and sickles, hay knives with badly split handles. It was only her cheese-making and dairy equipment which still gave her cause for pride. She touched the salting-trough and cheese-press, handled the hairsieves and the beautiful marble dishes for cream which her mother had once donated. She came to the milking stools and shoulder-yokes, and saw how the elm and willow wood had been worn, smooth as satin, from all those years of handling by herself and Loveday. Several broken tines had devalued the harrow; the wooden plough had rotted, its iron share and coulter thick with red rust.

The children were to wait out that last day in Loveday's cottage. Eliza watched them go down the lane towards Cherry Furlong, a sad little group, each child holding on for comfort to the hand of a favourite brother or sister. Mina walked with Jackie, Annis with Simeon, Candace carried the baby Louis in her arms. Blanche walked alone.

Eliza looked for Philip and saw his tall bowed figure

going uphill towards Pickett's Copse. Her eyes sought the shotgun and found it still racked above the inglenook fireplace. But she had already known that he would never have the courage.

Suamico, Brown County.

Dear cousin Eliza,

It is some years since I last wrote and much has happened in that time. As you know, a sister of mine, Elizabeth Vickary, left Buckland some years ago and came to America. She lives with her family in Suamico, Brown County which lies West from Chicago. After the deaths of Mr Salter and Eddie, I was persuaded by Elizabeth to move from Chicago, and settle in Suamico. This I did, and with happy outcome. I became acquainted with a Mr James Black, who had been an Army Lieutenant in the Civil War, and we were recently *married*. I received considerable Assets from the Sale of Mr Salter's Meat Business in Chicago, and have been able to purchase The Farm I have always wanted.

This is a Beautiful Country. Having only lived in cities I was surprised to see the lakes and forests as we travelled West to Suamico. I am well-settled here with Mr James Black, who is *Steady* and *Reliable* and a *Good Father* to my three children. George is now eighteen, Rosalind sixteen, and John nine. John still delicate in health, but have great hopes of Country Air.

I hear no news of you and Philip. As you know, it was ever my dear Father who was the letter-writer in our family, and since his sad Death, few letters do come from England. I am kept very busy with the Farm, also Sewing. The winters very cold here, and I am busy Quilting. Shall need to make at least three new Quilts before next winter, also dresses for self and Rosalind, store-bought goods being expensive and not always *Good*. Mr Black kept busy with the Farm, and the building up of a New Church here in Suamico. Have done *Sewing* and held several *Suppers* to raise money for our new Church which is *Badly Needed*.

Kind regards to all,

Your affectshunat cousin, Rhoda.

They came bowling up to Larksleve in their hundreds, on horseback and phaeton, on farmcart and waggon, all of them cheerful, joking and laughing like people on an outing. They remarked on the fineness of the April morning, anticipated the chance of a knock-down bargain. Eliza, alone, had remained on Larksleve. She sat in her rocking-chair and heard the voice of the Taunton autioneer as he disposed of her life. There was a sudden silence, and then the shuffle of many feet as people moved towards the house. Eliza, who had hardly eaten in the past two weeks, now experienced the revulsion of feeling in her stomach. She stood up, swayed towards the window, and felt the scalding bile burn her throat. God give me strength, she pleaded, God help me through this coming hour!

She followed the crowd through the rooms of the farm-house; Eliza studied the eager faces, saw the flicker of old spite, heard the gloat of satisfaction thicken bidding voices. She caught a sight of Samuel Greypaull, the furrows deeper in his face just lately, his eyes anxious. Under the hammer went the oaken settles, the kitchen table, the dresser packed with everyday china, the cooking-pots, the fire irons. They moved on to the parlour. Eliza saw the last of her flowered carpet, her horsehair sofa, and the tasselled windowblinds which had preserved their colours for so many years. Her piano, that special item, had been left until the end. The farm wives of Buckland gathered eagerly around it, jostled for position and fixed their reluctant husbands with determined gaze.

'A fine piece,' said the auctioneer, 'well-cared for, and in perfect order. Rosewood, inlaid with tulip. A valuable item and one that would grace any discerning lady's parlour.' The discerning farm wives began to bid, one against the other, slowly at first, and then rashly. Eliza Greypaull's piano was the prize of the auction. A flurry of hands pledged their hard-earned egg-money, then their childrens' school fees, and their husbands' savings. The final, outrageous bid was made by a stout, red-faced matron from Broadway. The auctioneer raised his gavel. 'Going,' he shouted, 'for the last time of asking, who will give – '

Eliza came forward. In her hand was a piece of paper. 'The piano is not for sale,' she said firmly, 'it is my own property, bought from Mann's Music Emporium in Taunton and given to me by my father-in-law, Daniel Greypaull.' The auctioneer lowered his gavel. 'A woman's property becomes that of her husband upon marriage – you knows that as well as I do, Mrs Greypaull. The piano is in the sole ownership of Philip Greypaull and, as such, is tendered legally under the conditions of this sale.'

'No,' said Eliza, 'the piano was purchased after our marriage. It was a personal gift to me.' She handed over the bill of sale and her marriage certificate. 'Compare the dates,' she insisted. 'My father-in-law's intention was quite clear.'

The auctioneer looked confused. 'Is Daniel Greypaull here?' he demanded. Philip's father came forward. 'Is this true, Mr Greypaull? Did you give this piano to your son's wife?' Daniel chuckled. 'Matter o' fact, thass exactly what I did! 'Tis Liza's own property – looksee! Her have got the bill to prove it.'

There were angry mutterings among the farm wives. 'Trust they Greypaulls to find a way round the law,' said one. ''Tidden legal,' said another, 'I be sure that piano

302

don't belong to her – ' Still arguing and complaining, they moved through the hall and towards the spiral staircase, and Eliza, all courage spent, stepped outside into the front porch. She could not bear to see the sale of the canopied bed in which all her seven children had been born. She walked out into her garden and saw how the snowdrops and crocus which formed the name of Larksleve had withered and died in the past two weeks.

The sale was completed at midday; the farmcarts rolled away down the lane loaded up with bargains. Samuel Greypaull remained. He had come that morning with his largest waggon; he had bid for the canopied bed, the oaken settles, the everyday china and cooking-pots, the feather beds. When Philip came down from Pickett's Copse he saw the loaded cart and his brother standing beside it in conversation with Eliza.

Philip tried to smile. 'Whass all this then, bor? Is you at last setting up your own establishment away from our dear father? Cud it even be that you is getting married?'

They turned grim faces upon him. 'Your brother,' said Eliza, 'hev bought back everything what us'll need for the life in Taunton. We shall always have your Sam to thank for the beds we lie on, for the china, and the pots we cook with, for the very chairs we sit on.'

Philip turned away. As always, her sharp tongue, her facial expression, her tone of voice had unmanned him. All his life he had been saying thank you to somebody for something. Until now, escape and forgetfulness had been his option. But no more. For the first time in all the years of their life together, Eliza would be going with him down to Taunton.

Meridiana had sought escape from grief and found none. To be Rom was to believe in the survival of unquiet spirits; here

303

in this house, this village were the memories which would not let her go. She would look to the conical Hill and hear Luke's blood cry aloud, for hadn't he died violently and before his time? Her people had moved out from Norton Fitzwarren as soon as their dead had been buried, and the smallpox scourge at an end. She felt that same urge, that need to be up behind the grai, leading-reins in her right hand, and the drom stretching out, long and white before her.

But there were others to be considered, and Meri, who had lived until now in the belief that to be Rom was all that really counted, began, once again, to assess the effects of a wandering life upon her three children. Luke's wishes must be kept to; he had wanted Charles and Henry hidden safe away from all evil. She had worked long and hard in the fields, hoeing and turnip-singling, apple-picking in the season so that she might purchase their quiet retreat.

There was Jye. The boy had more gorgio in him than she cared to recognise. Oh, but he was beautiful to look upon! So much like Luke. Jye was tall for his age, contained and sure within himself: there was even a dignity about his silence. He would not be persuaded easily to leave Montacute and travel. He had sought and found the necessary acceptance and understanding of his handicap in the crowded house of his grandmother, Charity Carew. On a table beside his bed, Jye treasured his father's tools: Luke's old sharpening stone, all his mallets and chisels, kept rust-free and polished, wrapped in a piece of soft cloth. 'A few more months,' the boy had told his mother, 'and then you shall pay over my shilling. I shall start to be a mason on the very first day of my twelfth year.'

'And so you shall,' she had promised, 'but jus' now I needs you to go with me to a big town called Taunton. My mother and father died and was buried, a long time ago, in a place called Norton Fitzwarren. I never bin back, Jye. Never

304

bin able to lay a single flower atop their grave. Go with me, Jye. Let we ride together on the steam-train, and I shall show you the bender-tents of my Rom people.' They rode the train down to Taunton; sat stiff and proper in their mourning clothes, and spoke to no one. They passed through Athelney; through that low wet country where the withy-beds lay deep beneath the spring floods. They came to a stretch of the track where the flood-water entered the carriages by one door and flowed out by the other. They lifted their booted feet from the carriage floor and laughed to see the brown water rushing through the train. 'That cudden never happen in a waggon,' said Meri, 'us 'ud take a drier road.' She pointed to Glastonbury, to the Tor which rose to dominate the landscape. 'I went there once,' she told him, 'afore you was born. I went to find the boy Jesus; I felt the earth move on that hilltop.'

His mother's strangeness frequently disturbed him. She had visited far-off places, she talked about Dorset and Devon as if they were within reach, just a short step up the road. Jye had no wish to travel. He had never even made the four mile walk into Yeovil. There were tales, often told by his mother, of an evening when she, at the age of seventeen, had halted on the summit of Babylon Hill and looked down upon Yeovil. Somerset, so his mother had said, was for her like the Land promised by God to Abraham and Moses. Dorset was a dangerous county, where gypsies were often murdered. Bristol was a great and wicked city, where the people died of starvation and wore rags. It all sounded wild and dangerous to Jye. He gazed at the stationary clouds, the flying fields, the wispy steam that streamed past the window, and wished himself at home, eating cabbage-and-bacon in his grandmother's cottage.

Badgers Lane was empty. Meri studied the patteran of twigs

and leaves which had been left at the roadside and knew that Loveridges had recently pitched there. She knelt to touch the circle of wood-ash, and found it still warm; and that old restlessness crept beneath her skin, making her impatient with Jye. She gripped his shoulder and spun him around to face her. 'We hev missed 'em by minutes,' she said carefully, 'but there is others what can never leave Norton Fitzwarren.'

They walked to the churchyard where gypsy mounds took up one whole corner. A hawthorn bush had been planted on her parents' grave. Meri pulled a handful of scarlet ribbons from her pocket and began to thread them through the hawthorn's branches so that they streamed past her in the wind. She anticipated Jye's question. ''Tis the custom,' she began, but Jye had already walked away towards the road. She followed him, angry and disappointed at his inattention. She could never be quite sure how much of his deafness was assumed.

They started back towards Taunton, and it was good to be upon the open road again, even though she wore boots and widow's black. She looked down at Jye who trudged silently beside her and remembered Granny Loveridge saying of Luke, 'Him idden no traveller. Him got his feet planted in ground.'

She halted suddenly and turned Jye around to face her. She saw the unease in his features, his sad eyes. 'What is it?' she asked him.

'I don't like all this walkin' about. It do make my legs ache. Let we go home to Montacute, Ma! Let we bide there for always.'

Meri took his hand. 'You'm just like your father,' she said quietly, 'he always did know what was in my head long afore I did. Us'll go back, Jye. No more wandering for we two, eh? I once promised Luke that I'd stay with him, in his village, for ever, and thass what I'll do.'

306

They came up to a crossroads and saw four drovers who were attempting to drive a flock of sheep in the required direction. Netted carts filled with squealing pigs rumbled past them. A man led a pair of oxen on a long rope, and Meri remembered the name of day. 'Why, 'tis Friday! No wonder the roads is crowded. Thass market-day in Taunton.' They waited for the road to clear, and Meri watched without too much interest until a high-sided waggon came into view and stopped beside her. It was obviously heading towards Taunton. Several children were perched on the load of furniture and bedding. Two men walked, one on either side of the horse's head. But it was the woman holding the reins who caught and held Meri's attention. Small and thin, the red hair curling from beneath her white cap – why surely, it must be Eliza!

'Eliza,' cried Meri, 'Liza Greypaull!' The woman looked down from her place high up on the waggon. Meri could see how her freckled hands tightened on the traces. 'Meri,' she cried, 'Meridiana!'

Eliza climbed down from the cart. They stood together at the roadside, the tall and dignified gypsy, the tiny farmer's wife. Meri pressed close up against the hedge and felt the blackthorn's shadow fall across her. All the evidence of Eliza's disaster: the scarred cheek, the sightless eye, the remains of her home loaded on a farmcart, had appeared before Meridiana as if such a meeting had been preordained. She said awkwardly, 'Whatever happened to 'ee, Liza?'

Eliza gestured towards the stooped, grey-haired man who was Philip Greypaull. 'He pledged away Larksleve – to settle a gambling debt for a friend.' There was incredulity in Eliza's voice as if she still could not accept that such a thing had happened. ''Tis all lost, Meri. Every stone of Larksleve – every acre.'

'What happened to your face?'

Eliza raised a hand to cover her left cheek. In the same

307

tone of disbelief she said, 'The phaeton turned over, and the side-lights set fire to some straw. I got burned. I can't see no more in my left eye.'

'But you got healthy chavvies?'

'All alive, Meri. All strong and growing.'

'Give me back my coral!'

Eliza's hand slipped down to cover her bare throat. 'I can't. The bailiffs robbed me of it.' She reached an apologetic hand towards the gypsy. 'I was hard-pressed at the time. Can't you understand? I had no choice.'

'When did you part with it, Eliza?'

'Before Louis – before my last child was born.'

'Well, I'm sorry to hear that. For your sake and the sake of that chavvie.'

The threat in the words made Eliza turn around and look fearfully at Louis. 'He's all right,' she said swiftly, 'Dr Priddy said so.' Eliza smiled placatingly at Jye. 'You had another son?'

'Aye.'

'He's a handsome boy. He looks exactly like his father. You see, Meri, the lack of the coral did you no harm after all!'

Meri placed a hand on her son's shoulder. 'Poor Jye be stone-deaf, and Luke is already dead. He was killed by a fall of stone.'

'Oh, Meri!'

'They tells me in chapel that 'tis the Lord's will. I don't believe that. We makes our own bad luck in this life. That chop for the blue bowl was never a fair one, Liza. You cheated me!' Meri looked towards the farmcart. Her fierce gaze fastened on the face of Blanche. 'You!' she said, 'you with the proud looks! The day shall come when you will try to get close to me and mine. But you be a bad one.' The listening children sat transfixed and full of fear upon the waggon.

Meri said, 'This matter of the pendant 'idden never finished betwixt you an' me, Eliza. There'll be no peace for any of us until that pendant is round my neck, where it ought to be.' She stared up at Candace and Madelina who shivered and clung close together. The compelling gaze roved across the cart and only softened at the sight of Annis.

'You, maid,' said Meri gently, 'Whass your name, then?'

''Tis Annis, ma'am.'

'So, Annis Greypaull! Remember this day when you met up wi' a gypsy, for 'tis you what'll put this matter right betwixt me an' your mother.'

Eliza shook her head in disbelief, she moved from the blackthorn hedge and climbed back on the farmcart. The road cleared suddenly and the waggon moved on. Meri watched it grow smaller and vanish from sight around a bend in the road. But the image of the evicted family still burned in her mind. She would never have known the stooped grey-haired man to be Philip Greypaull, but Eliza had been instantly recognisable: but for the scarred cheek, she had hardly changed at all. Meri closed her eyes and called up the waggon; she counted the children who had perched on feather-beds and settles. There had been seven of them, all strong, all straight and without blemish. She thought about Charles and Henry, recalled their crooked spines, their aged faces. She looked down at Jye, withdrawn again, into his world of silence. Meri stepped into the middle of the road. 'Eliza,' she called, 'you cheated me! That never was a fair chop.'

Jye took his mother's arm and led her back along the hedge-side. ''Tis time we found that old train, Ma,' he said gently, ''tis time we was getting home.'

Father let it be known that he had pawned his silver-topped stick in order to buy them respectable seats in a first-class compartment. 'I won't have you sitting wi' the riff-raff,' he had said. With tears in his eyes he had impressed upon them the fact that with these same tickets they could also return to Taunton. 'If you don't like it in London, then you must come straight home.' It was at this point that Father's tears had brimmed over and Mina, greatly touched, had taken his hand in both of hers and wept tears of her own. Carried away by this new emotion, she had cried, 'Oh Pa! It do grieve me to leave you.'

Candace watched from the far side of the platform as her father and Mina acted out their farewells. She stood guard on the two shabby bags which contained their darned under-wear and patched dresses. One night spent in Hunter's Court had confirmed the need for her own and Mina's removal to domestic service in London. Their bed had been a make-shift affair on the kitchen table, with Annis and Simeon whimpering together in a truckle-bed in the corner. The baby Louis had cried all night, and this morning's departure had been a chaotic business, with the little ones getting underfoot, and no privacy for washing and dressing. Candace had looked into her mother's white face. 'Don't you fret, Ma,' she had whispered, 'us'll be right as rain in London. I'll send back some money as soon as they pay me.'

'Go quick,' her mother had answered, 'and don't cry, maid. You know that do only upset me.'

The train pulled into Taunton station. Seen close-to, it was a fearsome object, all fire and steam. Father stowed their bags onto the rack provided for travellers' luggage. He handed them into their seats, and kissed them on both cheeks as if they were important ladies. Mina wept again, but Candace said nothing at all, not even goodbye. Father warned them not to talk to strangers, at least not until they reached London. They would be met, he said, by uncle Robert's footman, who was to take them to Mayfair, to their new situation. The tears poured down Father's face as

310

he said this, but Candace turned her head away and refused to look. Her last memory of Taunton was that of a brightly coloured hoarding which invited the traveller always to use Coleman's Mustard.

The seats of the train were covered in brown plush, above them was set an oval-shaped mirror which was flanked by two pictures, one was a photograph of Weymouth sands, and the other a sketch of Exeter Cathedral. The window blinds were made of dark brown leather, and the words GREAT WESTERN RAILWAY were printed across the carriage doors. Candace and Madelina sat in opposite corners of the compartment and dared not move a limb. The train stopped and started again; people left and entered the compartment. Mother had packed a little basket with pasties and two apples, but they were both too shy to eat in front of strangers. They travelled for what seemed like hours in an uneasy silence, until at last the train pulled into a station, and porters ran up and down the platform shouting, 'Bristol! All change here for London.' The guard, who had already been tipped by Father for this service, escorted them to the London train, and this time they had a compartment to themselves.

Candace began to unpack the basket; she handed a pasty across to Mina, 'Better eat it,' she advised, ''twill be a long time before us gets to London.'

Mina nibbled at the crumbly pastry. 'You wasn't very nice to Father, you never even said goodbye.'

'When was Father ever nice to me?'

'He brought us presents when he could afford it!'

Candace folded her thin lips into a straight line. 'If it wasn't for Father's gambling and drinking us should be still on Larksleve.'

'He's sorry about what happened. He told me so. He cried about it.'

'Tears is cheap, Mina! And what a short memory you

got! I minds that time when you had no flour to make bread; I minds the bailiffs coming up to Larksleve and taking away Mama's lamps and pretty china. Have 'ee forgot so soon that he was drunk when the phaeton over-turned? That Mama lost the sight of her left eye, and got her face all burned? That he pledged away Larksleve?'

'I didden forget. I shall never forget. It's just - well, I don't think that Father is all bad.'

'You must be the only one left in the world what believes that.'

'I know he pledged away our home - but he never done that for his own gain. 'Twas done to help a friend in need.'

Candace leaned forward and tapped her sister on the knee. 'You silly liddle creature! 'Twas Mama, and his seven children, that was most in need. Can't you see that?'

Mina began to cry. 'I don't want to go to London. I be frightened, Can'. Let we go home again; Pa said we could if we was unhappy.'

'No! Grandfather have fixed up for we to work in London, and that is what us got to do. 'Tis high time for we to stand on our own two feet. There's more to the world than Larksleve Farm - '

'You wants to go to London,' accused Mina, 'I do believe you was glad to leave Taunton.'

'And so should you be! There's nothing for girls like us in that town. You saw that Court, that liddle hovel!'

'It won't be no better in London.'

'Yes, it will. We shall have a bedroom, shared between us two, and a nice uniform, and enough to eat. Mama said so.'

'It won't be like Larksleve.'

'Nothing in all the world is ever going to be like Larksleve. We was the lucky ones, you and me and Jackie. We shall remember all our lives how lovely it was to live in Buckland. But it's over, Mina. Best turn your foot and your face towards London.'

They stood close together on the crowded platform. People jostled and pushed them.

'How shall us know for sure if 'tis uncle Robert's footman?'

'Who else 'ud know that we was coming up from Taunton?'

The young man who finally found them was wearing an overcoat of light blue with matching cap. In his hand he held a card which was engraved, 'Mr Robert Greypaull. Barrister.'

'Miss Greypaull?'

'That's right,' said Candace.

'I'm your uncle's footman. My name is Jenkins.' He held out the card, and Candace studied it carefully in order to show him that she was no fool.

'I've been told to take you to Berkeley Square, Mayfair. Is that correct, ladies?'

'Quite correct,' said Candace.

He led them towards a brougham which had the initials R.G. inscribed in gold-leaf on its door. He stowed their luggage, handed them up into the carriage, and then climbed in with them. 'Best settle back and enjoy the drive,' he advised, 'it's a fair way from Paddington to Mayfair.'

Jenkins sat facing them; he studied their patched boots, unfashionable dresses and shabby cloaks. 'You just come up from the country?' He was, thought Candace, being over-familiar for a footman. She was frightened, but dared not show it. To reveal the extent of her terror would be to invite the prompt collapse of Madelina.

'We come up from Somerset this morning.'

The footman grinned. 'Well now, ain't that interesting! I wonder what you two ladies'll find to do in Mayfair?'

Candace sat up very straight in the brougham. 'Some

advice, young man,' she said coldly, 'you'd do well to mind your manners and your own business.'

'No offence, Miss, I'm sure.'

'And none taken.'

They had left the broad thoroughfare which led out from Paddington Station and turned into a maze of narrow side-streets.

'Where are you taking us?' Candace demanded.

'Just a short-cut,' said Jenkins, 'but p'raps you young ladies had better shut your eyes. This ain't exactly the poshest part o' London.'

Madelina closed her eyes at once, but Candace leaned forward and stared deliberately about her. She had thought that the hovel in East Reach, Taunton, would be the worst kind of habitation she would ever see. But the piles of blackened bricks in these streets could hardly be classed as dwellings. Surely nothing human could move and breathe in such squalor; why, on Larksleve, she thought, we had our horses better stabled. The narrow passages which linked one street with another were filled with rotting refuse and heaped-up filth. Every door stood wide open; babies and children sat or lay on doorsteps. It was mid-afternoon, and every man and woman they passed was drunk and almost incapable of walking. A group of older children had gathered, and they began to run alongside the brougham, shouting and demanding money. Candace looked down into their childish faces and found them already brutalised and bestial. The driver whipped up the horses and within minutes they had passed through the slum and were out again and travelling in cleaner air and sunshine. Candace nudged Madelina, 'You can open your eyes now,' she whispered.

Candace thought that they must be coming closer to Mayfair. The buildings here were larger and more imposing, the streets cleaner. The footman waved his hand at a stretch

314

of grass which lay behind railings. 'That's Hyde Park,' he said proudly, 'ain't it lovely?' Candace glanced at the rough green acre, and sniffed. 'Thass nothing special,' she told him, 'you shud see the Blackdown Hills in springtime.'

They passed by an archway. 'Marble Arch,' announced the footman. Candace looked deliberately unimpressed. 'Where's this Mayfair place?' she demanded. The footman spoke reverentially, 'Why lor', Miss, that's just about the poshest part in all o' London.' She began to take notice of the place-names. Park Lane, Grosvenor Square, the Coburg Hotel, and now the houses were tall, with balconies which overhung the streets and window boxes full of spring flowers. They came into a large square, and the brougham slowed down and then halted.

'Number Seven is the one you want,' said the footman. He lifted down the shabby bags and set them beside the two sisters. He grinned. 'Shall I ring on the doorbell for you ladies?'

Candace glanced at Mina. 'You can be on your way,' she said sharply, 'us is quite able to find the front door wi'out your help.' They stood without moving until the brougham had turned the corner. Mina picked up a bag and began to mount the steps to Number Seven.

'Not that way, you ninny,' said Candace, 'remember what Ma said. Servants' entrance is always below ground.' She turned to the area steps, dragging Mina with her. ''Tis what is known as coming-down-in-the-world. Us had better get used to it, Mina.'

Respect was not easily given by the inhabitants of Hunter's Court. To begin with her neighbours had been hostile towards Eliza; slops and refuse, tossed from open doors and upper windows, had a way of landing in front of the Grey-paulls' closed door. It seemed that everybody in Taunton had heard the dramatic tale of The Pledge, and the subsequent loss to the Greypaull family of Larksleve Farm. Eliza's ownership of a piano, her clean and healthy children, her regular church attendance, and the Parson's early visit to her house in Hunter's Court did not endear her to these people, who saw her thin, indomitable aspect as a living condemnation of their way of life.

The women of the Court were slatterns, their morals as loose and inadequate as their clothing. It grieved Eliza, that thrifty farm housewife, to see children gnawing on the bones from half-cooked meat, to smell potatoes burning. Even when they possessed sufficient money to buy food for their families, still they lacked the ability to turn cheap ingredients into nourishing meals. The daily battle with dirt and disease had not so much been abandoned here, as never begun.

The miracle of gaslight had shown up and led to the eventual removal of the open drains and sewers which had once run through the main streets of Taunton. Pipes had been laid, and light cast in shops and places of business, and in many private houses. The coming of light had galvanised people, streets were cleaner now, the populace more alert.

The courts still dwelt in their original darkness. Dips and snuffers were in use, the rushlight and candle being solitary sources of illumination. Daylight rarely penetrated the tiny windows of houses which crowded so closely together. Eliza, accustomed to sunlight streaming through open casements, could only imagine the filth and livestock which lurked in every crevice and corner of Number Two, Hunter's Court. Her use of lye to kill the bugs and assorted vermin, and her subsequent whitewashing of all inside walls caused astonishment, disbelief, and then hilarity among her neighbours. But the laughing stopped abruptly, and the people paused to listen on that first Sunday evening when

316

the rare sound of piano music came from behind the Greypaull's closed door.

To part with Jackie was as painful as she had always known
it would be. Eliza had delayed his departure to the Bishop's
Hull Stables for as long as she dared. The excuse that the
boy had nothing suitable to wear was sufficient for her to
hold on to him for another week or even two. She had taken
what remained of Philip's fine clothing, the woollen
breeches and worsted jackets, and cut them down to fit the
tiny thirteen-year-old boy. The sight in her remaining eye
was not good, and the hours of stitching by a flickering
rushlight had made her head ache. But to see him go warmly
clad and with a set of spare breeches into his new life was all
that she wanted at that moment. To believe that he might
be happy was not possible. All his short life had been lived in
the belief that he would, one day, inherit Larksleve. She had
tried, while fitting him for a new cloth jacket, to discover
his feelings. She had pinned a sleeve into a shoulder opening
and, without looking at his face, she had asked gently, 'Do
'ee mind very much, Jack? Going away, I mean?' She had
felt his bony frame grow stiff.

'You never asked the girls,' he said, 'you told 'em they
cudden stay to home no longer.'

'That was diff'rent,' said Eliza, 'girls usually go away
from home, sooner or later.' She knew that he was remembering Madelina's tears, still mourning the absence of his
beloved sister. 'Mina do have Candace to rely on; she is not
alone in London.'

'But you never asked her if she minded. You told her
what she had to do.'

Just like your own mother when she ordered you to
marry Philip, the guilty whisper echoed inside Eliza's head,
but she would not listen to it. ''Tis diff'rent with maidens,'

317

she repeated. 'Mothers always know best what is good for their daughters.' Jackie looked doubtful. 'I wondered,' said Eliza, 'if you had set your heart on having Larksleve? Ever since you was a baby it had been promised to you.'

'No, Ma!' He swung around to face her; pins flew in all directions. 'I never wanted Larksleve, but nobody ever asked me. All I ever wanted was the horses; to live with 'em, to ride 'em.' His small thin face lit up with such joy that she was reminded briefly of Samuel Greypaull and the smiles they had once exchanged. 'I want to go to Bishop's Hull. I want to train for a steeplechaser!'

''Tis a dangerous job, Jack. Promise me that you'll be careful.'

'There's no sense in being careful, Ma. That do take all the life out of living.' And now he sounded exactly like his father, Philip.

Eliza sighed, 'You'll come back and see us when you get your day off?'

'Let me know when Mina's likely to be here, and I'll be over to see her.'

2, Hunter's Court,
Taunton.

Dear cousin Rhoda,

It is with heavy heart that I pick up my pen to write this letter. The *Final Blow* have fallen upon me, and Larksleve *Lost*. Philip *Pledged* our *All* to cover a gambling debt for a Friend, and was *Let Down*. So, dear Rhoda, this finds me in a bad posishun. We are come to a two-down and one-up *hovel* in the lowest part of this wicked town. My only hope is in Our Saviour, and in my good girls what have stood by me and never once complained. No, dear cousin, not even when they was tole that they must go away to work as *domestics* in London.

318

Oh, it did grieve me, Rhoda, to see them go. Philip put them on the train last Monday fortnight, and wept, as so he should, it all being *His Fault*. They have been fixed up in a good situashun by our Uncle Robert, who, as you know, is a barrister, and knowed of clients who wanted servants.

It is not so much the work that do grieve me. My girls is well trained and obedient. They is easily governed and do not *Answer Back*. No, Rhoda, the work is to be no Shock to them. But the lowering of their selves to the station in life of *skivvy* is what they could never have expected. They was always the Miss Greypaulls of Larksleve Farm, and us had our own pew in Church. I never did allow them to go to Church in darns and pattens. Even when we was at our *Lowest Ebb* my girls did hold their heads up. What will become of them in London? I spoke very strict before they left, but both are young Ladies and not *Flirtatious* which is a Blessing, since we all knows where *that* leads to.

My four youngest do still grow and do well, but for how long, I must now wonder. There is still smallpox in parts of this town, and the open drains in some streets is dreadful after the sweet air of Buckland St Mary. This is a bad house, but it is rent free from Daniel Greypaull and I must be thankful. Even with Candace and Madelina gone, we is still very cramped together. The other houses in this Court do lean very close to us. The people are rough and do shout from the upper windows. Sometimes the men do lie drunk all night in the Court, and my feare, dear Rhoda, is very great for Blanche. She is growed very tall and is *Developed* for her age. The child is a Great Beauty which was easy to hide on Larksleve. But even tho' I do bind her figure, and cover her as best I can, the men in this Court have Noticed and do already call out to her. My feare is very great for Blanche, and I keep to hand

Philip's riding whip which did not *Go* in the *Sale*. She is a wilful child and was never biddable like her sisters. But I must *Protect* her, and am ready to Whip any man what lays a hand on her. This letter is full of my troubles, dear cousin, for which I am sorry, but my heart is heavy and so much missing my dear Larksleve, which I know I shall never see again. Now I know how you must have grieved for home when first in New York, even tho' Mr Salter was a good Husband and Devoted to You. Would that I had been so Blessed, but it was not to be. My regards to dear Mr Black and your three children. I was thankful to know that you had married again, to a *Good Man*, and safe in a foreign Country. The life in Suamico do sound much like the life in Buckland St Mary.

Next week I shall have to part with my oldest Son. Poor Jackie is only thirteen, but I have been persuaded to let him go to a Stables in Bishop's Hull where he will live-in and be trained for a Steeplechaser, which do sound *Dangerous* but is what he Wants. It is *not* only *Death*, dear Rhoda, what do take away our children from us. Philip have hardly spoke a Word to any of us since the move to Taunton, save to shed tears at the going of Candace and Mina, which is all *too Late*, as I told him, and do help *Nobody*.

I have left this house only once, to take a letter of introducshun from the Rev. Soames to the Vicar of Trinity, which is the Church for East Reach. Feel safer to know that the Church is close to hand, and Vicar likely to call in near future, but feel shamed to receive callers in this *Evil Court*, some houses having neither *Doors* nor *Window glass* and all people's rubbish left lying in the Yard.

Am resolved to *Keep* up my *Standards*. Have whitened my Step, and washed all walls and floors from top to bottom with *Lye* and *Whitewash*, hung Clean Curtains, and polished the Doorknocker, this being the only house in the Court to have a Doorknocker, and have told Philip that he must fix a strong *Bolt* right away. My *Piano* a matter of great envy by the neighbours, altho' it do take up a lot of room in this *Hovel*. An Annuity, paid for by Grey-paulls in Buckland, mostly my Brothers, is to bring in *One Pound* a week, which is not riches but can be *relied* on. This house rent free from Philip's Father, but shall not *Bide* long here if something Better can be found.

So, dear cousin, this is my present situashun. Have still my health which is a Blessing and a *Wonder* to me. But the need to protect my young ones very urgent in this wicked town. I could not Bear to see any of them *Turn Out* like their Father.

My kind regards to Mr James Black, and to your three dear children.

I am, as ever,
Your affectshunat cousin, Eliza.

The reappearance of Mina, late one night, in Hunter's Court, was not entirely unexpected. The provision of her return ticket had been the only matter upon which Philip and Eliza had agreed in a space of years. The small weeping figure, accompanied by an outraged railway official, was handed over to Eliza with the observation that she 'should take better care of a child who was clearly only sixpence-in-the-shilling' and had not even known her own address in Taunton.

It had taken hours of patient questioning by her mother before Mina's story was told. How could she have been expected to know her address in Taunton, wept Mina, when she had only spent one night in the dreadful Hunter's Court hovel? The recital of all that had befallen in London and the reason for her flight from the house in Mayfair was so bizarre, and beyond Mina's capacity for invention, that

Eliza was obliged to believe that every word she spoke was the truth. Eliza's children had always possessed a tendency to see their lives in terms of high drama. Mina's tale was accompanied by a wealth of histrionic gesture and meaningful glances, but stripped of exaggeration it was still a remarkable story.

The house in Mayfair consisted of a basement and four upper storeys, at the top of which was a room roofed with glass called a studio. The studio was forbidden territory to servants. The master of the house was a famous artist. It was in this studio that his priceless and important masterpieces were painted. This information, said Mina, had been impressed upon herself and Candace within minutes of their arrival in Berkeley Square, Mayfair.

The cook-housekeeper was a fat and jolly woman called Mrs Chumley. She was strict, but not too strict, and had appreciated straightaway that here were two country girls, farm-bred to hard work and not in the least likely to prove flirtatious or untrustworthy. The house, said Mina, was beautiful beyond description, something like the parlour at Larksleve, but multiplied a thousand times. Mina's first task every morning was to clean the firegrates and light the fires in all the rooms except the studio, which, she was told, had a coke-burning stove, and was attended to by the master himself. The mistress of the house was said to be delicate and rarely left her room. There were several young men, sons of the artist, at whom Mina had never dared even to glance.

The first few days had been confusing; so many staircases, rooms, and corridors to get used to, so many buckets of coal to be carried, fireplaces tended, and woe betide the servants who allowed a fire to go out! She had wept every night from weariness and homesickness. It was different for Candace; she had always done the hard jobs, and in any case, she had wanted to leave home and go to London.

The second week had been slightly better. Surer now of

her direction when she answered a bell, or mended a fire, Mina had begun to look about her, to take notice. The thought of the artist painting in his glass-roofed room at the top of its own private staircase was intriguing. She grew curious. Several times, she had crept to the foot of the narrow little staircase, but had seen and heard nothing, until that afternoon when the mistress had suddenly collapsed and Mina had been sent up to the studio to fetch the master.

She had crept mouse-like to the studio door and tapped upon it. 'What is it?' a voice had shouted, and she had replied, 'It's Madam. She's fallen to the floor and Mrs Chumley can't revive her!' He had thrown open the door and, for an instant, Mina had seen the interior of the glass-roofed room. It looked, she thought, like the Larksleve kitchen on a washday, when the weather had turned wet and Mother forced to put up the indoor clothes-lines. But here there were pieces of thin white paper, instead of linen, hanging up to dry. The master had closed the door swiftly and she had been bundled helter-skelter before him down the narrow staircase.

She had gone back to the kitchen to find that the afternoon tea was being prepared. She had been told to exchange her coal-smeared dress and apron for the lilac uniform in which she was to serve tea. She had carried the heavy tray to the boudoir where the mistress, recovered from her swoon, was sitting up on the sofa and talking to the master. As Mina entered the room she heard the words 'not very bright, my dear. Just up from the country', and thought that it was probably her own intelligence which had been under consideration.

They had glanced keenly at her, and so she had dropped things, fumbled the teacups, apologised and looked stupid. They had dismissed her shortly, showing signs of irritation, but there had been something in their attitudes towards her which confirmed for Mina that what she had glimpsed in that

323

upper room had been both significant and important.

The secret had been huge and exciting. It grew larger and more portentous with the keeping of it. But caution had forced her to wait until the candle had been blown out and she and Candace lay side by side in the darkness of their own room. Only then had Mina whispered of all she had seen and heard that afternoon.

'Have 'ee told this to anybody else.'

'Course I haven't.'

'I think I know what he's doing up there, Mina.' Candace spoke slowly, her voice hushed with fear. 'Did they bits of paper have writing on 'em?'

'I cudden properly see – 'twas on'y a quick look – and then the door shut. I seem to recollect a sort of pattern, in black ink – '

'Banknotes! Thass what he's doing! He's making his own money!'

'I don't know about that. I never did see a banknote.'

'Well, neither did I, you ninny! But what else could it be? I once read in the *Taunton Courier*, about a Bristol man who made his own banknotes. 'Tis against the law. You goes to gaol if they catches you at it!'

'Oh Candace – whatever shall us do? He's a famous man. Cook did say that his paintings is hung in a gallery in London, and that he do paint important people. Whyfor should a man like that have to make his own banknotes?'

'Greed! The rich is always greedy! Remember uncle Francis down to Devon? He grudged giving Mama they five liddle sovereigns and, quite rightly, she threw the money in his face. Some folks is very tight about money, Mina.'

A long silence fell between them, until Mina whispered, 'What do 'ee think, Candace?'

Her sister's voice had been almost inaudible, 'You must never tell a living soul what you saw this day. 'Tis dangerous information. It could see the two of us lying dead in an alley, wi' our throats cut!' The whisper halted, and then began again. 'I likes it here, Mina. It do suit me very well to bide in London. But you is a silly, nervous sort o' maiden what'll blab out all what you know. Be better if you goes home to Mama. Safer for both of us.'

'But what about our uncle Robert? He got us this situation. What will he think?'

'You shall leave a note on your pillow. Thass what girls do in books. You shall write that you was homesick and couldn't bide no longer.' Candace giggled. 'They be sure to believe it. You bin crying every blessed day for the past fortnight!'

'And so I run away, Ma! I took my ticket and left that house early in the morning. I asked people where was the station called Paddington, and they showed me.'

Eliza studied the soft, pretty features, the pursed lips and dark curling hair.

'You done quite right, maid. That was no place for you. I never should have sent you there. I can see that now.'

'But what about Can'?'

'Your sister have made up her own mind. Her is seventeen – going on eighteen. If her was of a mind to come home then you would have arrived together. If what you says is true, then letters between us could be risky. Us must bide our time. 'Tis likely that you was both mistaken, and the great man only drawing maps – or something.' Eliza took both of Mina's hands and held them. 'But never tell anybody else about this business. Remember! Your sister's life could well depend on us keeping quiet.'

That retribution would always be visited upon the sinner was Eliza's firm belief. 'If you do harm to another living

325

soul – then that'll be sure to rebound upon you – fourfold!'
This had been her mother's favourite malediction, and how
many times had Eliza seen it come to pass. She remembered
Will Gardner, and the way Daniel Greypaull had sold him
up, in order to pay off Larksleve debts. Just to look at Philip
these days was confirmation enough of her mother's words.
If the sale of the farm and the move to Taunton had been
shaming for Eliza, then how much more must he be suffering now. Oh yes, he had been brought low, forced to live in
cramped quarters with a wife he despised, and ridiculed by
his friends for his naïvety in giving his pledge in this, his old
stamping-ground of Taunton.

Philip went out from Hunter's Court every morning, and
returned late at night. How he spent his time she neither
knew nor cared. Without asking his permission she had
cut down his decent clothes to make outfits for Jackie. Philip
was now obliged to wear the flannel shirts and moleskin
trousers of a working-farmer, the irony of which was not
lost upon his family, especially his daughter Blanche. Her
vindictiveness towards Philip far outstripped that of Eliza,
who still tried to show some Christian charity towards him.

Daniel Greypaull had come around on market-day to
collect his Hunter's Court rents. He had also collected his
grandson, Jackie, and ridden with him to the Bishop's Hull
Stables. 'The boy'll be all right,' he told Eliza. 'No call for
'ee to worry, maid. This one's a born jockey if ever I see'd
one!'

'But 'tis so dangerous,' said Eliza, 'all that jumping, and
the fences so high. What if he falls? What if he gets
damaged?'

'I won't fall, Ma. Did I ever fall on Larksleve?'

'This'll be diff'rent Jack. Folks bet their money on
steeplechasers.'

But he had ridden away leaping up behind Daniel and
mounted on a fine bay mare. A part of Eliza's life had gone

326

with him; only now could she measure how many of her hopes and dreams had been rooted in the promise of hope once given to her by James John Daniel Greypaull.

Jackie had gone away, but Mina had returned, which still left seven of them to manage in a three-roomed dwelling. Compared to their neighbours, the Greypaulls lived in luxurious space. The rooms in Number Two, Hunter's Court were tiny and very dark, and without the items bought-back in the sale by Samuel they would have suffered even greater hardship. Only now, was Eliza beginning to appreciate the possession of feather beds, a table, china cups and plates, and the amount of status bestowed by a piano. Her standing in the Court had risen week by week. The slops and refuse were no longer tipped from upper windows to soil her clean front door. Even the surliest of her neighbours allowed her the grudging title of Missus Greypaull. Philip, who was rarely seen and never heard, was discounted for a fool and totally ignored by them.

Applications of strong lye and whitewash were gradually subduing the vermin resident in all walls and woodwork. There would always be the nightly need to examine her daughter's long hair with a nit-comb, to hang her washing on lines suspended from the bedroom window, instead of drying it in the clean winds of Buckland. But with the rusty iron range polished up to a gleaming black, with a bright fire burning and her pegged-rugs on the floors, Eliza could pause, draw breath, and evaluate her position.

Work of some kind must be found for Mina. Eliza would have to overcome her aversion to the streets of Taunton and go out of the Court to seek paid employment for her daughter. The weekly pound, allowed by the Greypaull annuity, would need to be spent with great care. Everything in this town of Taunton must be bought and paid for by coin of the realm. Gone were the days when she could send her children out to gather firewood; never again would they run to bring her the blossom, the nuts, and the wild fruits. Milk was brought to her door by a man with a horse and cart who ladled out a bluish-looking liquid, measured from a grubby churn into her flowered milk-jug. Food must now be bought in quantities of a halfpenny-worth, instead of by the sackful. No hams or baconsides, no eggs or butter, no cheeses. It was cheaper to buy the baker's shop-made bread, to fetch ready-dipped rushlights from the tallow-chandlers. Eliza had finally reached the place where even her life was likely to be made sweeter by a farthing's worth of sugar.

2, Hunter's Court,
Taunton.

My dear cousin Rhoda,

No answer come yet from my last letter, you being took up now with the work of your new farm, which I do very well understand having once been in that situashun. My last letter to you being all full of trouble, I pick up my pen to inform you that I have mastered my *Nerves* and put my trust in our Saviour, what do make a lot of *Difference* in my ways of going on.

Candace still working in London. Madelina come home after two weeks, being *Homesick*. Jackie gone to Bishop's Hull, but against my better Judgement. Philip now a *Broken Man*, as well he might be. Have put away all thoughts of Larksleve, except that summertime do recall our Harvest, and the Reapers stretched out in line all across the field. The sun *must* shine sometimes on Taunton, but I don't *never* seem to see it. Madelina is gone to work in the collar-making factory at Poolwall. Long hours, but she is home every night, and brings out-work with her which do keep Blanche and Annis busy sewing, and brings in an extra shilling or two for food and coal. Blanche, Annis and Simeon don't go to school, and never have done, which do grieve me terrible, Rhoda. I have tried to show them to read and write, but they don't want to. Simeon is full of *cheek* and gets *unruly* him playing with the children in the Court, but what can I do?

It is not the same *Life* at all, but God and the Greypaulls have provided, and I must be thankful. Message came from Buckland last week, that my mother and father both took sick and died in two days of one another. All lands and money Willed to my four brothers. Please write a line or two when you have the time, dear Rhoda. My thoughts often with you in Suamico. Regards to dear Mr Black and your children.

Your affectshunat cousin, Eliza.


Suamico, Brown County.
My dear cousin Eliza,

Your two letters come to hand, and I must now take up my pen, our first Harvest being safely carried, and all straight before winter.

The *tone* of your second letter being more *cheerful* I have hopes that you will *Survive* the *Evils* of Taunton. Glad to hear that your three Oldest are settled in employment which is *Very Necessary* for the young ones. Cannot believe that your Mother and Father could have Cast you Off without a Shilling. Whatever could they have meant by it, dear cousin, when all that took place on Larksleve was *Not*, and never could be, *Your Fault*. You are in all our Prayers, dear cousin.

We are on the verge of winter here, and Rosalind and I busy sewing Quilts and Quilting them. We never seem to have enough. Rosalind now aged sixteen, pretty, though

I do say so. George a good boy and a hard worker, like his father. John, my youngest, remains delicate in his health, in spite of *Fresh Air* and *Good Food.*

Mr Black and I still much involved with the raising of a New Church. Many Sewing Evenings held, when ladies gather together for talk and company. Have done most of my Mending this way, also turned all my Sheets sides-to-middle, which pleased me greatly. Have dried several pounds of blueberries this year, and salted down and smoked a deal of hog-meat.

You are much in my thoughts, dear Eliza. We have no very near neighbours.

Please write when you can.

Kind regards to all,

Your affectshunat cousin, Rhoda.

One day lived in Hunter's Court was very much like another. Every year became a matter of endurance, but without the compensations she had found on Larksleve. The season, for Eliza, was always to be winter in this dreadful place. She rarely ventured on to the streets of Taunton. The spectacle of Philip, loafing on street corners along with the drunkards and ruffians of the town, was to be avoided. Bad enough to hear the stories brought back by her children, to see Madelina's shame at her father's behaviour, to hear Jack's story of his father seen begging for halfpence on the Taunton racecourse, to witness the contempt of Blanche towards Philip, and the fear in the eyes of Simeon and Annis. Letters came from Candace who was still in the employment of the suspect artist; but Candace had always been the close one, and the letters gave no hint of her state of mind.

It was only Louis, now aged four, who seemed quite unaffected by his situation. Eliza, with so many other

330

burdens to carry, had avoided close scrutiny of this, her seventh and last child, but now the truth could no longer be denied. In spite of his flaxen curls and dark blue eyes, his regular features and contented smiles, there was something very wrong with Louis. He spoke just a few words. He called her Ma-ma, he attempted the names of his brothers and sisters. But he was clumsy and uncertain in all his movements, and quite unlike her other children who were all deft and nimble-fingered.

Eliza remembered the coral pendant and herself, not yet pregnant, handing it over to the waiting Bailiff. ''Tis an ugly lookin' piece,' he had said, 'reckon as how you'll never miss it.' Then there had been the accident: the fall from the phaeton into burning straw, the loss of sight in her left eye, and Louis born that same night. She remembered Meridiana, all those years ago, slipping the pendant across her dark braids, and hanging it around Eliza's neck. 'Thass for nex' year,' she had crooned, 'an' for a safe birthing.' All her children had been born safe and healthy, save for Louis. It was at such moments that Eliza longed for Loveday, for the motherly comfort of those broad arms. Embarrassed as ever by the tears of others, she had never dared to say goodbye to Loveday. She had ensured Jed Hayes' continued occupation of the cottage, and work for his wife would be found within the family. More than this she could not do.

Some of Eliza's children were more obedient than others. She had no wish to dominate them as she herself had been dominated, but in a two-down, one-up hovel, a certain degree of obedience and docility must be expected. The easily governed child, taught Eliza, was the one who would, one day, inherit the Kingdom of Heaven; and it was love and only love, she insisted, which made her draw them close, which made her bind them to her.

❦

Blanche Greypaull was quite willing to forgo the delights of the Kingdom of Heaven for the more tangible pleasures to be found in Taunton. She resented the binding of her developing figure, her mother's watchful care. Against the expressed wishes of Eliza, down had come the length of Blanche's skirts, and up had gone the glorious dark red hair. But her plea to be allowed to work in the collar-factory with her sister Mina had been unsuccessful. 'You can bide to home and sew, with me and Annis,' her mother had said, 'I don't trust you to go amongst the men in that factory. You do have a bad tendency to flaunt yourself, Blanche!'

'But I shall be with Mina,' she had protested. There would be no danger of straying down the primrose path in the company of Mina, who was walking-out quite seriously with a Sunday School teacher called David, and who always attended church three times on Sundays, and Bible-Class on a Wednesday evening. But her mother had not relented, and Blanche, already as tall as her father, with a full high bosom, a narrow waist, and long slim legs, had needed only to pile up her auburn hair on the top of her head in order to drive the young men of Taunton to a pitch of frenzy.

Three brothers lived on the opposite side of the Court, all of them good-looking fellows, if not very clean. They watched her whenever she strolled with her water-buckets to the standpipe. They whispered things to her whenever she passed them in the narrow Court. It had amused her lately to bend down low beside the water-bucket and let it fill slowly, while she eased away her mother's careful binding and allowed the front fastenings of her blouse to fall open. With her back turned towards her mother's window, and the three young men leaning open-mouthed against the opposite wall, it had been a game to play on breathless summer evenings when she was tired of sewing shirt-collars and listening to the bickering of the younger children.

Annis could hardly remember the unhappy times on Larksleve. Four years lived in Hunter's Court had stolen memory and encouraged fantasy, so that she equated Buckland St Mary with the promised joys of the Kingdom of Heaven. Sometimes, when she and Mama sat sewing, when Simeon and Louis slept, and Blanche fetched water from the standpipe, Annis begged a story. The tale had always to be told about Larksleve, about haysel and harvest, and the Lord of the Reapers, about the deep snows of winter when Buckland people walked on the tops of hedges and tree-crowns, about the apple-picking and the cider-making. The stories she loved best were those of Harvest Home, and the dancing and feasting in her grandfather's great barn. 'And do 'ee remember, maid?' her mother would ask, 'that morning in spring when we two was in the garden on Larksleve, and I showed you the name of your home writ in snowdrop an' crocus?' Annis would always answer, 'Yes, Mama. I minds it well.' And a picture would come into her mind, of herself at the age of eight, yellow curls tossing in the breeze, dressed in a starched white pinafore, and holding tight to her mother's hand. It was a memory that was to bind her for always to Eliza. 'Yes,' her mother would continue, 'we was standing together, looking at the flowers, when the bailiffs came riding down the lane towards us. I shall never forget that minute, Annis; not in all my life. I knowed straight away in my heart that Larksleve was lost.'

'I knowed it too, Mama. I was only little, but I remembered the bailiffs once taking our lamps away, and Candace and Jack hiding all the feather-beds under straw in the barn. I thought that this time they might take away us children.'

'No, maid. I would have shot any man who laid a hand

on one' of my children. You is my only good crop of all what ever growed on Larksleve.'

The form of words would vary slightly from telling to telling, but it was a conversation of which Annis never wearied. She loved that picture of herself and Mama bound inextricably together in the beautiful garden about to be cast out of Paradise by the bailiffs; and Papa, like Lucifer the Fallen Angel, the root cause of all their misfortunes. Annis resolved that she would always be the easily governed child, the only one of her mother's daughters who could truly be relied on to regain her birthright, and the Kingdom of Heaven.

Simeon hated all his family, save Mama and Annis. He could not abide the sanctimonious Mina, who was always telling him to say his prayers and wipe his nose. His brother Jack, who should have been an ally in this house full of women, had abandoned him years ago and gone away to be a jockey. Blanche, according to Mina, was 'getting too proud by half and riding for a fall'. Simeon was not quite sure what this meant, but it sounded appropriately nasty. Louis was good for nothing. He could neither speak nor play games. He was a burden to Simeon and Annis having always to be looked after and protected from the wild boys in the Court.

It was only by looking at Annis that Simeon could recognise himself. 'Two peas in a pod,' people said. Identity had been hard to come by in a family of seven, and Simeon had a desperate need to know who and what he was. Annis held the key; she opened the door. She explained all the complicated stories told to them by Mama. Blanche, so people said, would turn out to be a great beauty. But Simeon and Annis together, walking hand-in-hand to the corner shop, could also draw admiring glances. 'The liddle dears!' old ladies would murmur, 'jus' look at their flaxen curls an' big blue eyes.'

He had once roamed away by himself. He had left the Court and walked up the steep hill of East Reach. He had come to the steps of the London Hotel, and sat down and wept from weariness and hunger. A fine lady had stepped down from her carriage and patted his head. 'What's the matter, little man?' she had asked, and Simeon, having spied the sixpence in her hand, had sobbed louder. 'My Ma an' Pa is both dead an' buried, an' I never had no food for three days.' The lady had parted easily with the sixpence, and he had run straight home to share the prize with Annis. One lie had led him to tell another. 'I found sixpence in a crack in the gutter – I jus' looked down – an' there it was!'

They had spent the sixpence at the bakery on a slab of doughcake filled with currants and topped with icing. They had eaten it on the way home, cramming their mouths with the rare treat so that they should not have to share a crumb of it with Blanche and Louis. But the true pleasure for Simeon had been the telling of the lie. You could get any- thing you wanted in this life, he thought, if only you knew how best to go about it.

These children of Philip and Eliza had always had a tendency towards exaggeration. On Larksleve there had been space for them to grow, to indulge their inclination towards histrionics and quick temper. But here in Taunton, in this dark little house in a crowded Court, Eliza watched Simeon grow sly and evasive, her girls sharp-tongued and vitriolic. They were becoming envious and intolerant of one another. They vied endlessly for her attention and approval.

The trouble with Blanche had come sooner than expected. It was a winter's night of bitter frost, and Blanche had thrown down the collar she was stitching. 'I'll go up to the standpipe and fetch water. It could all be fast-frozen by morning, Ma, and then what shall us do?'

Eliza had said no, it was too cold and dark. But Eliza had been weary and had not noticed the eagerness of Blanche to be allowed to go outside. The girl had ignored her mother's protestations; she had wrapped a shawl about her head and shoulders, grabbed up the bucket, and closed the door behind her.

It had been several minutes later when the screams were heard by Annis and Eliza. Annis had picked up the oil-lamp and run into the Court, followed closely by her mother, who carried the hunting-crop in one hand and a coal hammer in the other. They came upon Blanche at the top of the Court. She had failed to reach the standpipe. Eliza recognised the three brothers from the opposite cottage. Blanche was pinned up against the wall held by the two younger men, while the oldest brother was intent on tearing the last garment from Blanche's body.

'Let her go,' said Eliza. She had only needed to speak quietly. Perhaps it was her scarred cheek, her sightless eye, the fierceness of her red hair which quelled them. Eliza threw the coal hammer at one retreating back, and brought the riding-crop down in quick succession on the shoulders of the other two. As they ran, they shouted at Eliza, ''Tidden us what you shud whip – 'tis your bitch of a daughter. Ask her, Missus! She bin askin' for it, ever since last summer.'

There were times when the burning pain in his stomach would ease a little and the mist clear from his mind. It was then that Philip Greypaull remembered the debaucheries of his youth: the licentious and disgusting acts which had only been made possible by strong drink taken; and then he would fear for his sons, tremble for his daughters. There were things that he should tell them, warnings that must be voiced. He would look at each one of these children, born of his unwilling union with his cousin Eliza, and he would see himself in every face, in every pair of eyes that looked back at him.

He had risen late that morning, had staggered from his bed, felt giddy and unsteady upon the stepladder which led downstairs from the bedroom. The morning hours were the hardest; it was difficult to live through that space of time until he could cadge or steal a few pennies from Eliza to pay for the first healing drink of the day.

It was Maytime. The girls had taken chairs out into the Court, they had found a patch of sunshine in which they could sit and sew at collars. Simeon had been sent on an errand, and Eliza and Louis remained indoors. They had rarely spoken to each other since leaving Larksleve. Eliza's scarred cheek, her sightless eye had already said all that was ever to be needed. He would ask her for money and be refused or rewarded according to her purse and temper. He would leave the house to spend his day wherever a drink was to be found. He usually came back in the early hours, when the children were asleep.

The art of talking, he thought, had never flourished between himself and Eliza. Words, in fact, had been responsible for more divisions than had been their silences. He sat down at the table, and she placed a cup of weak tea before him. 'Food?' she enquired. He shook his head. Her speech, when it came, was so unexpected, that he scarcely took in the first few words.

'Blanche,' said Eliza abruptly. 'Blanche is goin' to end up in trouble!'

'Blanche?' he replied.

'Your daughter! The one with the auburn hair and violet eyes – remember her, do you? The one that you named for your fancy harlot!'

'Yes,' he said, 'yes, I remember.' He looked through the window to where Blanche sat, head bent towards her sewing. He saw the perfection of her white skin, the

337

classical profile, the amazing curve of her neck and bosom, and he remembered Blanche Sablon.

'What is it?' he asked quickly, 'did somebody - ?'

'Not yet. But 'tis only a matter of time.' Eliza gestured towards the Court. 'Animals,' she cried, 'animals, the same as you were in your young days. I be keeping 'em away from her so far with your horsewhip. But I can't always be watching. She is growing up to be a tease and a torment. It do please her to see the men crazy for her. There's something cruel in Blanche; her got no loving kindness.'

'Blanche loves you, Eliza.'

'Loves me?'

'Aye. Didden' you never know it?' His head drooped upon his chest. 'I would have given all I had to be loved by Blanche. She was always my favourite child.'

'All that you had, Philip? But you never had nothing to give, did you? Not to me, not to your children. You even took from us the little comfort what we had.'

'I've paid for what I did. Look at me, Liza! Sick in body, broken in spirit.'

'You've paid? Oh no, cousin. Your reckoning is yet to come, when you is face to face with your Saviour.'

'Us never should have married. 'Twas one disaster after another.'

'So you noticed, did you?' Her voice was sharp, her finger pointing. 'Did you ever bother to look at your last child? Look at him, Philip? He can't speak a word of sense, he can't wash or dress himself, he don't even know what his own name is!' All her pent-up bitterness of years, came flooding out. 'Better that I had put a rope around my neck, and hung myself in my father's stable, than allow myself to be wed wi' you, Philip Greypaull.'

He looked up at her, and his eyes were anguished; his voice, when he spoke, was a whisper. 'In all my life,' he said, ''twas only my mother what ever loved me.'

338

'Thass right,' said Eliza softly, 'oh, thass quite right, Philip; and I'll tell you something else. 'Tis the mothers who love their sons too dearly who cause most of this world's mischief.'

'Still quick to blame, eh Eliza? A true Greypaull if ever I see'd one. Is that what your Parson teaches? Or do I recall some story about sinners bein' forgiven?'

She sat down at the table, and covered her face with her hands.

'I did forgive you,' she cried, 'many times. I looked for reasons, made excuses for you,' she raised her head, 'but then I thought about all my children, and 'tis for their sakes now that I can not forgive you.'

'They all be housed an' fed.'

'No thanks to you! We live here by the grace of God and Daniel Greypaull. Why! we got your Samuel to thank for the cups we drink from, the beds we sleep on.'

'Our Samuel,' he said quietly, 'Oh yes. You shud have wed wi' our Samuel. He shud have bin the one to farm on Larksleve. I was nuthin' but the Joker in that cardpack of Greypaulls.' His face took on a rapt expression. 'I once came close to runnin' away from it all. An important man heard me sing. "A beautiful voice," he said. "You got a fine presence, young man. Let me take you to the music-halls in London," he said. 'You'll be sure to make your fortune."'

'So why didden you go with him?'

'Our weddin' was all arranged, Larksleve furnished, and weddin'-presents given. I talked about it to Sam.'

'And what did Sam say?'

'He said that Father 'ud never forgive me. That if things went wrong in London, I cud never come home.'

'Samuel advised you to wed me?'

'Aye. He said I shud keep my promise to you.'

The bright stain of anger appeared in Eliza's face.

'Dreams,' she cried, ''twas only dreams you once had about singing in London. It would have all come to nuthin', like everything else you've ever tackled. You've spoiled the lives of nine people with your silly fancies. 'Twas the ploughing and seeding that you was meant to do. God showed you the path – all you had to do was walk in His Ways.'

'You walked in His Ways, didden you, Liza. But you never did get me to walk with you.' He tipped his head sideways. 'You was always too good for me, cousin. A truly good woman. But you take warning and watch out for your children. I do look at 'em sometimes – there is a streak of me in every single one, save Mina.'

'We began by speaking of Blanche.'

He began to laugh. 'Don't never come to the Devil for advice Eliza, when you wants to know how to stamp out sin.' He clung to the arm of the settle and struggled to stand upright. 'I need a drink; all this talking – '

She fetched her purse and gave him a penny. 'I hope you know,' she said sharply, 'that your girls must sew at least one dozen collars to earn that much?'

He grinned. 'Thass no cause for complaint, eh Liza? You always did tell me how the Devil finds mischief for idle hands.'

The strange conversation with Philip had stirred memories in Eliza, had recalled other words spoken long ago when they had both been young and hopeful. To go back to the beginning, to that first year at Larksleve, was to call up the vision of Meridiana, triumphant in love, dressed in plaid and hung with coral and amber, the coloured ribbons flying about her head and shoulders; and that shout of triumph was how love should be, thought Eliza. She watched her husband leave Hunter's Court; saw him sidle guiltily past his two daughters, clutching tightly to the penny which had

340

been earned by their diligent sewing. She thought about the patteran left by the gypsies. That arrangement of twigs and grasses, particular to each travelling family, which showed to the ones who came behind which way had been chosen, which route had been followed.

She thought about Philip's recent boast, or had it been his warning? Watch out for your children, he had said. There is a streak of me in every one of them, save Mina. The patteran left behind by Philip Greypaull was, she thought, an evil arrangement of faults and weaknesses, of indecisions and a need for the gratification of every sinful pleasure; and it was much too late for Eliza to do anything about it.

Jye Carew, at the age of sixteen, had completed four years of his mason's apprenticeship. He was already more skilled in his handling of the stone than Luke, his father, had ever been. Jye brought an extra sensitivity to his work, a feeling for the Ham stone which surprised the older masons. Deafness had isolated the boy; he attended the Baptist Chapel because it was expected of him, but his true interest lay in the churches of the district. Buildings, thought Jye, grew not only from stone, but from a man's need of them. In the year of 1879 he had given many hours of his own time to the raising of the new Baptist Chapel. To express that need in the loving restoration of the churches built by the medieval masons was what he longed most to do. 'One day,' he told his mother, 'when my time is served, I might even go to work in London.'

'That don't sound like a good idea, Jye. You don't rightly hear what people say to you. That cud be a hindrance.'

He held up his hands and smiled at her. ''Tis my fingers I do hear with.' He spoke the truth; she watched him at work in his father's garden, saw the level rows of peas and beans,

341

the early potatoes. His passion for the roses far outstripped that once felt by Luke. A single rose-bush, cosseted in an unused corner, was never to be enough for Jye. He planted, fed, took cuttings and grafted, until the multi-coloured bushes marched in a straight line across the top width of the garden. From the upper windows of her house, Meri could see the Montacute churchyard. Jye had set a square of Ham stone at his father's head; on it he had chiselled the words, 'Thy Will be Done.' He had taken Meri to see his handiwork, and had told her the meaning of the carved words.

'And you believes that, do you, Jye? That 'twas God's will to take your father from me?'

'What else can us believe, Ma? My grandfather died accidental – '

'Aye. Luke's father was trampled to death by a drayhorse. My parents died of the smallpox.' She looked at her son across the newly set gravestone. 'I shan't never make old bones, Jye.'

'You've bin saying that, Ma, for as long as I can remember, I don't reckon you knows your exact age.'

'Yes, I do. I must be – well – something close to forty, give or take a year.'

'You'll live a long life, yet, Ma. You'll live to see grandchildren, and great-grandchildren.'

Jye's words stayed with her. Spoken, as they had been, at his father's graveside there had been a ring of prophecy about them. Grandchildren, and great-grandchildren; and Luke not there to share it with her. Was she to be condemned to live on to a great age? To continue to wake in the night and ache for the comfort of Luke's arms about her; to feel that old pull of the open drom in springtime, that restlessness in the blood that she had never mastered. She thought about Charles and Henry who lived in deliberate and sullen isolation; about Jye, whose deafness was now almost total; and as always such thoughts led her back towards the chopping of her coral pendant for Eliza Greypaull's blue china bowl.

She remembered that April evening beside the black-thorns when she had chopped a love-token that had been intended to enslave Philip Greypaull. The fleecy shawl, handed over by Eliza, had given Meridiana Loveridge the best of the bargain.

Philip had gone missing for a day and a night. He had been delivered to Eliza that morning by a neighbour, who had demanded a penny from her for the service. She had assumed, quite naturally, that he had acquired drink by some means or other. Believing him to be drunk, she had stripped off his drenched and filthy clothing, washed him and dressed him in a clean white nightshirt. With the help of Simeon and Annis she had wrestled the inert form up the step-ladder which led into the upper room. With her attention divided between the demands of Louis, and the urgent need to sew shirt-collars, it was late in the evening when she remembered Philip, and went up to observe his condition. She had thought him already dead, and then a slight rise and fall of his chest made her call out to Annis. 'Do 'ee go and fetch the parish doctor for me, maid! But mind you tell 'un that us can't pay. Hurry now, Annis! Your father's in a bad way.'

For a full three weeks he had lain, robbed entirely of speech and movement; the canopied bed, too large for the tiny room, was already his catafalque, his bier. It was strange how, towards the end, his looks had become almost saintly. The grizzled curls turned a snowy white, and the seizure had driven the mottled purple from his face. His eyes lost their bloodshot stare and became enormous in his wasted face. Lying between sheets, propped up on pillows, he belonged finally and absolutely to Eliza. Now she could give him the reassurance that she had denied him in all their years together.

''Tis all right, my dear,' she would whisper in the long nights of his pain. 'I be sitting here beside 'ee. I won't go away.' No longer capable of speech, he could not deliver those jeering words with which he had mocked at her faith in God. Now, she could pick up his hand and stroke it. 'Let we pray together for forgiveness, Philip. For all the damage we two have done to one another.'

A letter was sent to Candace in which Eliza insisted that the girl should return home. The agent who now collected the Hunter's Court rents was asked to inform Daniel Greypaull of his son's condition; but not a soul came down from Buckland St Mary.

When Candace came home she was looking so white and exhausted that Blanche was ordered by her mother to give up her comfortable half of the bed she shared with Annis.

'And where am I supposed to sleep?' demanded Blanche.

'On the kitchen table,' said Eliza, 'there's nowhere else, unless you fancy the floor.'

Blanche had refused to help Eliza with the nursing of her father. She made-up her makeshift bed on the kitchen table and, in the hour of Philip's passing, she was heard by her brothers and sisters to shout at the ceiling, 'Die, Philip Greypaull! Die, damn you! You should have been dead these many long years!'

Samuel Greypaull came to Hunter's Court. He had brought a coffin loaded on a farmcart. He came into the little house where nobody truly mourned. His eyes sought Eliza. ''Tis all over then?'

'How did you know, Sam?'

'The agent sent word up by the carter.'

'I sent for you Sam, but you never come.'

'I cudden, Liza. Father's in a bad way lately. I cudden leave him.'

She nodded. 'We be all getting older, Sam.'

'How old was Philip?'

'He was fifty-one,' she said. 'Do 'ee want to see 'un, for the last time?'

'I've brought his coffin, Liza. Father do want his body brought back for burial in our own churchyard. I said I would ask you what your mind was on the matter.'

She thought about it, but only for a moment. 'Take 'un with you, Samuel. Bury him alongside his mother. 'Tis where he belongs, after all. He never was mine.'

The farmcart pulled away from Hunter's Court. It bore the coffin which contained the remains of the man called Philip Greypaull. Eliza followed it out into East Reach; she watched the wheels turn, saw the coffin pass out of view as the farmcart breasted East Reach Hill; and so, in the end, he was to be taken back to Buckland St Mary. She lifted a hand to her sightless eye, but found no tears.

2, Hunter's Court,
Taunton.

June 18th 1881

Dear cousin Rhoda,

I have picked up my pen many times in the past few days with all intenshuns of writing, but then could not. There is no easy way to tell of a death, so I will only say that Philip passed away on the 10th of June. I should like to think that he had died in the Lord, but cannot truly believe that. I felt sorrow at his passing, us having lived for twenty-four years together. But then I began to see the hand of the Lord in all what have come to pass, and I took strength, Rhoda. I still have my seven children, and useless grieving over what can't be helped was never in my nature. Samuel Greypaull took Philip's body back to Buckland St Mary for burial beside his mother. None of us went with him.

Me and Madelina sewed black dresses for us all, and armbands for the boys. That was a struggle to buy so many yards of material, and I had to *pawn* my Wedding Ring to do it. Nobody have yet noticed that the ring is gone. That was my first time inside a pawnshop and you can imagine my shame. But black have got to be worn, and respect showed for a dead husband, and the *heart* must keep its *secrets.*

Thinking back over what happened to Larksleve is still a sorrow to me. On Larksleve I could lift up Mine Eyes unto the Hills, but in Taunton all I can see is my neighbours' brick wall. But I *will not complain.* I know that the Greypaulls will never charge me rent for this house, and the Annuity do bring in One Pound a week regular, what is riches compared to most of my neighbours what do live *On the Parish*, and is in *Dire Straits.*

My other News do concern Blanche. She is to go for a kitchen maid in London, and work in the same house alongside Candace. I sometimes think, Rhoda, that the Lord in his Mercy saw my affliction and have at last lifted both my burdens from me. Not that I *don't care* about Blanche, but when I look at her I can hardly believe that she is a child of mine. Blanche is not to be *blamed altogether* for her wild ways. The girl is a great beauty, and with such looks must come temptations what such as I can never understand, having always been a very plain and homely woman.

My other children is all well behaved and respectful.

346

Madelina is to marry a Wesleyan, Jack do prosper in his proffeshun, Simeon is a trial but kind-hearted, Louis do bide childlike no matter how big he grows. Annis stays close beside me. She is ever my liddle maiden and always will be. Yes, Rhoda, I think myself well blessed in my situashun. To have come thru such a Valley of Tribulation and be still Strong in Faith and Hope is indeed a Blessing. I can hold my head high in Taunton Town, dear cousin, sure in the belief that *I* have never *shamed* the name of Greypaull.

The Reverend Payne is a regular visitor to my home, what have been a great comfort to me in this Time of Trouble. Certain ladies in the Church have also offered to visit, but like I told the Vicar, I can't never receive genteel lady visitors while I live in such a place as this evil Court. There have been Times, dear Rhoda, when my head have bowed and my foot faltered, and I have dowted if the Lord still remembered His servant. But the Reverend Payne have explained to me how the Lord only puts to the test them he knows can stand the heaviest burdens, and that every fresh Trial have only made me grow the stronger. I have kept up my piano playing, tho' mostly only for our hymns on a Sunday evening. The music always soothes poor Louis, what do get very fretful sometimes. Things will have to get very bad indeed, dear Rhoda, before I ever think of parting with my piano.

I look forward to the years to come. Life will get easier with the children earning, and when they marry there will be grandchildren and oh, how I look forward to that, too.

I often think about you and Mr. James Black in Wisconsin. What sort of crops do you grow, and how big is your dairy herd? Your harvest will be starting soon, and the salting down of your hog meat, what I think must be pork as we say it here. I will be glad of a letter when you have the time, but I know how full your days must be, having worked myself in the dairying line of business.

Oh yes, dear cousin, the Lord do work in a *Very Mysterious Way* His Wonders to Perform, and them as *Lives Longest* do *see* the *most*. Poor Philip have only reaped the bitter Harvest what he sowed in his young days, and may God forgive him.

Love and best regards to Mr James Black and your dear children.

Ever your affecshunate cousin, Eliza.

*Glossary of gypsy words*

| | |
|---|---|
| Beng | the devil |
| chal | lad |
| chavvie | child |
| chie | gypsy girl or young woman |
| chittie | the iron hook from which the cooking pot is suspended |
| chop | to exchange |
| chovihanis | witch |
| chuchi | rabbit |
| cosht | piece of wood |
| cratch | food cupboard |
| diddecoi | derogatory term for gypsy. Half-breed gypsy |
| diklo | neckerchief |
| drom | road |
| dukerin | fortune-telling |
| gavvers | policemen |
| gorgio, gorgie | non-gypsy |
| grai | horse |
| kitchima | tavern |
| kushti-tan | comfortable camp |
| lavengro | word master |

| | |
|---|---|
| mokardi | unclean |
| O dordi! | Oh dear! |
| patteran | pattern of twigs and grasses showing the direction a gypsy family has taken |
| rai | young man |
| rawnie | lady or wife |
| Rom | gypsy |
| tan | camp |
| vardo | caravan |
| | |
| nammet | a Somerset dialect word for snack or lunch |

All Futura Books are available at your bookshop or newsagent, or can be ordered from the following address Futura Books, Cash Sales Department, P.O. Box 11, Falmouth, Cornwall.

Please send cheque or postal order (no currency), and allow 55p for postage and packing for the first book plus 22p for the second book and 14p for each additional book ordered up to a maximum charge of £1.75 in U.K.

Customers in Eire and B.F.P.O. please allow 55p for the first book, 22p for the second book plus 14p per copy for the next 7 books, thereafter 8p per book.

Overseas customers please allow £1 for postage and packing for the first book and 25p per copy for each additional book.